A PANSY RESTING ON ITS LAURELS

PRIVATE

JOSEPH LINDSAY

CRANTHORPE
MILLNER
PUBLISHERS

First published by Cranthorpe Millner Publishers (2025)

ISBN 978-1-80378-263-8 (Paperback)

www.cranthorpemillner.com

Cranthorpe Millner Publishers

For Marilyn

I hope you enjoy reading this as much as I enjoyed writing it.

Joseph Lindsay

For my brother, Steve, whose career I mirrored for a while.

18/03/25

PART 1

RECRUITMENT

JON COMYN
1982-1983

CHAPTER 1

The Intelligence Corps has, in its relatively short history, been known by various names, one of them being 'The Eunuchs', due to it having no Privates, a rather crude sexual pun that wasn't exactly true, as Jon Comyn found out when he went into the Army Careers Office on Hanover Street in Edinburgh to acquire some information about joining 'The Professionals' – as the British Army referred to themselves.

Jon was in his third year of a course at Napier College of Commerce and Technology, where he was studying – if that was the correct term – for a Higher National Diploma in Printing. Safe to say, it was not going well... hence his visit.

It had seemed like a good idea when he had first applied, as he had been bored out of his mind in his job as an 'indoor salesman' – read 'order clerk' – for Wiggins Teape (Stationery) Ltd. Despite having the advantage of sitting across the desk from his boss' lovely secretary, Anne, whom he had fallen hopelessly in love with, that hadn't made up for the tedium of doing next to nothing for six and a half hours per day, five days a week. Wiggins Teape Ltd. may have generously given its office employees an hour and a half for lunch each day, but the world of envelopes and cards had entered a quiet patch, and Jon had been presented with minimal work to keep him busy.

As a result, he had responded favourably when one of his flatmates had suggested they all become students for a bit of a laugh. The printing course had caught his eye, and it had seemed to offer the twin advantages of escape from the tedium of office work and a better career than in the printing industry. Unfortunately for Jon, technology caught up with him, and he had realised at the beginning of his third year that the course he had spent the last two years doing was, in effect, obsolete. It had also come as a nasty shock to discover that the previous year's graduates – those who had found work, that is – were earning about the same as he had been getting at Wiggins Teape Ltd. as the lowest paid worker in the office.

He had taken to drinking quite heavily following this realisation, frequently missing classes, to such an extent that he'd had an official warning about his attendance. His classmates had been gradually falling by the wayside and only the hardcore students were left, most of whom were dedicated and studious and didn't tend to socialise a lot. Jon's girlfriend had ditched him after she'd finally realised that he wasn't going to marry her, and he'd blown his chances with the lovely Anne from the office by turning up at her flat drunk, although thinking back on it she had still been very welcoming and maybe he should have been a bit braver and asked her out. He had never summoned up the courage to do so, and now it was probably too late. Such was life.

Thus, he had found himself walking towards the Army Careers Office one Wednesday morning, when he was supposed to be having typing lessons. It wasn't that he didn't see typing as a useful skill, he just couldn't get his head round the whole QWERTY business and had to look at the keys before pressing them. Not to mention it reminded him of his old man, who had been a typist in the Royal Air Force during his national service, though to hear him speak one would have thought he was a war hero, like *his* father, who'd survived three years in the trenches and been recommended for a Victoria Cross. The only reason Jon's grandfather hadn't been awarded the VC was because so many men were committing acts of bravery that staying overnight in a shell crater with a wounded officer and then helping them to safety wasn't seen as quite heroic enough. Consequently, he had been awarded the Military Medal and *Médaille Militaire* instead.

As Jon pushed open the front door of the Army Careers Office (covered with gaudy posters) and walked inside, he discovered a threadbare grey carpet, a rack of recruiting pamphlets, and two faded pictures, one of Queen Elizabeth II and the other of her husband, Prince Philip. Alongside the rather sparse furnishings sat three gunmetal-grey desks, at which sat an army Colour Sergeant, an RAF Flight Sergeant and a Royal Navy Petty Officer.

The three pairs of eyes turned to Jon as he hesitated in the doorway. It was like being observed by hungry vultures.

"Army, navy or air force?" enquired the Colour Sergeant, with a brevity of speech that was positively laconic.

"That should be 'navy, army or air force'," interjected the Petty Officer. "We are the *senior service*, after all."

"I thought those were cigarettes," joked Jon.

There was an awkward silence. The Petty Officer was obviously not amused, staring coldly at him.

"Yes. Well..." the Petty Officer finally said. "Which one is it?"

"Er... army," said Jon, hurriedly trying to cover his embarrassment.

The Colour Sergeant's face lit up with a triumphant smile.

"Good choice, son," he stated, giving the other two a grin. "This way," he added, standing up and gesturing towards a small office off the main room.

Jon followed him in and took the proffered chair, sitting awkwardly and not knowing where to start.

The Colour Sergeant pre-empted him by asking, "What regiment did you have in mind?"

"Er... I don't really know," replied Jon. "The Army Air Corps sounds interesting."

The Colour Sergeant gave him an appraising look. "Got any qualifications?" he asked, in a tone that made it sound as though qualifications were some sort of disease.

"I'm doing an HND in Printing," Jon responded, trying to justify himself. "I thought I might go for a commission."

"You want to be an officer?" the Colour Sergeant queried, the smile draining from his face as he saw a potential infantry recruit disappear, along with his bonus for bringing one in.

"Yes, that's the idea," said Jon brightly, totally oblivious to the frosty atmosphere being projected by the scorned Colour Sergeant.

"OK. If that's what you want," continued the Colour Sergeant, as if Jon had turned down something special. "Corporal Christy!" he shouted.

A small, smiling, red-haired Corporal, wearing the badge of the Women's Royal Army Corps on her beret, came into the office.

"Yes, Colour?" she asked.

The Colour Sergeant gestured to the seated figure of Jon. "This young gentleman is interested in becoming an officer. Set up an interview with the Colonel, will you?"

"Yes, Colour," replied the Corporal. She turned to Jon. "Come with me, please."

They re-entered the main office – where the naval Petty Officer and the RAF Flight Sergeant were each trying to persuade a thin, spotty youth who had foolishly entered their lair that theirs was the best organisation to join – and crossed over to a smaller office, which was obviously where the Corporal worked, and also made the tea and coffee.

"Would you like a cup of tea, sir?" she asked, politely.

Jon was slightly shocked to be called 'sir' but decided that it actually felt rather nice.

"Yes please."

"NATO standard?"

"What's that?"

"Oh, sorry, sir. White with two sugars."

"Yes, that would be very nice."

While she was making the tea, he looked around the office. Hanging on one wall was a framed board with cap badges from the various army units, and on the desk was a wooden shield. It had a stylised rose with a crown on top inside a laurel wreath, and the words 'Intelligence Corps' underneath. Opposite was a framed picture of the same red rose with the motto '*Manui Dat Cognitio Vires*' underneath.

"Knowledge gives strength to the arm," he translated aloud, pleased that he could still remember any Latin at all.

The Corporal turned to him with a surprised look. "You know the motto of The Eunuchs?"

"Eunuchs?"

"The Intelligence Corps," she explained with a giggle. "It hasn't got any Privates. Except for recruits."

"Even officers?"

"No. If you go for a commission, you become an Officer Cadet. That's below a Private."

"I didn't think there was anything below a Private," mused Jon.

"Only Officer Cadets," came the reply.

The Corporal arranged for Jon to have an interview with the Colonel, ushering him out of the office with a ream of literature about the various units, and a vague thought that the Intelligence Corps sounded quite interesting.

The following Wednesday, Jon went to Edinburgh Castle for his interview with Lieutenant Colonel Carstairs, who dealt with applicants for a commission in Her Majesty's Armed Forces. He walked briskly up the castle esplanade, glancing briefly at the workmen who were busy putting up scaffolding in preparation for the Edinburgh military tattoo, held every year.

At the main gate, two sentries wearing Parachute Regiment berets stood either side of drawn back wooden doors, holding the British Army rifle (known as an SLR) with fixed bayonets. As Jon approached, they came to attention in a general salute. Jon wondered what they were doing, and then realised that they had mistaken him for an officer. He was wearing a tweed jacket, corduroy trousers and black brogues. Officer clothes, he supposed.

"Thank you," he said as he walked past them.

Lt Col Carstairs' office was on the second level of Edinburgh Castle, and he ushered Jon into a room far plusher than the threadbare office on Hanover Street.

"Well, well, Comyn," he said jovially, gesturing for Jon to take a seat in a comfortable armchair. "So, you're after a commission in the British Army?"

"Yes, sir," replied Jon. He was treating this meeting as if it was an interview for a job, though he was actually just after more information, rather than committing himself to a three-year contract he couldn't walk away from.

"So, which regiment would you like to join?"

"Well, I was thinking of the Army Air Corps."

It was almost as if a buzzer had sounded 'wrong answer'.

"Ah! The Army Air Corps," stated the Colonel in a tone that indicated that this definitely *was* the wrong answer. "Not many places in the Army Air Corps," he continued. "Do you have any flying experience?"

Christ! I thought the whole point of joining the fucking unit was to learn *to fly,* thought Jon.

"No, sir," he said instead.

The Colonel grimaced. "Well, I know of a chap who already has a pilot's licence who's applied, and he probably won't get in, so I'm afraid you haven't got much of a chance," he said with a complete lack of regret. "Any other regiment?" he continued, with the stress on 'regiment'.

"How about the Intelligence Corps?" Jon offered.

That went down like a ton of bricks.

"Got a degree?"

"I'm doing an HND."

The Colonel grimaced again, as if he was terribly disappointed to have to shoot down Jon's hopes, though he wasn't quite able to hide his glee. "That probably won't be good enough. They're very choosey, you know."

Jon sighed. "I suppose the Infantry."

A smile appeared on the Colonel's face. Obviously, this was the correct answer. "Any particular regiment?"

"My grandfather was in the Gloucester's."

Wrong answer.

"My brother was in the Black Watch," Jon tried again.

Wrong answer.

"I was in the Territorial Army. Royal Scots."

A huge smile appeared on Carstairs' face. "Excellent choice," he said.

Not really surprising, thought Jon. After all, Lieutenant Colonel Carstairs was a member of the self-same regiment.

"The next intake is July, which will be too soon for you to attend the Regular Commissions Board. The one after that isn't until January, so would you like to do an O-type commission?"

"What's that, sir?"

"It's a ten-week course designed to help chaps like you pass the RCB."

It was as a consequence of this conversation that Jon found himself signing on as a Private in the Royal Scots regiment a couple of months later. In true British Army tradition, he was paid the modern equivalent of the Queen's shilling the day he signed on... and immediately went out and drank it.

Jon looked down at the tubular, metal-framed bed with its four grey army blankets and two white sheets, neatly folded, sitting on a rather thin, striped mattress. On top were a pair of navy-blue shorts, a white V-neck T-shirt, a pair of black gym shoes and a pair of green army socks. This was what they had to wear to the stores to collect the rest of their uniform. He wasn't sure whether it was designed to be humiliating, or it had just always been that way. You could never tell with the army.

He had arrived at Milton Bridge Training Camp at 0900 as instructed, and his name had been ticked off by the Corporal in the guardroom. He had then been told to go to building 101 to meet the rest of the intake of Scottish Divisional Squad 14. As he was walking through the camp, lugging his baggage, he wondered if there was any significance to the building being numbered 101. He hoped not, although the camp didn't fill him with a warm, fuzzy feeling.

He had done his Territorial Army basic training here some years before, and it hadn't changed much. Milton Bridge Training Camp had been built during the First World War, and the huts, which is what they were, were built of clapboard with metal-framed windows. He remembered the thirty-man billet, with alternate beds and lockers running along both walls. At the end was a small room for the Platoon Corporal, the Platoon Sergeant having his own room in the Sergeant's mess, which was in the more modern Glencorse Barracks in Penicuik, the oddly named town just outside Edinburgh.

He found building 101 relatively easily, following the painted numbers on the other buildings and, to his relief, he realised that it wasn't a thirty-man billet, but the old officers' mess. Four other recruits were already waiting, and there was a slightly nervous air about their conversation. A Corporal wearing a tam-o'-shanter with the cap badge of the Queen's Own Highlanders, who they found out later was named 'Dusty' Millar, told him to wait with the others as there was still one more member of the team due to arrive.

Jon introduced himself before stashing his suitcase and rucksack next to a pile of luggage that was neatly stacked against one wall. He took a seat in a square armchair with scuffed, brown leather upholstery and studied his new colleagues. They were all about the same age – roughly late teens – and all but one had posh accents.

"Anyone done any fitness training before they came here?" asked one of the two blond youths.

They all admitted that they hadn't, as they expected the army to get them fit. Jon had been a runner when he was at school, and still walked most places, but he'd never been interested in going to the gym. In fact, he had never really liked what he thought of as 'pointless' exercise. He considered himself to be fairly fit, but didn't have anything to compare it with, except comparisons with the average man on the street, who seemed barely able to run for the bus.

The final squad member turned up a short while later, and the Corporal showed them to their accommodation, which consisted of four, two-person rooms in a rundown clapboard hut, painted in peeling emerald-green with the remnants of roses growing up a decaying trellis bordering the front door. Each room had two single beds, two wardrobes, two small chests of drawers, and a basin with a mirror that had seen better days. There was a toilet block which was clean, if rather primitive, and smelled of strong disinfectant. They were told to change into Physical Training kit and to parade outside the hut in twenty minutes.

"Is it just me, or does anyone else feel ridiculous in this?" Jon asked as the team lined up, fifteen minutes later.

The rest of them smiled and agreed, though Andy, whose tanned skin made it look as if he had just come back from a long period in a hot country, didn't look quite as bad as the rest of them, with their lily-white legs sticking out from their oversized navy-blue shorts.

"It won't be so bad when we get our uniforms," stated Richard confidently.

"Don't be too sure," warned Jon. "I was in the TA and army uniforms tend to fit where they touch, as the saying goes."

At that point, Corporal 'Dusty' Millar arrived and herded them down to the Quartermaster's stores in Glencorse barracks.

They were issued with two pairs of plain green trousers, two pairs of combat trousers, a combat jacket, two green shirts, a green army pullover, a green plastic belt, four pairs of green socks, two pairs of boots, a tam-o'-shanter and cap badge of their respective regiments, and a small, grey suitcase that looked like it was made out of cardboard, alongside a green sack-like holdall to carry it all in.

When it came to Jon's turn, there was only one pair of size nine boots left, so the storeman gave him the choice of taking a free second-hand pair or making do with one pair until the new stock arrived. The boots were worn but serviceable, and when Jon tried them on, they fit him perfectly. He was quite happy to have a second-hand pair, as they were already broken in and hence would give him less trouble than two brand new pairs.

"These are perfect," Jon said happily.

The storeman gave him a grin. "You're a fucking lucky soldier then, aren't you?"

Once they got back to Milton Bridge they changed into their 'working dress', which consisted of the plain green trousers, green shirt and jumper. Corporal Millar lined them up and gave them a once-over, before asking Andy, the blond recruit with the impressive tan, to stand on the table, so he could demonstrate the correct way for them to wear their 'puttees' – long strips of cloth that wrapped around the ankle to hold your trouser legs in place, with a triangular end that pointed backwards and had stitching that lined up with stitching on the boot. An attached tape was used to hold them in place and was tied off neatly behind the tip of the triangle.

"Anyone in the Cameronians?" asked Millar.

The Scottish Divisional Squads (SDS) were made up of recruits from all seven Scottish regiments in the Scottish Division, but only the Royal Scots, the King's Own Scottish Borderers, the Gordon Highlanders and the Queen's Own Highlanders were represented in SDS 14.

"No, Corporal," came the reply.

"Why?" asked Jon.

Millar grinned. "The Cameronians are the only regiment to wear their puttees the other way round," he explained.

"Why's that?" asked one of the squad. "Are they special?"

Millar's grin widened. "No," he said. "Historically, a regiment belongs to its Colonel, who decides what uniform is to be worn. The story goes that the Colonel of the Cameronians got pissed in the mess one night and turned up on parade the next morning with his puttees on the wrong way round. The guys in his regiment all had to turn their puttees the same way, and it stuck."

"Wow," said James, the recruit who had arrived late. "It must be great to have your own regiment."

"Cost a fortune, though," said Jon.

"More than I could afford," agreed Millar. "Does anyone know why the Queen's Own Highlanders wear a blue hackle?"

"I know that the Black Watch wear a red one and that they don't wear a cap badge because they mutinied," said Jon.

"True," said Millar. "The reason the Queen's Own have a blue hackle is 'cause they asked if they could wear one."

"That's it?" exclaimed Richard, who had enlisted in the Queen's

Own Highlanders.

"Aye," said Millar. "You'll get more lessons in regimental history later on. There're loads of little snippets about each one. That's what I love about the army."

"Not the fantastic food and the superb pay then, Corporal?" asked Jon cheekily.

"No. It's the traditions that make it great. You'll all need to know them, if you're going to be officers."

The Platoon Commander, Lieutenant Archie MacGregor, who was also a member of the Queen's Own Highlanders, turned up later, introducing the squad to its Sergeant and explaining the outline of the next ten weeks. There was to be a mix of military and adventurous training, leading up to a Pre-Regular Commissions Board (Pre-RCB) testing weekend. If the guys passed the Pre-RCB then they would attend the Regular Commissions Board proper, a three-day assessment consisting of a series of physical and mental tests, to assess their fitness to be admitted to the Royal Military Academy Sandhurst. If they passed the RCB then they would go to Sandhurst and, hopefully, become Second Lieutenants or, if they failed, they could stay on as Privates in their respective regiments, or be given a free discharge.

CHAPTER 2

The following morning, they started their military training with a uniform inspection, followed by a room inspection. They were formed into a squad, albeit a rather small one, and marched to the parade square, where they were introduced to the joys of drill.

"You're a wanker," the Sergeant shouted at James, as he made a mess of turning right for the third time. "What are you?"

"I'm a wanker, Sergeant," James yelled back.

"I can't hear you," shouted the Sergeant.

"I'm a wanker!" screamed James at the top of his voice.

"Yes, I know that. You don't have to tell me," replied the Sergeant, to universal sniggering from the rest of the squad. "Now go and stand at the side of the parade square."

James marched off the square, halted, about turned, and stood at ease as the Sergeant marched the rest of SDS 14 around the square.

James tried his best but drill just wasn't really his thing. In fact, he was beginning to think that the army in general wasn't his thing. They had spent the previous week square-bashing, weapons training and doing physical training. He couldn't seem to do anything right, although the rest of the squad, particularly Jon, who had previous experience from being in the TA, did their best to help him.

"Why the fuck won't this fucking shirt stay ironed?" James had exclaimed on the first night while they prepared their kit for the next day's inspection.

"Here. Give it to me," said Jon, taking the offending item from James's hands and laying it out on the ironing board. "It's all about getting it flat and using plenty of starch."

"I've used loads."

"Yes, but not in the right place. If you use too much it looks like you've got dandruff, but you need to get the creases right or they'll never stay in place. It could be worse, they could be shirts KF. We used to call them shirts 'hedgehog'. They were made of wool and were really scratchy. Some guys used to shave theirs."

"You're joking?"

"No, deadly serious."

James looked downcast. "Why do they always do things backwards?" he asked plaintively.

"What do you mean?"

"Shirts KF. Boots DMS. That sort of thing," protested James.

"Oh, that. It's all to do with the stores and how they log kit. You start with the main item, for example a box, then you start adding descriptors to tell you what's in the box. So you get 'Box, Document, Security', or 'BDS', as opposed to 'Box, Ammunition, Small Arms', or 'Box, Ammunition, Mortar'."

"Okay," said James. "I suppose it makes sense. I wish it was like the old days when you could buy a commission, so I wouldn't have to go through all of this."

Jon looked at him. "Are your family rich?"

James gave him a smile. "Yes, very," he admitted.

"Fair enough," said Jon. "Mine aren't."

"Oh," said James. "I thought we were all from the same stock."

"No," clarified Jon. "You, Andy, Ian and Richard are. Me and Dave aren't."

"But you sound well-educated," protested James.

"My old man was an English teacher," explained Jon. "I got a scholarship to the Royal High."

"I went to Harrow."

"Not really a surprise," said Jon. "We're all Piccadilly

Highlanders."

"Piccadilly Highlanders? What's that?"

"We're all English, looking to become officers in Scottish regiments. That's known as being a 'Piccadilly Highlander'."

"I thought you were Scottish?"

"I am, on my mother's side, but I was actually born in Middlesbrough. We moved to Edinburgh when I was eight. My grandfather on my father's side was from Cheltenham."

"Oh, OK."

Unfortunately for him, James never did get the hang of ironing and polishing boots. He didn't take criticism very well either, particularly as both the Sergeant and Corporal Millar were obviously working class.

Sergeant Patterson, which he pronounced without the double T, had only been in the army for ten years, almost unheard of for an infantry Sergeant. He was destined for great things and would probably make Regimental Sergeant Major before he was forty. He was only twenty-five, a couple of years older than Jon, who was three years older than anyone else in the squad and the same age as Lieutenant MacGregor.

Things came to a head after an exhausting two-day overnight infantry patrol, the morning after which Sergeant Patterson made the squad double march back to the camp from the training area. This meant that they were, in effect, jogging, albeit a slow jog. James had been lagging behind and Sergeant Patterson was 'encouraging' him to keep up.

James foolishly made the comment, "It's all right for you, you haven't been out all night", which enraged Sergeant Patterson, who made a gesture that James took as a threat, raising his rifle to ward off the blow. Sergeant Patterson grabbed the rifle off him and, red faced with anger, marched the squad into the camp and halted them outside the accommodation.

"You. Come with me. Leave your kit," he shouted at James, who shamefacedly dropped his webbing and large pack. Sergeant Patterson turned to the rest of SDS 14. "Stay there and don't move until I come back!"

He then marched away with James, leaving the squad wondering what the hell was going on.

They stood in the hot morning sun, sweat dripping down their backs, wondering what was going to happen next. Jon didn't like the feeling of being completely controlled by someone else, though he understood this was part of being in the military and a necessary part of their training. He imagined that the other guys were feeling the same way too. *Is this the way it's going to be for the rest of my career?* he wondered. *Or will it get better once I become an officer?* Hopefully the latter. Only time would tell.

A short while later, Corporal Millar arrived and stood them at ease. "Go and sort your kit out," he said mildly. "The OC will be back soon."

Still in the dark about what was going to happen to James, the squad did as they were told, spending the rest of the day on edge.

Later that afternoon, a Sergeant from the Argyll and Sutherland Highlanders appeared and asked them what they were doing.

"Waiting for orders, Sergeant," said Jon.

"You've got the evening off. Go into town," he said. "Parade tomorrow at 0800."

"Yes, Sergeant."

The pubs in Penicuik were out of bounds to soldiers, so Jon and the squad caught the bus and went into Edinburgh. Jon had lived in the city since childhood, so he took them on a mini pub crawl to a few famous places that he knew. The first was the Ensign Ewart at the top of the Royal Mile, next to Edinburgh Castle. It was a small, traditional pub, named after a member of the Scots Greys who had captured a French Eagle at the Battle of Waterloo. They had a pint of real ale and then went down into the Grassmarket.

There were a number of pubs in or around the Grassmarket, and Jon took them to the White Hart Inn for a pint of Belhaven 80 Shilling ale. Finally, they went to the Nips O Brandy in Cowgate, just off the Grassmarket. Their feet stuck to the carpet as they walked in from all the beer spilt over the years, but the pub had decent beer and a brilliant jukebox.

Once they had relaxed a bit, they discussed the events of the day. It was easier for Jon's colleagues to accept the strict army discipline as they had all been to public school, apart from Dave, and were used to being told what to do all the time. Jon realised that he had become used to being his own boss, but he enjoyed the camaraderie with the others, and they all agreed that what had happened to James was something that you just had to put up with if you wanted to be in an organisation like the army.

No one wanted to risk getting drunk, so they left at 2200 to catch the bus back to Penicuik. James had not returned when they got back and there was no one about, so they all went to bed, still wondering what was going on.

The following morning, James reappeared just after 0800 as the squad was being dismissed from parade by the new Sergeant. He joined them in the common room as they were having a cup of tea and narrated his story.

He had been taken down to the guardhouse and put into a cell, and then Sergeant Patterson had stormed off to find Lieutenant McGregor, the Officer Commanding. One of the Privates who was on guard duty had warned James that sometime during the night the Guard Sergeant would provoke him, so that he could be beaten up, but in the end the Guard Sergeant got drunk, and it never happened. In the morning, James had seen Lieutenant McGregor and explained what had happened, then been told to go and rejoin the squad.

Later that morning, Lieutenant MacGregor appeared and told the squad that Sergeant Patterson had gone back to his regiment. Sergeant Davies was now the Squad Sergeant, and that was the end of it.

Three days later, James put in a letter of resignation and left, having come to the conclusion that the British Army wasn't for him.

It was Monday morning, and the day was cold but bright with the promise of sunshine. Traditionally the wettest month of the year in Scotland, August was at present staying remarkably dry, as if to prove the statistics wrong. Jon peered out over the top of the tower down onto the parade ground below. It was only about forty feet, but that was high enough to get seriously hurt or even killed if you fell. They were going to abseil off the top of the tower and were just waiting for Lieutenant MacGregor to arrive before they proceeded.

"You look nervous," Corporal Millar said to Andy with a grin. He was not personally taking part, so could make jokes with impunity.

"I am nervous," said Andy, who had an innate fear of heights.

"Don't worry, you've got a safety rope," said Jon encouragingly.

"Safety rope?" asked Andy, his face pale.

"Yes. That thing tied to your waist. You'll end up hanging upside down, but you won't fall," said the Corporal gleefully.

"It could be worse," Jon mused.

"Worse?" squeaked Andy.

"Yes. When I first tried abseiling, we didn't have safety ropes. If you let go with the wrong hand, you plummeted to your death."

"Oh, that makes me feel so much better," Andy muttered.

"Where was that, then?" asked Millar.

"The Royal Marines sent me on an outward-bound course in Towyn, Wales," Jon said. "We did our abseiling in a disused slate mine. It was pissing with rain and really slippery."

"What were you doing with the Royal Marines?"

"I originally went for a commission in the Royal Marines," admitted Jon.

"Why didn't you join?"

"I was too young," explained Jon. "They asked me to go back and try again, but by that time I'd discovered booze and women, so I didn't bother."

"And so, you ended up in the Bogging Royals," grinned Millar.

"Aye. Such is life."

"Bogging Royals?" asked Andy.

"We're called that 'cause we don't wear spats on our brogues," explained Jon.

"Are there any units that don't have a disparaging nickname?" Andy wondered.

"Not the Queen's Own," said Millar, smugly.

"That's 'cause you're too young," interjected Jon.

"Too young?" asked Richard. "When were they formed?"

"1961," Jon informed him. "A mere twenty-one years ago."

"Unlike the Bogging Royals, who were Pontius Pilate's bodyguards." Millar smirked.

"You what?" Dave asked.

"It's an old story that the Royal Scots," recounted Jon, "who have served kings and queens for over three hundred years continuously, were serving the King of France during Cromwell's time and were arguing with the French Picardy Regiment about who was the senior. The Royals claimed that if they had been on guard the night of the crucifixion, then Christ's body would never have disappeared. Hence the nickname Pontius Pilate's Bodyguard."

"What a load of bollocks," said Dave.

"You can't talk," countered Jon. "Apparently your regiment raised recruits by the Duchess of Gordon offering to kiss anyone stupid enough to join the Gordons."

At that point, Lieutenant McGregor turned up and the conversation was halted as the abseiling lesson began.

They were instructed to lean back as far as possible and let the rope brace them, though Lieutenant MacGregor did reassure them that they might find it a challenge to start with, especially if they didn't have a head for heights. As expected, it took a while for Andy to overcome his initial reluctance to go backwards, but eventually he managed it, and found that he rather enjoyed the experience. All in all, it wasn't a bad day.

After the first couple of weeks, the frequency of uniform and room inspections had steadily declined, though there was still an inspection by Lieutenant McGregor, the Officer Commanding (OC), once a week. The squad would parade at 0800 every Monday morning, outside the accommodation block if the weather was dry or, if it was wet, inside along a corridor that ran the length of the building.

That Monday, Andy, the week's duty student, brought them all to attention as Lieutenant McGregor came into the building, followed by the Squad Sergeant. Andy marched smartly up to them and came to a halt at the regulation three paces from him. Unfortunately for him, the floor, which was covered in ancient linoleum, had earlier been buffed to a smooth polish, with a huge device that looked like a rectangular wooden box with an elongated broomstick as a handle. Instead of stopping smartly, Andy's rubber-soled boots slid him along the floor and he put his foot through the wall. Thankfully, Lieutenant MacGregor saw the funny side of the incident and Andy didn't get charged for mess damages.

With the vast majority of British Army officers being quite young, typically in their late teens to early thirties, mess damages were charged at a rate of 7:1 in order to deter bad behaviour. Despite this, the combination of youthfulness, drink and lack of women often led to rowdy mess games and fights which could be quite riotous and there were stories of mess dos where, after the meal and the speeches, officers had pulled out their issue handguns and started shooting chandeliers and other furniture, shouting, "I'm rich enough to be able to do this." If any Other Ranks, known as OR's, had dared to attempt such a thing, it would have been called vandalism, but the officers were simply considered to be in 'high spirits'.

Fortunately for Andy, his faux pas wasn't seen as careless enough to warrant him paying for it. Besides, their accommodation at Milton Bridge was so old that mushrooms were growing through the floor in some of the rooms and the linoleum in the hallways was warped and twisted. Still, at least it was mostly rain-proof.

Jon was quite happy with his room, which he had to himself now that James had gone. The other guys still shared rooms (despite there being enough for at least two of them to have their own rooms) as this meant the work was shared between two. Of course, Jon had to clean his room without help, but he didn't really mind.

Things were going quite well, and the course members had settled into the routine of military training with lectures and projects.

One evening, the team had been watching an episode of *The Professionals* – a rerun of a television series about a fictional Intelligence unit called CI5; nothing to do with the British Army – when Richard suddenly burst into the communal area.

"Guess what I've found," he said with a huge smile.

"What?"

"I was in the OC's office," he declared excitedly, "and I found his desk drawer open."

Richard was the duty student for that week and was responsible for checking that the classroom and office were locked up and tidy, amongst other things.

"And?"

"I've found the programme for next week."

"What's in it?"

"I didn't risk taking it," admitted Richard. "But you know they were talking about going swimming on Friday?"

"Yes, what about it?" prompted Ian, the other blonde recruit.

Richard smiled. "It's a cover for an initiative exercise."

"I heard about that from someone who did this course a few years ago," said Andy. "We get searched, they take away all our money and then send us out to find stuff."

"Bugger. I don't want to be left without any cash," Dave grumbled.

"Sew it into the seam of your Y-fronts," replied Andy. "That's what my friend's team did."

Looking back, there were a number of hints that something was up.

They had been told to hand in their sleeping bags to be dry-cleaned, which should have been the first clue. Then they were told to wear casual clothes to go swimming. Before, they had always been encouraged to wear 'smart civvies' – i.e. a shirt and tie – when going outside the camp, not in uniform.

On the Friday morning, they had paraded in their civilian clothes, before being told to wait in the communal room. They were sitting in the room's leather armchairs when Lieutenant McGregor, the Platoon Sergeant and Corporal Millar burst in.

"Get down! Get on the floor," Lieutenant McGregor shouted, and instinctively they all obeyed.

It was amazing how quickly they had become accustomed to doing what they were told without question.

Once they were all on the floor, they were individually told to stand up and take off their clothes. Jon felt surprisingly unembarrassed as he removed his Y-fronts and stood stark naked in the centre of the room. He supposed that part of it was that it had been half expected and the other was that there was nothing sexual about it at all.

He smirked to himself as Corporal Millar took the offending item of clothing gingerly in his hands. Jon had purposely worn the same pair for three days, as he had a five-pound note stitched into the seam of the underpants and didn't want anyone looking at them too closely.

Once they had all been searched, they were told to get dressed, and had pillowcases pulled over their heads. Jon felt a momentary anxiety as the cloth restricted his breathing but forced himself to stay calm and not panic. He was led into an ante room and had his hands tied behind his back, before being gently lowered to the floor, which reassured Jon that no actual harm was going to come to him.

He recalled a story that his cousin, who had been a Lieutenant in the Royal Signals, had told him about SAS selection. He said that one of the Sandhurst intake the year that he joined had been a Trooper in the SAS and had told him that, as part of selection, they had done an escape and evasion exercise. When he was caught, he had been interrogated but had refused to talk. One of the interrogators had told him that if he didn't talk, then they were going to take him to the small lake near the entrance to the training area and throw him in. He still refused and so they threw him in with his hands tied behind his back. The pool was only ankle deep, but he said that the experience had changed him. Jon thought about that as he lay on the floor. There were some really nasty bastards around, but luckily the

Lieutenant, Sergeant and Corporal were decent guys.

He calmed his breathing and waited, counting as the door opened and closed and more bodies were laid on the floor. He could tell by the sounds that the other guys were also trying to control their breathing. After a short while, he felt himself lifted to his feet and was told to start walking. He was prevented from walking into the door and was guided to the back of what must have been a four-ton truck, the British Army's standard transport vehicle. He was laid down again.

The vehicle started off and Jon tried to guess the direction in which they were moving, but soon lost track after the first couple of turns. He moved his wrists and found that the string with which his hands were tied was quite loose. He gradually eased the bindings off with the intention of loosening the pillowcase.

"This one's got free."

A heavy stick whacked across his hands and the string was removed, then whoever it was started tying Jon's thumbs together.

That's a bit unnecessary, he thought, so he tried to go floppy and pretend he was unconscious.

"Is he OK?" asked the slightly worried voice of Millar.

Good old Dusty.

"I really don't give a shit," said a posh, unknown voice. "He's not a proper officer yet."

You fucking bastard.

He wondered who it was. He didn't recognise the voice, but he decided then and there that he disliked him.

The truck came to a halt and Jon was hauled up and guided to the back of the truck. Millar took off the pillowcase but couldn't undo his thumbs; the unknown person had tied them too tightly.

"Get him down, Corporal," shouted McGregor.

"I can't, sir, his thumbs are tied together, and he'll fall," said Millar.

"Who did that?" McGregor demanded in an angry voice.

"Don't worry, Archie, I'll cut it off," said the unknown person.

Jon looked around to find an overweight, red-faced Lieutenant with a King's Own Scottish Borderers' cap badge, sneering at him.

"For fuck's sake, Bill, we've got time constraints," cursed MacGregor.

"Calm down, Archie," drawled the Lieutenant. "I'm on it."

He pulled out a small, army-issue penknife and cut through the bindings. Once Jon's hands were free, he jumped down off the back of the truck.

"You OK?" asked MacGregor.

Jon smiled. "Fine, sir. Fucking funny way of going swimming, though."

MacGregor smiled back. He handed Jon a black, plastic bin bag and a clear plastic envelope. Inside, was a sheet of paper with a ten pence coin Sellotaped to it.

"These are your instructions," he said. "See you on Sunday."

"Cheers, sir."

"Have a good swim," added a drawling voice from the back of the truck.

"Thank you, sir," said Jon as the vehicle vanished into the distance.

Jon looked around. He was on a small country road somewhere in Scotland. He knew he could only be a few miles from Penicuik. They hadn't travelled that far, so he was probably on the Biggar Road which led from Edinburgh west to the A74.

He looked in the black bag and found his sleeping bag and a white cardboard box containing a packed lunch, which consisted of ham and cheese sandwiches wrapped in polythene, a similarly wrapped sausage roll, a packet of the cheapest crisps he had ever seen by an unheard of brand, an apple, a Mars bar, and a can of a soft drink by another manufacturer that obviously only existed to supply the army at the cheapest rate possible. The plastic envelope contained instructions of where he was to go and what to pick up, and the telephone number to call using the ten pence piece in the event of an emergency.

Jon scanned the list of locations that he was supposed to visit. Penzance was the furthest away (not that you could actually get much further and still be in the UK); Tidworth, near Salisbury was the depot of the Queen's Own Highlanders... but where the hell *was* Tidworth? Windermere – that was stroke of luck. He had worked as a waiter in Bowness on Windermere during his summer holidays as a student, so he could go and see the boss. The other locations were either places he'd never heard of or had no idea how to get to. It was strange how few places in England he had actually visited. All his geographical knowledge was of Scotland or, at best, the North of England. There was no real choice but to pick a direction and start walking.

After a few minutes, a truck passed him and pulled into the side of the road. The passenger door opened, and the grinning face of Dave peered out

"Hi, Jon. Want a lift?"

Jon passed his black bag up to Dave and clambered in. "Thanks, mate," he said to the driver, who was already engaging first gear and pulling back onto the road.

"Nae probs, pal," replied the driver in a soft Scottish accent. "Where're you going?"

"Ultimately Penzance, but Windermere will do for a start, if you're going that way."

"You're in luck. I'm on my way to Lancaster. I can drop you at Kendal."

"Perfect. Thanks."

Kendal was about ten miles from Bowness-on-Windermere, which was a decent distance to walk, but Jon was pretty hopeful of getting a lift. There was normally a lot of traffic, from both holidaymakers and locals. At worst, he could do the ten miles or so on foot if he had to.

"Where are you going, Dave?"

"I don't really know. I've never heard of half these places."

Dave was from a small town in Suffolk and had joined the King's Own Scottish Borderers – otherwise known as 'The Kosbies', which was said to be a Cypriot word for 'cunt' (although it may have just been the pronunciation of the initials KOSB) – because his grandfather had served in the regiment during the Second World War. Consequently, he didn't know the geography of Scotland any better than Jon knew that of southern England.

"Here, let me have a look at your list," Jon offered.

"I've heard of Fort William," Dave said, as he passed over the list.

Dave had been sent north, and Jon recognised Glencoe, Fort William, Spean Bridge and Glenfinnan. Most of the places had a military significance, with Glencoe being the scene of the famous massacre of the MacDonalds by the Campbells; Spean Bridge having a memorial to the Second World War Commando Forces, and Glenfinnan being where Bonnie Prince Charlie had initially landed at the start of the 1745 Jacobite rebellion.

"It's not too bad," said Jon, passing the list back to Dave. "What you need to do is get to Glasgow and then get a lift to Fort William. All the others are either on the way, or not too far away. It's just as well that you're not in the Black Watch, though."

"Why's that?" asked Dave, studying the list with a look of distaste.

"The Black Watch is considered to be a Campbell regiment, so you wouldn't get a welcome in Glencoe."

"Why not?"

"The Campbells massacred the MacDonalds of Glencoe after accepting their hospitality. It was considered a heinous crime, even for those days."

"You're no' a Campbell, are you?" asked the driver.

"No!" exclaimed Dave, indignantly. "I'm a Bentley. Like the car."

"That's OK then. My mother was a MacDonald."

"Oh," said Dave, not quite sure how to respond to that.

The driver gave Jon a secret grin to show that he was joking.

"It could have been worse," interjected Jon. "It could have been the Fort William in Calcutta."

"Calcutta!" shrieked Dave in disbelief.

"Yes. It was built as a barracks in 1781. In fact, there's a story that Redford Barracks should have been a hospital in India, but the plans got mixed up and what was the hospital got built instead."

"I could believe that," agreed Dave.

"Yes, the place is far too light and airy to be a normal British Army barracks. It would make a great hotel, if they ever sold it."

They carried on through a number of small Scottish towns, although most of them were little more than villages, until they reached Crawford Services on the A74, which ran north to Glasgow and south to Carlisle, where it became the M6. Dave got out at this point with instructions to find himself a truck heading north to Glasgow, Inverness or, if he was lucky, Fort William.

"See you on Sunday," he shouted, waving to the driver, and clumping off through the car park in search of a lift northwards

"Ready to go?" asked the driver.

"Lead on, MacDuff."

The A74 from Glasgow to Carlisle was a rather bleak road, but being a dual carriageway, it was fairly fast moving and was the main arterial road from Scotland to England. In the east, the A1 ran south from Edinburgh, passing near York and ultimately leading to London, but the west coast serviced the main industrial centres of Liverpool,

Manchester and Birmingham, and was far busier.

Jon sat and watched a squally rain spattering the windows as they headed over Beattock Summit and hoped that it would be dry further south. He didn't really fancy trudging for miles in the pissing rain, as he only had a waxed waterproof jacket and not the matching trousers.

Soldiers weren't allowed to wear the army-issue waterproofs on patrol, as they were manufactured from a material which made a loud rustling noise. It was said that they were actually made of the same material as crisp packets. Notwithstanding the noise, they were waterproof and were actually quite warm, if not breathable, but they did tend to make you sweat.

Jon had bought a black, waxed cotton jacket that he could wear over his combats to keep him dry. This was considered acceptable as it was 'tactical'. Army-issue uniform and equipment were fairly basic, so in general, if soldiers were willing to shell out their own cash, they were allowed to use non-standard equipment providing it was 'tactical'.

The driver went out of his way and dropped Jon off in the centre of Kendal so that he could get a lift to Windermere, wishing him well with a 'cheerio' before driving off, leaving Jon to pick up his black bag and head for the road to Windermere. Jon reckoned that it would take him about three hours to walk and it was still only mid-afternoon, so he hooked the bag over his shoulder and started out.

In the event, it was only about fifteen minutes before a car stopped and gave him a lift. The car dropped him off outside the Old England Hotel and from there it was only a short walk to The Lake View Café on Kendal Road.

Jon had enjoyed his time working as a waiter there during his college summer holidays, though he had always wondered how the café got its name; there wasn't really a view of the lake. He supposed it was poetic licence. They used to joke that if you stood on a chair in the far corner of the café you could just about see the lake. Maybe, when it was built, the buildings opposite weren't there, but he didn't think that was true.

The café was virtually empty when Jon went in. The coach tours that were the mainstay of the business during the season had obviously stopped coming, and there were only a smattering of customers having afternoon tea in the interval between lunch and dinner.

The café always closed for winter each year and the owners, Fred and Marsha, would normally head off into the sun for a couple of months' holiday in Spain or Florida. Fred's father had retired to an apartment in Alicante, and Jon had dropped him off a bottle of malt whisky on his way south to Morocco on a backpacking holiday a few years before.

It felt good to return to one of his old haunts.

"Hi, Jon. What are you doing here?" asked Marsha, as he walked through the door.

Invariably cheerful, Marsha was an outgoing, middle-aged blonde, although she admitted that it was out of a bottle.

"Hi, Marsha," he replied. "I'm on an initiative exercise."

"And you happened to have The Lake View Café as one of your targets?" she asked with a smile.

"Actually, yes," said Jon. "Well, not The Lake View Café, per se, but I'm supposed to get a postcard of the lake."

Fred and Marsha were both ex-military and so she understood what an initiative exercise normally entailed.

"That's a stroke of luck, since we sell them."

"Isn't it?"

"Fancy a drink?"

"It's a bit early to start drinking, isn't it?"

"It's never too early," said Marsha, with a touch of desperation.

Jon looked closely at her. She must have been beautiful in her youth, but time was beginning tell... that and the drinking and smoking. Jon could see the beginnings of unnatural redness on her cheeks, where the tiny threads of broken veins from too much booze were becoming noticeable.

"Is everything OK?" he asked.

"We have our ups and downs," she admitted.

He could see a sadness in her eyes, though someone who didn't know her as well as he might have easily missed it. "Well, I suppose one drink wouldn't hurt. What have you got?"

"I've got a bottle of white open. It's in the still room "

"Great. I'll just pop up and see Fred first."

"All right," said Marsha. "He'll be in the lounge."

The café kitchens were on the second floor, but it had been built against a hill, so the back door opened out on to ground level. It was actually a three-storey building with two bedrooms on the top floor. Jon had lived in the café during his last year working there as accommodation in and around Windermere was ridiculously expensive. Rich people had bought up the vast number of holiday homes, and the locals and lower-paid were priced out of the property market.

"You could have stayed here and carried on working for us, you know," said Marsha, when Jon had come back from saying hello to Fred.

Jon took the glass of wine and had a sip. It was no worse than he remembered. They'd had a real laugh working together in the café, and Marsha had often opened a bottle of cheap white wine that they had bought from the off-licence further up the road.

He looked into her grey-blue eyes. "It wouldn't have worked," he said, simply.

"Yes, I know," Marsha admitted with a wan smile. "But it would have been fun."

At that point Sue, one of the waitresses who worked for Fred and

Marsha, returned from her break and Marsha went back into the café to take payment from a couple of customers who were leaving.

Jon was left with his thoughts and sat staring out the window at the passing tourists as he sipped the white wine.

When the café closed, he helped Fred and Marsha to lock up and they took him back to their house which was a short walk away. Later that night, they went to one of the local hotels were Fred insisted on paying for all the drinks.

When Bob, one of their friends, heard that Jon was on an army initiative exercise, he got a bit self-righteous and said that if it was him, he would be walking all night to achieve his objectives.

"Don't be daft," countered Fred. "How far would that get you?"

Bob huffed and puffed a bit, but he had never really liked Jon, who had thrown him to the floor one night when he had 'playfully' grabbed him from behind. Bob, who was over 6ft and heavily built, couldn't believe that Jon, who was only 5ft 8ins and slim built, had been able to overpower him, and his embarrassment over the incident had never really gone away.

They left the bar fairly early, and back at the house Jon unrolled his sleeping bag and slept on the sofa. He had decided to leave early in the morning and didn't want to wake everyone else up. Marsha woke him with a cup of tea at six o' clock whilst it was still dark.

"Fred's still asleep. He's going to have a bit of a hangover," she explained.

Jon got up and sat with Marsha as they drank tea together, before leaving the house silently and making his way back to the road towards Kendal. The sun was just beginning to rise and there was just the faintest hint of frost on the grass. It was going to be a fine morning. The air was still, and the world had a freshness that only comes with the early morning.

Jon was halfway up Crag Brow when a car pulled up and a smiling woman rolled down the passenger window.

"Want a lift?" she asked.

"Yes, please."

As he was settling himself in on the back seat, the woman turned round.

"What are you doing here?" she asked.

"I'm on an army initiative test."

"Oh, how wonderful," said the woman. "Where would you like us to drop you?"

"The motorway would be handy, if you're going that way."

"Yes, we can do that, can't we, dear?" said the woman, turning to her husband who was driving.

"Yes, of course," he replied.

Do I know these people? Jon wondered.

He couldn't place them, but they might have seen him in the café, or it might be a case of mistaken identity. He just didn't know and didn't want to ask in case he offended them. He had a slightly unusual way of folding his arms, with his hands holding his biceps, and a couple of customers had mistaken him for someone else and told him that he was identical to that person, so maybe this was another instance

The couple dropped him at Killington Lake Services on the M6 motorway and cheerfully waved him away. He looked about for a truck heading south, then headed towards one with a driver at the wheel.

"Any chance of a lift?" he asked.

"Yes, OK," said the driver. "Where are you going?"

"I don't suppose you're going to Penzance?' asked Jon optimistically.

The driver laughed. "No, I'm heading for Southampton."

"How about Tidworth?" said Jon.

"Yes, I could drop you off at Tidworth, it's almost on the way," said the driver.

Jon was astounded. This was a stroke of luck.

"Great! Thanks," he said.

"Whereabouts in Tidworth?" asked the driver.

"I don't suppose you know where the Queen's Own Highlanders are?"

"No, but I'll drop you off at the guardroom. They'll know."

As it was, the guards at Tidworth Garrison Guardroom were members of the Queen's Own Highlanders.

"Who sent you?" asked one of the Corporals.

"My OC is Lieutenant MacGregor, and Corporal Millar is the squad Corporal," answered Jon.

"Dusty Millar!" said the Guard Sergeant. "How's he doing?"

"Fine, Sergeant," replied Jon.

They stamped his paper to prove that he had got to Tidworth Garrison and offered him some transport to help him on his way. By this point, it was getting late on Saturday afternoon and Jon realised that even if he made it to Penzance, there was minimal chance of getting back to Milton Bridge by Sunday evening.

"Anything going north?" he asked.

The Sergeant looked at the transport roster. "We've got a pick-up in Oxford, if that's any use?"

"Sounds good to me."

The driver was a Private in the Royal Corps of Transport, who talked incessantly about the army, which whiled away the time until he dropped Jon on the outskirts of Oxford.

The sun was beginning to set, and Jon doubted that he would be able to hitch a lift in the dark, so he looked around for somewhere he could spend the night. There was a dry ditch running along the road near a roundabout on the ring road and Jon reckoned that that would be as good a place as any. He had seen a carry-out Chinese restaurant and he bought himself a cheap meal of Chinese curry and chips with the money that he had sewn into the seam of his underpants. He unrolled his sleeping bag and tucked it into the black plastic bag to keep off the dampness and then took off his shoes and relaxed and went to sleep.

When he woke, it was early in the morning and a damp mist was covering the ground. It had rained in the night, and he found he was lying in a pool of water. British Army sleeping bags were made with a waterproof bottom, which had kept out most of the water, but he still felt damp. Partially that was due to the condensation from the black plastic bag, but also from the mist and rain. He got up and rolled up the sleeping bag and tucked it back into the black bag.

Amazingly, the first car that came along stopped for him and the driver gave him a lift to the M40 near Bicester. The car had its heating on full and Jon managed to dry out by the time he was dropped off, so he was feeling quite cheerful as he approached a truck in a layby near the turnoff for Bicester.

"Going north?" he asked.

"Yes, hop in," said the driver. "Manchester OK?"

"Great, thanks," said Jon.

Jon had never really hitchhiked before and found that it was quite easy, if you had the nerve to open the door first, before asking. Few drivers seemed to be willing to say no once you had the door open, although no doubt there were some unpleasant bastards who would have done. *It's probably a lot riskier for a woman*, thought Jon, but he felt pretty capable of defending himself in the event that things turned nasty. The army gave you that confidence.

He made the mistake of going into the centre of Manchester and had no idea which way to go, but fortunately he found a coach full of Territorial Army soldiers returning from an exercise and hitched a lift to a service station on the outskirts of the city. His hopes fell when he saw some graffiti saying that the services were a 'desert for lifts', but that proved untrue when he found a truck that took him all the way back to Edinburgh.

He arrived back at Milton Bridge just before midnight on the Sunday evening and Andy told him that there was a debrief at 0900 in the mess the following morning. With that, he went to bed in what felt like home, even if it was a dilapidated wooden shed with a metal-framed single bed.

CHAPTER 3

The next morning washed and shaved, the squad sat in the leather armchairs in the mess and recounted their tales of adventure and derring-do.

Jon had been the only one who had been sent south and, although he had only managed to get to two of his destinations, he was quite pleased with himself for doing so and managing to get back in time.

Andy recounted how he had got to his first checkpoint to discover that it was the house of Lieutenant MacGregor's mother. She had taken Andy in, fed him and then got one of her staff to ferry him around to the other checkpoints.

"Damn," said Lieutenant MacGregor with a laugh. "I should have told Mother not to do that." He looked around at the others. "Anyone get their end away?"

There was a short silence and then Dave spoke.

"Yes, actually. I did."

"Really?" said the Lieutenant. "One person usually does. Come on, spill the beans."

"Well…" Dave began. "There was this woman in a black Saab who stopped for me and then took me back to her place."

"Well done," congratulated the Lieutenant.

The initiative exercise seemed to have gone down well with the directing staff and the squad were beginning to feel accepted, rather than being considered as a bunch of wasters. Their first hill-walking exercise back at the beginning of their training had been a nightmare from start to finish, with Richard having to be casevaced and the whole three days being spent in soaking misery. After that, the debacle with James had soured the atmosphere for a while, but now they seemed to have turned a corner and were all enjoying themselves a lot more.

"Right," said the Lieutenant. "The rest of the week will be for finishing off projects and a prison visit, and then we've got one more field exercise and we're into the home straight. Well done, everyone."

They knew that the final week included the two-day Pre-RCB and the final party, so that meant that the next two weeks were the last official training of the ten-week course. They were a lot fitter than when they started, and it seemed like a lifetime ago that they had paraded in the ridiculous physical training kit to get issued with their uniforms.

Almost there, thought Jon.

He was actually surprised that he had made it this far. He'd almost packed it in at the same time as James but was now glad that he hadn't. He was starting to really like Lieutenant MacGregor and could visualise him as a friend as well as a colleague later in life.

He could have done without the visit to Saughton prison, though; it was a pretty grim place.

Located in an area called Saughton, hence Saughton prison, its correct name was HMP Edinburgh. It reminded Jon of George Heriot's School for Boys, which had similar iron balustrade balconies. Jon had gone there once after being persuaded to play in a chess competition when he was at school and hoped never to go there again. It was a bit like that with Saughton prison.

The staff were very friendly, at least to Lieutenant MacGregor and the squad, but the whole ambience of the place hinted at vague menace and threat, which Jon supposed was the purpose. You weren't meant to *want* to be in prison after all, so it was unlikely to be a place that felt warm and comfortable.

They were ushered around the various wings with the prison staff explaining the facilities. It was a bit unnerving to be locked in such a place. The warders had bunches of keys chained to their belts and each section was locked before the next was unlocked. The cells were pretty basic, but no worse than some army accommodation, and if you considered that Private soldiers were held to their three-year contracts and couldn't leave the army until their time was up, there were close parallels between the two groups of people. The main difference was that you volunteered to join the army, whereas not many people intentionally get themselves locked up in prison.

Jon was glad to leave the place as the heavy metal door slammed shut behind them with a loud clang.

Potential Officer (PO) hopefuls started to arrive early on Friday afternoon for the two-day Pre-RCB. They had been picked up from Waverley Station in the centre of Edinburgh and ferried out to Milton Bridge in an army minibus. Jon and the rest of the squad watched as the latest batch of young men were ushered into the mess and ticked off the list.

It was surprising how few were actually Scottish, considering that they were all intending to join Scottish regiments. The reason was apparently that Scottish schoolboys tended to be quieter and more reserved than their English counterparts, and this was interpreted by recruiting officers as a lack of confidence and leadership qualities. The gathering group, therefore, came over as a bit brash and arrogant and Lieutenant MacGregor, who was a true Scotsman, eyed them critically.

"You lot shouldn't have any trouble standing out from this crowd," he noted to the team. "Just be yourselves and don't panic."

It was getting towards midnight when the final batch were processed, and Jon was happy to flop into his bed with the prospect of a fairly packed couple of days of tests ahead of him.

Reveille was at 0600, and they started the day with a three-mile run. Some of the candidates were surprisingly unfit, which didn't bode well for their chances of impressing the directing staff. Lieutenant MacGregor was reputed to be thinking of applying to join the SAS, and he had little time for people who couldn't cut the mustard physically.

Jon remembered the first field exercise that they had done, soon after starting the course. Richard had struggled with the weight of his haversack. MacGregor had impatiently taken it off him and carried both Richard's and his own at a faster pace than anyone else in the squad could match.

"Never force me to do that again," he'd told Richard at the end of the march.

Richard was in the Queen's Own Highlanders and would be a close colleague of MacGregor's once he had passed out from Sandhurst and been commissioned, so it was fairly personal.

What had impressed the squad most was the fact that MacGregor had apparently been suffering from a dislocated shoulder and had still able to outpace the team.

At the end of the run, they were numbered off and allocated to syndicates based on their placings, which meant that there was a mix of fitness in each one, rather than risking all the fitter members being in one syndicate, which might skew the results.

They had breakfast in the main cookhouse, which had been opened for the weekend. Previously the squad had always gone to Glencorse Barracks for meals, but since the attendees were all civilians and potential officers, it wasn't considered acceptable for them to eat with the Other Ranks i.e. Private soldiers. Jon reckoned the food was better in Glencorse, which wasn't really a surprise considering it was a major infantry depot.

Jon heard one or two of the students complaining about the

quality of the breakfast and wondered just what sort of lives they had lived prior to coming on this weekend. Judging by their posh accents, some of them were obviously from the higher echelons of society. It was an accepted fact that most regiments were commanded by officers whose fathers and grandfathers had been Lieutenant Colonels. You no longer purchased a commission, but having family connections helped.

The day was broken up into a series of mental and physical tests, designed to mimic the three-day RCB assessment. Jon thought he had done fairly well, particularly when he was approached by the depot commander, Lieutenant Colonel Leitch, who was attending as an observer, and told that he had sounded very knowledgeable during a test where subjects were introduced to the syndicate, who then had two minutes to discuss them.

It came as a bit of a shock, therefore, when an elderly Major wearing a kilt told him that he thought there was something missing from his personality, although he couldn't put his finger on what it was.

He was a bit despondent when MacGregor got them all together to debrief them. He wasn't sure that he should tell the Lieutenant what had been said, but Ian said that the same Major had told him that he didn't think he should bother going to the RCB as he didn't think he would pass.

"Don't worry about that old fool," said MacGregor. "He's been away from his battalion for twenty years and, from what I've heard, they don't want him back."

That came as a relief to them all, but particularly to Ian and Jon, who had borne the brunt of the Major's criticism.

"What's more important now," continued MacGregor with a smile, "is the end of course party. If you do that well, then you're all through."

Since he had lived and worked in Edinburgh for a fair length of time, Jon was given the task of organising the said 'end of course party'. He ordered a nine-gallon barrel of real ale, known as a firkin, from a supplier just off the Grassmarket, and invited all his female friends and acquaintances. The last thing that they needed was more men, particularly non-military ones, as there would be a fair number of staff from both the course and the depot who would need to be invited.

The buffet was provided for by the cookhouse in lieu of an evening meal and the team made decorations for the mess from camouflage netting and bunting. Music was provided by Dave's cassette deck, with him acting as an impromptu DJ.

All in all, it went down very well and there were no embarrassing incidents, and no one was sick – at least not openly.

The following day, the last day of the course, was an open day for parents. Only Jon's parents and Dave's mother actually attended. Andy's father was a diplomat and was serving overseas, and Richard and Ian came from the south of England, so their parents couldn't make it.

There were a series of lectures about the events of the course, slightly censored, and then a buffet lunch with the Commanding Officer and the Second in Command of the Depot. It was whilst talking to Major MacIntyre, the Depot 2 i/c, that Jon's mother suddenly spoke up.

"His brother's in military prison for desertion, you know."

Jon couldn't believe his ears. Was his mother purposely trying to destroy his career?

"Oh! I'm sure it will be fine," said the Major. "Don't worry about it."

But Jon couldn't help wondering if that throwaway comment would come back to haunt him.

The next day, the squad left Milton Bridge, saying goodbye to Lieutenant MacGregor, Sergeant Davies and Corporal Miller.

"Good luck, guys," said the Lieutenant as they left. "See you all in the mess, sometime."

They were given a lift into Edinburgh and Jon left them at Waverley Station, where the rest would catch their trains homewards. Jon was the only one who actually lived in Edinburgh, though Andy had gone to boarding school just outside the city.

"See you at Westbury," said Jon.

They would get their instructions to attend the RCB in Westbury by letter sent to their homes. Until then, they were on leave.

Jon slung his rucksack on one shoulder and picked up his suitcase. He could get a bus almost to his door from just outside the railway station. There was soft rain falling as he made his way to the bus stop and fortunately it was covered, and since there weren't many tourists at this time of year it was also fairly empty. He went upstairs on the bus after loading his kit into the space provided and spent the journey wondering what the RCB would be like.

In a way, he was looking forward to it. After all, it was the culmination of the ten-week course and the Pre-RCB, and passing would open a door into a new world.

The RCB was held at an old estate in Westbury, Wiltshire. Leighton House belonged to the Phipps family, who had bought it from the Earl of Abingdon in 1791. In 1939, it was bought by the War Office, and since 1949 has been used for Officer Selection Boards.

Jon and Dave were on the same board, although they were put into different syndicates and barely saw each other during the three-day process. Andy, Richard and Ian had all attended another selection board that had been held the previous week and were awaiting the results.

As his syndicate lined up, waiting for their photo to be taken, Jon looked around at the other members of the team. They had all been issued with numbered bibs, which they wore over their clothes, allowing the directing staff to easily identify them. No names were used, only numbers.

There were seven other hopefuls with Jon and six of them seemed to be civilians, with no prior military experience. Jon doubted that any of them would pass. The seventh member of the syndicate was quite different. He was smaller than Jon, with bandy legs and arms that he seemed to be unable to straighten. Jon assumed his physique would be seen as a distinct disadvantage for someone wanting to join the Grenadier Guards, except that just after the initial interview, when the whole intake was given an introductory brief, the board president, a Major General, singled him out.

"Hello, Charlie. You'll have to tell me how your father's getting on."

Charlie's father, it turned out, was a Brigadier, who was a close personal friend of the board president.

Well, he's going to pass, then.

The others seemed to be nice guys.

Jon had just completed a ten-week course that, looking back on it, was specifically designed to help him pass the RCB. The first assessment proved him right.

It was a five-minute lecture on a subject of the syndicate member's choice, and the non-military members of the syndicate floundered. The pre-lecture briefing stated that the directing staff member would tap the table when there was a minute to go and that the lecture was to be no more than five minutes in length.

Jon's lecture was one that he had previously given during the SDS course, and so he already knew what he was going to say. He was just waiting to hear the tap.

As soon as he heard it, he wound up the lecture and asked for questions, thus allowing him to finish well within the allotted five minutes.

He sat in agony as the other guys hummed and hawed through their lectures or overran the time. All except Charlie, of course, who had also been trained in how to pass the board.

The assessment then moved on to command tasks. Jon was made syndicate leader for a task that appeared to be relatively simple. The obstacle was an imaginary gap, which had to be traversed using various lengths of planking to form a bridge between the small platforms which dotted the 'gap'. No piece of equipment could be left behind, and if a platform was used and vacated then it couldn't be used again. There was a metal-tubed framework to the left of the imaginary 'gap', but Jon couldn't see a use for it, so he ignored it.

"What's your plan?" he was asked.

"We'll use the planks to form bridges between the platforms and go over the obstacle in stages, bringing all the personnel and equipment with us," he said.

"Do you envisage any problems?"

"No, sir."

"OK," nodded the infantry Captain directing the exercise. "You have twenty minutes, starting now."

Jon called the syndicate together and explained his plan. He stood back, directing the members, and everything was going fine until the lead member, number forty-one, stopped.

"The plank won't reach the next platform," he said.

Bugger, thought Jon. This was obviously intentional. The command task had been designed in such a way that they wouldn't be able to tell that the planks were too short until it was too late.

"OK," he shouted. "Will it reach the framework on your left?"

"Yes," replied number forty-one.

"OK," Jon repeated. "Put it on the apparatus and go across and stay there."

Jon quickly calculated that they could still reach the other side using the framework.

"Number forty-six," he yelled. "Do not, under any circumstances, move until I tell you!"

He was just directing the rest of the syndicate towards the framework when the Captain shouted, "Halt!"

Everything stopped and Jon looked quizzically at him.

"Number forty-six has left the piece of equipment, and it now cannot be used," the Captain explained.

Jon spun around, furiously. Number forty-six, in his excitement, had followed number forty-one onto the framework, but in so doing had vacated the piece of equipment that he had been standing on, which now couldn't be used by any other syndicate member.

He had just completely ruined Jon's plan.

Jon almost exploded in a fit of rage at the disobedience of his order, but caught himself just in time.

Gritting his teeth, he took a few calming breaths. "OK," he said, looking quickly around. "Number forty-four, grab that plank and put it on the platform to your left."

He looked up to see the Captain watching him carefully. He realised that swearing at the unfortunate number forty-six would not have been a good idea and was glad that he had managed to restrain himself.

"Time's up," shouted the Captain. "Bad luck."

Jon felt a surge of disappointment. His one chance to impress had been blown by a useless civvy who didn't know how to obey orders. He helped the team put the equipment back where they had found it, and they moved on to the next task.

There wasn't enough time for every syndicate member to do an individual command task, and Jon noticed that Charlie wasn't tasked to do one. *Is that intentional?* he wondered.

He was happy with his overall performance during the three-day assessment, but he left Westbury wondering if it had been enough. Or had he blown it?

Potential recruits could attend the RCB twice, although there had to be an eight-month gap between attempts. Alternatively, the directing staff might decide that although a potential recruit hadn't gained a straight pass, they were good enough to be sent to a pre-Sandhurst course called Rowallan Company.

They had discussed Rowallan Company at the end of the SDS course and reckoned that it was a nightmare scenario, although after going through the ten-week SDS course with Lieutenant MacGregor, Jon thought it might not be that bad. It would be the disappointment that would be the worst thing. That was much more likely to break his will to carry on than the actual physical effort.

CHAPTER 4

A week later, a fairly plain brown envelope dropped through the letterbox.

Jon knew what it was. He had received a phone call two days before to tell him that he had been accepted to go forward to the Standard Military Course, starting at the Royal Military Academy Sandhurst the following January. It was a single sheet of paper, and rather plain at that, but it was his passport to a commission in the Royal Scots.

Andy phoned to tell him that he and Richard had passed, but not Ian, or Dave. Ian wasn't going to carry on, but Dave had decided to stay with the King's Own Scottish Borderers as a Private.

The three of them were given one week's leave and were then told to report to Bridge of Don Barracks in Aberdeen: a training base for junior soldiers. As the Royal Scots were serving in Northern Ireland, and the Queen's Own Highlanders were in the Falklands, neither regiment was considered suitable for Potential Officers. The other option would have been an attachment to a regiment based in West Germany, but the powers that be had concluded that posting the three of them to Aberdeen would be considerably cheaper, so they took the train north.

Aberdeen, known as the Granite City due to many of the old houses being built out of local granite, was freezing cold in winter. The wind that blew from the east came directly from Siberia, with nothing in its way as it blasted across the North Sea. Bridge of Don Barracks was located in the northern part of the city, an easy walk from the centre.

Andy, Richard and Jon were billeted in the 'band' block: an old, granite-built tower that, as its name suggested, housed the regimental musicians. Each regiment had its own band, with the bandsmen traditionally acting as stretcher bearers on the battlefield. Scottish regiments also had pipe bands, paid for by the regiment's officers, as it was unthinkable that a Scottish Regiment should go into battle without the skirl of bagpipes to inspire them. The sound of massed pipes and drums would make anyone with the slightest hint of Scottish blood in them want to fix bayonets and charge the enemy.

Be that as it may, the 'band' block was warm and dry, and the granite building seemed to be more than capable of blocking the bitter, howling wind that blew in from the sea. They each had their own room as, being Potential Officers rather than mere Privates, they were treated differently from normal infantrymen. The occupant of the room opposite Jon was an old Corporal, who was a couple of years from retirement. Soldiers could sign on for twenty-two years and spend all of it as a Private, but this guy had obviously made it to the heady rank of Corporal and then got no further. He seemed perfectly content with the arrangement and said that he had known several twenty-two-year Privates who had been happy to stay at that rank.

On the first Saturday night, Andy, Richard and Jon braved the freezing temperatures and went out on the town. Andy knew a girl who was studying at Aberdeen University and who had invited them all to a party. They had a few in the local pubs and then made their way to the address that Andy had been given. Richard left early and Andy seemed to be heavily involved with his student friend, so Jon went for a lie-down in one of the bedrooms that had been used for coats. He awoke to furtive whispering.

"Who's that?" asked a voice.

"I don't know, but I think he's a soldier," whispered another with a trace of fear in it.

"Oh!" said the first voice. "Maybe we'd better leave him alone, then."

Jon realised that it was the early hours of the morning, and that he was taking up someone else's bed, so he levered himself up and staggered to the communal lounge. Andy had vanished and the party seemed to be over, so he left the flat and made his way back to the barracks. Fortunately, it wasn't too far away, and the guards grinned at him as he signed himself in.

He woke up to wan sunlight shining through the thin curtains and made his way to the parade ground, where the Regimental Sergeant Major had volunteered them to man a regimental float for an army open day.

He had a stinking hangover, but Richard hadn't been drinking so he managed to cover for Jon and Andy, who had arrived just before the RSM made his appearance.

"I thought you had a steady girlfriend?" Richard said to a grinning Andy, later that morning.

"Yes, but she's in Edinburgh," replied Andy, as if that justified doing the dirty.

His latest conquest was called Anne and Andy had apparently known her from school. He was an incredibly good-looking guy, blond with startlingly blue eyes and a strong but not overbearing upper-class accent and was typically the first of them to garner female attention in any scenario. He said that he had once been to a do – hosted by his father, who was in the Diplomatic Corps – and had been asked by one of the guests if he wanted a career as a porn star. He smilingly told Richard and Jon that he had considered it. His father apparently held the equivalent rank of Major in the Intelligence Corps and, in the event of war, would take up the position of military attaché in whatever embassy he found himself.

"Did you not think of joining the Int Corps, then?" asked Jon.

"No. I didn't get enough O-levels," admitted Andy.

They all agreed that the infantry was where they wanted to be anyway, being real soldiers.

The staff at the barracks didn't really know what to do with three potential officers who were Private soldiers, so they were attached to the training team and given odd jobs to do.

One day they went out to Black Dog Range, to the north of Aberdeen, where they helped set up the firing range for a General Purpose Machine Gun (GPMG) demonstration. The North Sea oil industry was in full swing, and Aberdeen was its base, meaning personnel were being ferried back and forth out to the oil rigs by helicopter. A pilot had complained about potentially being hit by stray rounds, so a team from Bridge of Don Barracks had been sent to the ranges to see how high a stray round might go.

They had used the GPMG because it fired a 7.62 mm round and had a range of 1800 metres in the sustained fire role, though the test was to use tracer rounds, which would burn out at 1100 metres. Given that helicopters often flew as low as 150 metres above the city, they were technically well within range if any rounds were to stray.

The machine gun was set up on the 300-metre firing point, using a heavy tripod rather than the fixed bipod with which the weapon was issued, as the weapon was being used in a 'sustained fire role'. The butt was replaced with a back plate and the firer sat behind it instead of lying down. In this manifestation it could fire 750 rounds per minute, and there were stories of the barrel actually melting or becoming so hot that it was possible to see the rounds going up the barrel.

In this test they were using a one in five tracer method i.e. every fifth round was a tracer round. To help evaluate if the rounds would go straight up, they had placed a piece of corrugated iron, otherwise known as 'wriggly tin', on the range as the target.

Jon watched happily as one of the Corporals from the training team opened fire and a stream of red flashes shot towards the target. Occasionally, one would ricochet upwards, proving the point that it was feasible for a round to go to a theoretical 1800 metres. All that meant, really, was that commercial helicopters would have to avoid flying over the ranges when they were in use. There was no way that the army was going to stop using the ranges for live firing, and it would be up to the oil companies to cover the cost of flying around, rather than over, the location.

Andy, Richard and Jon were hoping to get a shot at firing the GPMG, but it was never offered, and they didn't have the confidence to ask.

Pity, Jon thought. It was unlikely that he would ever get the chance to fire one in a sustained fire role, as officers didn't do that sort of thing. Their job was to lead the troops, not to get involved in the actual fighting.

He wondered what it would have been like during the First World War when machine guns like these were used to massacre hundreds or even thousands of men. The British weapon in those days was the Vickers machine gun – a water-cooled beast that could fire 600 rounds per minute. There was a record of one being fired continuously for twelve hours. It was belt-fed, and the belts came in nine-yard lengths, leading to the expression of giving the full nine yards.

Jon did a rough calculation that that a .303 round being a third of an inch meant that the 'full nine yards' would require around a thousand rounds, or about two minute's worth of fire. These days, the GPMG is fired in three to five round bursts. The problem was carrying the ammunition. It was bloody heavy. They had been told that during the Falklands conflict, the Paras had carried nothing but water and ammunition when they went into combat and had still run out of ammunition, to the extent that most of the Argentinian casualties were the result of bayonets.

The following week, the three of them were 'invited' to join a three-day exercise, which was the culmination of the junior soldiers' infantry training, before they went on leave for Christmas. They were attached to different platoons, and Jon found himself with Sergeant Richardson, who had a reputation for being a real hard bastard. Jon had been told by one of the junior soldiers that Richardson had been known to come up behind them on field exercises and piss on them to make sure that they didn't move while on sentry duty, so Jon was a bit apprehensive about being part of his platoon.

The exercise started from the parade square in Bridge of Don, where an RAF Westland Wessex helicopter from RAF Lossiemouth landed to pick up the platoon. The exercise was to protect the airbase from enemy attack, the enemy being made up of a unit from 45 Commando, Royal Marines. Jon was made stick leader for his side of the helicopter and his job was to signal to the pilot when all his troops had embarked. It all went well, and he was quite enjoying his first helicopter flight, when he saw Sergeant Richardson gesturing at him. He was puzzled about what the Sergeant meant. He was pointing straight at Jon and then pointing downwards. Jon tried to interpret what he wanted and then glanced sideways. To his horror, he realised that the junior soldier next to him was about to be sick, the result being that vomit would soon be spread around the inside of the aircraft by centrifugal force. To prevent this, Richardson was telling the soldier to be sick into his combat jacket. Fortunately for the other occupants of the helicopter, he complied.

Maybe it's just as well Richardson's got a reputation, thought Jon, relieved. Being covered in vomit was not the way he had envisaged starting a three-day exercise.

They were dropped off a short while later and immediately took up guard positions around the airbase. Jon found himself in a small bunker on top of a hardened aircraft hangar, with two junior soldiers attempting to keep warm while watching out for Royal Marine infiltrators.

The next day was spent guarding the main gate, until they were informed that a fighting patrol was being sent out to try to locate the enemy's base camp. If this could be located, they would put in a dawn attack and then all go home for tea and medals.

It was pissing with rain and pitch-black, meaning the patrol, despite being led by an experienced Sergeant, couldn't find the location of the Royal Marines' base. They stumbled through marshy fields, tripping over tussocks of grass, known as 'baby's heads', and stepping into small streams, made faster flowing by the incessant rain. They had been allowed to wear army waterproofs under their combat jackets, but the rain managed to get through, down their necks and along their sleeves and they were all cold, wet and tired by the time the Patrol Sergeant finally gave up and turned for home – home being some concrete bunkers on the fringes of the airfield.

It had stopped raining, but it was still very dark with minimal moonlight and Jon had started to see flashing lights. They were ambushed from behind at one point and, in the chaos, Jon's weapon, an old SLR, jammed, partially due to excess moisture down the barrel but mostly because it was probably about twenty-five years old.

He had still not managed to remove the jammed round by the time the patrol returned to camp and the Sergeant lined them up to clear their weapons. He wasn't thinking straight, and instead of going through the correct unloading drill of putting the safety catch on, taking the magazine off, tilting the weapon to the right and cocking it three times before flipping the safety off and pulling the trigger, he took the magazine off and pulled the trigger, thinking that the chamber was empty. It wasn't, and the – fortunately – blank round went off with a loud bang.

"Who did that?" screamed the Sergeant.

"Me, Sergeant," admitted Jon.

He could have kept quiet and would probably have got away with it in the dark, but someone else would have taken the blame and he wasn't the sort of person who could let another be punished for his mistake.

Because he was a Potential Officer and not a junior soldier, the Sergeant didn't give him a punch as he would normally have done, and merely said, "That was an ND."

"Yes, Sergeant," said Jon, knowing that he'd fired a round without being ordered to do so – a 'negligent discharge'.

"OK," said the Sergeant. "We'll talk about this later."

"Yes, Sergeant," agreed Jon.

There was nothing more he could say.

The following day, the company patrolled out into the hills and lay waiting for three hours in the driving rain for a Territorial Army infantry unit (who were playing the enemy) to appear, so that they could spring an ambush. They never appeared, having gone over the wrong hill. With much muttering about how useless the TA were, the company finally made its way to the transport, consisting of 4-ton trucks that would take them back to Bridge of Don.

Sitting in the back of the 4-ton truck on wooden bench seats and soaking wet, someone gave Jon a hardtack biscuit and a cigarette. Oddly enough, he was happy.

Three hours later, they arrived at Bridge of Don Barracks. Jon's billet was lovely and warm, and he had a hot shower before putting his muddy, wet uniform into the washing machine and cleaning his kit.

"I hear someone had a ND," said one of the Corporals in the mess later that evening.

Andy, Richard and Jon used the Corporals' mess, since they were still Privates, not officers.

"Yes, that was me," admitted Jon, sheepishly.

The Corporal looked at him. "It's a case of beer for the staff."

"That's pretty reasonable."

"You were lucky that it was a blank. Don't worry, everyone has an ND at some point," he added, seeing the downcast look on Jon's face. "Just don't let it happen again."

The next day, they were told to go and see the orderly officer, Lieutenant Codrington, to give him a hand with setting up a room for the Christmas party. Because the junior soldiers were under eighteen, they were not allowed alcohol, but a magician and a hypnotist had been booked to perform. If it had been a normal infantry unit, there would probably have been a stripper, depending on whether there were any women in attendance, but this was a training unit for junior soldiers and not the Scottish Infantry Depot.

On the morning of the Christmas party, the officers, including Andy, Richard and Jon this time, carried on the tradition of serving the Other Ranks Christmas dinner. Although it was not actually Christmas Day, the Commanding Officer had decided that they would act as if it was. There were three newly commissioned Second Lieutenants who had come straight from Sandhurst, and they also were expected to join in.

At the end of the meal, one of the Corporals looked the new Second Lieutenants up and down.

"Look at the state of them," he remarked to Andy, Richard and Jon. "At least you three look like soldiers."

That was quite a compliment, thought Jon.

He looked at the three newbies. They did indeed look like three schoolboys rather than three leaders of men. They hadn't even bulled their shoes and, as one of the other Corporals pointed out, if a Private soldier had turned up at a CO's parade looking like that they would have found themselves charged with being 'in bad order'

The evening party went off quite well. There was no way that Jon was going to allow himself to be the victim of a hypnotist, but one of the Corporals found himself the butt of many a joke having been made to count to ten after being hypnotised to miss out the number seven. It was very clever, and Jon wondered how it worked. Maybe he would find out one day.

The following morning, Andy, Richard and Jon had a final interview with the Commanding Officer, who thanked them for their help and wished them well at the Academy.

"Maybe we'll see you back here, one day," he said, pleasantly.

They, in turn, thanked him for the posting and that was that. They were taken to the station and Christmas leave awaited.

The plan was that they would meet up in London for New Year's Eve, before spending a couple of days with Ian arriving at the Academy on 5 January. Andy was staying with Jon, as his parents were in the Far East, and they spent their time visiting local pubs, where Andy would invariably pick up the best-looking women. Jon didn't really mind. Andy's confidence with the other sex was beginning to rub off on him. He had always been a bit shy, but in Andy's company he could now comfortably start speaking to women whom he otherwise wouldn't have had the nerve to approach.

On New Year's Eve, Jon said goodbye to his parents, and he and Andy caught the train from Edinburgh Waverley Station to London King's Cross, though there had been a moment at the ticket office when Jon had thought the plan was all going to rat shit.

Jon had presented his travel warrant at the ticket office to get his ticket to London, and the man behind the counter had looked at it quizzically.

"This ticket is for Camberley," he'd said.

"Yes," Jon had replied. Camberley was where the Royal Military

Academy was located.

"Well, you can't go to London," the man had said officiously.

"Why not?"

"'Cause it's not the shortest route."

British Army travel warrants allowed for second-class travel by the shortest and cheapest possible route. Jon had never in his wildest dreams thought that there could be any way of getting to Camberley other than via London, but apparently there was.

"What's the other route, then?" he'd asked.

"It goes through Birmingham," the man had informed him.

Shit, Jon had thought. That would blow his plans.

"When does it leave?" he'd asked. *Maybe I can get back to London from Camberley.*

The man had rifled through his timetable. "It left last Tuesday."

"So, I'll have to go through London, then?"

"I suppose so," the man had admitted, reluctantly.

They'd got their tickets and caught the 1100 train to London, which had arrived into King's Cross at 1720, only twenty minutes late, which Andy and Jon considered to be fairly acceptable. It was dark outside, although with the streetlights and Christmas decorations it was well illuminated.

They got a taxi to Charing Cross Station, where they had arranged to meet the others, stowing their baggage before making their way to The Ship and Shovel in Craven Passage, next to the station. Ian and Richard were already in the bar with a couple of friends, and they had all obviously had a few.

"What's the plan, then?" asked Andy.

"We'll stay here until closing and then go to Trafalgar Square for midnight," Ian told them.

"Sounds good to me," said Jon.

The Ship and Shovel served the usual pub food, the beer was acceptable, and there was a good atmosphere. Everyone seemed to be in a festive mood. At one point, a man wearing a cowboy outfit, including a gun belt and Stetson, came in, which was a bit bizarre, but it added to the party spirit.

Just before closing time, they all pooled their cash to get a carry-out and then left The Ship and Shovel to make their way to Trafalgar Square. The crowd was huge, and people were standing shoulder to shoulder. The weather was suprisingly mild and the guys reckoned that they might even jump into one of the fountains, which was traditional for New Year's Eve. Jon had never particularly liked being in crowds and didn't really feel comfortable, so he told them that he would meet them after midnight at the fountain nearest the lion.

As he was making his way through the crowd, he noticed that every so often there would be a surge, as if a wave was passing through the throng of people. On one occasion, he was almost pushed over by the force of the phenomenon. He realised that if that happened, he could easily be crushed under a pile of bodies, like a huge rugby scrum, except those at the bottom would have no way of getting up again. With this in mind, he forced his way to the fountain and wedged himself against the rounded granite surround to wait for his friends.

After a few minutes, he found himself next to an attractive, dark-haired girl who appeared to be by herself. She smiled at him when she realised he was looking at her.

"Are you here by yourself?" he asked.

"No," she replied. "My brother has gone to jump in the fountain. You?"

"My friends are doing that too, but I didn't fancy it myself. My name's Jon, by the way"

"Marion," the woman reciprocated.

They carried on chatting and when New Year's Eve arrived, she gave him a kiss. After about fifteen minutes, there was still no sign of either Marion's brother or Jon's colleagues.

"Where are you meeting your friends?" she asked.

"We arranged to meet at the lion nearest the fountain," said Jon, looking around. There was still a huge crowd, and though he could see the lion, he couldn't see Andy, Richard or the others.

"There are two fountains, you know," Marion told him.

"Ah!" said Jon. He hadn't known that, nor obviously did Andy or Richard. "Which one are you meeting your brother at?"

"I'm not," she said simply. "We're meeting at the tube station. Do you want to come?"

Jon thought about it for a moment. He had lost his friends; he had spent all his ready cash and had no idea where the nearest cash machine was. He also had no idea where *he* was, apart from the fact that he was in Trafalgar Square, and that an attractive girl had asked him if he wanted to go with her.

She must have sensed his hesitation. "I can put you up for the night," she suggested. "I've got a flat in West Kensington."

"Sounds good to me," said Jon.

She linked arms with him, and they eased their way through the crowd that was still thronging the square, walking down Northumberland Avenue to the Embankment Tube Station. Marion's brother was already there, waiting outside the station.

"This is Jon," she told her brother. "He lost his friends and has nowhere to stay."

Marion's brother smiled. "Right, let's get back to your place, then. I'm freezing."

They got the District Line to West Kensington Station and turned left onto North End Road. To the right was a pub called The Three Kings, which Jon noted as a landmark. The lights were still on and there was obviously a lock-in party going on.

"You have no idea where you are, do you?" Marion asked, mischievously.

"No, I'm completely lost," Jon admitted.

"Then you'd better be nice to me," said Marion with a smile.

After a short while, they turned right onto Chesson Road, where Marion and a friend shared a two-bedroom flat. Marion's flatmate was there with her boyfriend, and they all had a couple of drinks and swapped stories until Jon yawned widely.

"Sorry," he said. "It's been a long day."

"You can use my bed, if you want," said Marion. "I'm going to stay up a bit longer."

"Thanks," said Jon and bade his goodnights before falling asleep in Marion's comfortable double bed.

When he woke up in the morning, Marion's brother had gone. She made him breakfast and they retraced their steps to The Ship and Shovel, where they found Andy, Richard and Ian nursing hangovers.

"Hi, guys. This is Marion," said Jon, cheerfully, as they stared, open-mouthed at him.

Marion had a quick Coke and then Jon walked her back to the tube station.

"I won't be allowed out for five weeks," he told her. "But if you want, I'll come and see you after that."

"That would be nice," she said, smiling at him.

"I'll send you a letter to let you know what's happening," he called as she stepped aboard the carriage for West Kensington and the tube hissed quietly away.

When he got back to the pub, his friends all looked at him.

"Well?" Andy asked.

"Well, what?" Jon replied.

"Did you sleep with her?"

"No," said Jon. "It wouldn't have been gentlemanly."

Their expressions told him what they thought of this reply.

"You must be the only person who could get picked up by a woman in Trafalgar Square on New Year's Eve, taken home, and still not sleep with her," said Ian.

Jon wasn't sure if that was a compliment or not, but he wasn't going to say any more on the matter. He had Marion's address and a vague agreement to meet up again in five weeks' time. That was good enough for him.

Ian lived in Kent, and they spent the next couple of days drinking in country pubs and meeting Ian's mates, before getting the train to Camberley and embarking on the next stage of their army careers.

CHAPTER 5

"Take a good look. That's the last you're going to see of the civilian world for five weeks," said the voice of the Corporal who had been designated to pick them up.

What am I letting myself in for? thought Jon, as he watched the leafless, winter-bound trees through the windows as they drove from Camberley Station to Royal Military Academy Sandhurst – their home for the next six months.

The Standard Military Course was a six-month programme designed to train young men to be Second Lieutenants. The course had previously been twelve months long, but it had been decided, as a cost-cutting measure, to split it into two, as a Short Service Commission (SSC) was only three years in duration. Those getting promoted to full Lieutenant, or who were on a Regular Commission (RC), would attend a second six-month course, known as the 'joined-up writing course', after they had served a couple of years with their units.

Female officers were all attached to the Women's Royal Army Corps, regardless of which regiment or corps they intended to serve in and did most of their training separately from the men. In a number of circles, it was still believed that women shouldn't be in the army at all, despite evidence that women could be just as good soldiers as men. There was a saying that the British Army was fifty years behind the times and the Scottish division was one hundred years behind.

A bit like Dundee, Jon thought.

Officer Cadets joining the army as army scholars, from Welbeck College, by passing the RCB, or having been promoted up through the ranks, were enrolled in New College, but those who joined the army after having completed a degree went to Victory College and did so as Second Lieutenants. This meant that they not only had an easier time than normal Officer Cadets, but they also passed out as full Lieutenants, and so jumped a rank. Jon didn't see how that was fair, but as he had already established, the British Army was rather stuck in its ways.

New College was a substantial set of buildings, but Arnhem and Rhine Companies used a conglomeration of portacabins, comprising accommodation, ablutions and classrooms close to, but separate from, Old College, which was the impressive building with the parade square, where passing out parades were held. Traditionally, the adjutant of Sandhurst, who led the Sovereign's Parade, would ride his white horse up the steps of Old College at the end of the parade.

Andy and Richard were posted to Arnhem Company and Jon went to Rhine Company. It was a bit of a shock to the system to find out that he was not only separated from his colleagues during training, but also during their downtime, as Arnhem Company was located in a different set of buildings and the two were completely isolated.

He was allocated a room, told that there was a briefing at 1700, then left to his own devices. On the standard metal-framed single bed were two stiff white sheets, four grey army blankets and a bed cover that could have doubled as a set of curtains. A yellow, typewritten sheet dictated exactly where every piece of kit should go and even detailed how one's hair should be cut, and the fact that they were not allowed to go on parade with shaving cuts.

Does that mean that if you cut yourself shaving, you don't attend the parade? Jon wondered. Highly unlikely. Everything just had to be pristine, including their faces. *Great! This is going to be like basic training, only worse.*

The briefing was held in the platoon classroom and the Officer Cadets were introduced to their Platoon Sergeant, Colour Sergeant McGovern of the Scots Guards. He was a huge, red-faced man with dark, greasy hair, though he seemed fairly pleasant to Jon.

Royal Military Academy instructors were all hand-picked and destined for greater things. The Platoon Sergeants were all Guards Division Colour Sergeants and were expected to make Regimental Sergeant Major in their respective regiments later on in their careers. This was the peak of the promotion ladder for Other Ranks, the next step being a commission to make them officers.

Colour Sergeant McGovern explained the programme, starting with the fact that they would make 'bed blocks' each morning, ready for room inspection. A bed block was a way of folding one's blankets and sheets into a neat, square block, with three blankets and the two sheets layered like a Liquorice Allsort and wrapped in the fourth blanket. It had to be exactly the right dimensions and placed exactly in the right location at the end of the bed.

The Colour Sergeant then explained that the next five weeks were the introductory phase, which would consist of drill, fieldcraft, tactical lessons, more drill, physical training, first aid, nuclear, biological, and chemical weapons training, weapons handling, and more drill. The culmination of the five weeks would be a drill parade, the successful completion of which would entitle the Officer Cadet to a weekend pass. Failure to pass the parade would result in a weekend of more drill.

There seems to be a theme to this, thought Jon. *I wonder if it has anything to do with drill?*

The Company Sergeant Major (CSM) was another Guardsman, but this time a Warrant Officer class two (WO2), who took the first parade the following morning. The platoon was lined up in the classroom as, being early January, it was still dark outside, and the staff didn't want any injuries at this early stage.

"My name is Sergeant Major Grant," he said, by way of introduction. "Since you are all Officer Cadets, I will call you sir and you, in return, will call me sir. The only difference is that you'll mean it."

Did he really say that? Jon had read about the clichés and standard phrases that they used during training sessions but had not actually believed that they would use them. Until now.

Despite this rocky start, the Company Sergeant Major seemed like a nice guy, unlike the New College Regimental Sergeant Major, Warrant Officer class one (WO1) I.P. Norris, who exuded an air of prickishness. Jon instinctively disliked him. Sandhurst also had an Academy Regimental Sergeant Major, who was the only Warrant Officer in the army who carried a sword, but Jon hadn't met him yet. He would be the one who inspected the Officer Cadets at the five-week drill parade and would decide if they got the weekend off or not.

That was the goal of the first five weeks: firstly, to survive, and secondly, to pass the parade and get the weekend off. Jon reckoned that he had a distinct advantage, having been in the Territorial Army and also having done the ten-week SDS course. He certainly had no real problems with the basic training, having done most it before. The one fly in the ointment was that Colour Sergeant McGovern was new to the post and was subsequently very keen to excel, whereas some of the other Colour Sergeants were far more laid back.

Colour Sergeant McGovern kept the platoon making bed blocks for the whole five weeks and no one was allowed to talk during 'shining parades', where they would sit for hours polishing their boots until they were 'black diamonds'. This meant that it was difficult to get to know the rest of the platoon, as they had no time to socialise. Jon only got to know those who had rooms close to his and became the unofficial protector of the 'overseas' students, who were regarded by some of the platoon as wasters, or worse.

One of his new acquaintances, Paddy, had been sent to the dreaded Rowallan Company before joining the Standard Military Course. The course had apparently been so tough that some of the inmates – "sorry, attendees," Paddy corrected, rolling his eyes – had T-shirts printed with '*vita est vacca caci*' on the front, meaning '*life is a bucket of shit*', and '*when I die, I'm bound to go to Heaven, as I've already served my time in Hell*' on the back. In actual fact, Jon knew the correct Latin should have been '*vita situla stercore*', but it didn't have quite the same fluency of prose, so Jon didn't mention that particular titbit to Paddy.

There were a couple of unpleasant physical tests during the first five weeks, including the dreaded 'milling', a three-minute round of boxing designed to test a person's willingness to fight, although it was peddled as a test for the intercompany boxing team. Jon had no interest in boxing and certainly did not want to spend extra time in boxing training, but he was happy to show willing.

The platoon was formed up in the gym in two lines, the theory being that opponents would be of roughly equal height and weight, though that didn't often translate into practice. When his turn came, Jon found himself facing a guy who looked noticeably bigger and heavier. Although Jon was average height, he struck it unlucky by being paired with a partner who looked like he had been on the school rugby team.

He didn't remember much of the bout, except that the three minutes seemed to last forever. He'd gone straight in fighting, to make a good effort, and had immediately been hit in the face. Everything went black, so he'd continued flailing about until, finally, the bell went for the end of the bout.

"Was it OK?" he asked Tim Forrest, who had the room next to him.

"I don't know about boxing, but it was a good scrap," said Tim with a smile.

That'll do, thought Jon.

The two things he learnt from the milling was that it was bloody painful, and that three minutes could seem like an eternity. Fortunately, he wasn't selected for the boxing team.

Another shock to the system had been the 'cold water swim'. They had been having swimming lessons once a week during physical training, but this was something different. According to their Physical Training Instructor, more members of the SAS had drowned than been killed in combat, so they needed to be introduced to combat swimming.

They were told to dress in fatigues, which meant their lightweight green trousers, shirts and boots. They double marched to the lake at the front gates of the academy and there saw the object of the lesson. They were to swim to a platform in the middle of the lake and back, along a slimy knotted rope that was strung between said platform and a peg on the lake's edge, which had been hammered into the ground.

Jon took his place in the line behind Aziz, a young Omani Officer Cadet, who had told him that he really wanted to be a banker, but that since he was the first son, his father had made him join the army – he was destined to be a Brigadier.

The first shock came when the water reached groin height, then chest height. Jon felt that he could scarcely breathe. He started swimming and could feel the weeds dragging his feet down. One of the instructors was in a kayak close by, but it didn't make Jon feel any better. He was about halfway to the platform when Aziz started screaming. There was nothing that Jon could do to help him; he was having trouble keeping his own head above water as it was, and besides, the guy in the kayak was on the case. He let go of the rope and swam around Aziz, who was clinging on for grim death. He managed to get back to the edge of the lake and crawled up the bank.

Jon was beginning to shake uncontrollably. It was February, and the water was barely above freezing. Jon was not exactly built for the cold, having been told at the medical that if he'd had any less body fat he would have been classed as underweight.

He got up and started moving to try to get some heat into his body before hypothermia set in. He had been told that no one actually suffered from hypothermia until someone invented it. Previously, people were just bloody cold and got on with it, but after the symptoms had been listed and the results given a name, individuals would start to recognise that they had it, but that didn't really help, in the circumstances.

He had also heard that one Officer Cadet got discharged from Sandhurst after going down with exposure, because it was considered to constitute a 'lack of moral fibre'.

There were some real bastards about.

The next week, having just about survived the cold water swim, they were given an even more gruelling task: the 'trainasium'. This involved a framework tower about 10m high, with a set of parallel bars attached to the top, which they had to climb up to and then shuffle across. The worst thing was that there were trees just far enough away to make them impossible to jump to, but close enough to emphasise the height.

The Paras had a test where recruits had to go up 30 m then jump from one plank to another. The instructors reckoned that if anyone couldn't do it, they wouldn't be able to jump out of a plane. Jon reckoned that would probably be easier, or at least no worse, than the shuffle bars.

Fortunately, after that, it was mainly drill, drill and more drill in preparation for the parade at the end of the five weeks.

Jon had written to Marion the week before the parade, to see if she was free that weekend, and she had replied saying that her flatmate was going away for a couple of days and that they would have the flat to themselves. All that was required now was to make a good impression on the Academy Regimental Sergeant Major.

The format was for the companies to form up by platoons, which would then be inspected. After the inspection, each platoon would march around the square, showing off their drill, and then each Officer Cadet would individually march out to where the Academy RSM and the Platoon Commander were waiting. They would then halt, salute and, after being dismissed, salute again and perform an about turn and march back to the squad.

They all marched down to the main parade square – where the Sovereign's Parade would be held for the pass-out of the senior division nine weeks later – and formed up in a waiting area to the side of Old College.

Out of the corner of Jon's eye he could see Officer Cadets lifting their feet backwards.

What the hell's going on?

When the inspecting officer reached Jon's platoon, he realised that they were checking the soles of the guy's boots in case a stud had fallen out. The Officer Cadets wore 'ammunition' boots for drill, heavy leather boots with thirteen studs in the soles of each. The story was that they represented the thirteen Victoria Crosses won by members of the Guard's Division, but Jon doubted this. *They must have won more,* he thought. They were supposed to be the elite of the infantry after all, but maybe it was true.

Whatever the reason, they were being checked, and failure to pass the inspection could lead to a failure to pass the parade. Jon started sweating even though it was a cold day. Had he checked that all the studs were there on his boots? He couldn't remember. In the event, the inspecting officer didn't check his boots, but Jon's nerves were still frayed.

His platoon was given the order, and they marched off around the square. It helped relax Jon a bit; he actually quite liked drill. When his turn came, he marched smartly out and halted the regulation three paces from the Academy RSM.

"Officer Cadet Comyn, sir," he stated, as per instruction.

"Are you related to the Gordon-Comyns?"

"I'm afraid not, sir," replied Jon. He had no idea what the RSM was talking about and hoped that his answer would do.

"Don't be afraid, Cadet," said the Sergeant Major, with a faint smile. "Dismissed."

Jon saluted and then turned on his heel to face away. This was the critical bit. He had to pivot on his heel and stand still for the regulation pause of 'two, three', before marching away. It was easy to wobble and make a mess of it, especially if a weekend pass rested on it. Jon did a perfect about turn and marched round the back of the platoon to take up his position.

He had passed the test and earned himself the weekend off.

Three members of the platoon failed the parade and despondently watched as their comrades left the academy for their first taste of freedom in five weeks.

Jon met up with Marion at The Three Kings and had a pint of real ale. They went for a pizza with one of Marion's friends and then went back to the flat to enjoy the rest of the night by themselves.

"Do you want some company?" Marion asked as they were getting ready for bed.

"That would be nice," replied Jon, giving her a smile.

CHAPTER 6

Lieutenant Colonel Leitch had a problem.

He called his Second in Command, Major MacIntyre, into the office, where two other Lieutenant Colonels sat in the square armchairs that the army provided for visitors.

"Yes, sir?" enquired Major MacIntyre.

"We've got a problem, Ian," Leitch stated. "The Royal Scots" – at this he gestured to one of the other Lieutenant Colonels sitting by the wall, who gave him a nod – "only have room for one more Short Service Commission for 1960, and they've now got two candidates."

Each infantry regiment in the British Army allocated its commissions on a system relating to the birth year of the applicants. They were allowed two Short Service Commissions and two Regular Commissions per birth year, which meant that if three people born in 1960 – or in this case, two – applied for a Short Service Commission, then only one was allowed it, and the other person would have to find a different regiment to join. It was a strange system, but it was supposed to mean there was a range of ages for officers, so that there wouldn't be a blockage for promotion. The promotion pyramid in an infantry regiment narrowed dramatically after Captain, and even more dramatically after that, as there was normally only one Lieutenant Colonel in each regiment who was the Commanding Officer.

"Which one do they want?" asked Major MacIntyre.

"They want the one who isn't already at Sandhurst," stated Leitch, bleakly.

"Bugger."

"Quite."

"Is there any leeway?" asked Major MacIntyre, knowing full well that there wasn't.

"I'm afraid not," said the Lieutenant Colonel of the Royal Scots. "Our preference is the son of Charlie Lawson. I gave him my personal promise that I would look after his boy."

Lieutenant Colonel Leitch looked at Major MacIntyre. "Is there anything in other one's SDS report that we can use?"

"No. He got a very good course report from Lieutenant MacGregor, and he passed the RCB with flying colours."

"Damn. How's he doing at the Academy, John?"

The Royal Scots officer, who was also the Regimental Liaison Officer, rifled through a notepad. "Unfortunately, very well, so far," he said. "He's passed everything and is very popular, especially with the overseas cadets."

"We'll just have to get his grading down then, won't we?" said the other officer. "Then we can get him to join another unit and the problem's solved. It's not as if he's got any family connections to the Royals, is it?"

Major MacIntyre was appalled but gave no sign. He had risen through the ranks and was horrified that these supposed 'gentlemen' were willing to potentially ruin a man's career for the sake of a vague promise given to a colleague, but these supposed 'gentlemen' didn't care.

"OK," agreed Lieutenant Colonel Leitch. "Nothing that we can help you with, anyway."

"No problem," said the Royal Scots Liaison Officer "I'll speak to one of the guys at the academy and get the ball rolling."

Jon arrived back at Sandhurst early on Sunday evening, having spent the day with Marion. From now on, they would be allowed out on alternate weekends, although they were required to sign in again before midnight. He kissed her goodbye and promised to let her know as soon as he had a fixed date for their next night together.

"What's on the programme for tomorrow?" he asked the duty student, as he wandered down the accommodation block to his room.

"Field craft. Section attacks," came the reply.

Sounds good, thought Jon.

He was sitting on his bed, polishing his boots, when McGovern's shape appeared in the corridor. Jon stopped polishing and looked up, ready to say hello, but McGovern hesitated and then moved on to Tom Forrest's room.

Was it something I said? he wondered, as he could hear Tim and the Colour Sergeant exchanging pleasantries.

The following morning, the platoon deployed to the training area for a day of field craft in old Bedford 4-ton trucks. They were given packed lunches in white cardboard boxes. Each one contained the standard sandwiches, an apple, a packet of crisps, a can of soft drink and a Mars bar. Early in the course, one of the cadets had told the overseas students that Mars bars contained pig fat which meant that they, being Muslims, couldn't eat them. It was a sneaky trick.

Typical of the public school-types in the company, Jon thought.

Some of the cadets were still pretty unfit, yet they would run like rabbits back to the mess to get a cream bun before anyone else. Jon considered it beneath his dignity as an Officer Cadet to do the same and usually arrived after they had all been claimed; you had to have some self-respect, even if the others didn't.

The first section attack was led by a cadet called Strong. He tried to take the cadets through a bramble-filled ditch, but they eventually found the enemy and fought their way through.

It was Jon's turn next. He put his section into an arrowhead formation and they started to cross a field. A shot rang out from somewhere ahead and, following drill, the guys ran forward to form a line and they all took cover.

"Does anyone know where that came from?" shouted Jon.

No one knew. It was likely that it came from a clump of bushes to their front, as this was the only cover in the field, but with it being a single shot, it was impossible to tell.

Jon was lying there wondering if he should order the troops to move forward again, when McGovern came running up.

"What are you going to do, Comyn?" he shouted.

Jon should have told him that he was going to try to locate the enemy, but McGovern was in one of his rages (he did this on the parade square, taking drill. He would be calm one minute and then fly into a red-faced rage, shouting and screaming and even foaming at the mouth).

"I'm going to go left-flanking," shouted Jon.

This would have been the acceptable manoeuvre if the enemy was indeed in the bushes, but what he really should have done was try to locate the enemy, even if he had to send someone forward to draw fire.

"Get on with it, then," screamed McGovern, panicking Jon into action.

Jon led his troops to the left and they started to advance towards the bushes, when another shot came from the direction of a clump of bushes further away.

Shit! thought Jon. *Where the fuck is the enemy?*

They had been taught that it was better to make a decision – be it right or wrong – than to make no decision, so he shouted, "Follow me," and charged towards the bushes which now appeared to contain the enemy.

They passed a Gurkha soldier playing dead as they swept through the bushes and reformed on the other side. McGovern went berserk, shouting and screaming, saying that was the worst section attack he had ever seen. Jon had to just stand and take it.

Christ! Jon thought. *I thought this was a training exercise.*

McGovern finally calmed down and nominated another Officer Cadet to take over. They carried on for the rest of the day with varying degrees of success, but apparently no one was as bad as Jon. Consequently, he was a bit despondent by the time they got back to the billets.

After that, he didn't seem to be able to do anything right.

The weather gradually got worse as February progressed into March, and they often found themselves wearing their army greatcoats when doing drill. They all seemed to be ancient, and buttons would fall off, usually just before a parade when it was impossible to do anything about it, leading to the offending Officer Cadet being put on 'show parade', which meant parading with the offending item, be it a dirty beret having been cleaned or a missing button reattached.

Jon didn't really mind show parades. They were a bit of a pain, but it wasn't as if he was doing anything else in the evening, and he had to prepare his kit, anyway. They had a standing joke about who could get the most show parades now. He was leading so far but Paddy, the Irish platoon boxing champion, wasn't far off.

It started to become obvious that McGovern had a favourite, whom Tim Forrest had nicknamed Lobo because he acted like he had had a frontal lobotomy, so Tim said. Every time Lobo got charged with something, Jon did too. This gave McGovern the opportunity to forgive Lobo and not actually have him punished.

McGovern had stopped speaking to Jon completely, except to charge him or to give him the odd command, but ironically it was another Officer Cadet who packed it in first.

Once you had actually got to Sandhurst, you were committed to an army contract. If you left by the eight-week point, it cost you £80.

(Officer Cadets were paid £48 per week.) If you got into the senior division, which was the second half of the course, it cost £300 to buy yourself out. And if it was the last month, that rose to a staggering £1000.

Robin had, on the surface, appeared to be quite happy and was getting on OK. Out of the blue, just before he would have had to pay £300 for the privilege, he bought himself out. It only cost him £80, and he left with a big smile on his face.

Jon was on guard duty with another Officer Cadet, who had been back-squadded due to injury, when Robin sauntered through the gateway to freedom.

"Cheers, guys," he said, giving them a smile.

"It's funny, you know," said the Officer Cadet to Jon. "I've seen plenty of people come and go, and not one of them has left without a huge grin on his face."

Jon knew exactly how Robin felt. Sandhurst was beginning to feel like a prison. It was almost as if a switch had been flipped. Up until he came back from the weekend break, he had seemed to be doing well, but then everything had changed. He was constantly on show parade and got charged for every offence that Lobo committed. He wouldn't have minded the show parades, but they were beginning to get monotonous. He had lost count of the number of times he had been done for 'dust on his beret'. It didn't matter if he brushed it the minute before he went on parade, he would still get done. It wasn't as if he could argue the case, either. This was the army and he just had to put up with it.

The problem was that it was beginning to affect him mentally, though he was OK when he was with the guys out in the field or doing lessons. Tim was a great guy, and they had fallen into the habit of buying each other a pint at lunchtime (when there was nothing on in the afternoon that would be affected by alcohol), and he had a good rapport with most of the others, particularly the overseas students.

But the platoon commander and McGovern were a different matter.

The platoon commander, who was an artillery officer, should have been Jon's friend. He came from Edinburgh, and they were both the same age. He suspected that the Captain was jealous of him, as he was much fitter and could easily beat him in a run. Jon had heard rumours that he had tried to join the infantry and had been turned down.

It was starting to affect his relationship with Marion as well. Whenever he got a night off, he would find that he couldn't think of anything to say and they would sit in silence, getting quietly drunk. She didn't really seem to understand his problem and when he had tried to explain it, she just appeared to write it off.

He got the results of his Army Knowledge 1 exam to find that he had scored 69.5, half a mark below the threshold for an A pass. What really got to him was that he was given a C for fitness. He was the best runner in the platoon and the third best in the company. He was only graded a C because he had had to pull out of a thirty-five-mile endurance march due to a bout of flu that was going around the company. He should have pulled out as soon as he started to feel unwell, but by that time they were well into the march, and he foolishly tried to soldier on. They were in a five-man patrol and the others were all trying to help him. He was doggedly sticking with it when the platoon commander joined them and advised him to give up. He did so for the sake of the rest of the patrol and then was criticised for it afterwards.

That gave him an overall C- grade, which was still good enough to get a commission, but he realised that he couldn't make any more mistakes.

At the three-month point in the SMC course, between the junior and senior divisions, there was a three-week break during which the Officer Cadets were to do an adventure training course. There were a range of activities, including parachuting and skiing, but Jon didn't want to risk being sent on a canoeing course, as he'd done canoeing before and hated it, so he volunteered for an outward-bound course in Tulloch, Scotland. Before that, though, there was the Sovereign's Parade for the previous intake who were passing-out.

The weeks before the parade were filled with rehearsals and drill practice, and McGovern was so engrossed with getting the platoon up to scratch that he left Jon alone.

Jon invited Marion to the event and, on a glorious day in late March, the platoon formed up, ready to take part in the parade. There is something magical about marching with music, and the Royal Military Academy Sandhurst had its own band. They marched with fixed bayonets, and King Hussain of Jordan was the dignitary who took the parade.

At one point, as the platoons were making a left wheel and two files joined together in a complicated manoeuvre to make it happen, Jon, who was the right-hand marker for his file, got pushed out when the two lines met and had to elbow his way back into the line. Fortunately, no one seemed to notice, even though the press apparently used to look out for that sort of thing.

At the end of the parade, he hung up his kit and walked with Marion through the academy's grounds to the station. He spent the night with her before getting the train to Edinburgh and then on to the Joint Service Mountain Training Centre, Tulloch. It was a ten-day course, and Jon had the rest of the three weeks as leave. He went back to Edinburgh at the end of it and stayed with his parents.

Almost as soon as he arrived back at Sandhurst, he was told that the Royal Scots Liaison Officer wanted to see him.

Jon turned up, expecting to talk about the Royal Scots as it was their three hundred and fiftieth anniversary. The Royal Scots had served kings or queens continuously for three hundred and fifty years from their raising in 1633 and had gone to France and served the French king rather than stay to become part of the New Model Army under Cromwell. That was why it was a royal regiment, unlike, say, the Green Jackets or the Northumberland Fusiliers. The British Army is not the royal army, like the Royal Navy, because they fought Charles I during the English civil war. Jon was proud to be a member of a royal regiment.

So, it came as a bit of a shock to be told that he wasn't good enough for the Royal Scots and that he should look for another unit. He wasn't even given the chance to improve. That was it. Something that he had set his heart on and spent almost a full year striving for had been snatched away, with no recourse, no appeal. That broke him.

Jon briefly toyed with transferring to the Pioneer Corps. It was the unit that he should have joined in the first place, he realised. They'd had a day at the academy where representatives from various units had given them presentations, and the Captain from the Pioneer Corps had seemed like a really nice guy. He was slightly scruffy, with hair longer than regulation length, and he let the Officer Cadets smoke during his presentation. But it was too late. The problem was that Jon had convinced himself that the Royal Scots was the one. To go from an almost elite regiment to what was considered the 'lowest of the low' was too much of a drop.

He carried on with his training, but his heart was no longer in it. He would spend all his free time lying on his bed, smoking and wondering where he was going. Ironically, the training had become a lot easier now that he was in the 'senior' division. There were no longer continual inspections, and they were free to go out every second weekend. He found himself becoming more and more anti-social and did the minimal amount of work to get by.

One Saturday night, he went with Marion to a restaurant called

The Coconut Grove in Leicester Square for her best friend's birthday. He bought the first round for the four of them – her friend's partner was also there – and was shocked to be presented with a bill for £10. That was all the cash he had on him, and he had to pay for the meal by cheque. During the meal, a pair of entertainers called Tik and Tok, who did robotic mime, did an impromptu performance. It was very entertaining, but Jon couldn't really muster any enthusiasm for it and generally stayed quiet. The one time he tried to join the conversation, Marion angrily turned on him and told him that he had said the wrong thing.

He wasn't unhappy to head back to the academy but missed the last train from Richmond station and had to get a taxi, which cost him £20.

In early May, he got a letter from his mother saying that his brother had served his sentence in the Military Corrective Training Centre (MCTC), Colchester and was living in London. Inmates would often tell people that they were doing a course at the 'Motorcycle Training Centre' rather than admit they were in army jail, but it was not unknown for soldiers who had served their time to be promoted soon afterwards, as the prison acted as a refresher training course.

Jon's brother had been offered a transfer to the Paras. He had deserted the Black Watch to join the French Foreign Legion because he was bored and had trained as a sniper with the Deuxieme Rep, the Second Parachute Regiment.

Jon's brother had had enough of the army and decided to get out. He was dishonourably discharged and was now working as a despatch rider for a company called Pony Express. Jon met up with him and they went to a bar called The Ship in the docklands to meet a friend who had been a Corporal in the Legion but had served his time and got out. They had a couple of drinks and then made their way back to Kenton in the Northeast of London, where Jon's brother rented a room. He stayed the night and, in the morning, borrowed his brother's motorbike and rode back to Sandhurst.

He got a bit lost and just made it in time. There was a church parade that morning. He threw on his Number two dress uniform and rushed out to join his platoon.

Church parade was mandatory for all Christians. It was held once a month, and if you were foolish enough to call yourself an atheist or were one of the Muslim cadets, you were allocated cleaning duties instead. Jon sometimes wondered if sweeping floors would be better than listening to some pompous army chaplain churning out religious platitudes.

They'd had a lecture early on in the course about the morality of killing, which, of course, goes against the Sixth Commandment, 'thou shalt not kill'. They got around it by rabbiting on about 'justifiable homicide', but it was a pretty weak argument if you were a true Christian. Saying that, if you were a true Christian, you probably wouldn't join the army and fight, but they seemed to need to justify themselves.

The chaplain had asked one of the Officer Cadets, who had been a Corporal in 2 Para and had been at the Battle of Goose Green in the Falklands campaign, if he had called on God when he found himself in danger and got a bit of a shock when the answer was no. The Corporal went on to say that you would call on *Mickey Mouse* if you thought it would do any good, which didn't go down too well. The lecture was cut short after that.

Jon was standing in line when he heard one of the other cadets saying that he had cut himself shaving.

Shit, he thought. *I haven't shaved!*

In his rush to get ready he had forgotten that he hadn't had a razor with him and had intended to have a wash and shave when he got back to the billet. He wondered what to say if he was asked if he had shaved. *Should he lie and say yes, or admit it and say no*? But if he said no, then what was he going to say? That he forgot?

Fortunately, there had been a Warrant Officer/Sergeants' mess do the night before and the duty Colour Sergeant never turned up, so the duty student marched them down to the church instead and Jon got away with it.

He knew he would have to get his brother's motorbike back to him that afternoon, so he sorted out his kit and drove back to London. They were due to go out on a three-day exercise starting the following morning, so he had time to return the machine and get back for an early night.

"Fancy a pint?" asked his brother, when he arrived.

He knew he shouldn't, but he was so sick of the army that he said yes and so they went to the local pub.

Jon found himself looking around at the other patrons, thinking that he just wanted to be normal again. Then he realised that he would need to leave if he was going to get back to Sandhurst in time.

He said goodbye to his brother and caught the tube to Richmond. Unfortunately, there had been a delay, and he missed the train. He was left with the choice of paying for a taxi or getting the early train. He couldn't really afford another £20 cab fare, so he got the tube back to West Kensington and walked to Marion's flat. She didn't exactly give him a warm welcome and he ended up sleeping on the sofa in the lounge. By the time he woke up, he realised that he wasn't going to make it back to the academy in time and was left in a welter of indecision. Should he go anyway, or should he try to get his brother to give him a lift? He tried to ring his brother but got no reply. It was now past the time when the company would be leaving for the training area, and he had visions of being locked up when he got back to Sandhurst.

Bollocks, he thought. He was going to have to face the music.

He got back to an empty billet and sat on his bed, wondering what to do. As he was mulling over his options, which were admittedly rather few, an unfamiliar officer pocked his head around the door.

"What are you doing here?" he asked, pleasantly.

"I missed the train and when I got here everyone was gone, sir," replied Jon.

"Have you reported in?"

"No, sir," admitted Jon. He hadn't really felt like being stuck in a cell, so he had come back to his room to try to work out what he was going to do.

"No problem," said the officer. "I'll let them know that you're here."

"Thanks, sir," said Jon.

A short while later, a Corporal turned up and told him that the College RSM wanted to see him. He went to Norris's office and knocked on the door.

"Enter," said a voice from behind the desk.

Jon marched smartly in and halted.

"So, what's the story?" Norris asked.

Jon told him the story and then waited.

"Why didn't you ring the guardroom?" enquired Norris, brusquely.

"I didn't have the number, sir," explained Jon.

Norris pursed his lips in disapproval.

"I'm putting you under open arrest," he said. "You're not staying here and eating rations for free. Go and get your hair cut."

"Yes, sir," said Jon and marched out.

Open arrest. That was OK. Jon had forgotten that, as an Officer Cadet, he was classed as an officer and couldn't be locked up. He could be put under 'close arrest', which meant being asked on his word of honour as an officer not to leave his room or, as now, 'open arrest', which meant that he lost all his 'privileges' but could still move about and do things. The only privilege that he had lost was the ability to use the NAAFI shop, from where he could buy cigarettes, newspapers and other bits and pieces, but that was a small loss. It all started to seem ridiculous, when he thought about it.

He put on a white belt, which the Officer Cadets normally wore with Number Two dress uniform, to denote that he was under open arrest, and went to the barber. Some members of the new junior division were in the waiting room, but he went to the head of the queue and had a twenty second hair cut that cost him 20p.

After that, he reported back to the RSM, who clearly didn't know what to do with him. Norris had absolutely no imagination. He was obviously very good at his job, which was why he had got to be a Regimental Sergeant Major, but apart from doing drill he seemed to have no skills at all, and he couldn't personally drill Jon until the company came back, so he sent him to sweep out the billet.

Jon spent the next three days doing trivial jobs and parading twice a day. He went to the head of the queue in the cookhouse at mealtimes and none of the junior division cadets questioned him about it, so he got the best meals that he'd had in his time at the academy so far. He knew that he would face the music when his company commander got back, but in the meantime, he was almost on holiday.

"Tell me what happened," demanded the company commander, as Jon stood at attention in front of his desk three days later. Jon told his story, as he had done with Norris.

"Is that it?" the Major asked.

"Do you want me to lie sir?" asked Jon.

"No," said the Major. "But in that case, it's going to have to go to the college commandant."

Two days later, Jon found himself standing outside the college commandant's door, waiting to go in. He was dressed in his Number Two dress uniform, but without his belt or beret, which apparently went back to the days of knights, when they would remove their helmet and sword before being allowed to see the king, or so he had been told.

He was marched in by the Company Sergeant Major and made

to mark time so that he would be out of breath, before being halted in front of the college commandant's desk. The college RSM was standing behind the desk, and Jon's company commander was seated to the right of it.

"You are charged with being seven and a half hours Absent Without Leave, and Conduct Unbecoming of an Officer Cadet at Sandhurst," read out the RSM.

Is that all? thought Jon but said nothing.

"Have you anything to say?" asked the commandant.

"No, sir," replied Jon. He had already told his story to the college RSM and the company commander and there wasn't really anything more to say.

The college commandant looked at him as he was standing rigidly to attention, trying to control his breathing. The speed march and being made to take off your belt and beret were done to try to humiliate the offender, but Jon didn't really give a fuck.

"Do you really want to be an officer in the British Army, Comyn?" the commandant asked, sarcastically.

"No, sir," Jon replied, without really thinking. There was a shocked pause.

"Then what are you doing here?" demanded the commandant in a querulous tone.

"I don't really know, sir," admitted Jon realising that he had spoken the truth. It was a fact. He didn't want to be an army officer anymore.

"Don't you think that you're wasting the army's time and your own time?" said the commandant in a high-pitched voice.

"Yes, sir."

"Well, what are you going to do about it?"

"I'd like to be discharged, sir."

"Twenty-eight days' restrictions of privileges. Take him away!" shouted the commandant.

And that was it.

The Company Sergeant Major started to call out the time to march him out of the office in double quick time, but Jon was stunned and almost sauntered out of the office. Twenty-eight days' restrictions of privileges? What the hell was all that about?

"Sergeant Major, sort that man out!" he heard the RSM shout, but he ignored it and just carried on walking.

"You'll do the twenty-eight days before you get out," said the CSM.

"Yes, sir," said Jon, numbly.

He would be here for ever, if that were so. Weekends and exercises didn't count, so it would take months to get out of there. Twenty-eight days would cover a minimum of six weeks, and there was a two weeks' exercise to consider as well, so that immediately took it past two months.

"Why didn't you tell me you wanted a discharge?" asked McGovern.

"I didn't think of it until he asked, Colour," replied Jon.

"OK," said McGovern. He had turned mellow now that the 'interview' was over.

In the event, Jon found out that he could leave as soon as he handed over £300 in cash, which only left him with the problem of how to get it.

Restrictions of privileges was very similar to being under open arrest. The only difference was a variation of wording during the twice-daily parades. Punishment parades were carried out at 0700 and 1900. Jon had attended so many in his time that the whole thing was a bit of a farce. He lined up on the right of the line. In battle it would have been an honour to be on the right of the line, ironically. He was wearing Number Two dress uniform, but this time with his beret and a white belt. As the duty Corporal/Sergeant came forward, each 'offender' would take one pace forward and then state the punishment: 'Officer Cadet [name], showing beret cleaned', etc.

Jon took one pace forward and slammed his steel-studded boot into the concrete floor as hard as he could.

"Officer Cadet Comyn. Twenty-eight days' restriction of privileges. First day. Staff," he shouted, as loudly as possible.

There were gasps from down the line as the other cadets took in the enormity of the punishment.

"What did you do? Shag the CO's wife?" asked the astounded Corporal.

"AWOL and Conduct Unbecoming," replied Jon, laconically.

After that, life became a bit easier for Jon.

He became a bit of a celebrity, because twenty-eight days' RoPs was the maximum that the college commandant could have given him, and the highest previous record was apparently fourteen days. The only higher punishment was fifty-six days, which could only be awarded by the academy commandant.

The only problem was that people kept asking him what had happened, and he got sick of telling them.

It took him three days to gather the £300 in cash by the simple expedient of using cheques guaranteed for £50 with his banker's card. The Royal Military Academy Sandhurst had its own branch of Lloyds Bank to cater for the three hundred or so Officer Cadets who attended the courses at any one time. Despite this, the branch had managed to pay Jon's money into another cadet's account one time which he found incredible, considering how unique his name was.

It was also a bit of an eye-opener. Kevin, a Zimbabwean cadet, had offered to lend Jon the whole £300 when he mentioned about swapping a cheque for cash, while the Honourable Jonathan Tarbuck, whose mother was a duchess and owned half of South

Kensington apparently, claimed that he was 'short of money'. This was despite Jon having done an extra guard duty for him when he had pleaded for him to do it so that he could attend some party or other.

Jon presented the cash to the Colour Sergeant, who gave him a chit saying that it had been paid, and then the discharge process began.

It was basically the induction process in reverse. He handed in his kit to the quartermaster's store. He took pleasure in smashing the 'bull' off the brown shoes that had had to be polished black because the company commander was a Gurkha officer and the Gurkha regiments wore black shoes, but he left the ammunition boots intact for the next poor sucker who would have to use them. For some reason, they didn't take his tam-o'-shanter or Glengarry headgear, but they had been issued at Glencorse and they weren't on the paperwork of the academy, so he still had his cap badge from the Royal Scots even though he had handed in his 'serve to lead' Sandhurst cap badge and beret. He had never paid for his Sandhurst blazer, so that went back too. Thinking about it, he didn't want it, anyway. The one time that he had worn the double-breasted blazer he had been mistaken for a British Rail employee and asked about train times by an elderly woman at King's Cross.

Pay and documentation didn't take long; there wasn't really much to do. His discharge papers would be sent to his home address in Edinburgh once they had been processed, and pay was automatically paid into a bank account.

The final process was a medical. Jon was told by a smirking medic that he couldn't leave until they said he was fit, and that was up to him.

Try and stop me, thought Jon. The guy was just being a prick. Basically, he was abusing his position and trying to be important, as if Jon cared.

He thought back to earlier that morning, which had been his last parade, when the duty Corporal had looked him up and down and said, "Not at all bad, sir." It was the only compliment that he could ever remember having received in all his months at Sandhurst, and for some strange reason it made him feel good. Maybe he wasn't such a failure, after all.

Finally, he said goodbye to his now ex-colleagues. There weren't actually that many who he would ever wish to see again. Ali, a friendly Jordanian cadet with a gold tooth, asked him what he was going to do.

"I don't know," admitted Jon. "Does the PLO pay well?" he asked, jokingly.

"I can find out for you," replied Ali with a grin.

"Too late, I'm afraid," said Jon, shaking his hand. "I'll be in touch," he said to Kevin.

Kevin had said that if he wanted to go to Zimbabwe, his father would put him up. Kevin's father had a 'small' farm, north of Harare. Small by Zimbabwean terms meant that was it was over 1500 acres.

"Will do," said Kevin, taking his hand.

Jon picked up his suitcase and a plastic carrier bag, which contained all his worldly possessions, and walked to the gate of the academy. They hadn't laid on any transport for him, which he thought was just typical. Now that he was no longer a member of the armed forces, they didn't want anything to do with him.

Fuck them, he thought, as he walked out the gate with a big smile on his face.

He was free.

PART 2

THE INTELLIGENCE CORPS

1989

CHAPTER 7

RECRUIT JON COMYN – EX ROYAL SCOTS OFFICER CADET

Things hadn't gone particularly well for Jon recently. He was almost broke and there was still no sign of a regular job on the horizon. He had come back to Edinburgh after working in London and he was starting to think that that had been a grave mistake. It wasn't that he didn't like Edinburgh, though the nationalistic undercurrent that had been growing since the discovery of North Sea oil was starting to manifest itself as a distinctly anti-English movement. This alone wouldn't have really bothered him (he'd had to put up with borderline racism after being the only English boy in a Scottish primary school when his parents moved to the city in the late 1960s). But this, combined with the fact that Edinburgh was the second most expensive place to live in the UK after London yet wages were nowhere near those of the UK's capital city, and the even more depressing fact that there seemed to be no jobs either, made it a dead-end place to be.

In desperation, he had started a gardening business, but he was getting rained off three to four days a week and couldn't make any money. It had been the same when he tried despatch riding in London after he returned from a stint in Zimbabwe working for Lonrho, as a security officer on a gold mine. Whenever he was on the verge of earning more than bread-and-butter wages, something would go wrong – his motorbike would break down or his landlord would decide to sell and he would have to find different accommodation and extra the money for deposits. He finally got sick of being cold and wet and packed the job in.

He rode from London to Edinburgh on a miserable November day and barely managed to get more than scrap value for his Suzuki GX 400 motorcycle when he took it to a local dealer. The poor thing had done him well but was on its last legs.

His only recourse was to sign on, but he knew that would be the first step on the slippery slope and he just couldn't bring himself to do it.

He sat watching the rain beating on the windowpane, knowing that yet another day would have to be written off, and wondered what he should do. Idly, he picked up the local paper, the *Edinburgh Evening News*, from the previous night and turned to the jobs section in the vain hope that there might be something that he could apply for. There was an advertisement for the army that he almost ignored, but next to it was one for the Territorial Army Intelligence Corps.

He wasn't interested in joining the TA, but the ad reminded him of a presentation that he had had when he was at Sandhurst. Two members of the Intelligence Corps, one male and one female, had tried to entice the Officer Cadets with stories about how the Corps was like James Bond. He was pretty sure that it was complete bullshit, but he wondered what exactly the Intelligence Corps did.

There was only one way to find out.

The army recruiting office had moved from Hanover Street to Prince's Street, but otherwise, it was almost exactly the same as when he had visited it all those years ago. The recruiting Sergeant was a lot younger than the one Jon remembered and the uniform had changed slightly. The green shirt looked a lot more comfortable than the old shirt – 'hedgehog' – and the boots were combat highs rather than DMS, but those were pretty minor changes.

"Hi," said Jon. "I'm interested in joining the Intelligence Corps."

"Do you know anything about it?" the Sergeant asked.

"No. That's why I'm here," replied Jon.

"Got any qualifications?"

"Seven O-levels, three Highers and a HND in printing."

"OK, that should be enough. Any military experience?"

"I was in the Royal Scots."

"Was?"

"Yes," said Jon. "I bought myself out."

"Bought yourself out?"

"Yes, I was at Sandhurst."

"You were an officer?"

"No. I was an Officer Cadet,"

"Ah. OK," said the Sergeant. "If you had been an officer, then you would have to go back in as an officer."

"Really?"

"Yes. That's the way it works. But since you weren't, then you can join again as a Private..."

Jon noticed the hesitation. "But?" he prompted.

"You didn't get 'services no longer required', did you?" asked the Sergeant.

'Services no longer required' was the form of words used on a soldier's discharge papers when they had been 'dishonourably' discharged. Jon's papers gave him an 'exemplary, based on nine months' experience' grade, which he thought slightly strange since he had been charged with being AWOL and Conduct Unbecoming of an Officer Cadet at Sandhurst. But he wasn't complaining.

"No," replied Jon. "Exemplary, based on nine months' experience."

"That's all right, then. How old are you?" the Sergeant asked as he began filling in paperwork.

"Twenty-nine."

The Sergeant sucked in a breath. "Just made it. The upper limit is thirty and you have to have had previous experience, which of course you have."

Jon had not really thought about his age. He had been one of the oldest at Sandhurst at twenty-three, but he hadn't thought that the army's age limit for entry would be so low. It was lucky that he had seen the advert because in a few months he would be thirty and it would have been too late.

"Got any medical problems?" the Sergeant continued, looking him over.

"No. I'm pretty fit," said Jon. *For my age*, he thought, but didn't say so out loud.

"Good. You'll get a full medical, of course, but you look OK. Taken any drugs recently?"

"What? Like dope, do you mean?"

"Yes. Illegal drugs. Taken any recently?"

"God, no," said Jon, surprised at the question.

"You'd be surprised how many potential recruits we turn away because they've taken illegal drugs before coming here."

"That's pretty stupid."

"Yes. It is, isn't it?"

There were a couple of interviews and some background checks along with the medical, but Jon must have passed them all because he got a letter saying that he had been accepted for enlistment into the Intelligence Corps and to report to Templer Barracks, Ashford, Kent for the start of his training.

He sat watching the rain beating on the windowpane. It might still be raining outside, but this time he had a smile on his face and a direction in his life. He would be a Private again, but only for the time it took him to get through the Intelligence Corps' basic training and then he would get promoted. The Corps apparently had the highest number of officers who had come through the ranks, and Jon thought that maybe one day he could get to the point that he had reached six years before and go past it to be commissioned and become an officer in the British Army.

But that was getting ahead of himself. First, he had to pass the year-long course and trade tests.

Don't count your chickens, he told himself, but he couldn't help looking forward to being in uniform once more. He realised that he had missed it – not that he regretted leaving Sandhurst, that was a heap of crap and was consigned to the past – but he had missed the camaraderie of the guys from the O-type. He wondered what the other recruits would be like.

No doubt he would find out soon.

CHAPTER 8

RECRUIT DAVE ANDERS – EX TA INTELLIGENCE CORPS SERGEANT

It was a bit strange for Dave to be back in Templer Barracks, this time as a Private. He had passed out from this very place six years before, as a member of the Intelligence and Security Group (Volunteers), the Territorial Army branch of the regular army Intelligence Corps, and had quickly risen through the ranks, passing his trade tests, drill and duties and attending the mandatory annual camps, and had ended up as a Sergeant before deciding to go regular. The drop in rank – and pay – was going to be a bit of a bind, but the training would be easy as he had done it all before. It would be like a refresher course, albeit a bit more in-depth than the Territorial Army.

He took the train to Ashford after exchanging the pink/purple travel warrant for a second-class rail ticket, and then caught a taxi as he was carrying a heavy suitcase and a Bergen stuffed with kit to ensure a comfortable passage through basic training.

A minibus was waiting at the station and Dave recognised it immediately. The driver was wearing civilian clothes, but they consisted of jeans, a sweatshirt and desert boots, which were a dead giveaway for army personnel. All that was missing was the 'Frank Zappa' moustache.

It's strange how quickly you get institutionalised, thought Dave.

He had heard that, until a few years before, some units had banned their members from wearing jeans, and due to the 'troubles' in Northern Ireland, you weren't allowed to leave barracks wearing 'mixed dress', which meant wearing bits of army kit with civilian clothes even though that would actually have been the perfect cover.

You could normally tell a squaddie by the way they looked, but he had expected the Intelligence Corps to be slightly different. Quite a few of the TA members dressed as if they were officers or university professors, which some of them actually were. There had been an amusing parade when the inspecting officer did his usual trick of asking the TA soldier what he did for a living, to be told, in all seriousness, that he was a brain surgeon. For some bizarre reason, TA Intelligence Corps officers were not expected to do trade tests, and many didn't even have a degree, which a lot of soldiers had. This led to some of the TA soldiers being better qualified than their officers.

"Corps?" questioned the driver, as Dave walked up to him.

"Yes," replied Dave, simply.

"Good. Hop in," said the driver, after ticking Dave's name off from a list which he took from his pocket.

"Many more to come?" asked Dave as he loaded his baggage into the back of the vehicle.

"No, not on this run. You're the last."

There were half a dozen pale-faced recruits already in the minibus and they looked up worriedly as Dave climbed in.

"Hi, I'm Dave," he said with a smile that seemed to break the ice.

They seemed to recognise that he was more experienced than them and one asked if he was an instructor. When he told them that he was a recruit like them but had been a TA Sergeant, they plied him with questions until they reached Templer Barracks, the home of the British Army Intelligence Corps.

RECRUIT DONNA COWES – EX EXOTIC DANCER

It was when the disabled man came all over her breasts that Donna finally decided that she'd had enough of being an 'exotic' dancer and should look for some other form of employment. Her problem was that she lived in a small town, and with only a couple of O-levels, employment was limited to shop work or being a cleaner. She could have applied for university (she had made plenty of money as a dancer, and instead of squandering it on drink and drugs, she'd bought her flat and saved most of the rest), but that would mean at least two years of taking A-levels to get the necessary qualifications. Besides, she couldn't think of anything she really wanted to study.

What prompted her to join the Intelligence Corps was a disparaging comment made by the owner of the seedy club where she worked when she said that she was thinking of leaving to do something more intellectual. She would show him, and everyone else, that she was clever and capable, and what better way to do it than by enlisting in the one unit in the British Army where you were actually paid to think?

The recruiting Sergeant had initially leered at her, expecting her to be just the usual blonde bimbo (she decided she would go back to her natural colour as soon as possible), but once he saw the results of her initial recruitment test, he grudgingly admitted that she could join any unit she fancied – except of course the SAS which didn't take women. The test had been laughably easy, and she wondered what level of intelligence you would have to have to fail it; you virtually got enough points to get into the infantry just by signing your name! Still, that was the first step out of the way, and she could move on to the culture shock of the rest of the army recruitment process.

Donna tried to do a bit of research into the Intelligence Corps but found that there was remarkably little of use that she could find. Most of the stuff was from the Second World War. She was quite surprised to find that the Intelligence Corps had only been formed in 1940 – she thought that it would be much older than that.

In actual fact, Intelligence has always been an important fact of warfare, even if it wasn't recognised as such until then. Sun

Tzu, who wrote the book *The Art of War*, talked about the use of spies, she found out. The British Army didn't seem to display much intelligence, hence the disparaging comment about Military Intelligence being a 'contradiction in terms' which people seemed to love to quote whenever she mentioned the Intelligence Corps.

Her friends seemed to fall into either those who thought the army was for losers or those who thought it was the best thing since sliced bread. She began to get sick of hearing the same comments over and over again, and stopped talking about the army, determined to find out for herself what it was really like

Donna toyed with spending some cash on equipment she saw in a military catalogue called *Survival Aids*, which had supposedly been started by two ex-SAS guys. When she realised how much it was going to cost her, she changed her mind and decided to do some actual army training before blowing a wad of money. She could always take the catalogue with her and order the stuff through the post.

No one she knew seemed to actually know anything about the army, let alone the Intelligence Corps. The British Army had fallen out of favour as an employer, what with the terrorist campaign in Northern Ireland, and the army hadn't really been involved in a proper war since Korea, back in the 1950s. People talked about the Falklands , but she read that it wasn't actually a war as such because the UK hadn't declared war on Argentina, so it was classed as a campaign.

She had been told to report to Templer Barracks in early September, so she decided to take a quick holiday beforehand as a reward for getting in. She persuaded a friend to go with her to Athens, as she had always wanted to see the Acropolis and was still young enough to get a student rail card, even though neither her nor her friend were students.

The trip was an absolute disaster from start to finish. Her friend only wanted to get drunk and talk about cosmetics. She had no interest in history, which she thought was for squares. Donna had purchased a copy of the *Thompson's International Train Directory*, which detailed train times for the whole of Europe. She planned the journeys so they could sleep on the train and not have to pay for hotel rooms, but her friend complained constantly.

They stopped in West Germany so they could get their clothes washed and have a night on the town in Munich, before getting a train to Thessaloniki in Greece via Yugoslavia. Anne, her friend, had a monumental hangover from drinking schnapps and they couldn't find their seats on the overcrowded train. They ended up sitting on their backpacks in the corridor, while families passed baggage through the windows at every stop on the trip south. Donna was sure that a crate of live chickens came through the window at one point, but she might have been hallucinating by then.

They were glad to get off in Thessaloniki and had a glorious couple of days sitting in sea-front cafés and lying on the beach. Unfortunately, Anne, who had been a great believer in fake tan, had forgotten that you need sun cream in the open air and got badly sunburned. She was miserable all the way to Athens and was no help when Donna got lost trying to find the Parthenon. It was worth it in the end, but Donna wished she had done the trip by herself.

They got an overnight ferry from Patras to Brindisi, and one of the most memorable moments of the trip was passing over the Corinth Canal on the way from Athens to Patras. It was like looking down a groove, cut dead straight into the earth, and a yacht was sailing in the azure-blue water. Donna read that there was no word for 'blue' in ancient Greece. Homer described the sea as being wine-dark, but Donna found this odd considering the colour of the water in the Corinth Canal.

The ferry from Patras to Brindisi was packed with German and Italian tourists, and they slept on the upper deck as it was an overnight crossing. Finally, they caught the train to Paris. Anne was supposed to change trains in Switzerland but didn't wake up in time and so Donna had to arrange another connection for her. She was glad when her friend left, and she was free to carry on by herself.

Donna was standing in the Gare du Nord railway station in northern Paris, waiting for the train to London, when she saw a strange bill poster. It seemed to be a set of steps with the legend: '*une aventure aujourd'hui avec la légion étrangère*'.

She slowly translated it and realised that it was a recruiting poster for the French Foreign Legion: 'An adventure today with the Foreign Legion'.

No thanks, she thought. *I'll stick with the British Army.*

The rest of the trip was uneventful, and she got home with two days to spare before she reported for duty.

RECRUIT CORPORAL PETER 'MICH' MITROVSKI – EX ROYAL SIGNALS

Corporal Peter 'Mich' Mitrovski knocked on the panelled wooden door and then waited.

"Come," said a loud, commanding voice which could be clearly heard through the closed door.

Mich steeled himself and then, turning the brass handle, opened the door and entered the room. He walked towards the desk, stopped in front of it and came to attention.

"Corporal Mitrovski. Reporting for interview, sir," he barked and then stood still.

"Take a seat, Corporal," said Major Donavan, the company commander. "Have a read through this and sign it if you agree with it." He slid a multi-paged form across the desk.

It was his ACR (Annual Confidential Report). Mich sat and read it. His initial feelings of pleasure at receiving a decent ACR turned to anger as he was, once again, shot down in flames with the final paragraph. All the hard work and effort that he had put into this job over the preceding year was nullified by a bland, seemingly innocuous comment that said, in effect, he was unsuitable for promotion.

This had happened over and over again. What should have been excellent reports were repeatedly rendered mediocre. 'Being damned by faint praise' was the expression, and it fitted perfectly. He knew the company commander didn't like him because he spoke his mind. He considered it moral cowardice to keep quiet while allowing injustice to reign, but he should have realised that there would be a price to pay for his honesty. He had been warned, but he thought that hard work and dedication to duty would overcome the obstacles. Obviously not.

"Thank you, sir," he said, signing the box with his name, rank and date and hiding his true feelings.

"Any ideas where you want to go for your next posting?" Donovan asked, without any enthusiasm.

"I thought I might try for selection," said Mich. Anything to get him out of here.

"The CO won't like that," said Donovan, stating one of the major problems with the regiment. The commanding officer, Lieutenant Colonel Phillips, had tried for SAS selection himself when he had been a young Lieutenant and failed miserably. He never forgot the humiliation of having to return to the jeering of colleagues who didn't have the guts to try themselves but were vocal in their taunting of others. It had taken years for the mocking epithet 'SAS Phillips' to fade, and he now had an innate hatred of 'special' units. He made it plain that he considered anyone who went for selection disloyal to the regiment, and it was an unwritten rule that they would suffer the consequences if they came back.

Mich didn't care. He was going nowhere with the Royal Signals, and he could either transfer to another unit or resign from the army. For all its faults, he loved the army; he loved the camaraderie and the friendly banter of trusted comrades. What he hated was the nepotism and favouritism that seemed to pervade this particular regiment.

"What about Special Duties?" he asked.

"Same thing. If you really want to do that sort of thing, you should have joined the Intelligence Corps," explained Donovan, offhandedly.

"OK. Thanks, sir," said Mich. "What about 9 Sigs?"

Donovan gave him a withering look. 9 Signal Regiment was based at Ayios Nikolaos in Cyprus and ran an Electronic Intelligence (ElInt) gathering station and was considered a 'plum posting'.

"I'll put you in for it," he said, condescendingly. "But I'm afraid that there's not much hope. There's a lot of competition for it."

Yes, and there's no way that you'll recommend me, thought Mich. But the Major had given him an idea.

"Thanks, sir," he said.

"Anything else?"

"No, sir," replied Mich, and his ACR interview was over.

Mich made an appointment to see WO2 Sally Stoner, the Warrant Officer in charge of the local Security section on camp, and asked her about transferring to the Intelligence Corps. She was very happy to oblige and helped him through the transfer process. The Intelligence Corps and Royal Signals had always worked well together and there was a close bond between the two.

Sally suggested that Mich could transfer to 14 Signal Regiment, which was responsible for Signals Intelligence (SigInt) and still stay in the Royal Signals, but Mich had had enough of Signals and wanted a change. The idea of being in the Intelligence Corps appealed to him and he could always go into 14 Sigs as an Intelligence Corps operator if it came to it. That way, he wouldn't be under the command of someone like Major Donavan, although he was pretty sure that there were people like that everywhere in the army. He just had to find a unit where that wasn't the case.

Mich was pleasantly surprised at how quickly his transfer went through. The Intelligence Corps was always looking for recruits and was very happy to take transferees from other units. Sally told him that plenty of people transferred in but very few transferred out.

He had a rather unpleasant interview with Major Donavan, who accused him of going behind his back in the case of the transfer, but he didn't really care. He was looking forward to a new beginning with a unit that apparently had the highest number of commissions through the ranks. Sally had also said that she was thinking of applying for a commission, as the Corps had a number of female officers, including those who had been other ranks. As a Warrant Officer, she would be commissioned as a Captain rather than a Lieutenant. Intelligence Corps Warrant Officers were considered to be slightly below Major and just above Captain in the army hierarchy, as indeed evidenced by their pay structure.

Mich was delighted to find out that he would keep his rank as full Corporal as he had passed his B trade qualifications and, because he was a trained soldier, was asked if he wished to skip the basic infantry training. He decided to do it anyway, as it would be a good refresher course and it would give him the opportunity to bond with the other recruits, who would be his colleagues in years to come.

RECRUIT SONIA SIZWE – EX SHOP ASSISTANT

The rain was beating down against the window, leaving it spotted with thick drops that ran slowly down the dirty panes of glass, and the howling gale was bending the trees and blowing litter along the road. Sonia watched a white plastic bag make its way between the parked cars to finally lodge in a stunted fir tree in someone's garden. She turned back to the three-page application form and continued to fill in the boxes in her neat, precise handwriting.

She wasn't sure if she was making a mistake applying to join the army, but she had had a secret hankering for it ever since she had found out that her grandfather had been a bit of a war hero during the Second World War and she had become interested in military history. She knew that the British Army, like a lot of British institutions, had a reputation for being institutionally racist. But if she was going to let that hold her back, then she might as well give up now and resign herself to being perennially unemployed.

Being black, she had had a rough time at junior school but had learned to cope with it by the time she reached secondary school, realising that a lot of it was due to unfamiliarity. The part of London where she came from didn't have a lot of ethnic diversity and so she had been a bit of an oddity, so to speak. But once she had got to know her classmates, they had accepted her as just another pupil, or at least most of them had. There was always the occasional person who couldn't seem to accept anything different, but she had reached the stage when she could let it wash over her and not upset her, as it had done when she was much younger.

She wondered if there would be any other black people in her unit or whether she would be the odd one out. There was only one way to find out.

Sonia completed the application form and sealed it in a large brown envelope with an extra line of Sellotape to secure it.

She seemed to have no trouble at any of the interviews and, as she was physically fit, she had no problems with the medical. She had been a runner at school. It had initially been a way of getting away from some of the other pupils, but then she had begun to enjoy the exercise for the pure pleasure of it. Going out early on a summer's morning when the air still felt cool and clean was a pleasure that you didn't often get living in a large, congested city.

She had been told that there was a thing called a basic fitness test (BFT), which consisted of a one and a half mile run or walk that had to be completed as a squad in fifteen minutes, followed by a second mile and a half run which was to be done in one's own best time. Women had to complete it in under eleven minutes, men had thirty seconds less. Sonia was determined that she would do it within ten and a half minutes so that she could not be accused of being given an advantage just because she was a woman

She mapped out a three-mile course and timed herself over the distance. She was quite pleased with herself for managing to complete it in less than thirty minutes, considering that she hadn't done any serious running since she had left school the year before. But she still needed to work on it if she was going to reduce it to twenty-six and a half minutes.

She did the same time the following day, but on the third day her legs were stiff, and she decided to have a rest day. The stiffness soon wore off, and over the summer she gradually got her time down until she could easily run three miles in twenty-five minutes.

In early August, she got a letter saying that she had been accepted for enlistment into the Intelligence Corps and to report to Templer Barracks in early September.

Sonia didn't really know how to tell her boyfriend that she was joining the army, and arranged to meet him for a 'special' night so she could tell him. They met up at a local pub called The Kings Head which was in Harrow-on-the-Hill. Sonia bought him a pint and a gin and tonic for herself, and they found a table away from everyone else.

Sonia's boyfriend started telling her about a possible job that he had lined up, saying that they could get married once he had sorted himself out. Sonia hadn't really thought about marriage and wasn't sure if she was ready for it. She was a bit surprised that he had assumed she would want to marry him. There was a pause in the conversation, and she decided that she would have to 'bite the bullet', so to speak, and tell him the news.

She was shocked by his reaction. He went into a rage and told her that under no circumstances would his woman join the army. She stared at him, wondering how she could have misjudged him so badly. She had thought that he would be supportive of her attempt to better herself, but he was too busy ranting to listen to her. Finally, he stormed out, telling her that she needed to get a grip of herself if she wanted him around.

She sat, red-faced, as he left the pub and saw the looks on the other patrons' faces. Wiping away tears, she followed him out, but he had already gone.

When she got home, her mother asked if she was all right and Sonia told her what had happened. Her mother gave her a hug.

"Don't worry, dear. You do whatever you feel is right. It's your life and I'm proud of you, whatever you do," she said.

"Thanks, Mum," said Sonia.

Over the next few days, Sonia thought about her future. Alex, her boyfriend, had told her that she was being stupid, and that the army was full of white trash who would treat her like a slave, and that she should stay with her own people, but she couldn't help wondering where that would leave her.

A visions of working in the local Tesco or having a string of kids, stretched out before her. Her own father had run out on her mother, leaving her to bring up Sonia by herself, and Alex didn't seem to be any more stable. He had had a number of dead-end jobs and had always seemed to be on the fringe of society, smoking dope and being involved in borderline criminality. He had always been fun to be with, a great laugh and the life and soul of the party, but Sonia wanted more out of life than that.

Alex had refused to speak to her unless she gave up her plan to join the army, so it was her mother who waved her off as she carried her suitcase to Harrow-on-the-Hill tube station to get the train to King's Cross and then to Ashford.

When she arrived at Ashford Station, she looked around, uncertainly. She had been told that there would be transport, but there was nothing that she recognised as a military vehicle. She saw a guy with a short back and sides haircut and a clipped moustache and took a risk.

"Do you know where to get the transport for Templer Barracks?" She asked.

"God, do I look that much like a squaddie?" he replied with a smile.

"Yes, I'm afraid so. In a nice way, of course."

He gave her a wry smile. "Thanks. It's this way." He indicated a grey minibus which was parked near the entrance. "I'm Jon, by the way," he said. "I'm a recruit, too."

"How do you know I'm a recruit?" Sonia asked, surprised.

"If you'd been staff, you would know the way. And if you had been regular army, you wouldn't have said 'Templer Barracks'."

"Why not?"

"You've just compromised yourself and admitted to me that you're army personnel. We have to be careful because of PIRA."

"What's PIRA?" she asked, bemused.

"The Provisional IRA," Jon explained. "Northern Ireland."

"Oh," said Sonia, a bit deflated that she had apparently already done something wrong.

Jon noticed her expression. "Don't worry. You'll soon learn."

"How do you know, then?"

"For my sins, I'm ex regular."

"Oh. Right."

Jon led Sonia to the minibus and the driver took their names. They were the only ones on this train from London, and he drove them straight to the barracks, which was going to be their home for the next year.

RECRUIT STEVE HAMPSHIRE – EX UNEMPLOYED

Steve had originally thought about joining the police, but he wasn't quite tall enough and couldn't see himself getting any larger, except sideways. He had liked the idea of becoming a bike cop; riding around all day on a souped-up Norton Commando and speeding through traffic with blue lights and a siren appealed to him.

Now that this option was out the window, he had to consider what he was going to do with the rest of his life. He was mulling over options when he suddenly remembered a school visit by a recruiting team from the British Army. He hadn't been particularly interested in joining as a squaddie, but one of the army staff had noticed that he was wearing a Norton motorcycle enamel badge and had said that he should join as they had despatch riders and a motorcycle display team. Unfortunately, that was all he could recall about the recruiting team, apart from the fact that they were wearing blue silk cravats. What part of the army they belonged to, was a mystery, and for the life of him he couldn't dredge up the name of the unit.

He put it out of his mind, and that would have been the end of it had he not been on his way to claim unemployment benefit and passed an army recruitment office. Sitting in the waiting room for his turn to sign on, he looked around at the other occupants. Some were fairly young, like him, some older but well-dressed, but the vast majority were obviously long-term unemployed. They emanated varying degrees of hopelessness and despair, which was not really surprising considering the dire employment prospects at the time. Steve had read that six hundred people had applied for a single job as a traffic warden, which pointed to a fairly high degree of desperation.

There were so many applicants for each job that HR departments had reportedly resorted to summarily discarding any application written in blue ink rather than black (or the other way round as the fit took them) in an attempt to winnow the numbers down to manageable levels.

You would see a job advertised in the local paper and apply, thinking that this could be the one. Then, after a while, when no response had been forthcoming, you would begin to realise that they weren't even going to get an interview and that another few weeks of your life had gone by, to no effect.

That was what had made Steve's mind up about joining the army. At least it would be better than sitting around all day, waiting in hopeless anticipation for an invitation to an interview dropping through the letterbox.

He stood up when his name was called and went forward to the shabby booth, where a member of the Department of Social Security waited to witness his signature on the UB40 form. It was telling that the stubby pencil with which you signed for your dole money was tied to the desk with a piece of string. He supposed that some people would steal anything.

"Done any work this week?" the bespectacled young woman behind the counter asked, in a peremptory tone.

"No," replied Steve.

"Sign there," came the command, and that was that.

The green giro payment would arrive at his home in a couple of days and could be cashed at the local post office. After he had given his mother almost half of it for housekeeping, he had barely enough to cover the cost of a few pints each night at his local pub. It was no way to live, and there was little or no prospect of it getting any better any time soon.

Boredom was giving way to apathy, as rejection after rejection sapped the will to even bother applying for jobs. He had got into a spiral of staying up late and then, because there was no reason to get up, staying in bed until 10 or even 11 o'clock in the morning. If he didn't do something soon, he was in danger of becoming one of the long-term unemployed.

There were families that he knew of where no one had worked in a proper job for two generations, and that was only because the third generation hadn't left school yet.

Steve stood up and turned to leave the dole office, with its smell of cigarette smoke and the faint taint of unwashed bodies and stale beer. He glanced at the waiting patrons, and the looks of despair on their miserable, dispirited faces convinced him that he had to do something to avoid becoming like them.

The army recruitment office was a brick built building with plate glass windows covered in posters, similar to most of the shops on Wembley High Street.

The recruiting Sergeant was a rather overweight, red-faced man wearing a faded green army jumper with cloth patches on the shoulders, and a huge, multicoloured badge consisting of a crown between two crossed Union Jacks on flag staffs above three stripes on his right sleeve. He smiled as Steve walked in and got up from behind his desk.

"Come to join the professionals?" he asked, pleasantly.

"Yes," said Steve.

"Good. Take a seat," said the Sergeant, gesturing to the rather utilitarian metal and plywood chair opposite his desk. "Want a cup of tea?"

"Yes, please. White, no sugar," replied Steve, taking a seat.

As he was waiting for the tea, he scanned the room. It was a very basic shop unit, consisting of an open-plan office with two desks and some shelving for pamphlets, and the statutory pictures of the Queen and Prince Philip on the walls. At the back was a small room which contained the tea and coffee-making facilities and next to that, a toilet; pretty basic with unsurprisingly minimal expense spent. The Sergeant came back with the tea and proffered a chipped mug to Steve.

"So," he began, "what unit do you want to join?"

"I don't really know," admitted Steve. "What are the options?"

"Well, the best is the infantry, of course, but there are plenty of choices. Have a look through these and see if anything takes your fancy," said the Sergeant with a smile, handing Steve a thick, glossy pamphlet.

He left Steve to look through it and he went away to do some paperwork.

The final unit caught Steve's eye.

"What does the Intelligence Corps do?" he asked.

"Ooh! The sneaky beakys," said the Sergeant. He didn't actually know what the Intelligence Corps did – it was a bit of a mystery – but he didn't want to admit to his ignorance, so he mumbled something about James Bond which left Steve none the wiser.

"What qualifications do you need to get in?"

"What have you got?"

"Seven O-levels."

"Oh, right. You could go for a commission with that lot. Become an officer."

"Not in the Intelligence Corps, Sarge," interrupted a Corporal who had come in with a bag of Greggs' pasties while Steve had been perusing the booklet.

"No?" queried the Sergeant.

"No," confirmed the Corporal. "You've got to have a degree to get into the Intelligence Corps as an officer."

"That's OK," interjected Steve. "I don't want to be an officer, anyway."

"Good man," said the Sergeant. "So, do you fancy joining the Intelligence Corps, then?"

Suddenly, it hit Steve that this could be the answer to his problem. He didn't really want to spend his time marching around or being shot at, which was all he could really think being an infantrymen was all about. Most of his knowledge of the army came from old Second World War films like *A Bridge Too Far* or *The Longest Day*, or the odd television docu-soap, so he had a slightly warped vision of what it actually entailed. But the Intelligence Corps sounded like something different, and like most men of his age, he was brought up watching *James Bond* films and there was a distinct attraction to being an international spy. So, he said, "Yes."

The recruiting Sergeant then passed him over to the Corporal, who made enquiries about the recruiting process for the Intelligence Corps. Joining as a serving soldier was considerably easier than going for a commission, but still entailed filling in a lot of paperwork. He wouldn't have to get vetted immediately, although that would come later – he only had to pass a basic security check to make sure that he wasn't an undercover Russian spy or had any serious criminal convictions.

Steve passed them all with flying colours, having lived a fairly quiet and conventional life, even though he thought he had been pretty wild as a teenager. He had never taken drugs, unlike most of his friends, and the worst that he had done was got thoroughly drunk and made a fool of himself at parties, but who of his generation hadn't done that?

A week later, he received notice of an appointment for a medical, and on a cold, blustery May morning, he left his house to catch the tube to Northwick Park Hospital. The hospital was conveniently located close to the tube station at Northwick Park itself, and Steve followed a group of students from the University of Westminster, which had a campus next to the medical complex.

One or two other people were straggling towards the reception area, and Steve briefly wondered from what ailments they were suffering, before forging on ahead to get to the reception desk first. As he entered the building, he caught the faint smell of antiseptic and vague illness that all medical facilities seem to give off. It made him feel slightly ill as he had foolishly gone out with some friends the previous night and drank more than he had intended.

His mates had come up with the usual jokes about military Intelligence being a contradiction in terms, and that he must be joining Intelligence because he hadn't got any, but it had all been light-hearted, although with an undertone of what Steve thought might have been mild jealousy that he was escaping from a world of unemployment and disappointment to an exciting new career.

Steve sat and waited for his appointment as the minutes ticked by on a round, white plastic clock attached to the wall. Every so often, an anonymous voice would announce someone's name along with the name of a doctor and the number of the room to which the patient was directed to go. Steve watched as the person named by the voice got up and went either right or left, depending on the room to which they had been directed. He played a game to try to guess which one would be next until, finally, he heard his own name called and was directed to Dr Robinson in consulting room five.

The room was a small, square cubicle with a standard medical bed on one side and a desk and chair tucked into one corner. Against one wall was a set of scales and a device for measuring height. The medical was going fine until the doctor, ticking off boxes on a list of ailments, asked, "Do you suffer from migraines?"

Steve, sitting in a post-alcoholic daze said, "Yes."

The doctor's pen stopped, mid-tick. "Oh," he said, ominously.

Shit! thought Steve.

"Do you get them often?" asked the doctor, peering at Steve through small round spectacles perched on the tip of his nose.

"No," replied Steve, slightly desperately. "In fact, I haven't had one for years."

"Hmm," the doctor murmured, tapping the form with his pen. "Headaches? Nausea?"

"Not badly," said Steve, seeing his potential career in the British Army disappearing down the plughole.

"OK," continued the doctor. "Having migraines doesn't debar you from joining the army, but we'd better get a specialist to check it out, just in case. They can be an indicator of strokes, you know."

"Is that bad?"

Dr Robinson gave him the look that people in the medical profession give to a layperson.

"If you have a stroke," he explained patiently, "then you not only wouldn't be able to join the army, but you wouldn't be able to drive, either. Do you drive?"

"Yes, I've got a motorbike."

"Nasty things," commented the doctor, unnecessarily.

Steve felt like his future was slipping away. He had built himself up with the thought of joining the army, and now it seemed like that future was going to be taken away from him, just like that. Dr Robinson saw the despondency on Steve's face.

"It might not be too bad," he said, encouragingly. "But we need to check, just in case."

"Yes, of course."

"Right. Let's carry on."

He continued rattling off ailments, most of which Steve had never heard of, and briskly ticking the boxes until he suddenly came out with, "Any history of mental illness?"

Steve hesitated and was tempted to say no.

What the hell? What have I got to lose by telling the truth? he thought.

"Yes," he admitted. "My grandmother was certified."

Dr Robinson looked at him. "Mother's or father's side?"

"Mother's," replied Steve.

The doctor shrugged. "That's not a problem, then," and carried on.

Steve couldn't really understand why having mental illness on your mother's side of the family was OK but not on your father's, but he wasn't going to complain if it wasn't going to stop him joining up.

The medical continued until Dr Robinson had completed all his forms, and then he arranged for Steve to see a specialist about his migraines. That was it.

Steve wandered out of the hospital in a daze and almost got run over by an ambulance, which would have just about completed the cycle of disaster. He was now feeling slightly sick as the effects of the hangover and lack of sleep worked their way through him. He would have to stop going to bed so late and drinking so much, but only if he could persuade the specialist that his migraines weren't too bad, otherwise it wouldn't matter, and he would have to find something else to do with his life.

When he got home, he had to tell his mother what had happened as she could tell from his face that there had been a problem. She was as sympathetic as she could be, but it didn't make Steve feel any better. The days dragged by, waiting for the specialist's appointment with a mixture of desire to get it over with and fear of the results.

In the end, the letter arrived early one morning, and Steve found that he had to go to Harley Street, of all places. He had heard of it but had no idea where it was, so he got out his London A-Z and looked it up.

Harley Street is in Marylebone, and the closest tube station is Regent's Park. The street itself consists of stone and brick buildings, with the odd modern block which replaced those destroyed by German bombers during the Second World War. The clinic was an imposing, three-storey block with a basement, sub-basement and what looked like a sub-sub-basement.

Steve went in and presented his appointment card and was directed to a waiting room with threadbare carpets and a pile of dog-eared magazines on a small, round table in the corner. The magazines all seemed to be about either posh homes and gardens, or hunting, neither of which interested Steve, so he sat and stared out the bay window, through the net curtains at the odd passerby, until he was called into the specialist's office.

The specialist looked exactly like Dr Robinson from Northwick Park and could have been his brother. He flicked through a pile of notes on his desk and then looked up at Steve.

"Can you describe the symptoms of your migraines?"

Steve thought for a moment and then said, "Well, the first thing is a tingling numbness in my right hand and the right side of my face."

"Yes. It's normally one side or the other," commented the specialist. "Do you get severe headaches?"

"No."

The specialist nodded to himself. "Go on."

"Then I get a sort of watery blurring in my eyes."

"Does it move?"

"Yes."

"Good," said the specialist, making a note on the form in front of him. "It's not a stroke."

"No?" queried Steve, a feeling of relief sweeping over him.

"No," continued the specialist. "If it was a stroke, then your vision would go dark and not move."

"What is it, then?"

"It's what is known as asymmetric migraine."

"Asymmetric?"

"Yes. You don't get headaches, which is a symptom of the classic migraine. You're quite lucky."

"Will it affect me joining the army?"

"It shouldn't, as long as you don't get them regularly."

"Oh, no!" said Steve. "I haven't had one for ages."

"OK. I'll send a letter to your doctor recommending that you are fit for active service."

"Thanks," smiled Steve.

His future was back on.

Three weeks later, he received a letter telling him that he had been accepted for recruitment into the Intelligence Corps, and to report to Templer Barracks for the September intake.

PART 3

MILITARY SKILLS

SEPTEMBER – NOVEMBER 1989

CHAPTER 9

Basic infantry training, or Mil Skills, is the first part of any soldiers training in the British Army, as all soldiers are considered to be infantry first and then tradespeople second. It is known as the CMS phase, standing for the Common Military Syllabus and is usually carried out at an infantry training establishment like the Guards depot at Pirbright.

Training consists of Drill, weapon handling, fieldcraft, first aid, Nuclear, Bacteriological and Chemical Warfare (NBC) training, map reading and fitness training.

The Intelligence Corps carried out their own infantry training at the Ashford Depot and had a specialist Training wing headed by an Intelligence Corps Major with an Intelligence Corps Company Sergeant Major. For some reason the Drill Sergeant was traditionally from the Pioneer Corps but other instructors were seconded from various infantry units where they would do a two year posting.

When Jon and his new colleagues arrived at Templer Barracks, they were met by a couple of Intelligence Corps Corporals who ticked them off a list and directed them to their quarters. They were told to dump their kit and to report to one of the classrooms for an initial briefing. This was done by Major Elswick, the head of the training wing, who welcomed them to the course and gave them an outline of the programme for the next six weeks. After that, they were told to sort out their kit and to parade outside their accommodation blocks at 0630 for breakfast.

Jon found himself sharing a room with three other recruits. Rob,

Paul and Colin were all much younger than Jon and had all joined the Corps straight from school. None of them had any previous military experience and Jon suspected that he had been billeted with these three so that he could look after them.

The room had four beds, two to a wall opposite each other, with a small piece of carpet between them, and each had its own wardrobe and chest of drawers

It's going to be a bit of a trial getting used to sharing a room again, Jon thought. (He had not had to do that since he was last in the army, many years ago.)

"Do you think we can go to the bar?" asked Rob after he had dumped his suitcase in the bottom of his wardrobe.

Jon stared at him for a moment. He was only about eighteen, although he looked younger because he had fair hair and looked like he didn't actually need to shave.

"Yes," he said, finally. "Although I wouldn't get drunk, if I were you."

"I thought that was what the army was all about," laughed Paul. "I was tempted to say that I was 'the scum of the Earth' and was only enlisting for the drink, when the recruiting guy asked me why I wanted to join!"

"The Duke of Wellington," said Jon, alluding to one of the UK's most famous General's more memorable quotes.

"So, we are allowed to go to the bar, then?" queried Colin.

"As long as you're over eighteen," replied Jon. "Which you must be if they've let you join the Corps. There's a saying that goes, 'What's not expressly forbidden, is allowed'. Unlike the Soviet Army, where it's the other way round."

"Oh. That's OK, then," said Colin.

They went down to the NAAFI. It was a large, open-plan room with Formica-topped tables and metal-framed chairs.

"God, it's not very plush, is it?" said Rob.

"Ashford is within easy walking distance," explained Jon. "So, most staff go there, rather than drink here."

"I don't really care, as long as they sell beer," put in Colin.

They made their way to the long counter which served as the bar and looked at the choice of drinks available. The only draught beer was John Smiths or Carling lager.

"I'll get them," offered Jon. "Lager or beer?"

Rob and Colin asked for John Smiths and Paul a bottle of Becks. Jon ordered the drinks and, as he was standing waiting for them, a burly dark-haired man sitting at the bar turned to him.

"It's traditional for newbies to buy the staff drinks," he said, without introducing himself.

Jon looked at him coldly. "Like fuck it is, Corporal," he said.

The man was slightly taken aback by Jon's tone and looked him up and down.

"What makes you think I'm a Corporal?" he asked. "I could be a Sergeant for all you know."

"Not in this bar, you couldn't," replied Jon. "This is the NAAFI."

"It could be an all-ranks' mess."

"It could be, but it isn't."

"You ex-regular?"

"Yes. I was in the Royal Scots."

"So? I'm an AIPT."

Jon wasn't particularly tall, but he was well-built and obviously fit, so he wasn't intimidated.

"And I did selection," said Jon, looking straight into the man's eyes.

"Oh. OK," the man said, looking faintly pale. "Well, we'll waive the drinks for you guys, then," he finished, lamely.

"Thank you, Corporal," said Jon, picking up his beer.

"What was that all about?" asked Rob, when they had all sat down at a table in the corner.

"That guy was trying to con the recruits out of free drinks," said Jon.

"What's an AIPT?" asked Colin.

"Assistant Instructor, Physical Training" explained Jon. "It means he helps out with PT, but he's not fully qualified."

"And selection?"

"I tried to join the TA SAS years ago. It's called SAS selection."

"What happened?" asked Colin, intrigued.

"I was too slow," said Jon. "Selection is all about navigating over the hills with a huge pack on your back and a rifle. I could carry the weight and do the distance, but I couldn't do it fast enough. So, eventually I packed it in."

"What distance was it?" asked Colin. They were all obviously fascinated and wanted to know the details.

"TA had to do fifty Ks in twenty-four hours, carrying a thirty-five pound pack and rifle. Regulars had to do it in twenty hours," said Jon.

"That doesn't sound too bad," mused Rob.

"Yes," agreed Jon. "It doesn't sound too bad until you have to do it. It's not fifty Ks on the flat. It's all up and down hill. It took three months for the scars from the Bergen to heal."

There was a pause whilst they digested this information and drank their beer. More recruits had come in and the Corporal at the bar had got himself a few free drinks.

"Christ! Will you look at that," the Corporal exclaimed, as Donna and Sonia came into the bar. "I'd shag that." He had obviously had a few and was worse for wear.

"Which one?" someone asked.

"The white one, of course," he replied.

"Fucking hell!" exclaimed Jon.

This didn't bode well for the intake. Not only was this guy a bully but he was a racist into the bargain. If he was one of the training staff, they were going to have problems. He probably should have kept his mouth shut and just bought the bastard a drink, but he wasn't made that way. What had looked like a good start was beginning to sour already, and he hadn't even started his training.

The guys finished their drinks, and they went back to the billet for an early night. Jon lay awake for a while, wondering if he should report the incident in the NAAFI or hope that it was an isolated event. With a bit of luck, they wouldn't see that Corporal again.

There were a few bleary eyes on parade the next morning as they formed up to go to the cookhouse. Some of the recruits had obviously overdone it and would pay the price for their lack of restraint.

The first army meal was a bit of an eye-opener for some. The cooked breakfast was always the same: one fried egg, two sausages of dubious content (so much so that when asked for vegetarian food, one of the chefs allegedly said, "Give them the sausages, there's no meat in them."), some fatty bacon, sometimes with the hairs still attached, tinned tomatoes and a piece of fried bread.

Jon was quite happy with this as it reminded him of his days as a student, but there were muttered complaints from some of the others, although not loud enough for the staff to hear.

The rest of the day was taken up with the issuing of uniforms and kit, paperwork and medicals. They formed a long queue at the Quartermaster's stores, waiting to be issued with the uniforms and equipment that they would need to carry out their roles as soldiers and tradespeople.

If they found themselves posted to a Security section in the UK, then they would rarely wear uniform and would be given a clothing allowance to cover the cost of suits, shirts and ties (or the female equivalent), but that would be at least a year in the future and was not an issue at present. The working uniform (or working dress as it was known) consisted of a cypress-green beret and Intelligence Corps cap badge, a green army jumper with cloth shoulder patches and epaulettes for rank slides (being Privates, they didn't need rank slides and wouldn't be issued with them until they passed out from Ashford), a plain green shirt and trousers, a green plastic belt, green socks and boots (combat high).

Puttees were no longer issued, and the bottoms of the trousers were rolled up and held in place by strong elastic bands (although specialist 'trouser blousers', which were stretchy green bands of elastic material with small hooks at each end, were beginning to be manufactured), and each recruit was issued with two pairs.

There were a number of other uniforms: Number One dress (ceremonial), Number Two dress, combat kit, PT kit and a range of other specialist clothing, to be worn as per Intelligence Corps' dress regulations.

Jon had looked up the regulations one time when he had had nothing better to do and been amazed to find that there were something like fourteen different types of uniform that could be worn, depending on what part of the world you were serving in, which unit you belonged to, and whether it was summer or winter, as well as the odd bits of kit that were unique to individual regiments and corps.

Jon had broken the heel off his issue brown shoes doing drill when he was at Sandhurst and found out that as he was an Officer Cadet, he was expected to pay for his own replacements. That was after being told by the college RSM that they should give it 'bags of strike' i.e. hitting their weapons and stamping their feet whilst doing drill, and that anything they broke would be replaced by the army. That was an object lesson in not believing everything that you were told, and Jon had never forgotten it. Jon had been lucky that the storeman was in a good mood and gave him a second-hand pair of shoes, otherwise it would have cost him a week's pay.

There was so much kit being issued that the recruits had to ferry it across to their billets to be dumped on their beds before going back for another batch.

"Are we ever going to use all this stuff?" asked Paul.

"Yes – if you stay long enough," replied Jon, who was carefully stowing his latest batch of uniform so that it wouldn't get any more creased than it already was.

"What's next?" said Rob, eyeing the huge pile of multi-hued clothing sitting on his bed.

"Webbing," said Jon, simply.

They went back across to the stores and Jon saw that the women were going in for their uniform fitting. They were issued their kit separately from the men because in the past there were complaints of being ogled as they were trying on the sometimes ill-fitting uniforms. The training wing had a female Second in Command who was an Intelligence Corps Captain. She made an appearance to check that no such activity was occurring on her watch.

Jon saw Sonia and gave her a smile as she caught his eye. He hadn't really had a chance to speak to any of the other female recruits yet, but Sonia, along with Donna, both stood out, albeit for slightly different reasons. The proportion of female to male recruits was about 40:60, which didn't really surprise Jon as the Corps was one of the few units where a woman had almost as much chance of advancement as a man. He wondered how many would stay the course and pass out. They had been told that there was no fixed quota and that it was possible for them all to get through, but he very much doubted that all of them would make it to the end. He had looked around at the young, anxious faces and tried to gauge their commitment, but it was impossible at this stage. Time would tell.

At lunch, Sonia and Donna came over to the table where Jon, Rob, Paul and Colin were sitting.

"Mind if we join you?" Sonia asked. The tables had six chairs and two were free.

"Sure. Help yourself," said Jon.

Rob, Paul and Colin were almost drooling as they watched Donna sit down, unable to believe their luck that she was sitting at their table. It wasn't that the other girls were unattractive, although some were definitely more on the masculine side, but that Donna had an innate beauty that shone through. Jon noticed that she was inevitably surrounded by a gaggle of male admirers whenever there was a break and wondered how she was coping with the attention. He supposed that she had got used to it over the years.

"I hear you spent some time in Africa," Sonia said to Jon, once she had got herself settled at the table.

He looked at her before replying. It was a sensitive area, and he didn't want to say the wrong thing.

"Yes. I worked in a gold mine in Zimbabwe," he admitted.

"Did you like it?" she asked.

"Yes. It's a beautiful country."

"Sounds fun. Why did you leave?" interjected Rob. He had torn his eyes away from Donna when he heard the words 'gold mine'.

"My contract ran out," explained Jon. "We were supposed to go to Tanzania to guard an emerald mine, but the job fell through, and I ran out of money."

"Would you go back?" asked Sonia.

"Not now. The country's gone to the dogs. When I was there you could get six-to-one sterling to Zimbabwe dollars, but the inflation went sky high. Also, odd as it may seem, I missed the cold weather."

"What do you mean?" questioned Sonia.

"I was in Zimbabwe for seven months and it only rained twice, that I can remember. It was all blue skies and sunny days. I eventually came to miss the UK's climate."

"Wow!" said Paul.

"Yes. Such is life," said Jon.

After lunch they went for their medicals. They sat around in small groups waiting for their turn to go in. It seemed like a complete waste of time since they had all had medicals before being accepted for training, but in some cases that had been months before and the army was now responsible for their health, amongst other things.

One of the girls came out of a consulting room and came across to the other and sat down.

"What was it like?" asked a dark-haired girl called Sandra.

"It was OK," replied the other. "But if you get a male doctor and he asks about breast cancer, tell him you know how to self-test. This one wanted to give me a demonstration on how to do it."

"Right!" agreed Sandra.

After their medicals they were told to stay in the waiting room and then were taken in small, single-sex groups to another area.

"I wonder what they're doing?" one of the recruits said.

"Probably drug testing," said Dave, who found himself attached to this group.

"Drug testing?" asked the recruit. "How do you know?"

"I was in the Intelligence Corps TA, and they were talking about the introduction of random drug testing before I came here," Dave explained.

"Is that why they're taking groups of men and women separately?" asked one of the girls.

"Yes," said Dave. "You have to piss in a bottle so they can get a sample, and they watch to make sure you don't cheat."

"I don't know if I can do it if someone's watching," complained another recruit, plaintively.

"They don't exactly watch you," said Dave. "But the door is open so that you can't slip in a clean sample. Or, at least, that's what they do for the men."

"Why would anyone be stupid enough to have taken drugs before coming here?" asked Sandra.

"You'd be surprised," said Jon.

"It can stay in your system for up to three months, apparently," continued Dave.

"Oh, OK," acknowledged Sandra. "You seem to know a lot about it."

"We had a lecture on it. Drugs are one of the seven levers for espionage."

"What's that?" asked another recruit.

"It's part of Security training. It's all about how to recruit someone to be a spy. You can either get them to do it willingly or you can blackmail them. Threatening to expose someone for taking drugs is one of the ways to blackmail them. That's why they're so keen to make sure we're all clean."

"What are the other levers?" someone asked him, but at that point the next batch was taken in for testing and Dave never answered the question.

Two recruits were found to have samples of illegal substances in their systems and were taken away from the squad and weren't seen again.

Two down. Thirty-eight to go, thought Jon, when he found out.

Back in the billet, Jon gave his roommates a lesson in shaping a beret. "The Intelligence Corps beret is described as being 'cypress green" he told them. "This is pronounced *sip-prus* rather than *sy-prus* (as in the country) and is made of felt with a cloth lining and a plastic square which covers the maker's instruction label. The first thing that usually happens is that the label is removed because it is reputed to cause a bald spot, although this may be urban myth. The next stage is to 'shape' it," he continued. "This is done by soaking it in warm water and then putting the sopping wet mass of felt on your head and manipulating into the desired shape. You then carefully remove it and place it somewhere safe where it can dry out. As it dries, it'll shrink and, if done correctly, creates a smart-looking piece of headwear that holds the Intelligence Corp cap badge depicting an Imperial king's crown surmounting a union rose between twin sprays of laurel; a scroll below bearing the insignia 'Intelligence Corps.' That's according to the Intelligence Corps museum or is 'a pansy resting on its laurels' according to some Second World War wit."

The following morning, now that they had all been issued with their uniforms, the squad had its first proper drill lesson. They were first introduced to standing at attention, standing at ease, standing easy, and left, right and about-turn. Then they were told to fall in with the shortest on the left and the tallest on the right. Jon was surprised to find that he was fairly close to the middle of the squad. At Sandhurst, he had been almost at the left of the squad, with only some of the cadets being smaller than him, but here he was taller than most of the women and some of the men. The tallest recruit was a Private called Johnny, who was huge. He must have measured about 6ft 6 or 7in, and towered over the next tallest, who was a respectable 6ft 2in.

One of the female recruits was about 6ft and had the longest legs that Jon had ever seen. He wondered how she had managed to get trousers to fit her. Mind you, judging by the state of them, she had obviously had to make do with a pair of men's trousers.

Sergeant Thompson, the Pioneer Corps drill Sergeant called them up to attention, which they did with varying degrees of success depending on their previous military experience (or lack of it, in most cases).

"By the right... Number!" he shouted.

There was silence.

"That means we start with you, big boy," said Thompson, moving to stand in front of the giant recruit to the right of the line. Thompson was about 5ft 5in. and had to crane his neck to look at the face of the nervous recruit.

"Sorry, sir," he said.

"Don't call me sir! I'm a Sergeant. I work for my money," said Thompson, causing a few smiles further down the line.

"Yes, sir. Sorry... Sergeant," came the reply.

"Right! Let's do that again," shouted Thompson. "By the right... Number!"

"One."

"Two."

"Three," called the recruits.

They went all the way down the line until the final recruit, a diminutive, black-haired female screamed, "Thirty-eight, Sergeant!" at the top of her voice.

"Good, well done," commented Thompson. "Let's see if we can get the next bit right. Odd numbers, one pace forward. Even numbers, one pace back. Wait for it! Odd and even numbers one pace... March!"

Amazingly enough, the squad did exactly as they had been ordered.

"Even better," said Thompson, happily. "The front rank will turn to the right. The rear rank will turn to the left. Front and rear ranks, left and right... Turn!"

The two ranks turned right and left, although one person in the rear rank started to turn the wrong way but quickly managed to spin round so that they were all facing in the correct direction.

"Right-hand, man. That's you, Private," said Thompson, addressing the tall recruit. "Stand still. All others forward... March!"

The two lines started to move and Thompson, pointing with his pace stick, directed them to their various ranks.

"Centre, rear. Front, centre, rear. Front centre, rear." he called out as each recruit marched towards him.

In this way the squad formed up into three ranks, with the tallest person being the right-hand marker and the smallest ones now being in the centre. Once they were all in place, Thompson addressed the troops.

"Look around you. This is your place in the squad from now on. I want you to form up like this whenever you hear 'fall in three ranks'. Understood?"

"Yes, Sergeant," came the reply.

"So far, so good," commented Thompson. "Let's see if you can march."

He turned them to the right and set them off.

"By the right. Quick march!" he shouted. "Left, right, left, right, left, right, left."

He called out at a blistering pace, and the squad soon lost any hope of keeping the step, but he carried on anyway.

"Left, right, left, right, left, right, left... Arms shoulder high... heads up everywhere... left, right, left, right, left, right, left. Abooout turn. Left, right, left, right, left, right, left."

Eventually he called, "Squaad, halt!" and the shambles that was the squad came to an abrupt stop.

"Squad, right turn! Stand at ease!"

The squad turned right and those that knew how to, stood at ease. The rest followed their example. A lot of them were breathing heavily and some were gasping for breath.

"Right," said Thompson. "Now that we've warmed up, we can slow it down a bit. What's the purpose of drill?"

"To build teamwork," said a voice.

"Correct," agreed Thompson. "To get you all working together, and also to get you used to doing what you're told to do and to obey it instantly."

They all listened attentively to the Sergeant while they got their breath back.

"You're all in the Intelligence Corps," he continued. "Which means that you're the only unit in the British Army that is actually paid to think. However, you still have to be able to obey orders and to do what you're told. That's what discipline is all about. Anyone know why?"

"Because if you don't, then you probably won't be able to work as a team, and a team will generally beat an individual," said Dave from the rear rank.

"Yes. Good," said Thompson. "It isn't about breaking you; it's about building you into a better player for the good of the team. Drill should be fun."

There were looks of disbelief on some faces.

"Not that it isn't hard work," he added. "But you're all smart people and you should be able to understand that."

Jon was amazed. He had never thought of drill as anything other than being a mild form of torture. Admittedly, he had enjoyed parades, especially to music, but the way that Thompson put it made perfect sense, and he wondered what might have happened had he joined the Pioneer Corps instead of buying himself out of the army. Still, that was water under the bridge, and no matter how hard you try, you can't go back and cross the same river twice, or so he had been told.

"Damn, it's gone again," complained Paul, as the oil-slicked mechanism slid through his fingers.

The squad were getting a lesson on stripping and assembling

the Sterling Sub Machine-Gun (SMG). This was a 9mm handheld machine gun, which was standard issue to the Corps as it was small, light and could be folded up when not in use. In fact, folded up SMGs were used as props for the weapons carried by the storm troopers in the early *Star Wars* films.

It was very simply constructed and the firing mechanism, or working parts, consisted of a cylindrical breech block with a strong spring attached. This was held within the body of the weapon itself by the curved cocking handle and the weapon's end cap, which had a tendency to slip through one's fingers as it was being assembled if it wasn't held properly. This could be very frustrating, and indeed deadly, if you needed to strip and assemble it under anything but ideal conditions.

"Who designed this thing, anyway?" said Paul in disgust.

"Someone who never had to use it," replied Steve, who had been attached to the group for weapons training.

"I can see that," agreed Paul. "What use is this thing, anyway?"

"It's good for drill," interjected Jon. "It's nice and light. Unlike the SLR."

The SLR (Self Loading Rifle) was a brute of a weapon. It weighed over 4kg, unlike the SMG, which was less than 3kg. Jon had been taught drill with the SLR at Sandhurst and he remembered wondering what would happen to him if he fixed bayonet and chased the college RSM off the parade square with it. During the Falklands campaign, the Paras had complained that many of the bayonets had broken and, since they had run out of ammunition, most of the deaths were therefore caused with broken bayonets.

"Well, at least it's good for something, then," said Paul.

"It's got no stopping power," said Mich in the group beside them who had overheard the conversation.

"What do you mean?" Paul asked.

"You could kill an elephant with an SLR round," explained

Mich. "It's 7.62mm, while this 9mm piece of crap will get stopped by wet webbing at 50m."

"What's it for, then?" queried Paul.

"Self-defence, mainly," said Mich. "It's good for enclosed spaces, and better than nothing, I suppose."

"A bit of a girly weapon, then?" said Paul, a little cockily.

"You'd be surprised," said Mich. "Wait until you've seen the girls on the range. You might change your mind."

It was an odd thing, but the women tended to be better shots than the men – at least initially – because they would do as they were instructed, as opposed to men, who thought they knew better. Mich had seen plenty of excellent female shots in his time.

"OK," came the instructor's voice, breaking their conversation, "pick up your weapons and form a single line."

They all got up and stood facing towards the classroom wall. On the other side were windows, but the side they were facing was blank, except for miniature pictures of the countryside which were pasted to the base of the wall and gave aiming points at various distances.

"With a magazine of no rounds, load," came the order.

The class went through the drill of checking the safety catch, opening an ammunition pouch, taking out a thirty-round magazine and slotting it into the magazine housing on the right-hand side of the weapon. After that, the pouch should have been closed again to prevent the loss of other magazines in the event of moving, but the slower recruits left them open as they fumbled with the unfamiliar weapon.

"Ready..."

This was the command to cock the weapon, which enabled it to be fired once the safety catch was released or, as sometimes happened with the SMG, if it was dropped or struck against a hard object.

"Aim..."

All the recruits pointed their weapons at the targets on the wall.

They were really for rifles, and the distances represented were too far away for an SMG to be effective, but that was beside the point.

"Fire!"

There were a series of clicks as safety catches were removed, and the class pulled the triggers of their SMGs, the working parts snapping forward.

"Cease fire," came the command, although because it was a drill and not the real thing, there had only been one time that the working parts had gone forward. If the magazine had contained live rounds, then the force of the bullet being expelled from the barrel would have pushed the working parts back, picking up a fresh round, and the process would have continued as long as the trigger was depressed, until the magazine was empty.

"Unload."

The drill was to put the safety catch on, open the magazine pouch, take the magazine off the weapon, tilt the weapon to the right and cock three times, catching any unfired round, put the magazine into the pouch and close it. "OK, that'll do for today. Well done, everyone. See you tomorrow. Dismissed," said the instructor.

CHAPTER 10

"Hey, Mike, come and look at this," the astonished weapons storeman shouted to his mate.

"What is it?" Mike asked, taking the SLR from his colleague's hands.

"He's managed to get the working parts in the wrong way round."

"But that's supposed to be impossible," stated Mike, with a touch of awe in his voice.

"He's slime," said the storeman. "They can do anything."

'Slime' or 'Green Slime' was a derogatory term for the Intelligence Corps that had apparently been started by the SAS as an insult to make up for the fact that Intelligence Corps personnel could cause them to fail SAS selection if they didn't pass the resistance to advanced questioning techniques phase which the Int Corps administered.

Paul 'Biff' Dobson stood miserably as the storemen had a good laugh at his expense. He tried his best, but he seemed to mess everything up. His nickname 'Biff' confirmed this. Though a partial joke, it demonstrated that Paul was on a slippery slope towards failure and dismissal from the Corps.

His latest fuck up was to put the working parts of his SLR in backwards which, as the storeman stated, was technically impossible. Paul couldn't have explained how he did it. He just seemed to have a knack of cocking everything up and, if it hadn't been for the heroic efforts of Jon and the other ex-regulars in the squad, he would have probably been voluntarily resigned (VR) by now.

The storeman managed to prise the rat's tail from the barrel of the rifle and turned the working parts around so that they slid easily into position.

"That's how it's supposed to be done," he said, showing the hapless Paul the correct way to reassemble the weapon.

"Thanks, Corporal," said Paul.

"No problem, Private," came the slightly condescending answer.

"Come in, Private Anders," said Major Elswick, the training wing Training Major.

"Have a seat," said Elswick, waving his hand towards the tubular, metal chair in front of his desk.

"Thanks, sir," replied Dave, sitting down.

Elswick gave Dave a long, hard look.

"We've got a bit of a problem with your vetting application," he said.

Ah, the vetting application! thought Dave. He had suspected that this was going to come back to bite him at some point, but he hadn't thought he would have to deal with it at such an early stage.

"What's the problem, sir?" he asked, innocently.

He could tell that Elswick was trying to weigh him up, and hoped his expression matched his voice.

"There appear to be gaps in your employment record."

Shit! thought Dave.

"Gaps, sir?"

"Yes, Private Anders. Gaps. For instance, what were you doing between 1984 and 1986?"

"I was in the Merchant Navy, sir."

"Yes. You put that on the form," Elswick paused. "What you didn't put on the form was what ships you were on and where you went. We need to know this, you understand?"

Dave understood perfectly but was caught in a cleft stick. If he told them what he had been up to, he would almost certainly not get clearance. He knew security well enough to know that. He had passed his A1 trade training, after all. He had hoped that he would get away with leaving it a bit vague, but obviously this was not to be.

"What do you need to know, sir?" he asked, dreading the answer.

"What we need to know, Private," stated Elswick, crisply, "is *exactly* which ship you served on and *exactly* where you went."

"Right, sir."

This is it, Dave thought. *I'm well and truly fucked.*

"Er... I can't exactly remember," he said lamely.

Elswick gave him a strange look that didn't bode well. He rubbed his left hand over his chin and pursed his lips.

"I'm sorry, Private Anders," he said, finally, "but that's not good enough. The DVA (*Defence Vetting Agency*) won't accept that, and without clearance you won't be able to progress with your training."

"OK, sir," said Dave. There wasn't much more he could say.

Elswick gave him a chance.

"Do you think that you will be able to recall the information?" he asked, not unkindly.

"I'll do my best, sir."

"Very well. You have three days to come up with the goods. That's all."

"Thanks, sir," replied Dave, and he left the room.

May as well go and get drunk, he thought. That was what had caused the problem in the first place, after all.

There was a small group of hardened drinkers in the NAAFI. The recruits weren't allowed to go out into Ashford until they had passed their CMS phase, and the four-person rooms could become a bit claustrophobic at times, so they tended to take refuge in the bar. It was the one place where they could air their grievances and discuss the elements of the day-to-day work without the risk of being overheard by a member of the directing staff.

"I really hate that guy," said Paul in low tones, indicating the burly Corporal who seemed to spend all of his free time in the NAAFI.

"I wouldn't worry about him," said Jon. "He's just a prick."

"Have you heard about the shit sandwich?" asked another recruit.

"No," said Jon. "What about it?"

"Well, apparently this guy" – the recruit nodded towards the Corporal sitting at the bar – "has been known to gross recruits out by eating shit sandwiches."

"You're fucking joking!" said Jon. "What, real shit? Not pretending chocolate is shit, or something?"

"No," continued the recruit. "I was told that he would wait until he has an audience, then go to the bogs and come back with a piece of bread with a layer of shit on it. He then puts another piece of bread on and eats it. He then says, 'Life is like a shit sandwich. The more bread you have, the less shit you eat'."

"It makes me feel sick just thinking about it," said Paul.

"And it's not quite true, either," interjected Mich. 'If you think about it, it doesn't matter how much bread you have, you still eat the same amount of shit. It just seems to be less."

"I'm surprised that Corporal didn't catch something. Did no one report him?" asked Jon.

"Everyone's scared of him," said the recruit. "He's a PTI and does powerlifting."

"Looks like he's on steroids, to me," added Mich.

"Why?" asked Paul.

"Spots, rapid weight gain, explosive mood swings," said Mich. "He fits the profile."

"How do you know about the rapid weight gain?"

"Dave told me," said Mich. "Apparently this guy is actually in the TA Intelligence Corps and is only here on attachment. Dave said he heard about him from a mate in their training team."

"If he's only on an attachment, maybe he'll fuck off soon," said another recruit.

"We can always hope so," replied Jon.

At this point Dave came in and joined the table.

"How'd the interview go?" asked Steve.

Dave looked at him before answering. "I think I'm fucked."

"Why? What's wrong?"

"I stupidly tried to cuff my vetting," admitted Dave.

"What do you mean?" asked Colin, who had otherwise been silent.

"I left out some details of some work I did, and they now want to know all about it," said Dave.

"So? What's the problem?"

"I was a bit wild when I was younger and did a few things that I shouldn't have."

"Like what?"

"Well, there was a time in Rio de Janeiro..."

Dave began to relate a story about when he had been given a week's shore leave and had gone to a house of ill repute. The local prostitutes expected their clients to use only their services for the time that they were in port and Dave, being young and stupid, had gone off with another woman. The first prostitute took great offence at this, and Dave was chased back to the ship by a knife-wielding whore who was vowing to remove certain vital organs. He made it back to the ship but had to stay on board for the rest of his leave.

"Is that it?" asked Jon. "It doesn't sound that bad."

"No, not exactly," admitted Dave. "Another time, I got drunk and got busted for drugs when I was in Panama."

"Ah! OK," said Jon. "Will they find out about this?"

"They will if I tell them which ships I was on," said Dave.

"How did you get away with it in the TA?" asked Paul.

"It was a different kind of vetting," said Dave. "We only needed a Security Clearance – it's a fairly low type of vetting - because we didn't really see anything classified above secret."

"But now?"

"Now they want to do Developed Vetting which allows you to see top secret and it's a lot more detailed."

"You'll have to drink your way out of this one," joked Jon.

"That's what got me into it in the first place," said Dave, despondently.

"I feel like I'm going to suffocate in this thing," one of the recruits said, as they tried on the S10 respirator.

"Wait till you get to the rubber gloves," said another.

"It could be worse," added Jon. "The Soviet kit is like a rubber cape and hood."

"I bet it makes you sweat," said the first voice.

"Fifteen minutes and you start dehydrating, by all accounts," agreed Jon.

They were trying out their 'noddy suits' or Nuclear, Bacteriological and Chemical Warfare suits. This was state-of-the-art protective gear that was said to be the best in the world. The British Army NBC suit consisted of a two-piece, charcoal-lined, green cloth suit of trousers and top which fitted over a soldier's normal uniform. Unlike its Soviet counterpart, it was breathable and was quite comfortable to wear. Rubber over-boots and gloves made the suit resistant to blood, blister and nerve agents when the S10 respirator was fitted, and the hood tightened around it.

"Britain has been a world-leader in biological weaponry

since World War One," their instructor told them "The Soviet Union considered chemical weapons to be no different from high explosives, and most of their artillery was designed to be used with chemical warheads. Subsequently, NBC equipment and training was considered vital in case the USSR finally decided to invade the West and sent 3 Shock Army across the inner German border from East to West Germany."

It was said that the research establishment at Porton Down could manufacture enough bacteriological weaponry in two days to kill everyone on the planet, but whether this was actually true or not Jon didn't know. It might have just been hearsay.

"OK, stand in a single straight line and we'll check the respirators," said the NBC instructor.

The recruits lined up and stood looking about through the goggle-like eyepieces of the respirators. The instructors went down the line, checking that the masks were fitted properly.

It was at this point that you generally started to feel uncomfortable in the knowledge that you now couldn't take your respirator off, unless you were under cover in an uncontaminated location. If you were unlucky, your eyepieces would steam up and you would be unable to see properly. This was made worse by any physical activity, including just walking at normal speed, and the idea of fighting in an NBC environment was most soldiers' worst nightmare. The only saving grace was that it would be ten times worse for the enemy, whose NBC kit was vastly inferior to anything the West had, Jon reckoned.

"Breathe in," the Corporal said to Jon.

He took a deep breath. It smelt of rubber and he could feel the edges of the mask being sucked against his head.

"Any problems?" the Corporal asked.

"No, Corporal," Jon answered, and the instructor moved on to the next person.

When they had all been checked, the instructor took the names of those who wore glasses. "The S10 respirator can be fitted with special eyepieces so that anyone who uses glasses to shoot can still do so without having to actually wear them under the mask. Or that is the theory," he told them. "We will be doing eating and drinking drills later, but I would suggest that if you find yourself in a real NBC environment, you don't eat. Drinking is a different matter as you have to stay hydrated."

They were given a smoke break and gratefully took off their masks.

"That was fun," said Paul.

"Wait till after the break," replied Jon. "We're going into the testing facility next."

"Oh, shit!" said Paul.

After the break, they formed up and marched in full NBC kit (less the respirator) to the training area, where the NBC testing chamber was located. One of the instructors was already there and had prepared the building for respirator testing.

The testing chamber was a small, enclosed room with a door at each end and a sealed window to let in light. They often have bench seats, as NBC drills can take some time.

"If you are going to survive a chemical or bacteriological attack, you must be able to don your gear quickly enough to avoid the effects of the agent, and then be able to change your respirator canister, eat and drink and decontaminate yourself, as well as being able to fight. To do so requires familiarity with the equipment and practice in a realistic environment," said the instructor.

Jon had heard a story about soldiers doing drills putting on their respirator in a room where an actual nerve agent was released, but he would have to question the sanity of anyone who actually volunteered for such a test. It was bad enough doing it in a room full of CS gas.

The recruits were told to form groups of twelve and then there was a short pause.

"Gas! Gas! Gas!" someone shouted.

Paul stood blankly for a moment, looking at everyone bending over and frantically grabbing for their respirators, and then suddenly realised that that was what he should have been doing. You had nine seconds, according to the manual, to put on their respirator on in the event of an attack, and he had already wasted about three of them.

Once the recruits had donned their respirators, they broke into pairs to check each other's kit. The army works on a 'buddy, buddy' system, where they help each other. After that, they were lined up and went into the chamber. There was nothing to see, as such.

"Chemical agents are generally colourless, although blister agent is more like blobs of jelly, with the consistency of paint stripper," said the instructor before lighting three CS pellets contained in a small container in the centre of the room. They didn't give off any smoke after they were initially ignited; there was just that feeling that they now *definitely* couldn't take off their respirators.

"Anyone feel the effects of the CS?" came the instructor's mask-distorted voice.

No one raised their hands, but Jon could tell from the body movements and wide eyes behind some of the respirators that one or two of the recruits were near to panic.

"Just stay calm," said the instructor, as if reading Jon's mind. "It's only CS. It won't kill you, unlike the real thing."

They stayed in the chamber for what seemed like a long time but was, in actual fact, only a few minutes, so that the instructors could be happy that the masks were working properly, and to accustom the recruits to being in a contaminated environment.

Finally, the instructor went up to the first recruit.

"Right. Take a deep breath. Remove your respirator. Say your name, rank and number and then you can leave the chamber," he said.

The recruit did so and ran to the door, which was opened by another instructor.

Once outside, they were told to take off their mask and to stand facing into the breeze with their arms outstretched. This apparently helped the CS dissipate. "CS is actually a compound, not a gas, even though it is called CS, or tear gas," the instructor told them as they slowly decontaminated. "It therefore sticks to clothing and especially skin. Some people are naturally immune to its effects, while others can be really badly affected, especially if, like you Private Dobson, you take off your respirator and then take a deep breath, rather than the other way round."

The instructor had let him out without saying his name, rank and number, because he didn't want Paul vomiting all over him, or to have to explain to the Intelligence Corps director that he had killed one of the Privates. The other recruits had a good laugh about it and were secretly happy that it hadn't happened to them.

"For fucks sake, don't point that thing at me!" shouted Jon as Paul 'Biff' Dobson let his Browning 9mm automatic pistol waver about.

"It's all right, it's not loaded," said Paul, defensively.

"There's been plenty of people killed by 'empty' weapons," growled Jon, angrily.

Biff was beginning to piss him off. Not only was he useless, he was now becoming dangerous. Jon did his best to help him, but he just seemed to have the knack of doing everything wrong. They had been put into syndicates for training and Paul was in Jon's, and his inability to do even the simplest task properly was starting to have a negative effect on the rest of the syndicate. They were constantly getting extra duties and punishments because of Paul's actions. It hadn't reached breaking point yet because they all liked Paul, but it was coming close.

Having been an infantryman, Jon considered that a rifle was a soldier's weapon and that handguns, or 'shorts', were merely dangerous toys. That had been borne out when he had been in Zimbabwe.

His boss, John Winner, had been a great guy, but he used to play with his 9mm Smith & Wesson. John carried it in a holster on his belt and used to practice his quick draw. One day, Jon had been sitting at his desk in the security office with two of his guards standing outside the door, his Sergeant just inside and the rest of the team sitting on a bench along one wall. John had come in and had done his usual, whipping out the pistol and pretending to shoot. He had half-cocked it and pointed it out the door in a safe direction but hadn't removed the magazine before pulling the trigger. It transpired that he *had* actually cocked it, and the weapon went off to his and everyone else's great surprise.

He had just missed shooting the Sergeant, and Jon felt the lead from the round ricochet past his head. There was a sudden, sharp silence until Jon shouted, "Sergeant, arrest that man!" Then everyone fell about laughing as the tension was released.

John should really have been charged with a firearms offence, but because he was the mine manager and as such the boss of the whole installation, he got away with it. Jon never forgot the incident, which could have ended in tragedy, and from that day onwards never really liked handguns.

"You should never point a weapon at anyone, unless you intend to kill them," interjected Mich.

"Oh. Sorry," said Paul.

"No problem. Just don't do it again," said Jon.

Most of the recruits thought the Browning was great and made them feel like *James Bond*. It was only when they got out on the range and actually fired it that they found out how difficult it is to hit the target with one, unlike in films.

Donna, Sonia and their two roommates, Sandra and Sue, were sitting drinking bottles of Becks lager and eating crisps from a family-sized packet. They had stopped going to the NAAFI when the Corporal was there, which appeared to be most nights. He had tried to chat up Donna on the first night and hadn't taken rejection lightly. There wasn't much that he could do as he was only an assistant PTI and could only take PT lessons under supervision, but he was a permanent fixture in the NAAFI and most of the girls tried to avoid him.

The NAAFI shop sold a range of alcoholic drinks, amongst other things, and they had started drinking in their quarters rather than risk a confrontation with said Corporal.

"I heard that Tony Cazanoe has asked Linda to go hillwalking with him when we get our weekend off," said Sue, taking a slug from a bottle of Becks.

"Is she the blonde one in room seven?" asked Sandra.

"Yes. She's the one who's doing the cap badge challenge, by all accounts."

The 'cap badge challenge' is when a recruit attempts to sleep with anyone who belongs to a different unit and hence has a different cap badge.

"Well, I suppose Cazanoe would count for the Intelligence Corps, but she must be desperate to go with him," said Donna, critically.

"He's pretty fit," countered Sue.

"Yes, but he's also pretty spotty," replied Donna.

"Mich reckons that's the steroids," added Sonia.

"When did he tell you that?"

"He didn't," replied Sonia. "I overheard some of the guys talking about it one time. I think it was Dave who said that he knew Cazanoe from the TA, and he was quite skinny when he first joined and then suddenly bulked up, almost overnight."

"He's certainly big enough now," said Sandra. "I wonder if he's in proportion."

This got a giggle from the rest of the room.

"I've heard that steroids make a man's dick smaller," said Sonia, putting the kibosh on that line of conversation. "It's apparently one of the drawbacks."

"That medic must be on overload, then," said Sandra. "He doesn't look like he's got one at all."

This started a discussion about the medic, who had joined them for a PT lesson and had indeed seemed to be lacking a bulge in the right place.

"Maybe he should just be called the 'me', then," suggested Donna.

"Because he's got no dic," finished Sue, to another round of laughter.

"Corporal Cazanoe doesn't like Jon, though," said Sandra, once the giggling had calmed down.

"What makes you say that?" asked Sonia.

"You can tell by the way he looks at him," continued Sandra. "He's also scared of Jon, from what I've heard."

"Really?"

"Yes. Biff told me that the Corporal tried to get them to buy him drinks on the first night and Jon told him to fuck off, and he did."

"Wow," said Sonia. "He's not that big compared to Cazanoe."

"No, but he's ex-infantry. Someone said he was in the SAS."

"No," corrected Sonia, "he said that he did selection but didn't pass. He said he could do the distance but couldn't do it fast enough, so he pulled out before he failed it."

"Whatever he did, Cazanoe is scared of him," insisted Sandra.

"I reckon Cazanoe's a coward," said Donna. "Bullies often are."

"He's a bit of a dark horse, isn't he?" interjected Sue.

"Who?" asked Sonia.

"Jon," replied Sue. "Do you like him?"

"Why do you ask?"

"He seems to like you."

"Really?"

"Yes, he always talks to you."

"He talks to everyone."

"He doesn't talk to me unless I talk to him," said Donna, slightly huffily.

"That's probably because you're always surrounded by a gaggle of men," explained Sonia.

They all had a laugh about that. Donna was by far the best-looking female recruit and the men were constantly seeking her attention. She had got used to it over the years, but in some ways, it was a bane rather than a boon because she could never really be sure if they genuinely wanted to speak to her or if they only wanted to sleep with her, and sometimes men whom she would like to have given her some attention were put off.

You can't win them all, she thought.

"What the hell happened to you?" asked Jon.

Biff had come into the bar sporting the beginnings of a cracking black eye.

"I was on the range and got hit in the eye by the sights on my SLR," he explained.

The SLR was a long, heavy rifle with a sloping butt. Unlike the old Enfield .303, which was straight and kicked straight back, the SLR kicked back and up. It was common for recruits to have their eyes blackened if they didn't hold the weapon tightly enough when they first fired it. When the SLR was introduced to the British Army in 1957, it was said that marksmanship would fall by 60% because of the weapon's kick. This proved to be the case.

Jon had used a slightly different version of the SLR when he had been in Zimbabwe. It was known as an FN due to it being produced by a Belgian company called Fabrique Nationale. It had a fixed cocking handle, rather than the folding one that the SLR had, and the foresight had been drilled down for competition use. Jon loved it and carried it everywhere with him. He became known as 'FN man' by the mine security guards, but he considered that a compliment, particularly since his colleague was known as 'Boss California' which, being American, he thought was great and Jon didn't have the heart to tell him that 'California' was slang for 'mad'.

"'The position and hold must be firm enough to support the weapon'," quoted Dave. "It's one of the marksmanship principals."

"Did you manage to hit the target?" asked Jon.

"Sort of," admitted Biff.

"What grouping did you get?" enquired Dave, innocently.

"I didn't exactly get a grouping, but I did hit the target five times out of five... eventually."

The initial aim of shooting is to 'zero' the weapon. To do this, you fire five rounds at the exact same spot, which is normally a white rectangle glued onto a figure eleven, or 'man-sized' target, roughly in the centre of the chest. The 'grouping' is how the rounds land, and the aim is to get them within fifty millimetres of each other. This grouping can then be used to adjust the sights of the weapon, so that the rounds will hit the target in the correct position. If you can't achieve a reasonable grouping, say two hundred and fifty millimetres, then it is impossible to zero the weapon and the rounds could go anywhere.

It is hard enough to hit the target at the best of times, and if someone is moving and you are getting fired at yourself it becomes even more difficult. This is why it can take hundreds, if not thousands, of rounds to kill someone on the battlefield. Gone are the days when lines of men would march towards each other until they could see the whites of their eyes and could hardly miss. They still did so even then, and until the invention of the machine gun, most casualties were, and still are, caused by artillery.

"Don't worry, Biff," said Jon. "A lot of people do the same when they first fire a rifle. You'll get better."

"Really?" asked Biff.

"Yes. If you pay attention to the marksmanship principals," interjected Dave.

"Oh," replied Biff, downcast.

Jon was a bit annoyed with Dave. He could see that Biff was taking it badly and had been trying to give him some encouragement.

"Here, have a beer," said Jon, handing him a John Smiths.

"Thanks," replied Biff.

CHAPTER 11

Jon was duty student for the day, so it was part of his job to march the squad to and from their various classes. The first lesson was PT, which started at 0600.

Jon had never understood why PT classes were held so early in the morning. They didn't have weapons training or first aid classes at this time, but for some reason the powers that be had decided that it was OK to send recruits out when they were cold, half asleep and sometimes hungover, to do strenuous physical exercise on an empty stomach. But there we are. They could rail against 'the slings and arrows of outrageous fortune', but it wouldn't do any good.

Because they were assembling outside the gym, the male and female sections of the intake would make their way there separately and then form up as a single squad. Jon had got the guys to march at double time by jogging to warm them up, as it was getting decidedly chilly in the mornings now that they were coming into October. Because of this, his section of the squad was a few minutes early. It is standard practice in the British Army to arrive five minutes early for any appointment. This allows the instructor/lecturer/higher ranking person time to arrive and have the audience ready to go, bang on the stated start time. Or so the theory goes.

Jon had been told by an 'old soldier' that if you were late, it was always best to say, "Sorry, sir, I was busy," without actually explaining the reason for being late. Most people can relate to 'being busy' and don't actually question any further. Of course, you always get the bastards who are just looking for an excuse to be nasty and this defence won't help, so it's best to turn up at the regulation five minutes early.

Jon could see the form of Corporal Cazanoe standing outside the gym doors, waiting for them. He was wearing lightweight green trousers with trainers and a blue PTI tracksuit top, which indicated that today's lesson would be outside.

Probably a BFT, thought Jon.

"Squaad... Halt!" shouted Jon. "Riight turn. Stand at ease. Stand easy. Morning, Corporal."

"Morning, Sass," replied Cazanoe, snidely. He had taken to calling Jon Sass when he found out that although Jon had done selection, he hadn't been badged SAS. It was not meant as a compliment.

"Where are the splits?" demanded Cazanoe.

"Splits?" asked Jon. "What do you mean?"

"Split beavers. Women," explained the Corporal. There were a few titters from the members of the squad who had been taken in by Cazanoe and thought he was the best thing since sliced bread.

"The *ladies* should be along shortly," replied Jon.

"Some of them certainly ain't ladies," came a voice from the ranks, to more tittering.

"Women shouldn't really be allowed in the Intelligence Corps, if you want my opinion," said Cazanoe. "We're almost teeth arms as it is."

'Teeth arms' was the term used to describe British Army units like the infantry and tank regiments who did the actual fighting. Combat support consisted of units like the Royal Signals and the Royal Engineers, who supported the teeth arms directly, and service support were the rear echelon units, like the Catering and Pay Corps. The Intelligence Corps was considered to be combat support though it would have liked to have been considered to be teeth arms.

Women weren't allowed to be on the front line, probably due to antiquated Victorian notions about women's roles in society. In a lot of ways, the British Army's attitudes were still stuck in the nineteenth century and hadn't moved on.

"What about the Israeli Army?" said Jon. "Women fight on the front line there."

Cazanoe turned on him with a withering look. "That's all right for foreign armies, Sass. This is the *British* Army."

"May I have a private word, Corporal," said Jon, quietly. They went aside and Jon looked Cazanoe straight in the eyes. "I'll tell you what, Corporal," he said.

"What?" interrupted Cazanoe. He obviously thought he had the upper hand as he was in the position of instructor and Jon was only a recruit.

"Stop calling me Sass, and I'll not tell anyone that you're wearing insignia that you're not entitled to."

"What do you mean?" blustered Cazanoe.

Jon pointed to his PTI tracksuit top, where his white T-shirt showed underneath.

"You wear a PTI Corps badge on your T-shirt," he said. "You're not even a proper PTI, let alone a member of the PT Corps. So, unless you want everyone to know that you're a *Walt*, I would suggest that you stop gobbing off, *Corporal*."

A 'Walt', or 'Walter Mitty', was someone who pretended to be something that they weren't. The term came from a 1947 film called *The Secret Life of Walter Mitty* which was based on a short story by James Thurber. 'Walts' exaggerate or invent incidents or service and often wear medals to which they are not entitled. The Americans call this 'stolen valour' and it is not the sort of thing that you would want to find yourself accused of, especially if you were a serving member of the armed forces.

Cazanoe stood there with his mouth flapping open but there was nothing he could say. He knew fine well that he wasn't a qualified instructor, but they let him wear the badges because they were

160

desperate for someone to help out with PT, and he had volunteered from the TA.

He was saved from saying anything as the female members of the squad arrived, followed a few minutes later by the regular PTI, WO2 Sanders.

"OK, troops. What we're going to do today is the BFT or basic fitness test," explained Sanders. "You've all done it before, but this one counts towards your fitness assessment for the course. Fail this one and you may find yourself back squadded."

"Nice of them to give us some warning," a voice from the back grumbled.

"That's PTI's for you," muttered another. "They're all bastards."

They were formed up into a squad and set off on a mile and a half march/double march pace that would take them fifteen minutes. After that, they had two minutes' rest and then they were set off on a second mile and a half that the men had to complete in nine and a half minutes or less, and the women ten minutes or less.

When Jon was at Sandhurst, they had run the BFT in boots and had had ten and a half minutes to do the second mile and a half, but now they ran it in trainers and had had a minute taken off the allowed time.

Jon set off at a steady pace that he knew would allow him to run the course in about eight minutes and fifteen seconds. His best time ever had been eight minutes dead, and that was wearing boots, but he had been challenged by another Officer Cadet who fancied himself and had had a real incentive to beat him.

Most of the squad passed him, but he resisted the impulse to try to keep up as this was an individual best effort and he knew that he would overtake most of them before the end. Halfway round, he saw one of the recruits throwing up at the side of the course. This was considered acceptable as long as he finished the course within the time allowed. It was the army, after all.

Jon passed Paul who was red-faced and struggling.

"Keep going, mate, you're almost there," he shouted on his way past.

Paul gave him a vague wave and plodded on.

Jon sprinted the last hundred yards to overtake three other members of the squad and came in third. Some PTIs reckoned that if you could sprint at the end then you hadn't pushed yourself hard enough, but others liked you to put in a final effort. There was no fixed rule either way, as long as you passed.

Of the two who had beaten Jon, one had done it in just over seven minutes. He was a natural runner and was unbeatable at this distance. The first of the women came in just after Jon. She was small and wiry, but Jon wondered if she would be able to carry the weight when they did the Combat Fitness Test (CFT) which was an eight-mile speed march carrying thirty-five pounds of kit plus helmet and rifle.

Paul made it with seconds to spare and collapsed in a heap just over the line.

"Get up," said Jon. "Stand up straight. It'll help your breathing."

Paul got to his feet and tried to do as Jon advised.

The stragglers were still coming in, although they were now BFT failures. Sanders walked up and down the line of the squad, eying them up.

"I'm sorry to say that I'm not impressed," he said. "One or two of you did well, but there were some disappointing results. You'll have to do better next time. Carry on, Corporal." With that he stalked away.

For some reason, a lot of PTIs seemed to have the attitude that they were fit and everyone else was a waster. They made little attempt to genuinely encourage people and seemed to take delight when they failed, rather than ensuring that they passed.

Maybe it's an ego thing, thought Jon, although an awful lot of them seemed to be the same.

Sanders wore a maroon Parachute Regiment beret, but rumour had it that he was actually in the Dental Corps and had only done an attachment with the Paras. Maybe this explained why he tolerated, and even seemed to encourage, Cazanoe.

Cazanoe strutted along the line and parroted Sanders. Jon wondered what *his* BFT time was. As an instructor, he had only run the first mile and a half and had then stood at the finish line taking times as the recruits came in. He was undoubtedly strong. Some of the guys had seen him powerlift 100kg kilos which was quite impressive, but he looked like a carthorse rather than a racehorse.

Maybe one day we'll find out, thought Jon.

The squad was now down to thirty-four from the forty who started back in early September. Johnny, the giant right-hand marker, had left due to injury. He had injured his back during a PT lesson which was exacerbated by the British Army drill that required participants to stamp their feet and to slam in their heels when marching. One of the female recruits had developed a knee problem which had required surgery and had been indefinitely back-squadded. This meant that she could rejoin the course at a later date, but it was dependent on her being fit enough to start again without the same problem reoccurring.

Another two the recruits had decided that the army wasn't for them and had been allowed to take voluntary resignation without having to buy themselves out, as Jon had had to do.

Everyone had expected Paul 'Biff' Dobson to either be kicked out or to be VRd, but he was hanging on in there, and Jon couldn't help but admire his dogged determination. He was still a complete fuckup and had become the squads 'shit magnet', which meant that he attracted unwanted attention, but it meant that some of the shit was diverted from the rest of the squad, who had started to treat him as something of a mascot.

"You could shag that," said Peter.

"*You* probably could, but no one else would," noted Mich, as he looked at the rubber dummy that lay on the floor.

It was known as 'Resussi Annie' and was shaped like the top half of a human torso and was used for CPR training in first aid classes.

The rest of the syndicate laughed good-naturedly at Pete. He was a tall, spotty recruit who the female section of the squad thought was probably still a virgin even though he was nineteen.

The squad was being taught first aid, the first principals being breathing, bleeding, breaks and burns, for the sequence of treatment.

"There is no point in treating a casualty for a broken leg if they have stopped breathing because they are probably dead or, at best, brain-damaged, so patients are triaged according to the severity of their wounds," said their instructor. "In battle, as an infantryman, you are taught to leave your casualties to the combat medics who follow on behind you. The theory is that if you stop to treat your mate, then the person who got him will get you next, and also by stopping to treat the wounded you will slow the advance. The best way to ensure that any wounded are saved is by taking the objective, thus preventing the enemy from creating any more casualties. There is a rule called 'the golden hour', which states that if the combat medics can get to a casualty within an hour of them being wounded, there is a very good possibility of them being saved. This was proven to be true during the Falklands campaign. The British Army medics are some of the best in the world. They might not actually fight the enemy, but are no less heroic as they often come under fire while treating their patients. However, not all casualties are caused on the battlefield and thus there can easily be cases where a knowledge of first aid will be useful in a non-battlefield scenario. So what's the first rule of first aid?" asked the instructor.

"To save life," replied one of the recruits.

"And?" prompted the instructor.

"To prevent further injury," added Sandra.

"Correct. Don't become a casualty yourself. So, what's the first thing you do when you come across the scene of an incident?"

"Grab his wallet!" said Pete.

This got a laugh from the class and also the instructor, a good-natured Pay Corps Lance Corporal who was also a trained combat medic.

"Check the surroundings to make sure it's safe," continued Pete, who was the squad joker but was also pretty capable.

"Yes," agreed the medic. "There's no point rushing into a building to treat a casualty if it's going to collapse on you. That's the 'prevent further injury' bit. Not only to the casualty but also to yourself. So, you've assessed the surroundings. What do you do now?"

"Check to make sure the casualty is breathing," said Pete.

"Good. And if he, or she, isn't?"

"Do CPR?"

"What about before that?"

"Ah! Check the pulse."

"Exactly. The patient might be dead. You have to be able to triage casualties. What do you do if someone is lying there with their leg blown off, screaming for help?"

"Treat the one who's not breathing?"

"Correct! The guy with the missing leg *may* die from loss of blood, but the guy who's not breathing *will* die unless you get him breathing again."

"That's a bit brutal, isn't it?" said one of the female recruits.

"War is brutal," said the medic. "I once saw a guy with all his face blown off from the mouth upwards."

"Did he survive?" someone asked.

"Yes. But the question is: would you want to?"

There was a pause while they all took in what the medic had said and then they got back to the lesson.

The sky was completely clear, and the stars were cold pinpricks of light. There was a hunter's moon and it was so light that Jon could almost see individual landmarks, even though it was 2200. He had always been able to see well in the dark and had never understood why they were so adamant on night exercises that you closed one eye if there was a light or if a flare went up. He didn't lose his night vision for long, unlike some people who took thirty seconds or more to get theirs back. Conversely, though, he couldn't stand glare and had been unable to ski if it was snowing because it resembled the effect of the Starship Enterprise going to warp. He wondered if it had something to do with the 'cones' and 'rods' in the eye that were receptacles for colour or black and white vision. He suspected that he had far more 'cones' than 'rods' and thus could perceive colour better than the average person. He never had any problems with the eyesight test where you looked at coloured dots and saw numbers, and he found that he had good colour perception across the spectrum, unlike most men who had the tendency to be slightly red/green colour blind.

"Where the fuck are we?" whispered Rob.

Rob was leading the team on a night exercise around the training area but had lost his way and now was completely disoriented.

"We've just passed the farmhouse that's marked on the map," said Jon.

"What farmhouse?" asked Rob.

"The one where you were supposed to meet the agent."

The task that they had been given was to navigate to a ruined farmhouse where they would meet an agent who would give them some information that they would take back to base.

"Shit!" swore Rob. "Why didn't you tell me?"

"I thought you knew where you were going," answered Jon. "You are supposed to be leading this patrol, after all."

"Fuck. What do we do now?"

"Get the patrol into all-round defence and go back to the farm," said Jon.

Surely, it's simple? he thought.

Rob didn't seem to have much initiative, or maybe it was that Jon, having been to Sandhurst, was just used to being in charge and giving orders. He had been trained to do that, after all.

"Right," agreed Rob. "Which way is the farm?"

"Do you want me to go?" asked Jon.

"Would you?"

"You can direct me, if you want," said Jon. "You are the patrol leader."

"OK," breathed Rob, obviously relieved that Jon had, in effect, taken command of the task.

Jon got them down into all-round defence. This meant the team forming a circle with their legs pointing inwards and hooked over one another so that orders could be passed silently.

"I'll be back in a bit," said Jon.

"Rightio."

Jon moved away from the patrol and knelt down. He felt something soft and realised that he had knelt in a cowpat.

Fucking great! That's all I need, he thought.

He orientated himself towards the farmhouse and made a note of the distinctive shape of a nearby tree so that he could find the patrol again, and then quietly made his way along the pathway towards the moonlit building.

"Is there anybody there?" he asked into the darkness.

"Said the traveller, knocking on the moonlit door," came a voice.

Intelligence Corps were like that. They liked to be intellectual and eccentric – or barking mad, depending on what way you looked at it.

"Birds fly south in winter," said Jon, repeating the code that they had been told to say when they met their agent.

"And in winter, the snow in Geneva comes up this high," responded the voice, obviously trying hard not to laugh.

"Cheers, mate," acknowledged Jon.

"You're welcome."

Jon retraced his steps and returned to the patrol.

"OK," he said. "We can fuck off back now."

"Which way?" asked Rob.

"Oh, for fuck's sake!" whispered Jon. "Haven't you got a compass?"

"Yes, but I thought it was light enough, so I didn't use it," said Rob in a plaintive voice.

"You've got to trust your compass," hissed Jon, echoing the words of his SAS instructor on their first night exercise of selection.

Jon showed Rob the route and put in the compass bearing for him.

God help him if he has to do this for real, he thought.

When they got back to the classroom, Rob went to report to the directing staff and Jon organised the rest of the group to write the patrol report. It was well after midnight when they got to their billet and Jon gratefully flopped into his bed and almost immediately fell asleep.

"Is it just me or is the beer in here getting weaker?" demanded one of the recruits plaintively, as he peered into the almost transparent depths of his pint of John Smiths.

"It's like making love in a canoe," said another.

"I know. Fucking close to water," agreed the first one.

It was Friday night, and the squad was in the NAAFI for close to their final time before being let out into the real world and the joys of Ashford, or even further afield. The military skills phase of their training was nearing its end and they only had a few more tests before they were pronounced qualified soldiers and could go on to the trade training part of their course.

Cazanoe was absent from the bar tonight, and word had got around, so that the recruits who would have normally avoided the NAAFI were out in force. They had spent the day doing field craft which was fairly physical, and it was nice to have had a hot shower and put on clean clothes before relaxing for the evening.

"Donna's looking good tonight," said Rob, through his beer.

"She looks good every night," agreed Paul.

"She'd look good in a sack," said another.

"Or in *the* sack," put in a third.

"I'm getting to the stage where even Louise looks good," said Peter.

"Jesus! How many have you had?" said Rob.

Louise was a thin, mousey-brown haired recruit who had, rather unkindly, been nicknamed the Cabbage Patch Doll. It was rumoured amongst Cazanoe's sycophantic followers that she must be a lesbian, as she had turned him down flat when he had drunkenly propositioned her one night, but Jon thought that that was actually an indication of good sense. She was a prodigious drinker who could outdrink any of the men, which was attributed to her coming from Scotland.

The course had split into distinct factions, between those who liked Cazanoe and those who couldn't stand him. Some recruits, like Steve or Mich, could alternate between the two, but most had taken sides early on and this had created divisions in the squad.

Cazanoe's group was looking a little forlorn as their hero was nowhere to be seen, and a number of tables held groups of female recruits who had formed their own cliques.

Jon was just musing on the implications of this for future postings when a strange group of half a dozen people entered the bar. The men were dressed in jackets and ties and the women in skirts or dresses, which was unusual attire for the NAAFI.

"Are you looking for the officers' mess?" asked one of the recruits as the group headed towards the bar.

"No," said one of the men wearing a tweed jacket and corduroy trousers. "We're all Corporals."

"Corporals?" queried the recruit, looking them up and down.

"Yes, we're TA," said one of the women, as if that explained everything.

"Oh. TA. Right," mumbled the recruit and edged away from them.

They ordered their drinks and came to sit at a table near Jon's. Jon looked over at them and caught the eye of one of the women. She was wearing a light blue, Laura Ashley dress and had long, light brown hair. She smiled at Jon over what looked like a gin and tonic. Finally, his curiosity got the better of him.

"Who are you lot, then?" he asked.

The women smiled again. "We're 22 company," she said, as if this explained everything.

"22 company?" he queried. "Intelligence Corps?"

"Yes," she replied. "We're the TA interrogators."

22 Intelligence company (Volunteers) was the Intelligence Corps Territorial Army Human Intelligence company. They were responsible for intelligence gathering by extracting information and

were trained in the various advanced questioning techniques.

The members of the company were mostly officers and Warrant Officers and were considerably older than most Intelligence Corps TA. They didn't tend to have many Corporals and Sergeants as they tended to be Russian linguists and one or two had even served during the Second World War, although according to legend, one of them actually served in the German Army. This story came about after a battlefield tour of the Netherlands, when the person in question was acting as a guide around Amsterdam. When asked how he knew the city so well, he replied that he had been there during the war. When someone pointed out that the British Army wasn't in Amsterdam very long, he allegedly said, I wasn't in the British Army'.

"So, what are you doing here?" Jon asked.

"We're on a training weekend," the woman, named Carol, said.

"Right. Where are you based normally?"

"The TA centre in Handel Street."

"Where's that?"

"Not far from King's Cross. We're co-located with 21 company. Imagery Analysts," she added, when he looked blank.

"Oh, right," he said, even though he had no idea what she was talking about.

"Are you staying in the NAAFI tonight?" Jon asked, thinking that it might be a chance to find out a bit more about the Intelligence Corps. The TA seemed happy to talk to the recruits, whereas some of the regular staff acted as if it was all classified information.

"No. We're only having one and then we're off out. Want to come?"

"I'd love to, but I'm on duty later," he lied, not wanting to tell her that the recruits were confined to barracks.

"Shame. Well, we might meet again sometime," she said, as her group finished their drinks as the arrival of a taxi was announced.

"See you later," she called over her shoulder.

"Cheers," he replied.

"Who were they?" asked Sonia, coming up to the table.

"TA Intelligence Corps," said Jon.

"STABS," muttered one of the recruits.

"What?" asked Jon. This was a new term to him, but it didn't sound very friendly.

"Stupid Territorial Army Bastards," explained the recruit, who Jon could now see was one of Cazanoe's group. "They're only part-timers."

"You know that Cazanoe is TA, don't you?" asked Jon.

"No way!" said the recruit.

"Ask Dave if you don't believe me," said Jon. "He was an Intelligence Corps 'STAB', and I was TA infantry originally, by the way."

"No offence, mate," said the recruit, hurrying away.

"That was nice," said Sonia.

"There's a lot of rivalry between the regulars and the TA," said Jon. "At least from the regulars' side. The TA seem to like the regular army."

"It doesn't really make sense, does it?" asked Sonia.

"It does to them," said Jon.

CHAPTER 12

The day of reckoning had come for Dave. He had tried to bluff his way through the vetting process, but it hadn't worked and, as the old saying goes, 'when you find yourself in a hole, stop digging'. He had been summoned to Major Elswick's office and told that his vetting application had been rejected. He was given the choice of resubmitting the application or a free discharge.

Dave had been thinking about it since the first interview and knew that there was now no way that he could claw back any credibility. He had lied and been caught out, and even if he told the complete truth now, it would only confirm that he was lacking in integrity, had been involved in criminal behaviour, and had tried, unsuccessfully, to cover it up. If he left now, there was always the possibility that he could go back to the TA and start again where he left off. So, he thanked Elswick for his time and went to pack his bags.

He wasn't the only one to have failed their vetting.

One was a female recruit whose grandmother still lived in Russia. It was considered too much of a security risk to allow her to carry on with the Intelligence Corps, both from her own risk of blackmail and the threat to her family still inside the Soviet Union. She was offered a transfer to another unit, where she would be less vulnerable, but decided to leave the army as she had set her mind on joining the Corps.

The other was a male recruit who had a minor criminal record for a drunken offence he had committed as a teenager. Unfortunately, it was within the three-year period that the vetting agency considered to be a 'live offence', and because it had an element of violence attached to it, his vetting was refused. He was also offered a transfer to another unit and decided that he would give the Paras a try.

They handed in their kit and said their farewells to the squad and then were given a lift to the train station in the grey army minibus, and that was that.

The squad was now down to thirty-one – nineteen men and twelve women. The training wing Major came into the classroom where the remaining recruits were gathered.

"Room, 'shun!" called out the duty student, and the recruits sat to attention with their backs straight and their arms outthrust in front of them, hands clenched.

"At ease," said Elswick, and they all relaxed. "Sit down, Private," he said to the duty student, who took her seat.

Elswick was a grey-haired man with a bushy moustache, now also grey. He was reputed to be one of the oldest serving Majors in the army, having come up through the ranks, transferring to the Intelligence Corps and getting commissioned. Being a 'ranker', he couldn't get promoted further than Major and had been at that rank for some time. He was about to retire and intended to take up the post of Permanent Staff Admin Officer (PSAO) with a TA Intelligence Corps unit, if it became available, to see him through until full retirement.

He had grown disillusioned with the army, having seen a number of what he considered to be incompetent officers promoted over his head and causing mayhem on their way. There was a belief that if an officer was good enough to be a Lieutenant Colonel in the Intelligence Corps, then they should be doing something else, but that still didn't explain why some of the people who had been promoted had got the rank. It was almost as if some joker looked out for the least competent officers and deliberately promoted them.

Maybe they did, he thought.

Elswick stood in front of the squad and twitched his moustache. He had no idea if he had been given a nickname by the recruits, but he hoped that if he had it wouldn't be as bad as some he had heard. He had stood, aghast, at an officer's mess do, listening to one such officer proudly telling his wife that the troops called him 'Sniper', when Elswick knew for a fact that he was actually known as 'Tangle Tits'.

Or even worse, the high-ranking officer, who was reaching the end of his career and didn't have a single medal to his name, and hence was known as 'NFM' which stood for 'no fucking medals'. The story went that he had gone across to Northern Ireland and had spent six weeks in the mess there so that he could obtain a Northern Ireland medal.

He looked over the recruits, who were all waiting expectantly for him to speak.

"You've all almost reached the end of your mil skills training," he began. "So, well done, everyone. Unfortunately, we've just lost three of our members, who failed their vetting. I'm not going to say why, just that it has happened."

He paused.

"We have also reached the point where you will no longer be able to get a free discharge if you decide to leave. That means that if anyone does have any serious doubts about being a member of the Intelligence Corps, they should think long and hard over the next few days about whether they want to carry on. That is not to say that I am advising you to leave, but from here on, the cost of your training increases exponentially, and the army likes to get its money's worth."

There was a round of soft laughter from the squad.

"You all have the ability to pass the course, and I hope you all will," he continued. "Thank you for your commitment, and good luck."

With that, he left the class slightly stunned that they had been given a compliment for a change.

The military skills tests were relatively easy.

The SMG has virtually no kick and is easy to aim. The weapon is fired from 25m, 15m and 10m ranges at a man-sized, figure eleven target. Even Biff managed to get a good pass.

They had already passed the NBC phase and the BFT, and those that had failed it were given another chance and passed on the second attempt.

The first aid test consisted of following the instructions in a printed handbook, even those which were wrong. The instructor told them to ignore that fact and to follow the instructions, regardless, which they all did.

The map reading exam was a twenty-question, multiple-choice paper that was designed for the infantry, who had a forty-five minute lecture on how to draw a straight line apparently and, as such, was pretty easy.

They would still have to complete a Combat Fitness Test (CFT) and be proficient at drill to enable them to attend the passing out parade, although there were rumours that, on occasion, recruits had not actually been on parade as their drill was so bad. But no one in this squad came anywhere near that, even Biff.

All that remained was the end of phase 'smoker'. This was a squad party which would be attended by the directing staff and a few select officers, and the recruits were warned not to get too drunk, or if they did, not to do as one recruit had done and pin the Intelligence Corps Director against the wall and tell him everything that was wrong with the army. Amazingly enough, the Director had taken it in good humour and the Private hadn't been disciplined for it.

Some of the female recruits sat in the NAAFI and planned what they would do for their first free weekend.

"I hear that Linda is still planning on going hillwalking with Tony Cazanoe," said Sue, in disbelief.

"Well, that's up to her, isn't it?" put in Sandra.

Sandra didn't like Linda anyway, so she wouldn't have much sympathy for her if the weekend turned out to be a disaster.

"What about you, Sonia?" asked Sue.

"It doesn't bother me what she does," replied Sonia.

"No, I mean what are you going to do for the weekend?" corrected Sue.

"Oh!" said Sonia. "I don't know. I hear that some of the guys were thinking of going over to France."

"Jon, you mean," said Sue, slyly.

They couldn't see Sonia's blush under her dark skin, which was just as well. She was hoping that the invitation to the France trip would be extended to everyone.

"They've asked if they can borrow a minibus," said Donna.

"Who has?" asked Sonia.

"Biff, by all accounts," replied Donna.

"Biff?" came the astonished response from everyone.

"Yes," agreed Donna. "Amazing as it sounds, he had the nerve to ask one of the staff and they said yes, as long as there's someone over twenty-five to drive it."

A few faces fell at that.

"Twenty-five!" exclaimed one. "Who's that old?"

"Jon's twenty-nine," said Sonia.

"How do you know that?" asked Sue, giving her a look.

"He told me that he was one of the oldest at Sandhurst when he was twenty-three, and that was in 1983, so that makes him twenty-nine," she said.

"Wow! He doesn't look that old," said another recruit.

"Looks can be deceiving," retorted Donna. "Unfortunately, I've got to go back up north."

"Why, what's wrong?"

"The boiler's gone in my kitchen, and I have to sign some paperwork for it, apparently," explained Donna.

"You own your own house?" asked one of the girls.

"Yes. I bought it, cash," said Donna, proudly.

"Where did you get the money?" asked another.

"I was a dancer," Donna stated, simply.

"You must have been good to get that much."

"Yes," admitted Donna, with a smile, "I was very good."

At that point, some of the male recruits came in and joined the conversation, which was moved in a different direction. Donna gave Sonia a wink. Sonia knew that Donna had been an exotic dancer, but she kept that a secret from the rest of the squad.

"Are you going to France, Paul?" Sonia asked.

"Yes, if we can get a driver," he said.

"What about Jon?"

"He said he's got to go back to Edinburgh."

"What for?"

"He didn't say, but it must have been important because he's gone already."

"Oh," said Sonia, slightly deflated.

"I'll drive, if you want an old man like me with you," offered Mich.

He was by far the oldest recruit, having served ten years with the Royal Signals before transferring to the Corps.

"That would be magic. Thanks," Paul turned to Sonia. "Want to come?"

Sonia hesitated. She was sort of hoping that Jon would have been there. Although there had been nothing spoken, she seemed to have a rapport with him and would have liked to have got to know him better.

"Come on, Sonia. It'll be fun," said Sue. "I'm going."

"In that case, I'd better go to keep an eye on you," replied Sonia, and that decided the issue.

They took the M20 to Dover and caught a P&O ferry to Calais. Some of the team went straight to the bar but Sonia and Sue went to the café for a cup of tea.

"Did you want Jon to come?" Sue asked her after they sat down at a table with a sea view.

"Oh, you know, it might have been fun to have him along," said Sonia, trying to hide her disappointment at his not being there.

"Sure," said Sue. "I saw the look on your face when you found out he had gone to Edinburgh. It seemed to be more than mild disappointment."

"I don't know," admitted Sonia. "We seem to hit it off together. I like his company."

"And?"

"There is no and," said Sonia.

Not yet anyway, she thought.

They returned to the minibus where a couple of the guys already seemed to have had a few.

"That was quick," commented Sonia.

"We haven't got time to waste," said one of them, with a smile.

Mich drove them to the centre of Calais and they booked into a small hotel across the road from Calais central railway station. It was cheap and cheerful, with a double bed and a pair of bunk beds in each room. The hotel had a small bar, but Mich said that Jon had told them about a place called The Pirate Bar which was just around the corner and stocked Stella Artois. That sold it for them, and they all piled in.

"'Twas bier, silver plate," tried Paul, attempting to speak French.

"It's OK, I speak English," said the barmaid.

"Oh, OK," said Paul, reddening. "Three pints of Stella, please."

"Of course," replied the barmaid, smiling. "Thank you for trying to speak French, though."

Paul smiled back at her.

"It's a bit cold to go to the beach. So, what else is there to do?" asked Sonia. She had no intention of sitting getting paralytic drunk before actually seeing a bit of the town.

"We're staying here, but there's some shops if you take the first left," said Mich. "The Hotel de Ville, which is the mayor's office and not an actual hotel, is a good point of reference. We'll meet you back here in, say, two hours and go for something to eat, if you like?"

"I'll come with you if, you want some company," said Paul.

"Thanks, Paul," said Sonia, "but it's OK. Unless you want to, of course."

Paul elected to go with her, and they stepped out of the bar. There was a bracing wind, and Sonia was glad that she had brought a thick jacket. The climate of Calais was similar to that of southern England. It was only when you got a lot further south that the temperature rose noticeably.

Jon got home late on the Friday night. He had got caught up in the London rush hour and just made King's Cross before the train left. He rang the doorbell rather than let himself in and his mother answered.

"Hello, Jonny," she said, giving him a hug. "We didn't know if you would come tonight or tomorrow."

"I got lucky with the train," he said.

"Are you here for long?" she asked.

"No," he replied. "I'll have to go back on Sunday. I only came back because I got a cryptic note from Aggie."

Aggie was Jon's sister, who he hadn't seen since she got married.

"Yes. She asked how to get in touch with you but wouldn't tell me what it was about," said his mother.

That was so typical of Aggie; she always had to turn a drama into a crisis.

"I'll go round and see her tomorrow," he said. "It's a bit late to give her a ring now."

"I think her phone got cut off again, anyway," announced his mother, despairingly.

Aggie was hopeless with money and her new husband wasn't any better. She was always cadging money off Jon's parents to pay bills just before getting cut off, but this time she obviously didn't make it. There was a public phone in Ashford, but it was difficult to get messages through to recruits, so they normally waited until Sunday morning to use the coin-operated phone just outside the guardroom.

"Want a cup of tea?" asked his mother.

"Yes. Thanks, Ma, that would be nice," he said.

Simon sat miserably in his bedroom and wondered what he should do. He really enjoyed being in the Intelligence Corps and, although he hadn't stood out, he had passed every test without difficulty. He was looking forward to the trade training and moving on to working as an intelligence operator, but he had a problem that wouldn't go away.

It hadn't been so bad when he was at school. He could hide

his sexuality from his friends because he was only a boy, but now it was getting to the point where it was more difficult and, to make thing worse, he had fallen in love. He hadn't meant to, but love isn't something that happens on demand. It either does or it doesn't, and he was in a dilemma about whether to share it with the person involved or keep quiet.

He would have liked to have gone to France with the other recruits; he really liked most of them. They weren't like the ones who hung around Cazanoe. He wondered if the Corporal was gay as well. He pretended that he liked women but that could just be a cover. He had glimpsed a pile of porn mags when he had been passing the Corporal's room one day and he was fairly sure, but not completely certain, that he had seen a gay magazine hidden between the others. Or maybe he was just imagining it.

At least he could go down to the local gay club and be himself this weekend. There was no one who would recognise him there and he would be safe from discovery. The problem was going to be when he went back to Ashford and resumed his training.

Donna went into a rage when she saw the state that the agent had let her flat get into. It wasn't as if she paid the bastard peanuts. She had left for Ashford thinking that at least she had a warm, comfortable flat to come back to if all went wrong. Thank God it hadn't, because her flat was close to being uninhabitable.

She rang one of her friends and went out to drown her sorrows. She would deal with this problem in the morning.

Steve sat in the bar, bored out of his mind. It wasn't that it was a bad place. The décor was nice, and the jukebox was playing all the latest hits. It wasn't that there was anything wrong with the beer either; this had been his local until a mere six weeks ago. It was just that he couldn't slide back into the company of what, until a short while ago, had been his circle of friends.

They hadn't changed – he had, he realised now. They seemed so shallow and mindless. He laughed at some inane joke and sipped his beer. He now wished that he had gone with the other guys. They would probably be pissed on French wine and scoffing oysters and frogs' legs by now. If he had to stay with this lot much longer, he was going to go nuts.

"Sorry, guys, I've got to go," he said. They didn't even seem to notice that he had gone.

So much for close friends.

He thought about his squad and how much of a laugh they all had, even when they were being persecuted by that bastard of a Corporal or run ragged on some exercise.

He made his way home and quietly opened the back door and let himself in. His parents were sitting in the lounge watching something on TV. He went to the kitchen and made himself a cup of tea. Sitting there, idly stirring the rapidly cooling brown liquid, he realised how much he had come to love the army. It was the best decision he had ever made, and the Intelligence Corps seemed to be a really interesting unit.

He had sat, fascinated while Jon, Dave and Mich had recounted tales from their previous units. There were so many interesting things to do and places to go. Thank God that he could get out of here. The thought of turning into one of his friends from the pub now filled him with horror.

He drank his tea and went up to his room. His parents wouldn't have expected him to be back for hours, but he was used to early nights and wanted to get up in the morning and go for a run. He was going to make sure that he got really fit. Who knows, he might even go for SAS selection at some point.

Sonia and Paul had wandered around the shops a bit and then had followed a sign which said '*plage*' which Paul thought meant 'beach' in French. There was a small patch of sand next to the harbour and they sat on the sea wall and watched the ferries come and go.

"Did you not want to get pissed?" asked Sonia.

"There's plenty of time for that," replied Paul. "We'll have to get some cheap booze to take back with us."

"There's a hypermarket somewhere near Calais, I think," said Sonia. "That'll have as much cheap booze as you can all handle."

"Do you fancy trying frogs' legs?"

"Not really," said Sonia, studying him. "Do you?"

"Apparently they taste like chicken."

"Doesn't everything?" Sonia laughed.

"Not army food."

"You've got a point there. I wouldn't mind something a bit exotic, though."

"Do you want to try one of these restaurants?"

"What about the others?"

"I reckon that they're going to end up having a liquid lunch," said Paul.

"You could be right," agreed Sonia. "OK. Which one?"

"How about that one we passed on the way here? It looked quite nice."

They walked back down the Rue Royale until they came to the Café de Paris.

"This one," said Paul, and they went in.

"What's French for two?" Sonia asked.

"*Deux*, I think," said Paul.

But he didn't even need to try to speak French as the waiter immediately came up and said, "A table for two, yes?"

"Yes please," they both replied at once.

They stared at the menu, which was printed in both French and English.

"You ever had steak?" Sonia asked.

"Yes. A couple of times," said Paul. "Special occasions, you know."

"I've never had a steak," admitted Sonia. She came from a fairly poor background and meat was a luxury.

"Well, have one now," suggested Paul.

"What are you going to have?"

"I think I might have a steak, too."

"Well, there you go, that's us decided, then," said Sonia. "What shall we have to drink? Wine?"

"Wine not?" quipped Paul.

"Do you know anything about wine?"

"No idea," Paul admitted. "Red or white?"

"I seem to remember reading something about eating meat with red wine and fish with white."

"OK, red it is, then."

The waiter came across and they ordered two medium-rare steaks (*à point*, as they say in France) and a bottle of red, which Paul chose by going for the middle of the wine list.

"Is this medium-rare?" asked Sonia, as her knife cut into the delicate, bloody flesh of the steak.

"That's what he said."

"OK... Mmm," she said, as she took a mouthful, "God, this is gorgeous."

"I concur," agreed Paul, delighted at the choice they had made. The wine was excellent, too.

They finished off with small cups of espresso which came with a chocolate-covered coffee bean.

"Wow, that was good," said Paul.

"Best meal I've ever had," agreed Sonia.

This trip was turning out to be a success.

They sauntered back to The Pirate Bar to find that most of the rest of the team were still there and happily drunk on industrial-strength Stella. They went back to the hotel and sunk into the comfortable armchairs, before wandering to their rooms.

"See you in the morning," Sonia said, as she put her key card in the door lock.

"Good night," replied Paul, before doing the same.

The following day, with a few members nursing hangovers, they stopped off at the hypermarket before making their way back to the ferry and, ultimately, Templer Barracks.

Linda didn't really know what to do. She had gone straight to her room when she got back to Templer Barracks and had been sick in the sink. She desperately wanted to talk to someone, but her roommate was in hospital with suspected appendicitis and the other previous occupant of the room had left after she failed her vetting application.

She didn't know if she should report the incident or just keep quiet about it and hope it went away. She felt dirty and guilty, as if it had been her fault.

I should never have gone with him, she thought.

She had been warned by Donna not to, but Tony had seemed so nice, and she had gained a lot of kudos being associated with him.

He had been drunk when he had sexually assaulted her and claimed that he didn't remember anything from the previous evening when she confronted him about it the next day, so she had sat almost silent on the way back from Wales, where they had gone hillwalking.

It had all started out so well. She had had great hopes that they might have had a serious relationship and had even fantasised about marriage (although years in the future when they were both Sergeants, or something like that). But it had now all fallen apart.

The room was cold, and Linda huddled on the bed and wrapped a blanket around her. She had heard reports that women who made complaints in the army were often ignored and even accused of either making it up or being at fault for leading the guy on. She didn't know what to do. She was badly in need of advice and there was no one around to give it to her, so eventually she curled into a ball and cried herself to sleep.

Jon sat alone in the NAAFI, nursing a bottle of Becks that was gradually losing its chill and becoming undrinkable. He hadn't bought it to drink, really, but as a prop so that he could sit and think without being disturbed.

It wasn't as if he was still in a relationship with Marsha, or even that he ever really had been. There had been a brief period where Marsha had talked about leaving Fred, but it was never going to happen. Jon was only a student, and Marsha was twenty years older than him.

It was doomed from the start, and eventually Jon had realised that he wasn't doing Marsha any good by filling her head with fantasies and had stopped it. The hardest part had been when Marsha phoned him up, pleading with him to go back to Windermere for one more year. He had heard the desperation in her voice but knew that he couldn't give in.

It would have been potentially fatal to them both. Fred was a big guy, with a violent temper when aroused, and had told Marsha that if she ever betrayed him, he would kill her with an axe and then do the same to her lover. Not that that would have stopped Jon, but the cold, hard realities of life had instead made him realise that there was no future for them, and they were on a downward spiral to destruction if they carried on.

And now she was dead.

He took a swig of the warm, flat beer and stared into the distance with his eyes unfocussed. That was the message from Aggie, delivered straight and with no preamble to soften the blow. Aggie hadn't known how close Jon had been to Marsha, only that they were friends from when he had worked for her and Fred. She had come across the obituary by accident while using an old newspaper to clean windows, of all things. She had been dead for almost a year before he found out.

Funny how things happen, he thought. Not that it was in any way amusing.

"Funny-peculiar, rather than funny-haha," as his mother used to say.

The bar was fortuitously empty, and it gave Jon the opportunity to sit and muse and remember times past before he would have to return to the present and deal with the day-to-day of life.

"Hi, Jon. How're you doing?" said a soft, pleasant voice.

Jon looked up into Sonia's large brown eyes.

"Oh! As bad as that, is it?" she said, reading the expression on his face.

He sighed before responding. "Yeah."

"Woman problems?" she asked, seeming to almost read his thoughts.

"In a way," he replied.

"Want to talk about it?"

"If you like," Jon said. In a way he did want to talk to someone about it, and he had always liked Sonia. She was very easy to talk to and didn't seem to make judgements.

She sat down opposite him and looked into his eyes. "Was she special?" she asked.

"Yes," admitted Jon simply.

Sonia felt a surge of disappointment at the thought that Jon was already claimed, but she hid it away deep inside. "You never know, it might work out," she said instead.

Jon looked at her. "It's too late for that."

"It's never too late," protested Sonia. "Can you not send her a letter or something?"

"No. Not in this case," said Jon. "She died."

"Oh... sorry," said Sonia. "What did she die of?"

Jon paused for a short while before answering her. "She drank herself to death," he said. "Although it was jaundice that did it." He saw the look on Sonia's face. "She had an unhappy marriage," he added.

"Oh... sorry," Sonia repeated.

"It's OK," said Jon. "Thanks for talking to me about it. It makes it better somehow."

Sonia smiled. "You're welcome. Anytime."

PART 4

TRADE TRAINING

NOVEMBER 1989 – JUNE 1990

CHAPTER 13

Once the military skills/basic infantry training phase is over recruits to the Intelligence Corps enter the trade training phase. Trade training is the process by which soldiers are taught the basic trade skills required to qualify them as Military Intelligence Operators and the course was known as the A3. As an Intelligence Corps soldier progresses through the ranks, they sit two more sets of trade training called the A2 and A1 courses. A2 qualifies one for the rank of Full Corporal and the A1 for Sergeant.

The A courses are divided into a Security (Sy) and a Combat Intelligence (Combat Int) phase. Each phase ends with trade tests that must be passed before the soldier can move on to the next one, and their successful completion earns a pay rise and completion of the trade tests and the Drill and Duties Three course (D&D3) promotion to Lance Corporal.

There are no Military Intelligence operators below the rank of Lance Corporal hence the joke about the Intelligence Corps being eunuchs because it has no Privates.

It was Friday 10 November 1989, and Major Elswick was waiting for them in the classroom along with Captain Case, his Second in Command and two Intelligence Corps Sergeants the recruits had never seen before. They filed in and stood behind their desks while the duty student (Sandra that day) marched up to Elswick and saluted.

"Squad Forty-Nine. All present and correct, sir."

"Thank you, Private Davidson," said Elswick, waving her to her seat. "Sit down."

The recruits all sat down and waited.

"You're now entering your trade training phase, having passed your basic training. But, before we go any further, you need to be aware that last night, the Berlin wall fell."

There were a few gasps but mainly silence from the room, as the recruits tried to take in the enormity of the statement.

"How will that affect us? I hear you asking," continued Elswick. "Well, in answer to that, we have no idea. We will all carry on as normal, but there may be some fallout over the coming months, and you can be certain that things will change, possibly dramatically, over the next few years. We'll keep you posted. In the meantime, good luck with your studies and I will leave you in the capable hands of Sergeant Knight and Sergeant Dante."

He nodded towards the two Sergeants and then, followed by Captain Case, left the recruits to the tender mercies of the two Intelligence Corps Sergeants.

"Good morning, ladies and gentlemen. I'm Sergeant Knight and this is Sergeant Dante. We're your instructors for the Security phase of your training," said the slightly overweight Intelligence Corps Sergeant, by way of introduction.

Knight went on to explain the course, which would be split by the Christmas break and would be interspersed with drill, PT and weapons training which would continue even though the recruits had passed the initial infantry basic training.

This would mean that some days they would only have a couple of lectures or a practical lesson, and there would be plenty of outside visits to ensure that the recruits could 'hit the ground running' when they passed out the following July and were given their first posting.

"Bugger, I thought we were done with infantry stuff," complained Paul, as they stood around in small groups during a smoke break.

"No. We've just scratched the surface," said Mich. "There's loads more that you'll need to know if you're going to understand Combat Intelligence, let alone survive, if you get sent over the water."

"What does that mean?" Paul asked.

"Over the water is the army term for Northern Ireland," Mich explained "a good number of the recruits here will find themselves going there as their first posting once they pass out from Ashford. Infantry battalions usually have their own 'Int' cell, made up of select personnel from within the regiment, but there is a vast network of agents and informers run by Military Intelligence, as well as the normal Intelligence cells that support headquarters units in their quest to prevent Republican and Unionist terrorism in the Province.

Int Corps personnel often join infantry patrols as a means of gaining 'ground truth' about the situation in their particular patch, and as a means of orientating themselves as to the geography and political leanings of the towns and cities in the region. To this end, they have to be able to patrol competently to avoid standing out as unprofessional or putting the patrol at risk militarily."

"I don't fancy that much," said Paul, as Mich explained it to him.

"Try to get yourself posted to a Security section, then," said Mich. "Most of the time you don't even have to wear uniform."

"That sounds more like it," agreed Paul.

"Best of luck, mate," added Jon. "The army has a way of giving you the exact opposite of what you ask for."

They trooped back into the classroom and were confronted by large folders, one for each person, on their desks.

"Welcome to the *Manual of Army Security*," said Knight, happily. "The regulations pertaining to army Security are written down in the Manual of Army Security or M.A.S. It is a four volume series of books covering every aspect of army Security, both physical and protective. They have a revolting, maroon-coloured cover and are big enough to use as a stepladder, if necessary.

"Everything you ever wanted to know about Security, and also probably a lot of things that you never wanted to know, are contained within the covers of these volumes.

"Once you get to know your way around these manuals, it's relatively easy, but initially it's pretty daunting, as even the index is classified.

"A lot of the job of the Intelligence Corps Security section is trying to interpret the regulations, which in some cases are totally straightforward and in others very woolly, to say the least."

Knight spent the rest of the morning trying to familiarise the squad with the said *Manual of Army Security*. Some of the male recruits found it really hard work although the female recruits generally had no problem. After what had seemed like an eternity in purgatory to Rob, the class broke for lunch, and they escaped to the dubious delights of the cookhouse.

"The only thing that I can remember from this morning is the colour of the damned manual, and even that's a bit hazy," said Rob, prodding at a wedge of quiche that sat wetly on his plate.

"I've heard that it is that colour because no one in their right mind would ever paint anything in that shade, and so it is unique," said Mich. "A bit like that shade of green that they use for safes and store cupboards."

"I suppose there's a certain amount of logic to that," agreed Rob. "Although I can't really see the point."

"OK," said Mich. "I'll tell you a great story that I once heard."

He had everyone's rapt attention as he told them his story.

"An Intelligence Corps operator turned up at a unit which had either lost the combination for their safe or, more likely, messed up trying to change it. He tried to open the safe but found that he couldn't, so he told the unit that they'd have to get the local blacksmith to cut the back off. They pulled the safe away from the wall in anticipation, only to find that it had no back. Another unit had obviously done the same thing, but instead of paying for a new safe, had pushed it back against the wall and painted a square of the wall the same colour as the inside of the safe. Great security, eh? But that's the army for you."

Once they had finished lunch, most of them wandered back to the billet for a snooze. A couple of recruits went to the NAAFI and had a drink. One was an ex-infantry full Corporal who had transferred in and had been exempted from the military skills phase due to his previous experience. He was accompanied by two of Cazanoe's sycophantic followers and another black-haired recruit who Jon had seen but did not immediately recognise.

"Who's that with Jock? he asked Mich. Corporal John 'Jock' Mackenzie was the Corporal who had joined the squad for the trade training phase.

Mich squinted his eyes to see the small group before they disappeared into the NAAFI.

"That's Simon Tollsland," he said. "Room on the next floor, which is why you've not really seen him. They call him Raven."

"Why? Because he's got black hair?"

"No. Because he's a ravin' homosexual," explained Mich.

"Ah!" said Jon. "Any proof?"

"No," continued Mich. "He's just a bit camp, I think."

"Poor bastard."

"Particularly if he keeps hanging about with that lot," agreed Mich.

Sergeant Knight took the lead on physical Security and Sergeant Dante on protective Security.

"Physical Security pertains to all aspects of Security relating to physical things," began Sergeant Knight "such as the thickness an armoury door needs to be, what sort of lock it needs, what height a Security fence needs to be in order to protect a class A unit, what type of lighting a military base should have, and whether the guard force should be armed or not.

"Whereas protective Security relates to regulations and laws such as vetting procedures and classifications, rules for security of passwords, lock combinations, and the protection of personnel," continued Sergeant Dante, "The regulations regarding army Security are all set down in the MAS and, if they are adhered to, should prevent any breaches of Security. One of the jobs of the Intelligence Corps is to ensure that these regulations are being obeyed, and to give advice and recommendations in the event of them being breached. Security has to make sense.

"If the Security regulations are too onerous, they *will* be bypassed. It can't be helped; it is human nature. I don't know whether it's that humans are inherently lazy or maybe it's just that humans will always look for an easy way of doing things. I suppose that if we didn't, we'd still be living in caves and beating clothes with a stone to clean them," Sergeant Knight concluded.

That afternoon they were given an introduction to the Combat Fitness Test (CFT). This was an eight mile forced march which needed to be completed in two hours, carrying thirty-five pounds including rifle, helmet and water. It was supposed to be carried out on a mix of roads and other terrain to simulate a forced march under combat conditions (without being fired at, of course).

Though that would have been a pretty good incentive to keep moving, Jon thought.

The biggest problem wasn't so much the distance or the weight, but that badly fitting boots could cripple you. Jon had seen the effect of doing a CFT on a gravel surface which had hospitalised one of the group, though they had still finished the course.

Women have a distinct disadvantage due to their height-to-weight ratio and the biological fact that women have less percentage of muscle than men, but they are given no leeway to compensate for this like in the BFT.

WO2 Sanders and Corporal Cazanoe were standing outside the gym wearing their blue PTI tops, and Jon could see that Major Elswick and WO2 Callahan, the training wing CSM, were also there, dressed as if they were taking part.

Because this wasn't an actual CFT, the recruits were told to carry their Bergens with twenty pounds of weight, which was enough to give them a good workout. Jon would have preferred to have had the weight around his hips rather than on his back, but it wasn't really a problem.

He noticed that Linda seemed to be avoiding Tony Cazanoe, but that may have been because he was acting as part of the directing staff.

They formed up into a squad and prepared to start. Jon found himself in the same rank as Sonia and gave her a smile. She hitched up her Bergen and smiled back.

"By the front... double march," came the command from Cazanoe.

"You can't take your dressing from the front, arsehole," muttered Jon.

Cazanoe didn't even know enough drill to be aware that the words of command to start a squad are by the left, by the right or by the centre, not by the front. It is all about from where you take your dressing (your left or your right). You can't take your dressing from the front because the front rank then has no one to take their dressing from.

They lurched away as Cazanoe jogged off.

"Fuck. This is too fast," Jon heard someone mutter.

The CFT was supposed to mimic a forced march, march being

the operative word. You weren't supposed to run and, in actual fact, if you completed it in less than two hours you would technically fail it because it has to be completed in exactly two hours, according to regulations.

The squad immediately began to stretch as the smaller men and women had difficulty in keeping up with the fast pace.

"Close up the ranks," Sanders shouted, and the squad concertinaed as those at the rear tried to catch up.

This was the worst possible way to do a forced march, and people rapidly started to fall back as the fitter ones overtook them in an attempt to obey the command to keep the ranks closed up. The only reason that the squad didn't break in two was because Cazanoe finally slowed the pace. Whether this was because he wasn't fit enough himself to carry on the rapid pace, or whether it was because he realised that he was going too fast, Jon didn't know, but he was glad on behalf of the poor sods behind him who were running in an effort to keep up.

It had taken its toll, however, and the rear of the squad was already becoming ragged.

"This looks like the retreat from fucking Moscow," shouted Sanders. "Close it up."

Bastard, Jon thought.

He had never liked Sergeant Major Sanders. He was one of those PTIs who seemed to try to fail people rather them to encourage them to pass.

He probably has an inferiority complex and tries to make up for it by belittling people, thought Jon.

He glanced around to see the dark-haired recruit, Simon, gradually falling behind. The Bergen was bouncing on his back and his face looked pale, emphasising his startlingly blue eyes. He was probably regretting going to the bar rather than taking a nap, like most of the others had done.

Major Elswick and the CSM were trying to encourage the recruits at the back, but some had already fallen out and had been picked up by the Biff waggon which followed behind. Paul 'Biff' Dobson was still with the squad, gamely plodding on, which was a surprise to Jon. He was definitely improving.

They reached the halfway point and Sanders halted the squad.

"Two minute break. Make sure you take in some water," he shouted.

On the way back, they obviously realised that they had gone too fast at the start, and they slowed the pace so much that it was agony. Jon couldn't remember the last time that he had been in such a badly run lesson, but whether the training Major would do anything about it was a moot question. They couldn't afford to lose Sanders, or even Cazanoe, so he supposed they were stuck with them.

Eventually the torture stopped, and they reached the doors of the gym.

"That was rather disappointing," said Elswick, which answered Jon's internal question. "Well done to those that passed but those of you who failed - and you know who you are - will have to do better next time" with that he strode off with the CSM.

"Christ! I thought that cunt was going to run all the way," grunted Rob as they sat at a table in the NAAFI.

"I don't think he's fit enough," commented Mich. "Did you see how red his face was when we slowed down?"

"I was so busy trying not to throw up that I couldn't see anything," said Paul. "That fucking quiche that I had for lunch almost came back."

"They're a couple of bastards," added Jock MacKenzie. "They shouldn't have done that."

"I quite enjoyed it, actually," said Donna, casually.

They all looked at her in surprise.

"Once I got over the initial shock, I didn't find it too bad," she added.

"Christ! You must be fit," said Rob, in disbelief.

"You have to be, to be a dancer," explained Donna.

"Is that what you were, before this?" someone asked.

"Yes," answered Donna. She hadn't meant to admit to being a dancer, it had just come out. She considered these colleagues to be friends and hadn't really thought about keeping it a secret from them.

"What sort of dancer?"

Ah! Here we go, she thought.

"Just a dancer," she said.

Fortunately, Sonia came in at that point and interrupted the flow of the conversation when she gestured to Donna to join her. They disappeared into a huddle and then left the bar. Jon watched them go, wondering what it was that Sonia had wanted to talk about that she couldn't say in public.

"What is Security?" Sergeant Knight asked.

"The situation where the commander can plan and carry out operations without undue interference from the enemy," said Mich.

"Yes, that's one definition," replied Knight. "Another is: the situation where personnel and materiel are protected from the threat to Security."

"What's the threat to Security?" someone asked.

Knight smiled. "I'm glad you asked me that question. The threat to Security is quantified, defined and laid out as: 'The threat from espionage, terrorism, sabotage and subversion'. Today, Sergeant Dante is going to talk about espionage."

"Thank you, Sergeant Knight," said Dante, coming up to the lectern.

She was medium height with long, ash-blonde hair tied in a bun and had beautiful, grey-blue eyes. She had a slight accent which Jon couldn't quite place but sounded similar to an old friend of his families who had come from Somerset. He wondered if, in fact, that was where she was from.

She paused for a moment surveying the class, and then started.

"Espionage is the technical name for spying," she said. "This is the *James Bond* stuff, although as far as I remember from the books, *James Bond* never actually carried out any espionage. What he did would actually have been classed as sabotage. That might seem weird, but it will be explained later.

"The definition of espionage is: 'The process by which a country or individual obtains, or attempts to obtain, information or Intelligence to which it is not entitled'. If it's done *to* you, it is called spying. If we do it, it's called Intelligence gathering.

It is generally carried out by specialist operators, known in the trade as talent spotters, who look for people who can be persuaded to spy for them. The Intelligence Corps doesn't generally get involved in espionage; that is left to the Security Service, commonly called MI5, and the Secret Intelligence Service, or MI6. That is, unless it involves military personnel, in which case we investigate it.

What the Intelligence Corps Security section is responsible for is preventing any would-be spies from being able to access military information or Intelligence, by the processes of physical and protective Security. Any questions so far?"

The recruits sat, enthralled, and no one could think of anything to ask.

"I'll talk a bit about recruiting spies, because this is the bit that could affect you directly and you'll need to be aware of it so that you can counter it, if it happens," she said. "Don't think that it won't happen to you, either. The Soviets are very willing to play the long game and will wait years, if not decades, for a chance to recruit someone. They will often target university students, in the hope that they will, one day, be in a position of power or have access to classified information that could be useful to them. Philby, Burgess and MacLean" – she paused and looked around the room – "has everyone heard of them?"

There were a few blank faces and shakes of heads, so she continued.

"Philby, Burgess and MacLean were all reputedly recruited at Cambridge University during the 1930s and spied for Russia. They all had access to highly classified information and worked for the Security services."

"Surely that sort of things doesn't happen now?" someone said.

"You'd be surprised," retorted Dante. "But in some ways, you're right, the *reasons* that people spy, changes – that's the only difference." She paused for a moment to watch this sink in and then carried on. "Has anyone heard of the 'seven levers'?"

"Yes, but I don't know what they are," came the reply.

Dante smiled.

"The 'seven levers' are the means a talent spotter will use to recruit someone to be a spy. They are: ideology, grudge, money, drugs, homosexuality, sex and excitement."

Jon's eyes flicked towards Simon as Dante mentioned homosexuality and he thought that the black-haired recruit reddened slightly, but he couldn't be sure.

"These levers are used to either hook the person, or they can be used to blackmail them," Gloria continued. "Philby, Burgess and MacLean were recruited because of ideology. Apparently, they actually believed in the Communist system. But sex, money, drugs, homosexuality and grudge are more common."

"Is that what a honeytrap is?" someone asked.

"Yes. And it can work both ways, *ladies*," she replied. "It's not only men who get caught out. So, you can see that you've got to be careful and why the vetting process is so stringent. Once you finish here, you may find yourself posted somewhere where you have access to highly classified information, and that *will* make you a target. Understood?"

That certainly gave them something to think about.

"At this point, it might be useful for us to look at the classification system," Dante said, checking her watch. "But we'll leave that until tomorrow. Carry on, duty student."

Sergeant Dante packed up her notes as they filed out of the classroom and formed up outside, ready for the duty student to march them away.

That was interesting, thought Jon, glad now that he had joined the Intelligence Corps rather than any other unit.

There was some excited chatter about the class during dinner, as the recruits took stock of what they had been taught. Instead of boring stuff like trying to decipher the *Manual of Army Security*, they were now finding out about the real spy stuff.

"I could see myself becoming a victim of a honeytrap," declared Peter. "A couple of women like Donna and Sonia, and I would be in real trouble."

"What? Both together or one at a time?" Rob asked with a smile.

"Cor," replied Peter. "Now there's a thought."

The banter continued around the table, with a few glances towards where Donna and Sonia were sitting with Linda.

Jon could see either woman easily bedazzling an impressionable young man, or an old one for that matter, and, presumably, the Russians would use volunteers who were willing to play their part for the good of the state.

How many male members of our squad would be able to resist? pondered Jon.

Well, maybe Simon, if rumour was true, but the rest, he didn't know. Including himself, if truth be told.

Jon was on guard that night, and at 2000 hours he reported to the guard commander, where he found that Linda was doing guard duty too, along with two other recruits.

Linda was another blonde, but unlike Sergeant Gloria Dante, who was naturally that colour, Jon could see the dark roots of Linda's hair. He wondered why so many women went to the effort of dyeing their hair blonde. He supposed that they were conditioned that way by magazines and the old adage blondes have more fun, and the film *Gentlemen Prefer Blondes*.

The guard force commander was an ex-infantry Corporal who had taken the job after retirement from the British Army. He gave the recruits a run-through of what their duties would be, regardless of the fact that they had already done guard duty at least once during their military skills training. He made Jon the guard commander for the recruits and briefed him on the rota.

"You go out in pairs, and you look out for each other," he told them, before leaving them to staff the guardroom overnight. They weren't expecting anyone to come in between midnight and 0600, so the guard commander told them he would be asleep in one of the back rooms if they needed him, but otherwise to give him a call about 0530.

One member of the team would be allowed to sleep while the other three did 'stag' (army slang for guard duty). There was a broom handle leaning against the wall in a small room with a double bunk, which they were told was for use by male members to wake female guards, to avoid any allegations of sexual assault.

"Is that really necessary?" asked the male recruit.

"Unfortunately, yes," Jon told him. "Just to be on the safe side. You never can tell."

Linda gave him a funny look.

"Not that I'm saying either of the ladies would make allegations, mind you."

Linda turned away and studied the signing-in book as if she found it fascinating.

When it was time to go out on patrol, Jon noticed that Linda wasn't wearing waterproofs.

"Haven't got any waterproofs?" he asked her, as she was about to go outside along with the other female recruit.

"No," she replied. "I didn't think that I'd need them."

"Here, take this," Jon said, handing her his Gore-Tex jacket and trousers.

"Won't you need them yourself?"

"I'll only be going out to check ID cards, so I shouldn't get that wet," he said. "If it rains while you're on patrol, you'll get soaked."

"Oh, OK. Thanks," she replied, taking the camouflaged bundle.

"If she wears it, it'll come back stinking of perfume," Ron, the other recruit said after the women had disappeared into the darkness.

"It's better than stinking of sweat," retorted Jon.

"Aye, I suppose so," grunted Ron.

Ron was a bit of a dour Scotsman and never seemed to be particularly happy. Jon hadn't had much to do with him as he was one of Cazanoe's gang.

Ron, whose turn it was for the sleeping watch, took hold of the broom handle.

"I wouldn't touch her with a barge pole, let alone this," he commented, before going into the room and shutting the door.

Jon sat at the duty desk and wondered what Linda had done to merit that remark. He had heard the rumours about Linda and the 'cap badge challenge', but that was her own affair, so to speak. If a guy had slept with several women, he would have been praised for it, but that was the difference between men and women; if a woman did it, she was branded a slut.

He wondered if Ron had propositioned her and been turned down. That made him think that maybe he shouldn't let them go out on patrol together and decided that he would adjust the roster to make sure that they didn't.

After about an hour, Linda and Georgina came back. They were both wearing waterproofs and rain was dripping off them. They peeled off the camouflaged jackets and trousers and hung them up on the coat hooks which lined the rear wall.

"Thanks for the loan of the gear," said Linda.

"You're welcome," replied Jon. "It looks like you needed them."

"Yes. It's absolutely pissing it down out there," said Georgina.

"It could be worse, you could be in a trench," commented Jon.

"What's it like?" she asked.

"It's not too bad when it's dry," said Jon. "You are sheltered from the wind by being underground, and it's surprising how warm a candle can make a slit trench, especially if you've got a bit of hessian sacking as a door. But when it rains it can be a real pain, especially if your trench floods."

"I can't say that I fancy the idea," retorted Georgina.

"That's why we're in the Intelligence Corps," said Jon, with a smile. "We generally don't have to play at being infantry."

"It makes me feel cold just thinking about it," added Linda. "I think I'll have a coffee. Anybody want one?"

They sat and drank coffee, but Jon noted Linda was very quiet and hardly said anything except for the odd comment. Georgina was the one who led the conversation, and she seemed to be far more outgoing, which was strange considering Linda's reputation. In fact, after making the coffee, Linda sat silently and merely watched as Georgina reeled off a list of questions about the army that Jon did his best to answer.

After a while, Ron reappeared and Linda was next on sleeping watch, so she went into the back room and closed the door.

The rest of the night was uneventful, and by 0630 they were on their way to the cookhouse for breakfast. Jon always enjoyed the first meal after a night on guard duty; it tasted better, for some reason. Linda claimed she wasn't hungry and didn't join them, instead heading straight back to her room.

Jon wondered what was driving her, as she seemed to have changed recently, but he couldn't put his finger on what it was. Since he didn't really know her very well, he didn't know how to take it forward, so he put it to the back of his mind and concentrated on getting his breakfast.

CHAPTER 14

"How many of you have a full driving licence?"

The question was asked on a Monday morning, as the recruits sat in a freezing cold classroom wondering what aspect of security they were going to be taught today.

There was an old army trick, where someone would ask whether anyone could play an instrument and then go on to say, "Good, you can go and move the piano from the storeroom to the officers' mess." Jon wondered if this was a similar con.

"Car or motorbike?" he asked.

"Car. The motorbike course is separate."

A tentative show of hands confirmed about half of the squad could drive.

"OK. Duty student, make a list," said the CSM "All Intelligence Corps Lance Corporals need to be able to drive. So, those of you who haven't already got a full driving licence will get lessons."

"What, for free, sir?" asked Peter.

"Free. Gratis. Compliments of the army," acknowledged the CSM.

"Wow!" replied Peter, smiling.

It wasn't often that the army gave you something for free, there was normally some catch, but this sounded pretty good.

"You'll start your lessons as soon as the instructor gets back off sick leave," announced the CSM.

"What's wrong with him, sir?" queried Jon.

"He had a heart attack," said the CSM, laconically.

There was a brief silence as the recruits contemplated being taught to drive by someone who might feasibly die on them while they were doing a hill start, but you couldn't win them all, and the excitement of getting driving lessons and the test paid for by the army overruled the worry about having to do CPR on their instructor.

"Thanks, Sergeants. Carry on," said the CSM, who then vanished out the door.

"OK, back to the acting," said Sergeant Dante. "Today's lesson is on classification. Before I start, what is the difference between information and Intelligence?"

"Intelligence is processed information," said Mich who had been a Corporal in the Royal Signals and had dealt with classified material before.

"Good. Spot on," said Dante, before going on to explain that information covered anything like documents, letters, telephone calls, conversations, etcetera, and once it was processed by means of analysis, collation and interpretation, it was turned into Intelligence.

There were four levels of classification of information/ Intelligence in the British Army, she informed them. These were (from the lowest to the highest): restricted, confidential, secret and top secret.

Restricted was the lowest level that anyone within the military, or who was linked to the military, could access. This allowed virtually anyone to access it, and a restricted classification was only meant to prevent non-military people from seeing sensitive information.

She paused briefly and then wrote on the whiteboard behind her in green ink 'Need to know' and 'Need to hold'

"These are two principals of dealing with classified material that you will need to know, haha," she said. "Need to know and need to hold are exactly what they say they are. Does someone need to know the information or intelligence and do they need a copy of it? The amount of people should be kept to an absolute minimum for the sake of security, but it's not always possible." She then went back to explaining the classification system, "The next level is confidential, which is used for more sensitive information/Intelligence like FCO Diplomatic telegrams or medical records, but not something so important that it could get people killed if it fell into the wrong hands.

"After confidential comes secret, by which time the information/ Intelligence is getting quite sensitive. Secret material needs to be properly protected as the ramifications could be very damaging, including 'severe loss of life'. Secret material has to be logged into a special register called a MoD Form 102, which itself could be classified.

"Finally, there is top secret. This is the stuff that gets a lot of people killed or causes real problems if it gets into the wrong hands – atomic secrets, battle plans and that sort of thing."

They had a short break and then Dante started again.

"Anyone with the right authorisation can access top secret information, so to narrow it down a bit, we use the 'STRAP' system," she began. "What does 'STRAP' mean?" she asked, almost rhetorically.

No one answered, although they all looked at Mich who shook his head slightly, indicating that he didn't know, either.

"STRAP doesn't actually mean anything," said Dante, triumphantly, having caught them all out. "It is merely a codeword that indicates who can access the information. STRAP 1 means anyone who needs to see it can do so; STRAP 2 means that only those within a closed circle can access it, and STRAP 3 means that it can only be shared with a single, specified person."

She went on to say that the problem with classification is that it can get out of hand at the drop of a hat, so to speak. There is a saying that Security must make sense. This means that things can't be too complicated, or they will just be ignored.

"I'm sure everyone has seen a fire door wedged open because it is the easiest way to get out of a building for a smoke," she said. "This is what I mean. If you put too many obstacles in the way, humans will ignore them, even if it puts their life in danger, because we tend to think it will never happen to us. So, what I'm saying is don't classify anything that doesn't *need* to be, because you will just cause problems for everyone if you do. Understood? Probably not, but you eventually will, particularly if you get attached to a Security section. That's it for today."

There were some relieved looks from the shell shocked squad. Jon looked around and saw a few bemused expressions, especially from the male recruits. It was obvious that a lot of what Dante had said had gone straight over the heads of many. Whether they could come to terms with the intricacies of Security remained to be seen.

The squad had a respite from the constant classroom work, as the next lesson was a revision of the Browning 9mm pistol. The two 'personal' weapons of the Intelligence Corps operator were the SMG and Browning 9mm. This was because they could be used in enclosed spaces and, unlike the infantry, the Corps was not expected to engage the enemy directly and thus did not need to carry the SLR.

Constant revision and practice with both weapons was explained as the need for familiarity to become 'muscle memory' where ones reactions become instinctive. This could be a matter of life and death, especially when the fog of war descended and panic threatened to steal away ones will. At this point drill takes over and the more entrenched the drill the better.

"I can't get my head round this Security stuff," complained Corporal John 'Jock' Mackenzie, as they sat in the cookhouse with a cup of coffee.

"Didn't you do stuff like this in the infantry?" asked Simon, with a puzzled look on his face.

"Not like this," replied Jock. "I was in the battalion Intelligence cell, but we didn't do this sort of thing."

"Combat Intelligence," interjected Mich.

Simon just looked at him, blankly.

"What we move on to next," explained Mich, "It's Intelligence in the field. That's the best way that I can describe it, anyway" he added. "I'm not an expert, but it's more about fighting the enemy than countering the threat to Security."

"Aye. That sounds about right," put in Jock. "What we did was all about where the enemy was, what their capabilities were, and where they were going to attack, rather than this Security shit."

They had just come back from doing a Security survey of the depot armoury and were now expected to produce a written report on the results.

Jock had spent twelve years in the Royal Anglian Regiment and, although he was called 'Jock', he had spent most of his life anywhere but Scotland. His father had been the Regimental Sergeant Major of the Royal Leicestershire Regiment, which had been amalgamated into the Royal Anglians in 1964 and, as a child, Jock had travelled around the world until he joined the army as a junior soldier in 1977.

"We'll be through the Security phase in a couple of months," said Mich, encouragingly. "After that, it's Combat Intelligence, and you should be OK."

"Aye, but what if I get posted to a Security section?" argued Jock.

That was a question that Mich couldn't answer.

"What the hell is the 'Talurit method'?" Jon muttered out loud.

There was a brief silence as Jon's syndicate considered the question. They were sitting in one of the classrooms, preparing their Security survey reports, poring through the regulations pertaining to arms and armouries found in the depths of the maroon covered

Manual of Army Security.

"Sounds like a sexual position to me," said Peter, to a round of universal laughter.

They all reckoned Peter was actually still a virgin, even though he talked as if he was some sort of modern Cassanova. The female recruits had discussed testing out the theory one night but hadn't been drunk enough to take it any further than a comical discussion.

"No idea," replied Rob. "Tell us?"

"It wasn't a quiz question," grunted Jon. "It's here in the regulations about how weapons can be secured to their racks with a wire rope and padlock using the Talurit method."

"Probably something nautical," said Steve.

They all turned to stare at him. Steve was fairly quiet and generally stayed in the background, just getting on with the job.

"I did a dinghy sailing course once," he admitted, reddening slightly, as if it was something to be ashamed of. "I think I remember something about it from then."

"Could be," agreed Jon. "It would fit with what it's being used for."

"What's that?" asked Donna.

"It's a way of securing weapons by putting a cable through the trigger guard and securing it to the end of the rack, instead of having to secure each individual weapon."

"God. I hate Security," grunted Peter.

"Is there anything that you *do* like?" asked Donna.

Peter leered at her.

"Men!" said Donna and turned back to her report.

They had been given the afternoon to complete the Security survey report, and by the end they were heartily sick of it. Just when they thought that they had covered everything, someone would make a comment or ask a question, and they would realise that there was something else to be added to the list.

Security reports follow a set format: introduction, main body, conclusions and recommendations. In a working Security section, you would generally use the previous report as a template and merely alter the relevant details as necessary, which saved a huge amount of time. But because the recruits were being trained in the basics, they were expected to do it from scratch so that they would be able to do so, if required. Everything they needed to know was set out in the *Manual of Army Security* and the format was laid down in *Joint Services Publication 101* (JSP 101) which was the regulations pertaining to what is known as service writing. The only problem is how to find the information they needed in the welter of other rules and regulations. Once you were familiar with the system, it was quite easy, but learning the system was the hard bit.

"Finished at last! *Pro Christo da mihi potum*," said Jon, closing the cover of the manual and putting his report into a neat pile.

"What does that mean?" asked Donna.

Jon gave her a smile.

"It was found written in the back of a fifteenth-century illuminated Bible," he explained. "It means for Christ's sake, give me a drink'."

"Hear! Hear!" concurred Peter.

"What is it? Latin?" Donna continued.

'It's a mix of Latin and Greek, apparently," said Jon. "Don't ask me why. I just like it."

"It would make a good slogan for our squad T-shirt," said Donna.

"Yes, I suppose it would," agreed Jon.

With that, they packed up and headed off to the cookhouse.

The recruits trooped into the classroom and sat down at their desks. There was no set rule about where anyone should sit, and Jon found himself next to Simon.

"What do you reckon we've got for today?" Jon asked.

Simon gave him a shy smile and just shrugged. "No idea."

Sergeant Dante came in and pointed to the whiteboard where 'The use of force to coerce for a political aim' was written in large, black letters.

"Anyone know what this is the definition of?" she asked.

There were no suggestions and so she simply said, "Terrorism."

All the recruits scribbled it down in their notebooks. This was the sort of question that they would be asked in their written Security paper at the end of the phase. The recruits would need to score 60% or more to pass the Security phase which was made up of the written paper and assessments of the various reports that they would write.

"Terrorism is the norm for warfare at the moment," stated Dante. "There aren't many conventional wars going on, and those that are, are pretty small-scale. So, what we're going to look at is the threat to Security from terrorism."

She went on to explain that terrorism is used as the first stage in what is known as asymmetric warfare. This is where the protagonist does not have a conventional army, or it is not strong enough to match the enemy's forces. It is the first stage of guerrilla warfare. Terrorism often involves the killing of civilians, either to terrorise them, or as the collateral damage of attacks on enemy bases or personnel. It is usually justified by the terrorists saying things like, 'They are all guilty', or 'They are perpetuating x regime', etcetera. Also what is classed as terrorism is very much dependant on your particular viewpoint. In the UK, the Provisional Irish Republican Army, PIRA or the IRA if you prefer, would be considered a terrorist organisation by the vast majority of the British people, but in the USA, they were often considered to be heroic underdogs, fighting the British Empire.

"Do you think that the fall of the Berlin wall will make any difference to terrorism, as it is practiced at the present time?" Dante asked, after the squad had come back from a coffee break.

"Yes," said Jon.

Most of the other recruits stayed silent, but Mich and Mackenzie nodded their heads in agreement.

"Why?" queried Dante.

Jon thought about it for a moment.

"The left wing terrorist organisations have just lost their justification."

Dante gave him a small smile.

"Correct. Organisations like *Baader Meinhof* and the Red Brigade no longer have a cause and thus will have trouble surviving. Let me explain."

She went on to talk about what was known as 'Scotch John's dictum'. "This is a proposal named after a TA Intelligence Corps Corporal called John, who was Scottish, and goes as follows:

If a terrorist organisation has a safe operating base (preferably outside the country in which it is operating), sufficient funding and a reasonable amount of support, it cannot be beaten."

There was a silence as the recruits absorbed this. Dante looked around the room with a small smile on her face.

"I can tell by the looks on some of your faces that some of you disagree," she said. "Prove me wrong," she challenged.

"What about Malaya?" said Mich from the back of the class.

Dante grinned. "Malaya – I knew someone would say that – the famous SAS Counter Insurgency operation led by the formidable General Gerald Templer, after whom this depot is named. The CT, or Communist Terrorists, didn't have sufficient support from the local people, therefore this campaign didn't fulfil the three requisites of Scotch John's dictum, and therefore was beaten, although that is arguable.

If you want another example of not having enough support from the local people, look at Che Guevara's abortive operation in Bolivia, in which he died."

She paused so they could absorb this.

"Compare these to the Provisional Irish Republican Army or PIRA. Their terrorist campaign fulfils the three requisites and, therefore, they can't be beaten."

"Then how do we stop them?" someone asked.

"There are two options," Dante said. "Firstly, we can kill everyone in Northern Ireland i.e. we commit genocide, or we change at least one of the three factors stated in Scotch John's dictum."

"I'll go for genocide," called out Peter, which got a bit of a laugh.

Dante smiled. "It's not that easy, unless you're Genghis Khan. Genocide is not really an option, so we have to try to knock away one of the three legs instead."

"How would you do that in Northern Ireland?" Mackenzie asked.

"Reunite the country," said Dante. "Take away their cause."

"Wouldn't that just lead to Protestant extremism?" asked Jon.

"Yes," admitted Dante. "But it would resolve Republican terrorism. I never said it would be easy. But back to the original question about communist terrorists. There are already indications that they have simply ceased to exist. They've no longer got a cause because communism is no longer seen as a viable concept. So, there you go."

"So, why do we carry on in Northern Ireland if we can't win?" asked Mackenzie, who had obviously been thinking of the various tours of the province that he had done.

Dante gave him a sympathetic look. "We do what we're told to do by our commanders, who do what they're told to do by our political masters."

"Shit!" muttered Mackenzie, almost under his breath.

"If you don't like it, become a politician," said Dante. "That's the only way to change things."

"Wow! That was a bit more interesting," exclaimed Peter later on in the bar that night.

"Yes. It's better than writing bloody stupid reports," agreed Mackenzie. "I still don't know if I want to do Security though."

"Time will tell," agreed Peter.

"Right," said Sergeant Knight, enthusiastically. "My favourite toy: the Manifoil Mark IV Security combination lock."

The class let out a collective groan as Knight whipped off a cloth from a box-like shape on the table at the front of the room, as if he was a famous prestidigitator instead of an Intelligence Corps Sergeant.

"I'm sure you've all seen a spy film where someone breaks into a safe by twirling the dial while listening intently to the noises made by the mechanism levers," he said, happily. "Wrong! It is actually quite difficult to open a safe, even if you know the combination and you're not under any pressure. I knew a regular Intelligence Corps Staff Sergeant who couldn't do it if anyone was watching him. It's a bit like going for a piss in a public toilet, I suppose.

Safes are generally made of thick steel plate with internal hinges and a Security lock. The *only* approved one for such things is the Manifoil Mark IV Security combination lock. The lock is a fairly basic device, but it has a three-figure combination, made up of three sets of double-digit figures, and is considered to be very secure.

The manufacturer's setting is forty, fifty, sixty, and you are supposed to change it as soon as you bring it into service. To open it, you turn the dial clockwise, going through the line marked on the front, four times, stopping on forty. This is after turning it at least five times to scramble the combination. With me so far? Good, it gets worse.

You then turn the dial three times anticlockwise, going through the line, stopping on fifty. Then, twice clockwise, going through the line, stopping on sixty. And finally, once anticlockwise, through the line, stopping on zero, twenty-five, or seventy-five, depending on where the lock was located in the safe. Then you open the safe? you ask. No. You've got to turn the dial a quarter-turn clockwise for it to open. This is where you find out if you've been accurate enough. If you stopped halfway between numbers, the safe won't open and you have to go through the whole rigmarole again."

Knight then got the recruits to take a Manifoil Mark IV dial mounted in a wooden frame back to their desks to play with for a while, so that they could get accustomed to it.

"It is part of your A3 trade test to open one of these things, and you have fifteen minutes in which to do it, which sounds fine, until you actually try," said Knight. "Imagine doing it when, if you get caught, you could be jailed or even killed, and you'll understand why spy films are a load of bollocks.

It is the responsibility of the local regular Int Corps Security section to deal with any problems that another unit might have with their combination safes or Box Document Security, known as BDS, and any of you who find yourself attached to a Security section might be tasked with going to help. Your credibility will be on the line if you can't do it," he concluded.

"Fuck me, I'm fucking fucked," complained Peter. "I just couldn't get the fucking thing to open."

He was drowning his sorrows in the NAAFI after a frustrating afternoon with the Manifoil Mark IV Security combination lock.

"You need to relax and take it easy," said Jon.

"If you fail the test, do you fail Security?" he asked, plaintively.

"I wouldn't have thought so. It's only one part of the course," said Jon, although he wasn't certain on the matter.

"Ask Sergeant Knight next time you see him," someone else added.

"I found it quite easy, surprisingly enough," said Paul 'Biff' Dobson.

Ever since he had passed the CFT, Biff seemed to have turned a corner and now didn't really merit his nickname, although he might have to live with it for the rest of his career.

"I think it's one of those things that you can either do straightaway or you have to practice like hell," added Jon. "You remember what Sergeant Knight said about the man not being able to open it if someone was watching? It's a bit like that."

"I fucking hope so," moaned Peter.

"It's a bit like driving," added Jon.

"I'm not very good at that, either," lamented Peter.

Jon had had the first of his driving lessons and was pleasantly surprised at how easy it was. He had passed his motorbike test, using a friend's 125cc Suzuki, six weeks after getting his licence, but hadn't got around to passing his car test as he either hadn't had the time, or the money, or both.

His only real problem was being able to judge the width of the vehicle. When he had been a despatch rider in London, he had removed one of the wing mirrors from his machine as this allowed you to get through narrower gaps. He had been able to judge the gap between two cars driving side by side sufficiently to overtake both by driving up the middle of them. The police probably wouldn't have approved of the manoeuvre, but it was standard practice for despatch riders in those days.

He had been allocated ten hours of lessons and given a slot for his driving test. He was quite confident that he would get through it by Christmas. He had found out that anyone struggling or who looked like ten hours of lessons wouldn't be enough to get them through the test (which appeared to be most of the non-driving recruits) would be sent on an intensive two-week course with the driving test at the end. Those who had already passed would have two weeks of adventurous training, and it had been suggested that a skiing trip was in the offing, which made it a bit of an incentive to get through.

The car lurched forward and stalled as Linda once again, unsuccessfully, tried to pull away from the kerb.

"No, no, no!" shouted the instructor. "Gently with the clutch, *gently*."

Linda was miserable. She didn't like cars and had no interest in learning to drive one. In fact, she had no real interest in anything at the moment. She had thought that things would calm down and she could forget the incident with Cazanoe, but she kept seeing him around the camp and it brought it all back in vivid detail. She had taken to drinking to try to get to sleep, but it meant that she had a hangover most mornings and couldn't really concentrate on her studies. It was lucky that there were so many recruits in the squad and that the likes of Jon, Mich and Jock MacKenzie stood out and, had she been aware, took a lot of the flak for the other less able members of the course.

She had tried approaching Tony, but he had avoided being alone with her, so she couldn't get to talk to him about what had happened. She was also worried because she had missed a period and was terrified in case she was pregnant. The only people she could talk to were Donna and Sonia, but they were often on different syndicates or were doing other things, and she needed to speak to someone *now*.

She tried again and, this time, managed to pull away from the kerb and carry on with her driving lesson.

The MLAT, or Modern Language Aptitude Test, was a test designed to see if recruits were suited to learning foreign languages. This was essential for any recruit who planned to go to 14 Signal Regiment, or possibly become an interpreter, and the recruits sat the test one afternoon after a morning of drill and weapons handling. Sergeant Thompson, the Pioneer Corps drill Sergeant, took them through the format of the passing out parade that they would, hopefully, be a part of on Corps Day on 15 July 1990.

Jon attempted the test but found it was completely beyond him. He had always had an interest in languages but had never really had any skill at learning them. He had hated French at school (or rather, he hated the way that French was taught) and had given it up as soon as possible. He had had to do a language to balance his science O-levels, so he had chosen Latin. He had managed to scrape a C pass, although he couldn't for the life of him work out how he'd managed it.

He looked around the classroom and noted that a few people seemed to be struggling; at least it wasn't just him, then. Once the test was over, they were given a break while the overseer, an Intelligence Corps WO2 from the Defence Special Signals School (DSSS, known as 'D triple S'), marked the results.

They stood in small groups outside the building, where those that wanted to could smoke. Jon had never understood how so many fag ends could appear when you were on cleaning detail, when everyone who smoked either took their fag ends with them or put them in the sand-filled containers that were sometimes provided.

"Languages aren't for me," he said to the group in general.

"Same here," agreed Peter.

"I thought it was all right, myself," said Donna. "I've always wanted to do a language."

"Good with your tongue, are you?" leered Peter.

Donna gave him a look. "No. I'm not a cunning linguist, like you," she retorted, to general laughter.

Peter reddened and left the group.

"Actually, I think I might like to go to 14 Sigs," admitted Donna.

"Speak to Mich," said Jon. "He knows a bit about it."

"Thanks. I might just do that."

"What about you?" Jon asked Sonia.

"No. It's not really my thing, either," she said.

"There seems to be plenty of choice," remarked Jon.

"Yes. We've got the Imagery Analysis test to do sometime, too," agreed Donna.

"Combat Int for me, I think," said Mackenzie. "At least I understand what that's all about."

The recruits were already starting to get an idea about where they wanted to go after basic training. They hadn't started the Combat Intelligence phase yet, but from what people like Mackenzie had said, it appealed to Jon, although he didn't really mind what he ended up doing.

The results of the MLAT test weren't really surprising. You knew if you could do it or not instantly, and those like Jon who had struggled, weren't really disappointed to find that they weren't being recommended to join DSSS. It didn't really seem like Jon's cup of tea, although he respected anyone who, like Donna, fancied it. It was reputed that linguists would get a pay rise due to the extra skills, but it would take more than that to persuade Jon to spend his life interpreting voice intercepts.

CHAPTER 15

"Well done, Private Comyn. You've passed your driving test," said the instructor.

"Thank you, sir," said Jon, breathing a sigh of relief.

It wasn't that the test was particularly difficult; Jon had driven a car before, although he vividly remembered losing control and ending up crashing through a set of bushes when he had been driving down a rutted dirt road in Zimbabwe. It was more that it would be embarrassing to have to tell everyone that he'd failed the test. In the event it had gone smoothly and, by accident rather than design, he had pulled in more than 50m from the corner at the end. (He had only remembered that he should do this when the instructor had asked him how far from the corner he was.)

He got out of the car and wiped his sweaty hands on his trousers. One more hurdle surmounted. It was a bonus that he now had a full driving licence. His mother had a licence that allowed her to drive just about anything, including a traction engine. She had been given it at the end of her service during the Second World War as a sort of thank you. Not that she would ever drive a traction engine – or a motorbike, for that matter – but she could have done had she so wished. Now, though, even if he left the army immediately, without doing anything more, he would have gained something useful from it. Apart from the experience, that is.

"How'd it go?" asked Sergeant Knight when he got back to the classroom.

"Passed, Sergeant," Jon announced with a big smile.

"Good, good. Well done," said Knight. "Can you just take the minibus back to the carpool, since you can now drive?"

I might have known, thought Jon, taking the keys and going outside to look for 'the beast'. That was what the course minibus was known as because it was a beast to drive. The clutch was shot to hell and had a tendency to lurch forward if you let it out too quickly. To make it even worse, it was parked in an impossible position, wedged into a corner between two other vehicles. Jon had to do a twenty-something-point turn to get it out and was sweating profusely by the time he did.

I'm going to need a drink after this one.

By the time he got back, the others had returned from their tests. Peter had failed his as his foot had slipped off the clutch as he was trying to do his hill start. It hadn't helped that they had been wearing army boots, which made foot control a lot more difficult. He was lucky that he hadn't hit anything, but it meant that he would have to attend the two-week driving course instead of ten days of skiing in Scotland.

Donna had passed with flying colours, demonstrating, once again, her competence and ability. Paul 'Biff' Dobson had also had no problems and sat, rather smugly, with a small smile on his face.

The following week was taken up with Christmas parties as the festive season was upon them. The upshot of this was that they had to do a fair amount of extra guard duty as there were dos in both the officers' and Warrant Officers'/Sergeants' messes.

On the weekend before the Christmas break, the latter's mess was used for the Territorial Army Intelligence Corps Warrant Officers'/Sergeants' mess function. The TA started arriving on Friday night, as they were holding a training weekend with the party on the Saturday night.

"They're not going to get much done on the Sunday, are they?" someone commented, which led to a discussion about TA and their effectiveness, or lack of.

Jon was amazed at how old some of them were or seemed to be. He was responsible for checking MoD Form 90s (the army ID card) and some of them were difficult to reconcile with the real-life faces of the personnel he was checking. The TA Intelligence Corps was one of the very few units in the army that was issued with its ID cards on a permanent basis. Normally, TA would be issued them where necessary and then hand them back in at the end of the exercise, or whatever deployment they had been on, but the TA Intelligence Corps were trusted to look after theirs.

"Thank you, sir," said Jon, handing back the ID card.

It was impossible to tell a person's rank from their MoD 90 except that a soldier's army number had eight numerals and an officer's, five. Jon thought about a time when he had heard someone say I am not a number, as if it dehumanised someone, but an army number is unique to the soldier; it is kept for life and never forgotten. Jon's mother could still remember her WRAF number from the Second World War.

"Thank you, Corporal," said the car's occupant, wrongly assuming that Jon must be at least Lance Corporal or Corporal because he was Intelligence Corps.

Corporal, thought Jon. *Yes, that sounds nice.*

He saw no other sign of the TA members until they drove away on Sunday morning, many of them looking worse for wear.

There were only a couple of days left before they broke for Christmas leave.

One or two recruits, like Mich and Jock Mackenzie, had their own vehicles and left under their own steam, but the majority got shuttled to Ashford Railway Station for the train to London. A group of them hit the bar at King's Cross while they waited for their respective trains, while those who came from London or surrounding areas disappeared off to the tube or local stations.

"I thought you lived in London?" said Jon to Steve, after he had come back to the table with a pint of lager.

"I do, but I'm in no rush to get home," said Steve. "I'll catch the tube when everyone else has gone."

"It's going to be strange not to see you lot in the morning," said Peter, already halfway through a pint of some fizzy brown liquid, which Jon assumed was beer.

"Yes. I'll miss you," said Donna.

"Really?" asked Peter, hopefully.

"Only if you don't aim at him," added someone else, to a round of applause.

"Where are you going?" Jon asked Donna.

"Newcastle, first."

"And after?" he prompted.

"A bog-awful place called Bishop Auckland."

"I know Bishop Auckland."

"Really?"

"Yes. My brother and I were almost killed there on a cycling holiday, years ago. He was sixteen and I was fourteen. We were trying to get to York," he reminisced. "It had been raining and our brakes failed as we were coming into the town. There was this huge hill with a single road going over a bridge and a Pickfords lorry coming over it. I still don't know how we managed to get passed it."

"So, you really like the place, then?" she asked, with a smile.

Jon laughed.

Jon was the only one who was going further north than Newcastle, and the effects of the journey and the lager were beginning to affect him as the train pulled into Waverley Station. It was already dark, even though it was only just after 1500, and a cold drizzle was beginning to fall – dreich they called it in Scotland. It was a beautifully onomatopoeic word that perfectly captured the damp misery of the day. It was no wonder that the Scots drank so much – who in their right mind would want to be outside when they could be in a nice, warm pub?

He climbed the flight of steps leading up from the station to Prince's Street, passing the shop where he had bought his first sheath knife at the age of fourteen. It was a lovely thing, with a leather-bound handle and a slim blade that was slightly curved at the tip. It had *I cut my way* engraved on it and Jon wondered how he remembered such small details; he hadn't seen it for years. He wondered if it was still somewhere at his parents' house. He would have a look, if he remembered. Jon caught the number eleven bus from the stop outside the station, which went all the way to Morningside, and got off outside The Canny Man's Pub. Its proper name was The Volunteer Arms, and it had a kneeling rifleman as part of its sign. His parents lived just around the corner, in Nile Grove, which his sister and her husband called 'the pyramids'.

His parents were in the lounge, and he could see them through the bay window as he went through the front gate. It looked warm and comfortable, and he was looking forward to a cup of tea.

Two weeks later, he retraced his steps and found himself waiting at Ashford Station for transport to Templer Barracks. He recognised the familiar faces of squad members as they made their way to the grey minibus, and he recalled the difference between this and the first time that he came to Ashford Station, which was only just over four months ago. It seemed like an awful lot longer and it was now almost like coming home. He had a sudden flashback to Sandhurst and how much he had hated the place, whereas this was so different.

Odd, he thought, *but not surprising.*

These were his friends and colleagues, whereas there was now no one from the Sandhurst days whom he kept in contact with. Even Kevin, his Zimbabwean friend, had gone his separate way.

His room was warm and still had the faint smell of mould that it had had when they had first moved in. He was the first to arrive and took the opportunity to unpack his kit and play the music he liked, rather than what his roommates thought of as music.

They kicked off the New Year with a lecture on sabotage.

"Sabotage is the denial of resources by means of physical damage or destruction of material and can, on occasion, include assassination," quoted Sergeant Dante.

She went on to say that James Bond was 'licensed to kill', and by killing an important member of an organisation you can, in effect, sabotage it. The word sabotage comes from the French Revolution when saboteurs would throw their shoes (sabots) into the moving parts of a machine to stop it working.

This was the sort of thing that the Special Air Service Regiment (SAS) were intended for – blowing up enemy airfields behind the lines, and that sort of thing.

This led to a discussion about the SAS and the Iranian Embassy siege, and how the SAS were generally not very good at surveillance. They tended to stand out, looking like stereotypes of themselves in their jeans, sweatshirts and desert boots to go along with their Frank Zappa moustaches.

The weather turned colder as January progressed and outside PT gave way to gym work. It was also almost impossible to do drill on an ice-covered parade square and so, reluctantly on Sergeant Thompson's behalf, drill was shelved.

Sergeant Knight had taken them through both the principals of physical Security and the practical aspects such as Security surveys and report writing. They had done a number of visits to Key Points (KPs) to see for themselves the numerous issues that physical Security raised in the design and use of various types of Security devices. Key Points were locations of a strategic importance that were considered vital to the defence of the realm. He assured them all that they had passed the practical element of the Security phase, and all that was left was the written paper, which they would take at the end of February.

It was lightly snowing, and the parade square was covered in a soft, white sheet. There was one set of footprints cutting straight across it, and Jon wondered what the repercussions would have been had someone dared to do that at Sandhurst.

They would have had the whole course out, sweeping the area, and everyone put on show parade, or some other such nonsense, he thought.

Why was it that Regimental Sergeant Majors seemed to think that the parade square belonged to them, and that no one was allowed to walk on it but them?

Sergeant Knight and Sergeant Dante were, unusually, combining their efforts with a visit to the FAWG site. No one seemed to be able to say for certain what FAWG actually meant, but Knight said it was the Forcible Attack Working Group and they took his word for it. Whatever it meant, it was the place where physical Security equipment like walls, windows, etc. were tested to destruction by a team from the SAS, who apparently went at everything with a chainsaw. The record for resistance seemed to be seven seconds. Jon couldn't help thinking that it would have been a pretty noisy seven seconds.

Knight explained that most physical Security measures were merely designed to buy time until a guard force could respond, and that the best site security was actually provided by a person with a dog, the principal being that the human could do the thinking but the dog, being unaware of the threat, would provide protection and give the human confidence.

Army attack dogs were specially trained and as long as they didn't get bored, which apparently they could in as little as twenty minutes, were excellent for guard duty. The downside was that because they were attack trained, they were unable to be used as either pets or anything else and were put down after two years. That seemed a bit harsh to Jon as it wasn't the dog's fault, but he supposed that you couldn't have savage dogs on the loose.

After the visit, the squad went back to the classroom to get warm, and they had a lecture on defence in depth. This was illustrated by a series of concentric circles, with the thing to be protected at the centre and protective measures written in the circles around it.

A bit like the nine circles of hell, mused Jon.

Initially, the protection was all physical, like the Box Document Security (BDS) or Security cabinets or safes, with, of course, the squad's favourite, the Manifoil Mark IV combination lock. After that, it was about doors, windows, etc., then walls, gates and lighting, followed by CCTV, guards, etc. Finally, regulations and Security protocols, and finishing off with the Official Secrets Act and other government legislation.

All these measures were designed to ensure Security, they were told, and it was the Security section's job to make sure that any breach of security was investigated and measures recommended to prevent further breaches.

It all seemed quite simple when described in that manner, and all the recruits understood it, even if they didn't really want to have to be in a Security section when it would be their responsibility.

The day of the trade test arrived, and the squad waited nervously for Sergeants Knight and Dante to appear, but instead, Captain Case and the CSM WO2 Callahan came in.

They distributed the papers, and when everyone had the single sheet face-down in front of them, Captain Case looked at her watch.

"All right. You have two and a half hours, starting now," she said, as if it was a race and not a written exam.

They all hurriedly turned over their papers and scanned the questions.

"Don't forget to put your name, rank and number at the top of the paper," Case called, and then sat down at the desk, scanning the room.

For what? Jon briefly wondered, and then turned back to the exam.

It was all handwritten and although two and a half hours seemed like a long time, the Sergeants had warned them not to waste any of it, as recruits often ran out of time before finishing the paper.

"If you can't answer a question immediately, leave it and go back to it, if you have time," Knight had advised.

Jon swiftly read through the questions and then went back to the top. He picked a question that he knew the answer to and started scribbling.

Two and a half hours later, he was still writing furiously.

"Five minutes to go," Captain Case called out. "I would suggest finishing up."

What seemed like mere seconds later, she spoke again.

"Time's up, pens down."

They all put their pens down as instructed, apart from one recruit who had already finished, but whether that was because he had actually finished answering the questions or that he had given up, no one knew but him.

"Fucking ran out of fucking time," snarled Peter.

They were, once again, sitting in the bar drowning their sorrows or congratulating themselves, depending on how their individual exams had gone.

"I didn't think it was too bad," said Donna, happily.

"That's 'cause you're good at Security," grunted Peter.

Donna shrugged.

"Don't worry, Pete," said Jon. "I think most of us ran out of time. I just can't write that fast."

They started to discuss the questions, as people who have just sat an exam have a tendency to do. Jon knew from his student days that this wasn't necessarily the best thing to do as he kept hearing things that he had forgotten to put down or had not remembered in the first place.

"Shit, shit, shit," was the most common phrase as the group talked over the paper. The only ones who seemed completely happy were Donna and Steve, who corrected the others when they had made a mistake.

"How come you're so good at this, Steve?" someone asked.

"I don't know," he admitted. "It all just seems to stay in my head."

"Ah well, it's done now and it's too late to do anything about it. Drink, anyone?" said Jon, with an air of resignation.

"When do you think they'll give us the results?" asked Paul.

"It probably won't be too long," said Mich. "We've only got a few weeks before we're supposed to start Combat Intelligence."

"Can you do it again if you fail it?" someone else asked.

"Yes. You get two attempts, so I've heard," said Jock. "Although you'll be doing Combat Int as well."

"What happens if you fail it a second time?"

"From what I've heard, you either get kicked out or you get back-squadded, depending on how badly you fail and whether they like you or not," replied Jock.

"OK. Let's get drunk."

"What's wrong with you lot?" snarled Corporal Cazanoe the next morning as he took the squad for a run.

There were a lot of pale faces, and a few recruits seemed to be on the verge of throwing up. He took them out to the edge of the training area and then, looking at his watch, said, "OK. Own best effort back to the gym. You're in your own time now. Go!"

The stragglers were in danger of missing breakfast, which was a punishable offence for recruits as it was considered to be a parade. Cazanoe had done it on purpose to get as many of them in trouble as possible. He seemed to be getting worse, his mood swings coming more rapidly, and Jon wondered if that was indeed down to steroids or whether he was just becoming even more of a bastard, if that was possible.

Fortunately for the slow ones, there was no record of who actually went to breakfast. The catering staff didn't care, and the duty student was one of the recruits, so he was hardly likely to tell on his colleagues, although Jon had come across people who would have done.

"Trained soldiers can turn up to work at whatever time is designated by the OC," Jon told them at breakfast, "but recruits are normally expected to parade at a set time, which is considered to be the start of the working day. This is supposed to instil a sense of timing in us, but wouldn't work outside a barracks environment, where the working day can, and often does, start at any time, day or night."

The lessons that morning were weapons handling and a first aid refresher.

"There is a thing called 'skill fade'," the instructor told them, "where you tend to start to forget training if it is not regularly used or practiced. New drills are constantly being brought in, partially as high-ranking officers use this as a means of appearing to be efficient in an effort to gain further promotion. This is nothing new.

"We trained hard but it seemed that every time we were beginning to form up into teams we were reorganized. I was to learn later in life that we tend to meet any new situation by reorganizing, and what a wonderful method it can be for creating the illusion of progress while actually producing confusion, inefficiency, and demoralization. Petronius Arbiter 27-66 AD," he quoted to emphasise his lecture.

The squad still hadn't received the results of the Security trade test when the list for those attending the two-week driver training course and those going skiing were promulgated. Almost half the course still had to pass their driving tests as there had been a limited number of places, and those deemed most likely to pass had been put forward first. That meant that fifteen recruits were eligible to go, which left a problem, as each minibus had to have a member of the directing staff with them, so only a maximum of fourteen recruits could go.

Mich volunteered to stay behind as he had an old knee injury and didn't want to hazard further damage that might cause him to fail the CFT. Jock Mackenzie also pulled out. He had decided that the Corps wasn't for him, and he had asked for a transfer back to the infantry. It was suspected that he had failed his Security paper and didn't want to admit it, but unless they broke into the OC's office and stole the exam papers, they would probably never know.

The fifteen drivers would go to Aldershot for the two-week

course and the others would head up to Rothiemurchus Lodge to go Skiing in the Cairngorms. Captain Case and Corporal Cazanoe were the directing staff or the skiing trip, which displeased the recruits no end when they were informed.

They were due to take two minibuses, and Jon volunteered to drive one as he knew the roads up to Aviemore. Steve offered to be the other driver, so he and Jon met up after breakfast at 0700 to do a first parade.

A first parade is the process by which all British Army vehicles are supposed to be checked over every morning to ensure that the vehicle is roadworthy, and the paperwork is correctly filled in. It is easier to do with two people as it can be extremely difficult for one person to check things like rear brake lights whilst they are pressing the brake pedal.

There is a set format for the first parade with a list of things to be checked: lights, brakes, fuel, oil and water, and the drivers' work ticket. If the work ticket is not filled in, then it negates the driver's insurance. It is amazing how many times they are left unsigned.

Steve and Jon shared the task and then loaded their kit and waited for the rest of the team. They had signed out skis and skiing gear from the stores on a MoD form 1033 and now they stowed them on the roof racks and at the back of the minibuses. As the recruits showed up, they stashed their luggage and allocated them seats so that when Case appeared they were ready to go. Or would have been, if Cazanoe hadn't been missing. They hung about, waiting, until Case lost her temper and sent one of the male recruits to find him. The recruit returned five minutes later, with a dishevelled Cazanoe in tow.

"Sorry, ma'am," he muttered as he stowed his gear.

Case gave him a glare and then ordered everyone onto the minibuses. Jon was in the lead, with Case and Steve following with Cazanoe.

They left Templer Barracks at 0830 instead of 0800 and hit rush hour traffic. Fortunately, they were close to the M2 and were soon heading towards London.

The route was motorway all the way to Glasgow, from where they would join the A9 via Stirling towards Aviemore. There was a turnoff for Rothiemurchus that should be quite easy to find, but then Jon had to locate a small backroad that led to the actual lodge. His plan was to drive for about eight hours and then swap over so that he could have a rest. He would then take over again near Kingussie, so that he would be driving when they came to the turn off for Rothiemurchus. That was the plan, anyway.

"I'll need to swap over drivers at some point so that I can lead the way to Rothiemurchus, as it'll be dark by the time we get there, ma'am," said Jon when Case appeared to have calmed down.

"OK, Private Comyn. Let me know when you want to do it."

"Will do, ma'am," he replied.

Lunch was provided as haversack rations from the cookhouse, and the recruits were given their white cardboard boxes with the standard contents of cheese and ham sandwiches, an apple, a packet of unbranded crisps, a can of unbranded fizzy drink, a packet of custard cream biscuits and a Mars bar.

They would worry about dinner when they got to the lodge, but it would probably consist of fish and chips from Rothiemurchus village or, at worst, they could go into Aviemore, which was a reasonable-sized town.

It started to rain shortly after they left Ashford and didn't let up until they passed Manchester. After that, it was sleeting all the way to Stirling, where it changed to snow. It was dark when they pulled into the petrol station in Perth to fill up the vehicles and change over drivers. It was only about another ninety minutes before they reached Kingussie and Jon took over again. The turnoff was the B970, but it was on the road to Aviemore, so it wasn't difficult to find. The entrance to Rothiemurchus Lodge was a bit harder. Fortunately, the snow had stopped after blanketing everything in white, and there was a full moon, so Jon managed to see the turnoff.

The lodge was ablaze with light as another unit was also using it. They had arrived earlier in the day and had made sure that the heating was on. They worked a deal with the other unit, who were a group of Royal Signals from HQ Army, Scotland, and joined their ration roll, which saved them having to cook for themselves. The cooks were delighted as it meant that they had extra cash to purchase whatever they wanted, and Case was happy not to have the responsibility of organising food for the troops. The Signals had also brought along their own bar and were more than happy to share it with the Intelligence Corps.

After they sorted out their accommodation, they all went down to the bar where a huge log fire was burning and settled themselves down for a few beers.

The Royal Signals turned out to be a section from the Communications Centre (ComCen) (the staff who ran the switchboard) who were doing some adventurous training. There were a mix of civilians and soldiers, men and women. Their OC was a slightly older, female Major and she and Case went off to plan the next few days together, leaving the recruits with the Signals.

"Hi. I'm Jenny," said the red-haired girl running the bar.

"And I'm Rab," added the Royal Signals Lance Corporal who was with her.

"I'm Corporal Cazanoe," he said, trying to intimidate the Signals' troops, who seemed to be in their late teens and early twenties.

"And I'm called RSM," said a cold voice behind him.

Cazanoe went red as he turned to see a burly individual with a WO1 badge on his uniform.

"Oh. Oh, sorry, sir," Cazanoe blustered. "I didn't know we were being informal."

"We don't have to be, Corporal," said the RSM. "It's up to you."

"Oh. Right, sir," he mumbled.

The Regimental Sergeant Major swept the room with his gaze. "We can all use first name terms here, as long as it doesn't get abused. Understood?"

"Yes, sir," came a chorus of replies.

"Very good. Carry on."

He left the room.

"Tony," said Cazanoe to Jenny and Rab, trying to cover his embarrassment.

"Right, what do you want, *Tony*?" asked Rab.

"Uh, I'll have a Becks, thanks," said Cazanoe. Taking his beer, he moved away and sat near the fire.

"Sorry about that," apologised Jon as he introduced himself.

"That's OK," said Rab. "What's his problem?"

"Apart from being a prick, you mean?" said Paul, coming up behind him. "He's an AIPT."

Jenny and Rab both laughed.

"Right. That explains it," said Rab.

They sat, relaxing with their beers, until Case came back in a short while later.

"Breakfast at 0800 tomorrow, briefing at 0900 in here. Pass it around, will you, and I'll see you tomorrow."

"Yes, ma'am," replied Jon.

CHAPTER 16

The car lurched forward as Sue tried to release the clutch.

"Gently does it," said the instructor, smiling across at Sue. "It isn't a race, you know."

Sue relaxed a bit. She was used to the Intelligence Corps driving instructor, who made her nervous, but the Corporal from the Royal Corps of Transport was a lot more laid back and made her feel comfortable.

"OK," the Corporal continued. "Drive up to the end of the road and do a three-point turn."

"What if I hit the wall as I'm turning?" Sue asked, tentatively.

"Ha!" snorted the Corporal. "It's an army vehicle. We won't make you pay for it."

Sue smiled at this and managed to do the three-point turn without any problem.

"Just take it easy. There's no rush," he encouraged. "Your test isn't until the end of the week."

Sue felt a flood of anxiety at the thought of the test, but Corporal Cowan's patient manner helped calm her nerves.

They had been at Aldershot for a week now and had all been pleasantly surprised by the relaxed attitude of the RCT instructors. They were told that the purpose of the two-week course was to teach them to drive and to get them to *pass* their tests at the end, not to fail them.

"If you don't pass the test, then it's our failure, not yours," they were told at the start of the course. "We're the professionals, after all."

They were allowed to drink but were advised not to overdo it as it would affect their driving the following morning.

"How much can you drink and still be safe to drive?" they were asked.

"Two pints," said one of the male recruits, confidently.

The instructor smiled. "Wrong! The answer is zero. There is no hard and fast amount that you can drink and still be safe. It depends on the person and the particular circumstances."

"What about the eighty milligram limit?" someone asked.

"That totally depends on one's height, weight and sex, and factors like how much you've had to eat," explained the instructor. "Also, you may be under the legal limit, but that doesn't necessarily mean that you are safe to drive. It also depends on experience and the road conditions."

The course attendees sat quietly, taking that in.

"So, if you are going to drive, it's best that you don't drink at all," finished the instructor, with a grin that acknowledged that was unlikely to happen.

"I heard that having a small drink before your test would calm your nerves," said Peter.

"Was that the man in the pub who told you that?" asked the instructor, to universal laughter.

"No," he continued, when the laughter had died down.

"Don't do that. If you have the slightest whiff of alcohol on your breath on test day, you won't be allowed to take the test, and you'll fail the course. OK?"

"Yes, sir," they all replied.

The army cooks had pulled out all the stops. The sausages even tasted like they were made of real meat and the bacon was more meat than fat. Jon was sitting at the bench tables in the dining area of the lodge, enjoying a proper cooked English breakfast.

Rothiemurchus Lodge was a well-built complex that could cater for large groups of service personnel. The extensive kitchen was attached to an eating area just off the main recreation room, which was furnished with a large open fire and a small television. It was a tri-service establishment, which meant that it could be used by all three services, although it would only be the Intelligence Corps and the Signals unit using it for the next two weeks.

The recruits had all piled in at exactly 0800 as they were used to arriving at the time they were told, but the Signals (some of whom were civilians) sauntered in, in dribs and drabs. The two groups were very different, and the disparity was obvious. The Signals were loud and boisterous, as if this was a holiday rather than training which to them, it was. They were all trained and qualified personnel doing their jobs, and the civilian element made them look like a normal group of workers rather than a regimented military unit.

Is this what it's like in a Security section? Jon wondered.

At 0855, the regulation five minutes early, the Intelligence Corps contingent formed up in the recreation room awaiting Captain Case. She arrived at 0900 and told them all to sit down. She went through the list of names and divided the group into two groups, depending on skiing experience.

As a qualified army ski instructor, Case would take the more experienced skiers. The beginners and people like Jon, who had skied once but not for years, would go with the Royal Signals beginners' group. Each day, a few personnel would be designated to help the cooks and then would be allowed to go into Aviemore for some rest and relaxation.

Jon was allocated to drive the minibus, with the Royal Signals RSM as the instructor, while Case took Cazanoe as her driver. That suited Jon perfectly as he hadn't really fancied being stuck with

Cazanoe after he had embarrassed himself in front of the Royal Signals and would probably take it out on the recruits, if he had the chance. It seemed like Case had been informed of the incident, as she gave Cazanoe a slight look of distaste. Jon got Simon to help him with the first parade and then they waited while the Regimental Sergeant Major rounded up his flock.

There were three people from the Signals unit, including the red-haired Jenny who, it turned out, was an ex-Royal Signals Signaller, which was their equivalent of Private, but was now a civilian contractor.

They drove up to the ski slope in Cairngorm and parked the minibuses. Case then took her team to the ski tow and the RSM led his group to the beginners' slope. It was what is known as a green run and is the gentlest slope, the next being blue, then red and finally black, which was only for very experienced skiers like Captain Case and one or two of the others.

Simon was among the group who had never skied before, and the RSM guided them through the process with varying results. They stopped for lunch at 1200 and went to one of the resort's cafés.

"You can put in a CILOR claim for this," said the Regimental Sergeant Major, as they ate.

"What's that, sir?" Jon asked. The RSM looked over at him.

"You can call me Bill when we're in a public setting. For security reasons, you understand?"

"Yes, Bill," said Jon.

Wow! I never expected to call an RSM by his first name, thought Jon.

"CILOR is Cash in Lieu of Rations," explained Bill. "You are entitled to lunch, but since that hasn't been provided, you can claim the cash instead."

"How do we do that?" asked Simon.

"Your Captain can either put in a collective claim when you get back to base, or you can fill in a 1771."

This earned him some blank looks.

"1771?" someone asked.

"MoD Form 1771 is the army expenses claim form," said Bill. "I'm surprised you lot haven't been told about them."

"We're still in recruit training," said Jon.

"Ah! That explains it," nodded Bill. "You'll need to know about them if you're going to a Security section. Who knows, some of you might end up at HQ Army, Scotland."

"What, in the actual headquarters?" exclaimed Steve.

"Not the HQ itself, but there's 29 Security section at Cragiehall," replied Bill. "We run the ComCen there."

"Do you all live there?" enquired Steve. "On the base?"

"I live in Edinburgh," put in Jenny.

"Oh! Whereabouts?" asked Jon.

"Albert Street, just off Leith Walk."

"I know it well," said Jon. "There's a pub at the end of the road that sells Bass beer."

"No. That's Robbie's Bar on Iona Street. It's the next one down."

"You could be right," admitted Jon. "It's been a few years since I've been there."

"Do you come from Edinburgh?" she asked. "You don't have a Scottish accent."

"No. I originally come from Middlesbrough, but I lived in Edinburgh for a fair while. My old man was an English teacher."

"That explains it, then."

After lunch, they went back to the slopes and did another couple of hours, before meeting up with the other team and heading back to the lodge. Although the weather was sunny and clear, it started to get dark at about 1530 and the slopes closed well before darkness fell. Jon cleaned out the minibus and made sure it was ready for the next day and then went for a snooze before dinner. The rooms held four double bunks, but there was enough accommodation that they didn't actually need to cram everyone in, and Jon had ended up with a room to himself. The adventurous training was going pretty well.

I just hope it stays like this, he thought.

"You can drive a bit faster, if you like," said Corporal Mike Bunyon, Sue's driving instructor.

Sue gently put her foot on the accelerator and brought the speed up to just over thirty miles an hour.

"That's better. Don't be afraid of a bit of speed," said Bunyon.

"But don't I have to obey the limit?" Sue asked, while trying to concentrate on her driving.

"Yes. But sometimes you need a bit of speed to get you out of trouble," Bunyon explained.

"Oh. OK," replied Sue.

"If in doubt, drop a gear and be ready to accelerate," he continued. "You'll get used to it. Don't worry."

The recruits were in the final week of the course, with some of them already having taken their tests. The results were very promising, and all those who had attempted the test, including Peter, had passed without any problems. The recruits had the opportunity to go on leave if they passed, but all had decided to stay with their colleagues to give them moral support. Those that had were being allowed to drive military vehicles like Land Rovers and were thoroughly enjoying themselves.

Only Sue, Linda and one other male recruit were left to pass, out of the fifteen who had started the course, and it was a matter of pride now that they would all do so before the two weeks were up.

"OK. Brake when I hit the dashboard," came the command.

Sue slowed slightly, but not too much, and Bunyon tapped the dashboard with his clipboard.

Sue hit the brakes and brought the car to a stop.

"Good. Well done! I think you're ready to do your test."

Sue smiled, proud of herself for getting this far, although she was also incredibly nervous of making a mess of it.

"I'll put you in for tomorrow afternoon," continued Bunyon. "We'll do a refresher lesson in the morning and then you can pass your test in the afternoon."

"Thanks, Corporal," she said, happily.

Jon and Simon found themselves on the roster for kitchen duties and Rest and Recuperation, better known as R&R. The duties were hardly onerous, consisting of helping with the washing up and mopping the floor after the cooks made breakfast. There was no formal lunch, so the only other task was a bit more washing up after dinner, and that was that.

Two of the cooks were heading into Aviemore to pick up fresh rations, so Jon and Simon hitched a lift and went to see what the town had to offer.

Aviemore was beginning to become a centre for Scottish skiing, which had started in the early sixties. Before that, no one had really considered Scotland as an alternative to the French Alps or Norway, and the snow tended to be much wetter than in the Norwegian resorts, but it was a damned sight cheaper to get there.

The town was still little more than the main street, although it was definitely expanding as the resorts increased. Simon decided that he wanted a proper haircut, so they found a barber off a backstreet, and Jon sat and waited while the barber did his business. The depot hairdresser wasn't that bad.

Not like the one we used to get at Sandhurst, thought Jon.

He remembered once timing him cutting the Officer Cadet's hair as if it had been a race. He seemed to recall that the record was twenty seconds for a cut, and that the barber used to leave his trademark of a small bald patch on the back of the head. Although, for 20p per cut, even in those days, you couldn't expect much better.

After that, they found a bookshop and split up to browse the shelves. Some of the recruits only seemed to be interested in sex and football, but the vast majority had an interest in books and Jon wasn't surprised that Simon shared his liking for reading. Jon toyed with buying a book, but he didn't have much cash on him, so he fought down the impulse. Simon didn't find anything that took his fancy, so they headed back onto the street to see what else Aviemore had to offer.

Unsurprisingly, there was a fairly large outdoor clothing and camping shop and, since it had started to sleet, they went in. Jon had always loved camping gear, ever since he had been a child. His family had never really taken to camping, going for static caravans instead, but Jon loved all the little bits of gear that you could carry, like mini stoves and coffee makers. When he had been in the infantry, he had tried to get a few bits and pieces, like a Teflon-covered frying pan-cum-lid for the army-issue mess tins, but he had found out that they rarely actually used individual equipment. Mostly, they got fed by the Catering Corps, and so it was a bit of an extravagance. He still loved looking through the gear, even though he would probably never use it.

They whiled away a good hour in the camping department before Jon suggested that they go for a coffee. He wasn't hungry enough for lunch, but he fancied a seat and wasn't in the mood for drinking this early. Simon seemed to be happy to follow his lead, which was something that he had noticed about the black-haired recruit. He was definitely a follower rather than a leader. There was nothing intrinsically wrong with this, although Simon almost seemed to be incapable of making a decision on his own.

The coffee was freshly ground and brewed and reminded Jon of when he had gone backpacking at the end of his HND course. He had travelled to the south of Spain and met up with a chef who had worked for Fred and Marsha and was spending the winter camping with his girlfriend.

Marcus, the chef, had had a little coffee maker. He put freshly ground coffee in the bottom, screwed it onto the upper part which contained the water, and then put it on a camping stove to brew. It made a couple of small cups of coffee which were delicious. Mind you, they all used instant coffee in those days, so real coffee was a treat.

He suddenly remembered that Marcus had turned out to be gay. He had also died of cancer some years before. Jon didn't know why this thought came to him out of the blue, but he gave Simon a slightly guilty glance who, fortunately, was looking the other way.

The sleet had got heavier, and they were getting wet by the time they reached the minibus, where the cooks were waiting for them.

"We haven't kept you, have we?" Jon asked.

"No. We've just arrived ourselves," replied one of the cooks.

It looked like they had been in the pub for most of the morning after doing their shopping, and Jon just hoped that the driver wasn't over the limit, but they got back to the lodge without any incidents.

The Royal Signals team was already back from hillwalking, having turned back when it started to sleet. They had been intending to go over the Lairig Ghru, a pass of 835m which runs along a narrow *arête*, but the instructor had decided that it was too dangerous to attempt in the winter, and so they had returned before the weather turned really nasty.

"You've got to watch it," he explained. "Minus two in Scotland is like minus ten in Norway. It's the wet that kills you."

Jon agreed with him entirely. As a teenager, he and his brother used to have a motorcycle run to the Loch Tummel Bridge Hotel in March each year. It was often icily cold, and they would stand by a fire in agony as their fingers and toes defrosted. They hadn't really been able to afford anything better than leather jackets and boots, so it was amazing that they hadn't gone down with hypothermia after some of the runs. Maybe they had and just not realised it. He hadn't heard the term until he joined the army. Before that, you were just fucking cold!

"Some of us are taking a sauna. Do you want to join us?" Jenny asked.

"Sounds good to me," replied Jon. He turned to Simon. "You coming?"

Simon turned red and mumbled something about feeling a bit tired and would give it a miss and then hurriedly disappeared.

Jon went to his room and, wrapping himself in a bath towel, went to the sauna. There were six members of the Royal Signals group with Jenny, and they had already started to pump up the heat. Jon loved dry heat; it reminded him of Africa. Wet heat, like in a Turkish bath, was a different matter. He recalled landing in Lagos, on the way to Harare, where the humidity was in the region of 90%. It had been hellish. He could hardly breathe – and that was late at night, too.

Gradually, the others all succumbed to the heat until it was only Jon and Jenny left.

"If this was Finland, we would run outside, naked," said Jenny with a smile.

"Yes. But here we'd be running into a muddy car park in the sleet," replied Jon.

Jenny laughed at that. "You seem to be able to handle the heat OK."

"I was in Zimbabwe for a while," explained Jon. "It was pretty hot there, most days. I got used to it. How about you?"

"I was an army brat," she said. "We spent a lot of time in Cyprus."

They stayed chatting for a while until it got too hot even for them, and then went for showers in their respective parts of the accommodation. Jenny suggested that Jon should get in touch the next time he was in Edinburgh, and he would definitely consider it.

Linda just couldn't concentrate. She had never really been interested in driving and wouldn't have come on the course if she'd had any choice. The two weeks had felt like an eternity, and she couldn't wait to get it over with. She was the last of the group to do her test and had failed it once already.

The instructors and her colleagues had given her as much support and encouragement as possible, but the pressure just grew with each lesson, and now she was on the final day and knew within herself that she wouldn't pass.

She woke up each morning feeling sick and had actually started to throw up which her roommate put down to nerves, but she knew in her own heart, without having to take the test, that she was pregnant. She came from a strict, religious upbringing and had gone a bit wild with the freedom when she had first arrived at Ashford. Now she was paying the price.

What made it worse was that the only two people that she trusted enough to tell – Donna and Sonia – had both gone skiing, as they had passed their driving tests easily. She burned with shame at the thought of having to tell her parents, knowing what her father's response would be.

Tears rolled down her cheeks as she stalled the car once again.

"Let's stop it there for today," said the instructor, not unkindly. "I don't think you're in the right frame of mind for it."

"Sorry, Corporal," she said, simply.

"It's OK," he replied. "Some people take longer than others to learn to drive. You've got a lot of other things to think about and you've still got time."

She thought about the kit that she had prepared. It was locked away in a secret place in her room, back at Ashford. Once she got back there, she could carry out her plan and it would all be OK.

It was the last day, and a party had been arranged. One of the Royal Signals had brought a cassette deck and they had trawled the group for suitable tapes to play. Some of the slightly more drunken members of the two units were already dancing and Captain Case and the Regimental Sergeant Major had made a tactical withdrawal, leaving the junior ranks to enjoy themselves on their last night at the lodge.

"Fancy a beer, darling?" Cazanoe slurred at Jenny.

"No. I've got one, thanks," replied Jenny, sliding away from his clutches. She went to join a group of the Royal Signals Corporals, who gave Cazanoe a warning look.

"Fucking lesbian," he muttered, and wandered off to try his luck with one of the female recruits.

Jon was helping run the bar as he was driving the following morning and didn't want to do so with a hangover.

"What a thunder cunt!" muttered Steve, under his breath.

Jon was quite surprised. Steve was normally very quiet and wasn't the sort of person to make comments about other members of the Corps, particularly X-rated ones. It just showed how disliked Cazanoe was. Even his usual sycophants seemed to have tired of him.

Or maybe they've finally seen through him? Jon wondered.

"Get me a beer!" Cazanoe ordered Simon, who had the misfortune to be standing near him.

Simon meekly went to the bar and asked for a bottle of Becks.

"Hang on a moment," said Jon, taking a half-empty bottle from the table next to him. He topped it up with water from the sink next to him and gave it to Simon.

"There you go. Free of charge," he said, and gave Simon a wink.

Cazanoe was so drunk he didn't even notice that he had been given a doctored drink. A short while later, he staggered outside and was sick in the car park.

"Well, that was a success," said Jon happily to Simon.

"Awesome!" came the reply.

"Never fuck with the barman," said Steve.

"And don't have the custard at the weekend," added Jon.

"Sorry?" said Simon.

"It's an old story about how they wank into the custard if they have to work the weekend," replied Jon. "I don't know if it's true or not. It might be an urban myth, but I do know that they caught one of the chefs shagging a joint of meat."

"You what?" Steve almost shouted.

"Yes," continued Jon. "This guy would take a frozen joint of meat back to his room and thaw it out on the radiator while he showered. He would then shag it and cook it. He only got caught because someone got jaundice, and they traced it back to him."

"Fuck me!" said Steve.

"I'd rather not, if you don't mind," quipped Jon.

"Christ! I think I'd kill the guy if he'd done that to me," Steve added.

"Yes," agreed Jon. "He was the chef for a Para battalion, and if the Royal Military Police hadn't taken him away, I think they would have killed him."

"God. Makes you think though, doesn't it?" said Steve, speculatively.

"Sure does."

Gradually, people disappeared to bed as the drink and the physical exercise took their toll. Jon washed up as he was going along, and Simon stopped to help him. Jon saw Donna, Sonia and Jenny all leaving together. They had formed a defensive group against Cazanoe, whose behaviour had soured the evening somewhat. Jon wondered if anything would happen about it, but then realised that because he was TA and not regular, there wasn't really much that they could do. It wasn't as if he could be given a poor Annual Confidential Report or, even if he could, what difference would it make?

Eventually, it was just Jon and Simon, and they closed up and turned the music off. The fire was burning low and could be safely left to its own devices.

"One last beer?" suggested Simon.

There were two opened bottles of Becks that would otherwise have to be thrown away.

"Yeah. Why not?"

They took seats next to the fire and watched the glowing embers. There is something magical about a real fire, something that goes back to primeval times. It is no surprise that many believed fire was a portal to another world when one watched flames dancing.

After a while, Simon looked at Jon.

"You know that I'm madly in love with you?" he said.

Jon's heart lurched; this was not what he wanted to hear. He turned to stare at Simon with his mouth open.

"I wish you hadn't said that," he replied, eventually. Simon looked hurt.

"I can't help it," he said. "It's true."

"It might be true, but I'm not gay, Simon," Jon said, as nicely as he could.

"I didn't think you were," said Simon, sadly. "I just thought—"

"You can't think these things," Jon interrupted. "Even if I was gay, it's illegal."

"It shouldn't be," protested Simon.

"That may be so," agreed Jon. "But that's beside the point. It *is* illegal in the army, and there's nothing that you can do about it."

"You can say that again," muttered Simon.

"I'm going to pretend that you never said anything," stated Jon. "It was a drunken joke, right?"

"But—"

"No buts, Simon," said Jon. "Did you not listen to the lecture on levers? You could get blackmailed for this, and if the vetting guys find out, you'll get kicked out. OK?"

"OK," agreed Simon. "I... I think I'll go to bed."

"Good night. See you in the morning," replied Jon.

Simon got up and walked away.

Jon sat staring into the fire.

Why the fuck did he have to pick me? he thought, although maybe it was just as well he had.

There was no way that Jon was going to repeat the conversation to anyone.

It wasn't that he was homophobic. Back when he was a student living in Edinburgh, one of his flatmates had been gay and that wasn't a problem. He knew that plenty of people in the army were also gay, they just didn't admit it. The problem was, as he had told Simon, it was illegal in the army, and Simon's career could be cut short if the wrong person found out.

One thing was for certain, though: Simon's nickname, Raven, proved the old saying 'many a true word is spoken in jest'.

Jon finished his beer and went to bed, troubled.

In the morning, Simon avoided his eye and got on the other minibus. They left at 0900 and drove back through drizzly sleet.

It was a good trip, apart from the ending, thought Jon, as he guided the minibus along Scotland's wet and windy roads.

They halted for lunch at Knutsford Services just outside Manchester, and Jon let Steve take over driving. He sat at the back of the minibus, staring out the window at nothing, until it got too dark to see, and then tried to sleep for the rest of the trip back to Ashford.

They arrived after 2000 and unloaded the kit before heading to the billet.

"We'll clean out the minibuses tomorrow morning," said Captain Case. "After that, you've got the weekend off. Well done, everyone. That was a good trip. Good night."

With that, she was gone.

Jon took the opportunity to spend the weekend in London with his brother, but his heart wasn't really in it, and he used the time to get drunk and to try to forget. It was better than hanging around the barracks, but not much.

CHAPTER 17

Linda felt an overwhelming sense of relief, now that the decision had been made. It was as if a great weight had been lifted off her shoulders and all the pressures that were crushing her had gone away. She actually felt happy for the first time in weeks and felt a small smile on her face as she anticipated a different future.

The recruits had got back from Aldershot early in the morning, cleaned the vehicles and then been given the rest of the day off and told to report to the classroom at 0800 on Monday morning.

Linda had volunteered to do guard duty for one of the other recruits so that the course could go out as one and celebrate the passing of their driving tests. She had watched them happily leave the barracks with big smiles on their faces. She was glad for them, although she knew that her own destiny lay in a different direction.

She wrote the letter explaining her decision and found the package that she had prepared before going on the course. She carefully unwrapped it to make sure that everything she needed was there and then stowed it in the bag she would take on guard duty with her.

She reported to the guard room at 2000 A steady flow of personnel was heading out into Ashford as it was Saturday evening and the pubs and clubs would be full of revellers, even though the weather was getting chilly. It looked like it would be a fine night, perhaps with a light frost in the early hours of the morning.

She spent the first few hours helping with checking people in and out until it was time to go on patrol. She hadn't seen her colleagues return as she had been on sleeping duty. She had slept for the allotted two hours, which were amazing, and she felt totally rested and ready for the task ahead.

"Let's go," said Simon, picking up his SMG.

He had volunteered for guard duty as he hadn't felt like doing anything since he had got back from the adventure training. He was in turmoil, his thoughts running around like headless chickens. He knew in his heart that Jon was right, and that he had a choice of whether to stay in the army and suppress his feelings, or to leave a job that he had come to really enjoy in the hope of finding love that he could express openly.

"You seem a bit distracted. Is everything OK?" Linda asked him as they patrolled along the fence line.

"Yes. I've just got a lot on my mind, you know. Combat Int, and all that," he lied.

"Don't worry, it'll all be fine," she said, happily.

It's all right for you, he thought, bitterly.

They were halfway through the patrol when Linda turned to Simon.

"Sorry, Simon, but I've got to go to the toilet."

"Can't you wait until we get back?" he asked, plaintively.

"No. Sorry. I'm desperate," she said and quickly walked off.

"Fucking great," he muttered to himself. "Now what do I do?"

Linda had picked this point because it wasn't too far from the gym, and she could get into the ladies' toilet there. She would have preferred to carry out the operation in the accommodation, where the light was better, but she didn't want to disturb anyone or have anyone come in while she was doing it. She eased herself through the side door and opened one of the cubicles. She sat down and took out her specially prepared kit from her jacket pocket.

She looked at the shiny new 9mm round that lay in front of her, with its polished brass casing and dull grey tip. She loaded it carefully into the magazine and slotted the black, curved magazine into the housing on the side of the weapon.

Lucky the SMG is short and light, she thought.

She lifted the SMG and, putting it in her mouth, pulled the trigger.

Simon pushed through the door into the guardroom. The guard Corporal looked up from his novel and nodded to him.

Where the hell has Linda got to? he wondered.

He dumped his kit and went into the back room for his two-hour sleeping shift. Thoughts kept churning around in his head and he lay awake for a while until he dropped off to sleep. It seemed like minutes rather than a couple of hours when his alarm clock went off, telling him that his rest period was over. There was still no sign of Linda, but the day shift was coming on and he assumed that she had already been dismissed.

He went to breakfast where a number of white-faced recruits were trying to deal with the effects of excessive drinking from the night before. He sat by himself and went through his options once again as he drank his lukewarm tea.

Was he the only gay person on the course? he wondered. He had heard rumours about one of the Intelligence Corps officers, but he couldn't prove it. *Maybe that was the answer. Maybe Jon was right.*

He finished his breakfast and went to his room. Today was a free day, so he played some music and drifted off to sleep.

Corporal Cazanoe thought that there was a strange smell in the gym, but he didn't recognise it as cordite, and it wasn't until Captain Case came in to do some weight training that they found Linda's body. No one had noticed her absence and, since she had a room to herself, she had no roommate to report her missing.

"Anyone seen Private Marks this morning?" asked the duty student, as the recruits formed up outside the classroom.

None of the female recruits said anything, so Simon piped up.

"She might have gone sick. She wasn't feeling well last night on guard duty."

"Well, she should have told someone," grunted the duty student, unsympathetically.

They filed into the classroom and sat down, waiting for the staff to appear. It was Major Elswick with an ashen-faced Captain Case who eventually arrived.

"There's been a terrible accident," explained Elswick. "It's Private Marks. When was the last time that anyone saw her?"

Simon felt sick, as if someone had kicked him in the stomach.

"She was on guard duty on Saturday night," he volunteered.

"Did anyone see her after that?" asked Elswick.

There was no response from the class as they all sat wondering what had happened.

"No one?" queried Elswick. "What about her roommates?"

"She didn't have any, sir," offered Donna. "I don't remember seeing her yesterday, but most of us didn't get back until last night."

The rest of the female recruits nodded or mumbled agreement.

"Did anyone see her this morning?"

Donna looked around at the other girls.

"No. She wasn't at breakfast."

"OK," announced Elswick. "Private Tollsland, come with me, please. You seem to have been the last person to see her."

"Yes, sir," said Simon, getting up from his desk with a feeling of dread.

"Under the circumstances, we won't be starting the Combat Intelligence phase today," said Captain Case, after Elswick and Simon left.

"Why? What's happened, ma'am?" Jon asked the question that

the whole course wanted answered.

"We don't know for certain yet," admitted Case. "But it looks like Private Marks committed suicide."

There was a stunned silence as the recruits tried to take this in.

"Why? What's happened ma'am?" Jon repeated.

"That's what we're going to have to determine," replied Case. "The Royal Military Police will be investigating, so if anyone has anything to tell us that could help with the inquiry, please let me know."

Donna and Sonia looked at each other.

"Can we have a private word, ma'am?" Donna asked.

"Yes. Come with me," said Case, and all three went to her office.

"Fucking hell!" said someone, and a discussion about what could have happened and what could have caused it broke out among the members of the squad.

The rest of the day was taken up with interviews and written statements, as the incident was investigated by a team from the RMP led by a female Sergeant from the Special Investigations Branch (SIB).

It was a very subdued group that night who sat in the NAAFI discussing the day's events in low voices. Linda hadn't been as well-liked as Donna or Sonia, but she was a member of the team, and a lot of the recruits, particularly the female ones, felt responsible for what had happened. Simon had taken it particularly badly, and Captain Case had asked Mich to watch him in case he did something stupid. She chose Mich because he was the oldest of the recruits and a Corporal and had experience of traumatic events like this one. Simon just sat, staring blankly at his beer and not saying a word.

Cazanoe had been questioned by the RMP, but had not, so far, been charged with anything, although he was warned that charges might be forthcoming in the future, depending on the investigation. He hadn't taken that well and was sitting in his usual place, muttering darkly about injustice to anyone who would listen.

Later that evening, Jon went up to Simon, who was still sitting silently, staring at nothing.

"Are you OK?" he asked.

Simon looked up at him with tears in his eyes.

"I should have done something."

"There was nothing that you could have done by the sounds of it," argued Jon. "It's not your fault."

"It doesn't feel that way."

"Once we find out what really caused it, it'll be different," asserted Jon.

"You think so?" asked Simon, with a faint glimmer of hope in his voice.

"Yes, I'm certain."

There was a pause while Simon looked into his glass.

"Look, I'm sorry about what I said to you. Can we still be friends?"

"Of course," said Jon.

Simon gave him a wan smile. "Thanks."

"No problem, mate," replied Jon.

The following day, normal training started again. It would take weeks, if not months, for the inquest and formal inquiry to produce its results, and life must go on. In war time, people die on a daily basis, and soldiers have to be prepared to accept death as part of normality, otherwise they would not be able to function. It's not that they become brutalised, but there is an element of desensitisation that allows them to carry on with their jobs. Civilians often don't understand this, nor the black sense of humour that comes with it.

Ironically, it is this ability that may be the reason why Post Traumatic Stress Disorder (PTSD) doesn't tend to kick in until sometimes as long as sixteen years after the event, and why old soldiers sometimes turn to drink or commit suicide for seemingly no apparent reason.

The Combat Intelligence phase of training was led by two different Int Corps Sergeants, with Sgts Knight and Dante now having finished their bit and preparing for the next squad of hopefuls.

Sergeant Donald Lott and Sergeant Peter Lewis were both cheerful characters, who were delighted to get two-year postings to Ashford as a break from their Int companys, which were based in West Germany supporting the British Army on the Rhine (BAOR).

They explained the format of the next few months, which mirrored the Security phase in that it would consist of lectures, practical demonstrations and exercises, as well as visits to military museums. At the end of the course would be the written trade test and a Combat Intelligence exercise, which included briefings, among other things.

"You generally either love or hate Combat Intelligence," Sergeant Lott explained. "Int company's are the poor relation to Security sections, as we do a lot of field exercises, but the beer's dirt cheap in Germany and you can buy a car tax free."

"Tax free?" someone asked.

"Yes," said Lott. "Because it's overseas, so there's no car tax or VAT, which makes it considerably cheaper. If you buy one and bring it back, you're saving about 20%."

"Wow. Sounds good," someone said.

"What about the beer?" asked Peter.

"Tax free if you buy it in the NAAFI, but it's still pretty cheap in the German bars. They do a thing called a 'tower'. It's five litres of lager in a glass tube with its own little tap."

"You can sign me up," replied Peter, happily.

"So, what actually is Combat Intelligence?" Sergeant Levis took over, asking the question rhetorically.

He went on to explain that in a nutshell Combat Intelligence is the process by which Intelligence operators gather, produce and prepare the information needed by a commander to try to predict what the enemy is likely to do so that they can counter it. It is driven by the Intelligence cycle.

"In a conventional war ie where both sides are relatively equal, it is like trying to put together a jigsaw puzzle with only a vague idea of what the picture on the box is. You get a couple of pieces which are blue, and you say, that's probably the sky. A couple more pieces will be grey, and you'll say, it could be an elephant. As you get more pieces, you'll say, ah, it's actually a whale, and the blue bits are the sea." He explained

"If you're not following this then I apologise, but Combat Int is probably not for you. Anyway, twice a day there will be a briefing, and the senior Intelligence person, normally a Major or Captain, will give the commander an Intelligence update on what has happened and what G2 (Intelligence) thinks will happen in the future. The commander then goes away, fights the battle and hopefully wins the war."

"Did you understand any of that?" Donna asked over dinner.

"I understood the bit about the beer and the cheap cars," said Peter.

Donna shot him a withering look.

"Apparently, women can have difficulty with Combat Int because you all played with dolls and not Airfix models when you were kids," replied Peter, a bit smugly.

"What do you call Action Man, if not a doll?" put in Sonia.

"That's different," Peter argued, illogically.

"Touché," said Jon from the side.

Donna turned to him.

"Did you understand it? You were infantry, weren't you?"

"Yes," he admitted. "I managed to follow most of it, but it's a lot to take in, in one go. We've got three months or so."

"I just hope it's long enough," muttered Donna.

The gym was still closed off as the investigation into Linda's death was still ongoing, so PT was outdoors instead.

Cazanoe's temper seemed to be getting worse, and Jon wondered if it was due to steroids or pressure from the investigation, or both. Cazanoe spent every evening in the NAAFI. He seemed to have no other hobbies apart from the gym, which was now denied to him.

Jon noticed that Cazanoe was having trouble keeping up with the pace that Sergeant Major Sanders was setting. The drinking seemed to be taking a toll on his fitness, although he had never struck Jon as a runner, anyway. He was definitely more of a carthorse than a racehorse.

The squad were being fitted for their Number Two dress uniform that afternoon, and Jon realised that meant the passing out parade and the end of the course was getting closer. It had seemed like a long way off when they had all first arrived, but that now seemed like a lifetime ago.

Intelligence Corps Number Two dress uniform consisted of a khaki-coloured, two-piece suit which was worn with a Number Two dress shirt and tie. Boots were to be highly polished i.e. bulled to a glass-like shine. The Corps wore their green plastic belts instead of the issue khaki cloth one. They would wear berets and carry SMGs as their personal weapon and any medals that they were entitled to.

Mich was the only recruit who actually had any medals. He had done a tour of Northern Ireland and had been in long enough to be awarded a Long Service and Good Conduct (LS and GC) medal (also known as the 'Long Service and didn't Get Caught' medal).

There were very few members of the armed forces who had anything other than LS and GC or NI (Northern Ireland) medals as there hadn't been a major war since Korea in the 1950s, and any personnel who did, tended to have done Special Duties, which included members of the Intelligence Corps. There were a few members of the Corps who had been awarded the Queen's Gallantry Medal (QGM) earned for undercover work in Northern Ireland. When one considered what awaited them (a drill to the kneecaps, among other things) if they got caught by the IRA, they deserved the awards.

They carefully took their uniforms back to the billet and hung them in their wardrobes so that they would stay uncreased, and then spent the rest of the afternoon polishing their boots.

"Does anyone know who created our modern map-marking symbols?" asked Sergeant Lott.

"Sun Tzu?" said a voice from the back of the class.

"*The Art of War*," quoted Lott. "Good guess, but hardly modern."

"Fredrick the Great," said Jon. He suddenly remembered this fact from Sandhurst.

"Correct! Fredrick the Great, King of Prussia 1740 to 1786. Or king *in* Prussia, if you want to be pedantic. That means picky, Private Jarvis," he added, making Peter, the class joker the butt of the joke and earning a round of laughter.

"Fredrick the Great, or 'Old Fritz', as he was known, developed the use of blue for friendly forces and red for the enemy that we still use today. NATO map-marking symbols are based on his system and you will need to know them. That was a hint, by the way."

Sergeant Lott and Sergeant Levis would often give the recruits hints as to what was actually going to be in the trade test. Whether the recruits took any notice was up to them, but they couldn't complain that they hadn't been given a chance. It was a godsend for the female recruits who, true to form, were finding Combat Int more difficult than the men. That didn't mean that there weren't some women who were very good at it, but initially they struggled with the terminology and equipment recognition, whereas the guys had learned it as children, playing with toy soldiers.

Lott went on to show them a myriad of little rectangular boxes filled with lines and squiggles that represented just about anything that you would find on the battlefield.

"Infantry are designated by a cross symbol, which goes from corner to corner like a St Andrew's cross, and is allegedly a representation of a soldier's cross belt. Cavalry, or nowadays recce, have a single, slanted line. Tanks, or armour, as we call it, have a track-like symbol, and engineers have an E on its side.

With me, so far?" he asked the sea of blank faces. "Ah, well. You'll get there in the end."

They were given a map-marking symbol aide memoire and were advised to get themselves a set of coloured pens and an old slide frame for drawing them.

"Right. We'll have a little map-marking test next time, so go away and see how many you can memorise."

"It just gets worse," complained Donna to her roommates.

"I can see the point of it, in a way, but how are we supposed to remember it all?" agreed Sue.

"In reality, you probably don't," said Sonia. "But, for the sake of the trade test, we'll need to know most of the common ones."

"What does this one mean again?" Donna asked, showing the track symbol.

"That's a tank, or armour," replied Sonia.

"How did you remember that?" demanded Sue.

"Tanks have tracks," replied Sonia. "I had brothers who played with them."

"I was an only child," said Sandra.

"I wish I had been," said Sue, with a laugh.

They had a break from Combat Intelligence when they did an Imagery Analysis (IA) lesson and test. The instructors came from the Joint Air Reconnaissance Intelligence Centre (JARIC), and the class was initially given small devices, which looked like a pair of spectacles mounted on downward looking frames, which they were told was called a stereoscope.

A stereoscope is a binocular optical instrument that allows the viewer to look at two aerial photographs simultaneously, so that features that are not noticeable in two dimensions appear in three dimensions.

Jon remembered that his grandfather had had a device that you slotted cardboard-backed photos into that would do the same thing. He had loved the one that showed a pool of boiling mud that appeared to actually be bubbling, and another that showed the inside of a U-boat. He wondered if his parents still had it; it would probably be worth something now.

"Can you see where the line goes through the hillside?" one of the instructors asked.

The instructors both wore glasses and were rather weedy-looking individuals, which fitted the stereotype of an Imagery Analyst that the Sergeants had laughingly told them about before the lesson.

A couple of the recruits couldn't see the line that the JARIC instructors were talking about, even when it was pointed out to them.

"You have stereoscopy blindness," they were told. "It happens with some people. I'm sorry, but you won't be able to become an Imagery Analyst."

The recruits didn't exactly look devastated to find out that they wouldn't be locked in a darkened cupboard, staring at satellite photographs for the rest of their careers. They sat through the rest of the lesson with big smiles on their faces.

The test itself consisted of interpreting a series of aerial photographs which took about two and a half hours. Jon quite enjoyed it, although he had no intention of volunteering to be an IA. At least, not initially. He fancied something a bit more warlike like Combat Int.

"I could go for that," said one of the recruits, later.

Each to their own, thought Jon.

They were told that they would get the results of the test in a week or so. There would be a visit to JARIC later on in the course, and anyone who fancied joining could put their name down for it. The two instructors then packed up their kit and left.

"So, who wants to get locked in a cupboard?" asked Lott. "Only joking. They're a great bunch of guys and gals at JARIC."

"Do they get paid any more for doing IA?" Peter asked.

"No. But promotion is pretty good, apparently," replied Lott. "Why? Are you interested?"

"I could be."

The rest of the recruits looked at him in surprise. You just never could tell.

The next day, the squad was introduced to the Intelligence cycle. 'Direction, Collection, Processing and Dissemination were written on the whiteboard in a large circle. The pen that was used was green. They were told that this was simply because the black pen was missing, not because green had any significance.

"Unlike in the SIS," Sergeant Levis added, as an aside.

"Could you explain that?" someone asked, bravely.

Levis looked triumphant. It was obviously one of his favourite stories and he had been looking forward to telling it.

"The head of the Secret Intelligence Service (SIS) or MI6 to you lot, is called C," he declared. "This is because the founder of the SIS was called Mansfield Cumming, and he always signed his reports in green ink. He was a Rear Admiral and was a bit eccentric, to say the least. Ian Fleming called *James Bond*'s boss M because of the Mansfield bit rather than C for Cumming. Did anyone know that?"

No one did.

"Anyway. Back to the Intelligence cycle. It's not the rusty old thing that the Major rides," he joked, "but the process that drives Combat Intelligence."

He went on to explain that the first stage, Direction, was how the whole thing started, with the process being directed by the Commander's Intelligence and Critical Intelligence Requirements determining what was to be collected. Hence the next step, Collection. That led to the collected information/Intelligence being processed by the means of collation, evaluation and interpretation. Then finally, the Intelligence would be Disseminated to those who need it in a timely manner. After that, the commander's Intelligence requirements would change, and the whole process would start all over again.

"Thus, keeping us in gainful employment," said Levis. "I would *suggest* that you try to remember the Intelligence cycle in its entirety. Hint, hint."

Donna and her roommates sat in varying states of despondency, with bottles of Becks and a liqueur called *Apfelkorn* that a friend of Donna's had brought back from Germany and given to her as a Christmas present.

"God. There's so much to remember," she said, passing the bottle to Sonia.

"We'll just have to drink our way out of this one," said Sue.

"At least we've got the *Apfelkorn* to help," added Sandra.

"Thank heavens for that," agreed Donna.

She had been near, if not at, the top of the course for Security but was struggling with Combat Intelligence like most of the rest of them, apart from Sonia.

"Well, I'm definitely inclined to 14 Sigs, after this lot," she declared.

"Security for me," announced Sue.

"Hear! Hear!" slurred Sandra.

"I don't know, I quite like Combat Int," said Sonia, quietly.

They all turned to stare at her, as if she had said she didn't like chocolate.

"You've got to be mad!" scoffed Donna. "It's all field exercises and muddy boots."

"Germany sounds fun, though," countered Sonia.

"And loads of desperate guys," added Sue.

"All guys are desperate!" said Donna.

"Not *all* of them," contradicted Sue.

"Well, most," insisted Donna.

"OK, I'll give you that," conceded Sue, taking another swig of the schnapps.

This led to a drunken discussion about the various men on the course, and men in general, until the Becks and *Apfelkorn* were both finished, by which time they were all ready to sleep.

CHAPTER 18

Aside from the two Sergeants, the recruits had lectures from various other members of the Corps, notably a certain Captain Addison, who loved artillery. They were in the phase where they were being taught doctrine and recognition and these, combined with the previous lectures, were beginning to form a picture that was at last making sense.

"Doctrine," he explained "is the name given to the rules that govern how any individual army – be it a huge force, like the Red Army, or a small terrorist cell – is organised. Doctrine lays out how the units are organised, known as Orbats, or orders of battle; where units should be located in the various forms of manoeuvre; advance to contact or advancing until you meet the enemy and start fighting, and the pursuit, etcetera. It can even include such things as how far a unit should move in a set time, or exactly how much artillery ammunition is to be expended during an attack.

Recognition is the process by which one learns what the various pieces of equipment found on the battlefield are used for. These are located on the map by use of map-marking symbols."

That morning, Captain Addison was talking them through the different types of artillery and where they could be found in the line of march (how the various units were lined up before commencing their movement).

"The Soviets love artillery almost as much as I do, and they have lots of it," Addison explained. "Down at the regimental level, there will be a battery of either D30, wheeled artillery, or 2S1 self-propelled guns, which will form the Regimental Artillery Group or RAG. On the next level up – division– there will be a Divisional Artillery Group, or DAG. Finally, at the Army Artillery Group there will be an?"

"*Aaagh!*" shouted out Peter, who was the squad joker.

"Close, but no cigar," said Addison, smiling, "not quite so many As. But you get what I mean."

Captain Addison was an eccentric genius who lectured at Sandhurst, among other things, but his main hobby and life's work was the study of Soviet artillery. He went on to explain that the Red Forces, the Soviet Army – or enemy, in this case – would pound a target remorselessly before sending in the armour and infantry to take the objective.

"I once played a wargame at NATO," he told them, happily. "And I destroyed BAOR with a creeping barrage."

"Do they have enough ammunition to do that?" asked Jon.

"Yes, they do."

"Bloody hell," Jon muttered. He remembered back to when he was at Sandhurst, he had been taught that if 3 Shock Army (which was the Soviet army facing the West just over the inner German border in East Germany) ever did decide to attack, then BAOR would initiate a preplanned defence involving three separate battle lines.

The first thing that would happen would be that the three Parachute battalions would be parachuted into battle in front of the advancing Soviet forces in order to slow them down. This was expected to result in a casualty rate of 95%. In other words, the Paras would be wiped out. This led to the paradox of Parachute Regiment officers, who were supposed to be some of the best officers in the British Army, being stupid enough to join a regiment that meant almost certain death if they actually went to war.

As the Paras were getting massacred, BAOR would deploy to pre-

prepared positions in what was known as the first line of defence. They were expected to take 75% casualties, which was almost as close to being wiped out as the Paras.

Anyone who could, would fall back on the second line of defence, which was expected to take 50% casualties. They would then fall back on the third line of defence, which it was hoped would hold until reinforcements from the USA could be flown across the Atlantic and the Territorial Army could be mobilised and deployed.

If this failed, then tactical nuclear weapons were expected to be used, and they had been told that the US would rather destroy Western Europe than allow the Soviets to win.

It was a pretty horrendous scenario and was made worse by what Captain Addison had just said about the amount of artillery and ammunition that the Soviets possessed.

Addison carried on brightly with the additional information that *all* Soviet artillery was designed to use chemical weapons; the only saving grace being that their Nuclear, Bacteriological, Chemical protection was several levels below that of the UK, and the use of chemical weapons could backfire badly on them if they did deploy such weaponry.

"How does the fall of the Berlin wall affect all this?" Mich asked.

"Good question, Corporal," answered Addison. "The answer is we just don't know yet. Time will tell, but it could make the Soviets even more dangerous."

"Why's that, sir?" someone else asked.

"The Soviets have always had a huge army. It comes from their paranoia about being invaded. They have been invaded three times in the last three hundred years. Firstly, by Charles XII of Sweden, next by Napoleon and, most recently, by Hitler.

Because of this, they haven't been able to buy the best equipment. It's all down to economy of scale. If you have an army of one million, then it will cost £10m to equip your troops with ten pounds worth of equipment. If, on the other hand, you have an army of 100,000, you can give them each equipment worth £100 for the same amount. As we saw in the First World War, technology gives you a real edge. So, if the Soviet Army becomes a lot smaller, then it could become much better equipped and thus more deadly. Have a think about that over lunch."

"Thanks, sir," said Peter, facetiously.

After lunch, the squad had an introduction to Soviet weaponry. An infantry Colour Sergeant, who was doing an attachment to the Intelligence Corps, was waiting in the classroom with a selection of Soviet small arms and infantry weapons. They were allowed to play with the equipment, stripping down and reassembling AK47s, Skorpion sub machine guns, Draganov sniper rifles and RPG7s, among others. It helped to actually be able to see the equipment that was listed in the Soviet Orbats so they could recognise them and brought home the simplicity of most of the Soviet weapons.

"Soldier proof," said the Colour Sergeant about the famous Kalashnikov AK47. "So simple to use and so reliable that you can, allegedly, bury it in sand, dig it up again and it will still fire. You can't say the same of the SLR."

Jon took up the Draganov sniper rifle. It was 7.62mm calibre, the same as the British SLR, but the Soviets used a shorter round so that they could use NATO standard ammunition at a pinch, but NATO couldn't use theirs.

"What's the range, Colour?" asked Jon.

"50% chance of a first-round hit at 300m."

Jon was surprised. British Army snipers were expected to get a first-round hit at 300m *every* time.

"That's not very good."

"No. Not compared to ours," agreed the Colour Sergeant. "And it's a five-round magazine. We use bolt action. That's generally considered better for accuracy."

In general, the Soviet equipment was cheaply and, it appeared, a bit shoddily made, but the Chinese have an expression: 'If a weapon's stupid and it works, it's not stupid', and this stuff seemed to work.

The day of the dreaded Combat Fitness Test arrived. The recruits carried their gear down to the gym and prepared for the test, weighing their kit and making sure that everything was stowed as comfortably as possible.

"Where's Corporal Cazanoe?" someone asked.

He should have been there to help out. This was the sort of thing he loved doing – humiliating recruits who struggled to march eight miles with a pack, helmet and rifle. No one had seen him, and he hadn't been in the bar for the past few nights. Finally, they found out that he had been admitted to hospital with a bowel problem and wouldn't be back any time soon.

"What a shame," said Donna, with a complete lack of sincerity.

All the training wing staff joined in the CFT as it was a requirement to do it once a year, although many units claimed that they were too busy and got by on a waiver.

Sergeant Knight looked less than happy. He was verging on the podgy side, and the recruits had often wondered about his fitness level. As the training Major was there and kitted out like the rest of the course, he could hardly avoid it.

"Slow down a bit, Sergeant Major," Major Elswick shouted, as WO2 Sanders tried to lead them off at a run. "I'm an old man and can't do it that fast, you know."

Sanders didn't really have any choice as he was heavily outranked and, although he was technically in charge of the CFT, Elswick was an officer and could make his life difficult had he so wished.

"I don't want anyone to fail this, myself included," he explained to the PTI as the pace returned to the normal CFT speed.

Due to Elswick's intervention, none of the recruits fell back as they had done on the previous march. The pace was hard but endurable, and they were all still together when they reached the psychological barrier of the halfway point.

There were one or two stragglers coming into the home straight, including Sergeant Knight, but they managed to catch up within the time allowed and no one failed the test, as requested by the training wing OC.

Sanders was obviously not happy and stalked off as soon as he could.

Why is he such a cunt? thought Jon. Some people were just like that, he supposed.

They held a celebratory piss-up in the NAAFI that night, with one more tick in the box towards their passing the course and becoming Intelligence Operators.

The Tank Museum at Bovington, Dorset was a three-hour drive from Ashford, so it was a daytrip away from the depot. It felt a bit like a school outing as they piled into the coach that had been hired for the day. The two Combat Int Sergeants sat at the front and the recruits, who were all in civvies, sat wherever they liked in the back. They had been issued with the dreaded haversack rations and the back of the bus was soon littered with white cardboard boxes.

The museum had a range of Soviet machinery, including tanks and armoured personnel carriers, both tracked and wheeled. It was interesting to see the vehicles in real life after studying them for so long. They had a dedicated guide, who told them in great detail about each vehicle, and then they had a chance to actually climb over and sit in them.

"You have to be under 5ft 5in. to comfortably man a Soviet tank," said the guide. "That way, they can be considerably smaller than NATO tanks, although NATO tanks are far more comfortable."

"Where do they get so many small people from?" someone asked.

"A lot of them come from the Stans – Tajikistan, Kazakhstan and Turkmenistan. But that can lead to real problems. There's a great story about a T55 having a collision with train because the driver didn't understand the tank commander's orders because he didn't speak Russian."

"Wow!" someone said.

"Yes," agreed the guide. "Most Soviet soldiers are conscripts and don't want to be there."

"A bit like us," said Peter, getting a laugh.

They spent three hours at the museum and then were back on the coach.

"Did that help?" Jon asked Donna, as they were on their way back to Ashford.

"It certainly helps," she said. "But I still can't get my head around all the line of march stuff."

"It might be easier after we've done the first Combat Int exercise," he said, optimistically.

Donna looked at him, doubtfully.

'Intelligence briefings' were the words on the whiteboard. They were used to green ink, but someone must have shelled out for a black pen, because the writing was in black today.

Beneath the heading, Sergeant Levis wrote: *Introduction, Vital*

Intelligence, Ground, General Enemy Situation, Enemy Operations in detail, General Comment, Questions.

"This is the format for Intelligence briefings," he said, pointing to the board. "Get yourself some index cards, cover them with plastic film, attach them with treasury tags, and there you go – you've got yourself a set of briefing cards. You can write the headings on the card before you cover them and then use lumocolours to write your notes," he instructed.

He then went through what the headings meant and how they should conduct the brief.

"At first, you'll be pretty nervous, but it gets easier over time."

"Will we be expected to do briefings for real?" asked one of the recruits.

"In reality, probably not," admitted Levis. "But for the trade test, yes."

"Will we be briefing you and Sergeant Lott?"

"No. Unfortunately not. They like to get people in from the headquarters and, if you're really unlucky, you'll get the Director."

"What!" shrieked Peter in a high-pitched voice, as if someone had stuck a pair of rusty compasses into his groin.

"Haha, only joking," said Levis. "No. It'll be more like the CSM or the training Major."

"God. That's just as bad," someone muttered.

"Don't worry. Just don't panic and stab the Commander with your pointer. Oh! You'll need a pointer, as well."

The recruits could see that Levis used what looked like an old car aerial as a pointer and wondered where he had got it from.

I wonder if I can nick his? thought Jon.

"In case you're thinking of taking mine," continued Levis, as if he'd read Jon's mind, "don't even think about it. You can get them from the carpool, if you ask nicely."

They spent the rest of the day practicing briefings, with everyone getting the chance to stand in front of the rest of the course and make a fool of themselves. Some were better than others, with one or two getting stage fright and having to be coaxed into carrying on.

This must be the worst part of the course for some people, Jon thought.

"Intelligence Preparation of the Battlefield, or IPB for short, is a relatively new concept that has come over from the US Army," said the Sergeant Lott. "It consists of a series of overlays called templates, which are placed over the briefing map to allow easier analysis, as it is very visual. Previously, the Intelligence section Second in Command, normally a Captain, would write the Intelligence estimate. This could be a lengthy piece of work and, as the old saying goes, a picture is worth a thousand words, and IPB is nothing if not visual.

There are three main templates. The first is the blue forces template, which shows Friendly Forces, and is obtained from Operations, or G3 in NATO parlance. The second is the weather and terrain template, which is the preserve of the Royal Engineers, and the third is the doctrinal template, which shows the standard Soviet Army line of march, and is produced by us.

From these templates you can assess the probable enemy objectives, their routes and possible choke points, which lead to a series of decision points and courses of action. The latter can then be used to brief the Commander."

The recruits were initially tasked to produce the weather and terrain template. They got to work with taping maps together so that they could be covered with thin acetate layer cellulose or (TALC) which was a fancy name for plastic sheeting.

"Does the army always have to use these bloody acronyms?" complained Jon, to no one in particular when told that the plastic sheet was called TALC.

"Yes," replied Mich. "They love their TLAs."

"TLAs?" queried Peter.

"Three letter abbreviations," explained Mich. "There's a whole ream of them in JSP 101."

"There you go, again," said Peter. "What's JSP 101, when it's at home?"

"*Joint Services Publication number 101* is the manual of service writing," replied Mich patiently. "It tells you exactly how any army documents should be written, from a letter asking for a day off to how to complete an AF 252 properly."

"Are you taking the piss?" Peter demanded. "What the fuck's a 252?"

"I'm surprised you don't know already, Pete," broke in Jon. "It's the army's charge sheet."

Mich was grinning like a madman. "That's the army for you. Never speak plainly, if you can speak in tongues."

Peter shook his head and went back to taping the maps together.

The British Army generally used 1:50000 mapping, where it could. This meant that 2cm on the map represented 1km on the ground and was detailed enough for briefings, without being either unwieldly or too small to see.

"What first?" asked Donna, as she started to prepare the weather and terrain template.

"No-go and slow-go'," said Mich.

"There's not really such as thing as no-go," argued Jon. "History is littered with examples of battles that were lost because one side thought the other couldn't go somewhere. Look at the Ardennes during the Second World War."

"I agree," said Mich. "But that's what we've been told to do."

"Fair enough," conceded Jon. "Black outline and crosshatching for no-go, black outline and single hatching for slow-go," he said to

Donna.

"Sorry," she replied. "I don't understand what you mean."

"It sounds like it's got something to do with chickens, all that hatching," put in Peter.

Jon smiled and took the black lumocolour pen from Donna.

"Here. Let me show you."

He drew the outline of a lake in black and then drew slanted black lines across it both ways, forming multiple crosses, or crosshatching.

"See what I mean," he said. "The edge of the lake isn't really no-go. You could probably drive a tank through the water. It depends on the depth of the water and what sort of material makes up the bottom."

"I think I understand," said Donna, finally. "Should we make the edge slow-go, then?"

"Therein lies the rub," answered Jon. "We don't know enough about the lake to say. We'd have to ask the Engineers, and if we start doing that, we'd never get this done."

"How do we do it, then?" protested Donna.

"We do our best in the time available," replied Jon, pragmatically. "I doubt the instructors expect us to get it exactly right. It's only an exercise, after all."

"And in real life, you've got people like the Royal Engineers who can give you the answers. There's a lot more resources available," added Mich.

"Oh! OK."

They worked on the template until the instructors called a halt and then there was a squad discussion about each syndicate's efforts.

Jon's team had done by far the best template, but that was probably because he and Mich understood what they were doing.

"Out of interest," said Lott, at the end, "the Soviets are reputed to have maps with all the forests and rivers in East Germany annotated as to whether you can drive a tank through them. Don't think that just because an area is thickly wooded that you can't get through it. There are normally tracks and even roads that you can drive vehicles through. Be aware of that when you're doing the template."

Lott didn't realise that he just confirmed exactly what Jon had been saying before.

"I really enjoyed that," Jon said, as they packed up the maps and rolls of TALC.

"You're weird, you are," replied Donna, with a smile.

Jon's knuckles were white as he gripped the Land Rover's steering wheel and tried to control the wildly veering vehicle. He had visions of crashing into a tree, which is what had happened the first time he had ever driven a Land Rover, although that was an armour-plated one on the mine in Zimbabwe.

The recruits had gone down to Aldershot for some advanced driver training. They had left Ashford early in the morning and driven in convoy, four to a vehicle, to the driver training area on Hankley Common.

They were now attempting to follow the instructor's vehicle as they drove through thick mud and hidden tank tracks. Jon had never realised how difficult it was to drive in conditions like that. He had driven down rutted, sandy tracks in Zimbabwe, but this was the first time that he had had to cope with deep pools of water and axle-deep mud.

"Go with the flow," said the instructor. "Keep it in a low gear and don't overcompensate."

Easier said than done, thought Jon.

They reached the end of the flooded area and moved out onto a slightly higher patch of ground, where the tracks were merely bumpy and not treacherous. Reaching the top of a steep rise, they halted.

"Well done," said the instructor, looking back to where one of the recruits had managed to get themselves bogged down.

"Ooh, I wouldn't like to be them," he said, happily. "The person who gets the vehicle stuck is the one who has to get out and sort it."

Jon was relieved that he hadn't made a mess of it and sat, letting his nerves calm and his tense muscles relax a bit.

They watched as the unfortunate recruit – Jon couldn't tell from this distance, but he thought it was Peter – reluctantly got out of the Land Rover and waded through the mud to the passenger door and climbed in. The instructor had obviously slid across to the driver's seat. There was a puff of exhaust as the instructor expertly revved the engine and reversed out of the hole that the Land Rover had got stuck in. It all looked so easy when they were just watching it.

"There you go. Easy as pie," noted Jon's instructor.

The next obstacle was river crossing.

"Firstly, stop the vehicle in a safe place and check the depth of the water," Jon was told. "Then, if it's shallow enough and safe to cross, pick your route and drive *slowly* and steadily across the obstacle. That's the secret. Driving slowly and steadily creates a bow wave but doesn't flood the vehicle, although you've got a raised exhaust so you wouldn't need to worry about that."

Jon did what he was told and got across the stream without any difficulty.

"You'd be amazed how many people go at it like a bat out of hell, thinking that they'll get across quicker. Wrong!" the instructor explained, with a smile.

Finally, they drove to the top of a small, steep hill that looked like it had been constructed which it almost certainly had.

"Stop at the top," commanded the instructor.

Jon put the vehicle in first and crawled to the top of the mound and stopped. It looked awfully steep on the way down.

"OK," the instructor said. "Put it in first gear and, once you're moving, take your foot off the accelerator and let it drive itself down the hill. Don't use the brakes and don't put your foot on the clutch."

Jon did what he was told, and the Land Rover slowly drove itself down the slope, the gearbox acting as a brake and keeping it under control.

"There you go," explained the instructor, when they reached the bottom. "First gear gives you the control. It is fast enough to get down but acts as a brake so that you don't lose control."

"Thanks, Corporal," replied Jon, glad that his bit was now over.

They swapped drivers and it was now Donna's turn. She did exactly what she was told to do and went through the exercise without any drama.

They had lunch and then some of them were given the opportunity to have a shot at driving an old armoured personal carrier. It was an FV 432 (or Fighting Vehicle 432) but was commonly called a Panzer. They were used by Intelligence Corps in Germany as mobile Combat Int cells. It was noisy and smelt of diesel, but it gave a feeling of security. Jon imagined himself sitting in one doing Combat Intelligence.

You never know, it might happen.

They all ended up covered in mud and it was raining again as they drove back to Ashford, but it had been an instructive day and those recruits who had recently passed their tests had been given a bit of confidence about their driving.

It was Steve's birthday, and the squad had decided to take him for a curry. They had booked a table for fifteen and the others were going to join them in a club later on.

"So, how old are you then, Steve?" Donna asked.

"Nineteen," replied Steve. "I was seventeen when I first applied to join."

"God. You're young," said Mich.

Mich was the oldest on the course, having served ten years with the Royal Signals before transferring.

"I can remember being nineteen," he continued. "I thought I knew everything."

"You still do," quipped Peter.

"Yes. But the difference is that I now *do* know it all," laughed Mich.

They've come a long way since they first joined, thought Jon, looking at the others around the table.

From a group of disparate youngsters, they had evolved into a group of confident colleagues. Even Paul 'Biff' Dobson was a 'biff' no longer. He had proven himself to be a competent operator and would probably pass the course without any further problems.

Steve sat across from Jon thinking similar thoughts. He had been quite shy, and still was in some ways, but he was glad that he had joined the Corps rather than the police and was happy to be in the company of this group of people, who would likely be his friends and colleagues for a long time, if not for life.

"Did you hear about Corporal Cazanoe?" someone asked.

"No. Do tell," replied Donna.

There was one thing that the squad loved, and that was gossip. Jon supposed it was natural that they would want to know what was happening; if they didn't, then they probably wouldn't make good Intelligence operators. He had once asked the question as to whether they would read someone else's mail – not open their letters but read a letter that had been left lying on a table. Most of them had admitted that they probably would.

"He's had to have part of his bowel removed and will have a colostomy bag."

"I wonder if steroids had anything to do with it?" remarked Paul.

"Who knows?" replied Donna. "But it means that he probably won't be coming back."

"Hoorah to that," said Paul.

Cazanoe hadn't made himself very popular with the recruits and there wasn't much sympathy for him. Donna and Sonia exchanged glances and Sonia nodded. Karma? Maybe.

They went on to a club in the centre of Ashford and Donna, who was a bit drunk by now, did a special dance for Steve for his birthday. He stood with a slightly glazed expression on his face, but whether that was the drink or the effect that Donna had on him was unknown.

They staggered back to the barracks at 0200 in small groups, past the litter of cans, broken bottles, spilt chips and piles of vomit that represented a Saturday night in a town centre, and went off to their various rooms.

They were woken the next morning, a Sunday, by someone loudly shouting drill instructions on the parade square.

"Who the fuck is that?" grunted Rob, as the sounds penetrated their hangovers.

"Fuckin' TA," replied Paul, trying to bury himself under the covers.

They tried to ignore the noise, but eventually gave in and got up. They found out at breakfast that it was the TA Intelligence Corps doing their Drill and Duties Two (D&D 2) course. The TA Intelligence Corps mirrored their regular counterparts with their training, the difference being that the TA did theirs over a weekend instead of over a couple of weeks.

The TA had spent the Saturday doing field craft and range work and then had had a regimental dinner on the Saturday night.

Regimental dinners were usually the preserve of Sergeant and above, but because the D&D2 was a precursor to promotion to Sergeant, the Corporals attending the course were being given an introduction to the delights of the regimental dinner.

There are set rules for regimental dinners in the British Army which vary from unit to unit, but they are very formal, and non-compliance with the rules generally leads to extra duties or some other such punishment.

Jon had always thought of them as a form of mild torture, one of the main rules being that one cannot leave the table until after the loyal toast and the speeches were over, which entails enduring hours of agony or resorting to such tricks as pissing in a glass or bottle under the table.

David Niven, the famous actor, relates in one of his books that he pissed in a champagne bottle while cutting cheese with his other hand during one such dinner.

The Intelligence Corps has a tradition called the Brown's recess. This was gifted to the Corps by a Warrant Officer called Brown who either had a weak bladder or had to leave a mess dinner to meet an agent (it depends on who is telling the story). A Brown's recess allows one to leave the table at an Intelligence Corps regimental dinner after the loyal toast but before the speeches without occurring any penalty.

Yet another reason to join the Intelligence Corps, rather than another regiment, thought Jon.

CHAPTER 19

At the end of another day's lessons on Combat Intelligence, the squad was told that they were going into London for a visit to the Defence Intelligence Staff (DIS). DIS was located in Whitehall in the old War Office building, opposite Horse Guards Parade where the trooping of the colour is carried out. They were told to wear jackets and ties (or the equivalent for women) and to parade at 0800 the following morning.

They took the train from Ashford Station to Waterloo and then got the tube to Embankment. They could have walked from Waterloo Station, but Sergeant Lott wasn't familiar with London and didn't want to risk getting lost.

"This way... I think," said Lott, as they came up the stairs from the underground and milled about in Embankment Station.

"This way's quicker," said Jon, pointing to the other entrance.

"How do you know?" demanded Lott.

"I used to be a despatch rider."

"Is there anything that you haven't done?" asked Simon admiringly.

Jon suspected that Simon still harboured feelings for him, but he had kept them to himself since the night in Rothiemurchus.

"OK," said Lott. "Lead on, MacDuff."

Jon led the group along Embankment Place, across Northumberland Avenue and then into Whitehall Place.

"Front or side door?" he asked.

"I've no idea," said Lott. "I've never been here before."

Jon took them to the front door of the Old War Office Building in Whitehall and they went in through the huge wooden doors.

"We're the group from Ashford," Lott told the security guard, proffering his MoD 90.

"Go to reception. That way." The guard gestured towards an internal auditorium. "They'll sort you out."

"Thanks, mate," said Lott.

"My pleasure," replied the guard.

They went to reception and waited while they were issued with temporary passes. They surrendered their MoD 90s and were given visitor passes which they hung around their necks.

"Your host will be with you soon," said the receptionist. "Just wait there, please."

They waited a few minutes as people dressed in suits and skirts came and went. Finally, an older man in a plain, grey suit appeared from some lifts and came towards them.

"Intelligence Corps?" he asked Mich, assuming that he was the leader because of his age.

"Yes, sir," replied Mich, uncertain of the individual's rank but erring on the safe side.

"I'm Sergeant Lott, sir," said Lott, hastily introducing himself. The man transferred his attention from Mich.

"Right," he said. "WO1 Jarman. Follow me, please."

He led them towards the lifts, but instead of using them, he took them through a glass door to the side of the lifts, using his pass to open it and keeping it open as they all trooped through.

"It would take too long to use the lifts," he explained. "They can only take four or five at a time. It's an old building."

"Yes. I can see that, sir," agreed Lott.

They went up a flight of wide, shallow stairs with black cast-iron railings and a dark wood banister. Their leather-soled shoes *click clacked* on the uncarpeted floor, which looked to Jon to be made of mosaic tiles and reminded him of the *Ipcress File*, the film starring Michael Caine.

They reached the second floor and were ushered into a high-ceilinged room with full-height windows draped in thick net curtains. They were so thick that although they let light through, one couldn't tell if it was sunny or raining outside.

"Have a seat," said WO1 Jarman, and turned to the room's other occupant. "Sergeant Lott and the recruits from Templer," he announced.

"Excellent. Thank you, Mister Jarman," the man replied.

WO1s in the British Army are normally referred to as Mister rather than Sergeant Major or Warrant by officers, due to their seniority.

The man was wearing a pinstriped suit and had a grey moustache.

"I'm Major Barrrat and I'm the DIS Liaison Officer for the Corps," he announced.

Barrat ran them through a list of departments, most of which went completely over their heads.

The Levant? Where the hell is the Levant? thought Jon.

He vaguely remembered hearing the term one time but couldn't place it. *Sub-Saharan Africa? What did that mean?*

He came to the conclusion that DIS was a place where officers did their Intelligence posting before being promoted to Lieutenant Colonel and that probably explained why they used these anachronistic terms, to showcase how clever they were.

There appeared to be a few posts for junior ranks, but Jon reckoned one would end up as a gopher for senior officers, rather than being allowed to do any meaningful work. Still, it wouldn't be a bad posting, working in this historic old building in the centre of London.

They were shepherded around a few more offices by WO1 Jarman and were then shown the door, almost literally, and found themselves at a loose end in London for the afternoon.

"We can walk to the Imperial War Museum from here," offered Jon, but most of the recruits decided to go to The Tattershall Castle instead. The Tattershall Castle was a ship that had been turned into a bar and was moored on the River Thames outside the MoD and was open all day.

Jon didn't really fancy starting drinking quite so early, so he asked Sergeant Lott what the timetable was and agreed to meet everyone else at Waterloo Station at 1500. That gave them enough time to get back to the depot for dinner.

Donna and Sonia opted to go with Jon and, as he was leaving, Simon came up and asked if he could go, too. They left the mob at the boat and walked down Victoria Embankment to Westminster Bridge. They followed Westminster Bridge Road until they got to the Imperial War Museum.

"I wouldn't have thought that you would be interested in this," Jon said to Donna, as they arrived at the museum.

"I'm not, really," admitted Donna. "But I didn't want to get drunk, either."

"Fair enough," said Jon.

On the way back, Jon pointed out the Union Jack Club, which was tucked down a side street near Waterloo Station.

"If you need somewhere to stay in London, that's your place," he told them. "It's a bit like a barracks, but it's cheap and clean."

Some of the recruits were half-cut by the time they arrived at Waterloo Station; they had obviously had a good session in the bar.

They all piled onto the Ashford train and some of them carried on drinking, while others fell asleep. Jon sat and watched the countryside go by and thought about all the crazy wars that the UK had been involved in over the years. In the museum, there had been displays of medals given out for heroic bravery in various conflicts around the globe, but Jon had begun to realise that an awful lot of the wars had achieved very little. They were mainly about keeping the balance of power between rival nations. What was it all about, really? When he had been younger, he had thought that it was fantastic when he read of soldiers sacrificing themselves for their comrades, or to hold some vital position. But, reading into it, an awful lot of these heroic defences had been pretty pointless as, at the end of the war, the governments had swapped bits of land and only the rich and powerful seemed to have benefitted.

Christ! I'm turning into a Communist, he thought, except that communism had failed.

The results of the Imagery Analysis test had come back and, unsurprisingly, not all that many of the recruits had passed. It was one thing being able to see what was in an aerial photograph, but another thing entirely to be able to interpret what you were seeing.

Jon, Mich and a few others had done well and had been recommended for a posting to JARIC on completion of their training, if they wished to. Their results were down to experience and an understanding of military tactics. The others would get better at it in time, but it was all still far too new for most people.

Those that passed were interviewed by Major Elswick and asked if they wished to put their names down for JARIC. Jon wasn't sure.

"We can arrange a visit to JARIC, if you would like," offered Elswick.

Jon agreed because he thought it might be interesting, and any experience was useful, in his view.

In the event there were only four of them: Jon, Paul 'Biff' Dobson, a recruit called Alan and, surprisingly enough from Jon's point of view, Sonia, who were interested.

"I didn't think that this would be your thing," Jon said to Sonia, as they sat at a table on the train to Huntingdon.

JARIC was located at RAF Brampton in Cambridgeshire. It had been decided that they should go by train rather than drive and so, clutching their pink travel warrants, they had made their way to Ashford Station for the train to London and thence to Huntingdon.

"I didn't think so either, but you never know until you have a look, do you?" she responded.

"Are you considering it?"

She thought for a moment. "Probably not," she said, eventually. "But it's an option."

"There is that," he agreed. "What about you, Paul?"

"Me? No chance!" said Paul. "I'm only here to get me out of Ashford for the day."

"Alan?"

"Yes," he replied. "I really enjoyed the test, and I reckon it's what I want to do."

Alan went on to explain that he wanted a real job; he didn't want a posting where he would just be sitting in Germany, endlessly training for something that now with the fall of the Berlin wall, would probably never happen, or writing pointless Security reports that no one would ever read.

"Wow! Where'd you get that from?" Jon asked.

"I met an Intelligence Corps Corporal who told me what it was like in a Security section," he explained. "He said that all you are is i/c photocopier until you get to at least Sergeant and even then, it can be mind-numbing."

i/c photocopier (in charge of the photocopier) was a term for a pointless, low status job which is often what a junior Intelligence Operator could expect to do. At least at first.

"He's got a point," said Sonia. "Security is a bit bookish. It's not like being in the army at all, from what I've heard."

They discussed the various options that they had heard about, but most of it was hearsay and until they actually experienced working in the various units, they would never know.

"Well, we'll all probably be sent to the last places we want to go, knowing the army," said Jon, eventually.

"That's why I'm keen on being an IA," said Alan. "They're really short of people, so if you volunteer and are accepted, then the chances of being posted somewhere else are minimal."

"I've heard that most of their support comes from the TA," put in Sonia.

"Really?" said Jon. "I wouldn't have thought that they would have had the commitment."

"Apparently they can do it at weekends," explained Sonia.

They were given a very warm welcome by an Int Corps WO2 and taken around the complex to be introduced to the personnel working there. They seemed to display a slightly different sort of personality than the other Intelligence Corps operators, which was probably because they did a distinct job, and a specific type of person tended to become an IA.

Jon was impressed with the setup. They were told that the Americans – who had all the satellite equipment but, for some reason, couldn't use it properly – would fly the product over to JARIC, where it would be analysed by British IAs and then sent back. This meant that they were doing a 'real' job, as Alan had suggested, but there were also IAs attached to anywhere there was a need, and postings included the US and SHAPE.

They left RAF Brampton with a fresh view of being an IA and with plenty to think about over the coming weeks. Time was moving on, and it wouldn't be long before they had to put in their posting preferences so that they would have a unit to go to, once they passed out.

"Two and a half hours. On your marks... Go!" said Sergeant Levis, as the recruits sat, waiting to start their Combat Intelligence trade test.

Jon turned over his paper and scanned the questions. There was nothing here that he couldn't attempt, although some of the questions were badly written and could be ambiguous.

Q: Name three types of report.

What exactly were they wanting from this? he wondered.

Presumably three types of Intelligence report, although the question didn't say so. He hated having to assume things. If you assume, you make an ass of 'u' and 'me', was the saying, but they didn't leave him with any choice.

Intrep, Intsum and PicIntsum he wrote down, hoping that Intsum and Picintsum wouldn't be considered to be the same thing, or that was one point gone.

They needed at least 60% in the written exam, the same as the Security trade test. There were other tests to come, too. They needed to score 75% in the recognition test, and the final Combat Intelligence exercise was a continual assessment, which meant that they could fall at the last hurdle. No pressure there, then.

Q: Draw the line of march for a Motor Rifle Regiment.

Jon took out his slide and drew a series of rectangles that he filled in with what he hoped were the correct map-marking symbols. *Should I do them with a double outline or use red ink to indicate enemy forces?* Yet another ambiguous question. Fortunately, he had a red pen with him, so he did them in red.

Q: What is the map marking symbol for supply?

You've got to be fucking joking, he thought. *Why the hell would anyone ever need to use* that *symbol?*

Luckily, he knew it, although why he had remembered it was beyond him.

Q: Where would you find Combat Engineers?
In a Combat Engineer unit, fuckwit!

No, they probably wanted the answer to be 'with the bridging equipment', or 'for mine clearing', but one never knew.

Q: How many tanks are there in an independent tank battalion?
Shit! Was it thirty-one or forty-one?

He went for forty-one.

Q: What do you associate with a ZSU 23-4?

Though one could put anything down at all for this, what they wanted was 'an HQ', as it was an air defence weapon.

Jon rattled through the paper and finished it in just over two hours. He then went back through it and agonised over some of the answers, until time was called, and he handed the paper in.

Sitting with the others discussing the paper, his heart fell as he heard answers that weren't the same as what he had put down.

Oh shit, I hope I haven't fucked this up, he prayed.

They had a few days before they went out into the field for the final Combat Int exercise. To take their minds off it, they rehearsed the pass out parade. They were beginning to get pretty good at it, as they had been doing the same thing for weeks now. Sergeant Thompson was getting fairly laid back, and drill was actually enjoyable. It was quite pleasant marching around the parade square on a fine afternoon in late May.

"You'll get to see the slide for twenty seconds and then you'll have another twenty seconds to write it down," came the instruction for the recognition test.

By this point, they would either know it or not, although some of the slides could show odd angles, but it wasn't designed to be difficult that way. It was the relentless slides, one after the other, that caused the pressure.

During their recognition training, one of the slides had come up with 'BRDM2' written along the bottom.

"I thought it was a trick," said the recruit who had assumed that it must be something else, and not written down 'BRDM2'.

"Don't always assume that we're trying to trick you." replied the Sergeant with a smile.

The first slide came up and Jon wrote down 'T62', immediately. He was beginning to be able to recognise the equipment instantly, which he supposed was the purpose of the training.

When he had originally been in the TA many years ago, an old Corporal who had transferred in had told him that as an anti-tank gunner, he had been taught to recognise NATO kit and kill anything else. That was one way of doing it.

PMP-3, he thought, as the next slide came up.

These things were so distinctive that the only problem was remembering which was which.

The test lasted for just over an hour, and Jon was happy that he had got his 75%. He had recognised most of the kit and there were only one or two slides where he couldn't instantly say what they were. There were a few glum-looking faces, though. Some people obviously hadn't had it that easy.

They deployed into the field in groups of four in Land Rovers for the final Combat Int exercise. They would use 12 x 12 tents and sleep in them as well, if they could. The exercise was due to last thirty-six hours, which allowed them to set up the cell before they had to brief the commander. Each of them would do a brief and they would be marked on the cell as a group, so teamwork was essential.

Jon was in a syndicate with Sue and two other recruits whom he didn't really know, one male and one female. They set up the tent and they allowed Jon to take over as the natural leader. He designated them tasks and they were almost ready to go when Sergeant Levis popped his head in.

"How're you doing?" he asked.

"No problem, Sergeant," replied Jon.

Levis nodded.

"Looking good," he said, and left.

There were smiles from all around at the compliment. One of the directing staff came in with a sheet of paper.

"These are your first serials," he said, handing them over.

Jon gave them to Sue, who had been designated as the log keeper, and read them over her shoulder as she neatly copied them onto the three-part log sheet. The first one would be the Intelligence cell record, the second would go to the map marker so that they could transfer the information to the map, and the third went to the cell chief so that they could keep abreast of developments and be ready to brief the commander at any point.

Tom, the male recruit, had been designated as the map marker and was busy writing the names of towns in large black letters, whilst adding in the enemy 'sightings' that would form the basis of the brief. They had been warned off that the first brief would be at 1600, with the next at 2000, then 0800 and the final one at 1200. This allowed for an extra couple of briefs in case anyone made a complete mess of theirs.

There are four posts in an Intelligence cell: cell chief, log keeper, collator and map marker. It is standard practice that in a four-person team, the logger and collator posts are amalgamated, leaving one person free to sleep or eat.

Jon had found himself as cell chief by default and, once the cell was set up to his satisfaction, he designated Anne, the other female recruit, as the floater. She sat with Sue at the log keeper's desk and kept out of the way as it was too early to sleep.

By the time 1600 came, Jon was happy with the progress that they had made and had his brief prepared. He was just marking the map with the briefing time of 1600, when he heard a noise behind him and a sort of collective gasp. He turned around to find that the Corps Director, a Brigadier, had come to take the first brief.

"Good afternoon, sir," he said. "Would you like a seat?"

"Thank you," said the Director sitting down on a fold-out canvas seat that was there for the purpose of briefing.

Jon felt his palms sweating and his mouth go dry. He looked down at his briefing cards. He had once made the mistake at Sandhurst of trying to go through the orders process without using the aide memoire because he thought he wasn't allowed to. He wasn't going to make that mistake again.

"How long have you got, sir?" he asked, following the headings that he had written down.

"Five minutes," replied the Director.

"Right, sir. I'll give you a quick, five-minute briefing. The briefing period is from 0800 to 1600."

He paused while he flipped over the briefing cards. He could see the others watching him and, out of the corner of his eye, he saw the figures of Major Elswick and the CSM standing just outside the tent.

"Vital Intelligence," he said. "There is no vital Intelligence at the moment."

"OK," acknowledged the Director nodding slightly.

Jon flipped over another card. "Are you familiar with the map, sir?"

"Yes. Thank you," came the reply.

It would be a poor show if the commander *wasn't* familiar with the ground, but you always had to ask just in case someone had just arrived in theatre. Next card. Jon fumbled with his cards as they wouldn't flip over properly.

"General enemy situation," he continued, reading off his cards. "Sir, facing you is 101 Motor Rifle Regiment."

The Director just sat and listened. He was playing a British Army infantry battalion commander and would expect to be confronted by a Soviet regiment that was three times bigger. Doctrine states that the enemy needs at least three times the quantity of troops if it is to succeed in an attack. Unlike the British Army, where a regiment is made up of as many battalions as it needs but generally only has one, a Soviet regiment is made up of three battalions.

Jon flipped another card.

"Enemy operations in detail," he read. "We assess that the enemy is advancing along a main axis, here."

With this, he pointed to the big red arrow that Tom had drawn on the map.

"And that the second axis is here."

This time he indicated a smaller red arrow.

"We assess that the enemy is still 100% combat effective. Possible enemy courses of action are that they could continue along the main axis, or turn north or south." Jon paused again as he ran his tongue around his teeth to moisten his mouth.

"Probable course of action," he continued. "The probable course of action is that the enemy will continue along the main axis, with the main objective being the bridge over the river at Tinsletown."

Christ! Do they have to give the places such stupid names? It's bad enough trying to brief without crap like this, Jon thought.

"That, sir, concludes my briefing. Do you have any questions?" he asked.

The Director glanced at the map. "Any idea where the RAG is?"

This was a typical question and Jon had expected it. The Regimental Artillery Group was a serious quantity of firepower, and a battalion commander would want to know where it was.

"Nothing definite, but we think that it may be located somewhere near here," bluffed Jon.

"Thanks, Private..."

"Comyn, sir."

"Thank you, Private Comyn. Good brief," said the Director and got up to go.

Jon let out a sigh of relief; he had got away with it. Major Elswick poked his head into the tent a couple of minutes later.

"Well done," he said, smiling. "This is the best syndicate – so far."

That set the stage for the others to follow and gave them a boost of confidence. It got easier from then on for Jon, as he had done his brief and was unlikely to be asked to do it again. At least, in a test scenario. He concentrated on getting the others through and coached them in the use of the set format headings and how to bluff, if necessary.

Sue did hers at 2000 and sailed through it. They were then relatively free until 0800 and started to have a bit of a joke, so much so that Sergeant Levis popped in to see what was going on. He could tell from the happy faces that the cell was running well and gave them a thumbs up.

Serials kept coming in during the night, and Jon decided that there was no point trying to sleep as there was nowhere comfortable or quiet enough. Anne had asked if she could do the brief at 0800 and he wanted to make sure that she had the best support that the others could give her.

Copious quantities of tea were drunk, and they sat up, chatting about possible enemy courses of action until dawn broke and Captain Case came in for the brief. She seemed happy and didn't ask too many awkward questions and Anne finished with a smile.

That only left Tom. He was a bit nervous. He had a slight stammer, Jon noticed, although that might have been brought on by nerves and lack of sleep. The day was promising to be bright and sunny, and it was getting quite warm when Elswick came in for his briefing. By that point, the enemy objective had become clear. It *was* the bridge, and the combat indicators like bridging equipment and air defence units were beginning to get reported, so they could give the commander a fair idea of what was happening and where things were.

"Well done," repeated Elswick, once the brief was over. "The only thing that I will say is that it's not usually this easy in reality, but that's not your fault."

With that, he went on to the next syndicate.

"You can start packing up," they were told by the CSM at 1400. "This syndicate won't be asked to do another brief, although Major Elswick wanted you to show the rest of them how to do it, but I stopped him."

"Thanks, sir," they all said, with relief.

It was a great compliment that Elswick thought they were good enough to brief the whole squad, but they could certainly do without the chance to balls up in front of everyone.

They found out later on that not everyone had done as well as them, and that three people failed their briefings. They were to be given the opportunity to try again while the rest of the squad went on a battlefield tour of Waterloo.

"What could be better than a weekend drinking Belgian beer and a tour of one of the most famous battlefields in the world?" asked Sergeant Lott, happily.

He was happy because Sergeant Levis had volunteered to stay behind to help the recruits who were still doing their briefings for their trade test, so he would be going with the majority of the squad across the Channel for the weekend and getting the army to pay for it.

They would leave on Saturday morning and drive to Brussels, where they would stay overnight before doing the tour and return on Sunday afternoon. What made it even better was that it was close to the anniversary of the battle which occurred on 15 June 1815.

The plan was to take three minibuses, and the CSM and Sergeant Thompson were going to be the directing staff for the trip. Jon once again found himself as a driver, although he didn't really mind. They would be driving in convoy and that meant that he couldn't really go that fast, as all three vehicles would need to stick together.

They set off on a warm, June morning in the knowledge that they had only their pass out parade to complete before they were qualified to be Intelligence Corps Lance Corporals. This meant not only a promotion but a double pay rise, as there was a pay increase for both passing the trade test and also on promotion to Lance Corporal.

They were in a festive mood, marred only by the fact that three of their colleagues were struggling, but Sergeant Lott told them that they had every chance of passing, and even if they didn't this time, there was still the opportunity to do so on the next course. The army had spent a lot of money on their training so far, and it wasn't an organisation that let that slip away, if it could be avoided.

They caught an early ferry at Dover and were on the motorway to Brussels by 0900. The motorway was pretty good until they crossed over into Belgium, and the change was fairly dramatic. The road was full of potholes, some of them quite large, and they had to slow down for fear of damaging the suspension.

They were booked into a small hotel on the outskirts of Brussels, but once they had dumped their kit, they were given the opportunity to drive into the city and look around. Jon's group had the CSM in charge and he seemed to know his way around. He guided them to a public car park in a shopping area and told them to be back in an hour. He then disappeared on his own, leaving Jon and the others wondering what to do. They wandered around the market and then went to a local café. They were reluctant to go too far from the minibus, for fear of not finding it again.

"He could have given us a bit of direction," complained one of the recruits.

"He's always been a bit funny," said another.

Jon didn't really know. The CSM seemed to be a nice guy, but they hadn't had much to do with him, as he always seemed to be busy with the training Major and rarely attended the recruits' lessons. He seemed quite pleased when he returned, and Jon drove them back to the hotel.

They had dinner in the hotel, which Peter claimed was horse meat, but it tasted great, and the beer was good. The next morning, they drove out to Waterloo and spent three hours wandering around the battlefield. It was a bit spoilt by the huge mound that the Prince of Orange had apparently had constructed after the battle, but it was a superb viewpoint for the surrounding area.

It was fascinating for Jon to see Hougoumont and the farmhouses at La Haye Sainte. He'd read about them and he was glad for the opportunity to see them in real life.

On their return, he noticed that Steve seemed very quiet. When they got to the ferry and went to the café, Jon asked him what was wrong, but Steve seemed reluctant to say. Eventually, he told Jon that he had knocked on the CSMs door to give him an early morning call, first thing in the morning and the door had swung open. The CSM was in the bathroom, but Steve had seen a magazine lying open on his bed. He had quietly shut the door without being seen and went back five minutes later to 'wake' him.

"So, what's the problem?" Jon asked, puzzled.

"It was the magazine," said Steve. "I didn't really get a good look, but it looked like child pornography."

"Oh, fuck!" said Jon. "Are you sure?"

"No," admitted Steve. "That's the problem."

That put a bit of a downer on the trip, to say the least.

PART 5

DRILL AND DUTIES 3

JUNE - JULY 1990

CHAPTER 20

When the recruits got back from Belgium, they found out that, true to what Sergeant Lott said, all three of the failures had now passed their briefings. This resulted in a huge piss-up in the NAAFI, helped along by duty-free booze brought back from the continent.

It was, therefore, with some major hangovers that the recruits filed into the classroom on Monday morning, to be told that they had to fill in their posting preferences. They were all now expected to pass out on 15 July, which was just over a month away.

Jon didn't really have any problem deciding what he wanted to do. His first preference was an Intelligence company, his second a Security section, and in third place was IA training. He had given it some thought, but Combat Intelligence was definitely his first choice and, if he didn't get that, then he didn't really mind either way. He was pragmatic enough to realise that the army would send him where it wanted him to go, regardless of his desires, so he wouldn't be disappointed if he didn't get what he asked for.

Major Elswick came into the classroom to congratulate them all on their Combat Intelligence trade tests. Jon was slightly disappointed to find out that he had actually done better in the written Security paper, where he had scored 81%, than he had in the Combat Intelligence paper, where he only managed 75%. He put that down to ambiguous questions and the irony of life. There were one or two recruits who had been borderline failures for the written exam, but they had been given a bye with some creative marking. Jon loved that about the army: one would expect it to be totally rigid

313

when it came to stuff like this but, if they liked someone, they would bend the rules for them.

"So, what did you go for, then?" Donna asked, as they sat around on the grass during a coffee break.

"I went for an Int company," replied Jon. "How about you?"

"14 Sigs, for me."

That wasn't really a surprise. Donna had professed an interest in joining the unit ever since she had heard about it.

"Same here," added Mich. Again, that was no surprise as Mich had transferred in from the Royal Signals.

"Security, for me," said Sue. Most of the female recruits favoured a Security section over an Intelligence company.

"How about you, Paul?"

Paul 'Biff' Dobson was a bit of a wildcard. He had started off badly but improved over time and was now considered to be one of the top recruits.

"I don't know, really," he admitted. "I put down for a Security section but we don't really know enough about it, do we?"

They all agreed on that, but they had had to state a preference and now it was done and only time would tell where they would end up.

Now that basic training and the trade tests were over, there was a feeling of being slightly in limbo. They still had to prepare for the pass out parade, but that mainly entailed doing drill and polishing boots. No one was expected to fail that part of the course. They had heard of the case of a recruit who was so bad at drill that they hadn't been allowed to be part of the squad in case they ruined the whole thing but had still passed out. They were Intelligence Corps after all, and not guardsmen.

"Go! Go! Go!" shouted Jon.

Sue dropped her bat and sprinted off to the first marker. They were having a game of rounders, which would be one of the contests in a sports competition that would be held in the run up to Corps Day. The opposition would come from the Territorial Army Intelligence Corps squad, which was due to pass out at the same time.

There was an ambivalent feeling towards the TA in the squad. Those recruits who had no experience of the TA, or had been influenced by Corporal Cazanoe, didn't hold them in high regard, but most of the others were prepared to wait and see.

Sue reached the first marker.

"Keep going!" yelled Jon.

Sue had made a really good hit, and she might make a home run.

One of the male recruits was sprinting after the ball but hadn't reached it yet. Sue carried on running. She was past the third post and on the home straight as the ball was thrown to the bowler. Fortunately, he fumbled it, and a red-faced Sue staggered past the fourth post and scored them a home run.

"Well done, Susie," Paul called.

Susie? Jon thought.

He had never heard her being called that before. He wondered if there was something going on between Paul and Sue. It was perfectly possible. There was no restriction on relationships between similarly ranked service personnel, as long as it didn't breach the service test.

The service test is the mechanism by which breaches in the army's values and standards are judged. It applies to everyone in the army, at all times, both on and off duty, irrespective of rank, and is summarised by the question: 'Have the actions or behaviour of an individual adversely impacted, or are they likely to impact, on the efficiency or operational effectiveness of the service?'

It is surprising how many people think that the rules only apply to other people and not to them, particularly the higher ranking members of the service, but that's where entitlement comes in.

Sue and Paul, both being Privates, were the same rank. As long as their relationship, if they had one, didn't affect their training, then there shouldn't be a problem. If Paul had been higher ranking, say a Sergeant or Warrant Officer, then it would have proven awkward if a disciplinary matter was involved.

"Keep going like that and we'll easily beat the TA," said Jon, to a round of smiles from the team.

They practiced all the different sports that would be included in the competition so that the best teams for each one could be chosen. There were still thirty of them left from the original squad of forty, so they had plenty of choice. The least sporty and least fit members of the squad accepted that they wouldn't be picked for the teams. It was a matter of honour that they didn't get beaten by 'part-timers'.

Jon had been given the nod that he, Mich and Steve were all in the running for best recruit, which meant that Sergeant Thompson took them in hand for extra drill, as they would be required to march out in front of the guests and staff to accept the award.

Donna had won the prize for the Security phase of the trade test, and a recruit called Andy had won the Combat Intelligence prize as he had done exceptionally well in the written paper, scoring over 90%. 'Most improved recruit' went to Paul 'Biff' Dobson, and 'best shot' went to Sonia.

It was eventually decided that Steve should get 'best recruit', as both Jon and Mich had previous experience. (Jon got the 'best at drill' as a consolation.) It pleased him greatly, as he remembered his

Colour Sergeant at Sandhurst constantly putting him on charges for mistakes in drill, which resulted in a charge of being inattentive on the parade square, oddly enough at the same time as the Colour Sergeant's favourite, and they were both let off with a reprimand.

He would have liked to have seen the face of his Colour Sergeant when he was awarded the prize, to show him that he was actually quite good at drill, but that was water under the bridge and the guy had probably left the army by now.

Steve asked Jon to go for a quiet drink with him that night. They went out into Ashford and found a small pub down the back streets.

"What do you think I should do about the CSM?" Steve asked, when they had their drinks.

Jon gave him a long look. "What can you do?"

"I can report it," said Steve.

"Who to?" queried Jon. "Do you have any actual proof?"

"No," admitted Steve, "but I know what I saw."

"Yes. But it's going to be your word against his. Look, I know this is hard, but you've got to understand that although you saw what you saw, you haven't got any proof, and this could turn nasty."

Steve sat and looked at him, his face a contradiction of emotions. "I can't just let it go."

"OK. Suppose you report it. Who are you going to report it to? The Major? The police? Who?"

"I... I don't know."

"I'm not trying to defend the bastard, but unless you've got something concrete, you're going to land yourself in trouble. Imagine what the Major's going to say when you accuse his CSM of something like this. Christ! He could be in on it himself, for all we know."

"You don't think so, do you?" Steve said, appalled.

"No. But that's what I mean. We just don't know."

"What are we going to do, then?"

"The only thing I can think of is to leave it and hope it was a one off. It might have been just that one magazine. He may have just bought it and didn't know exactly what was in it."

"Do you think so?"

"Unfortunately, no. But I can't see any good outcome for this."

"Shit," said Steve, with feeling.

They sat for a while, silently drinking and mulling over options and then, finally, Steve came to a decision.

"You're right," he said. "I'll keep it to myself, but will keep an eye out, in case I come across anything else. OK?"

"Agreed."

It felt like a lack of moral courage, but Jon had heard too many stories about miscarriages of justice to let Steve go any further at this time.

They finished their drinks and went back to the barracks.

"Today, you're going to get a couple of presentations about possible future deployments. So, I'd like to introduce Major Blanche, who's going to talk about Op Banner," said Major Elswick, as the recruits sat in the lecture theatre.

They sat on tiered seats that looked down onto a huge projector screen where, previously, they had endured interminable PowerPoint lectures on various subjects, but today sounded quite interesting.

Major Blanche smiled at Elswick. "Thanks, Doug."

He clicked on the projector, and the words 'Op Banner' flashed up onto the screen in large letters, on a background of brick-built houses and burnt-out cars, which they took to be somewhere in

Northern Ireland. Probably Belfast.

"'Op Banner' is the operational name for the British Army in Northern Ireland," he said. "Some of you will find yourself posted to Security sections or Intelligence companies and may find yourselves serving across the water."

He paused to let this sink in. Jon hadn't really considered Northern Ireland, although he should have. He assumed that joining an Intelligence company would mean that he would be deployed to West Germany, to do Combat Int with the Red Army as the enemy, but maybe not. The 'Troubles' had been going on since the late 1960s and had become background noise in the life of most people in the UK. It was odd, but he never really thought about it, unless something was reported in the press. It had almost become the norm.

"The Intelligence Corps," Blanche continued, "has a fairly major presence in the province, and I like to think that we have helped to keep things under control."

You might like to think that, but we haven't won, have we? thought Jon.

He remembered the lecture on terrorism and Sergeant Dante talking about Scotch John's dictum. From what she had said, the IRA couldn't be beaten.

"Before I go any further, I'd like to ask a couple of questions," he said and paused.

"How many counties are there in Ulster?"

"Six," came the reply.

Blanche smiled. "No," he said. "There are actually nine – Cavan, Monaghan and Donegal are in the Republic. So, Northern Ireland doesn't even cover the whole of Ulster. I know this because my wife's father was in the IRB."

He looked out at the blank faces.

"The IRB, or Irish Republican Brotherhood, was the forerunner of the Irish Republican Army, which split into the Provisional IRA

(PIRA) and official IRA (OIRA) in 1969, although nowadays we only talk about PIRA. Anyway, I'm not here to give you a history lesson about Ireland, but to talk to you about this."

He clicked a slide, and the words 'Op Maximise' came up beneath the heading of Op Banner.

"'What is Op Maximise? I hear you ask. Or do I?"

Mich was nodding.

"Does anyone know what Op Maximise is?" he asked, looking towards Mich.

"It's the operational name for selection for 14 Int," Mich replied.

"And 14 Int, although it's not called that anymore, is?" he prompted.

"Er... they're the undercover surveillance guys, I think."

"Correct! 14 Intelligence Company, or Joint Communications Unit Northern Ireland, JCUNI, for short, is the unit that does undercover surveillance in the province."

"Are they the agent handlers?" someone asked.

"No. That's JSG and I'll come to them later. You have to be at least a Sergeant to attempt Op Maximise, so that would come later in your careers but, as a Lance Corporal, you could find yourself doing analysis or working in the Intelligence cell that supports JCUNI."

Wow! That sounds interesting, thought Jon. *That's the real* James Bond *stuff.*

"So, you see, even as a lowly Lance Corporal in the Intelligence Corps, you have the opportunity to make a difference," continued Blanche.

They were given a break and when they came back into the lecture theatre, the words 'Op Samson' had replaced 'Op Maximise'.

"Joint Support Group, or JSG, is the unit that recruits and manages agents and agent handlers," Blanche told them. "It is a HumInt speciality and can be very dangerous. As an agent handler, you go out, often alone, to meet your contact, and there have been plenty of attempts to either ambush or capture the handler."

"What would happen if you got caught?" someone asked from the back.

Blanche pursed his lips. "It depends. If you can keep yourself alive, then the SAS will get you out. Otherwise..."

There was silence from the auditorium, as the recruits thought about the stories that they had heard about people being tortured. Kneecapping was a favourite, sometimes using a Black & Decker drill.

"Anyway," continued Blanche, "it is unlikely that you would have the experience to become an agent handler for a few years, but you could certainly be posted to JSG."

"As i/c photocopier," someone muttered.

Blanche smiled. "Well, someone's got to make the coffee, haven't they?"

"Don't fancy that, much," said Paul, at lunch.

"What running the photocopier, or getting your kneecaps blown off?" someone asked.

"Either to be perfectly honest," admitted Paul. "Doing a nice, safe Security survey is more my forte, methinks."

"Remember those two Corporals who got killed?" someone said. "I heard that they were JCUNI."

"No," disagreed Mich. "They were Royal Signals. The reason that the army didn't send someone to help them was because there was no official record of them being on an operation and the QRF never got called out."

"What's a QRF?" asked Paul.

"Quick Reaction Force," replied Mich.

"Is that true?" asked Jon.

"That's what I was told," said Mich. "It was a tragic mistake. They just happened to be in the wrong place at the wrong time. Could happen to anyone."

"I remember that," said one of the female recruits. "It was in the paper."

"Yes. What made it even worse was that one of the guys pulled out a 9mm pistol and the magazine fell off after the first round. Or so I've heard."

"Bloody hell!" exclaimed Paul.

"I suppose that most of you are too young to remember, but do you remember when that guy tried to kidnap Princess Anne?" enquired Jon.

"1974, wasn't it?" Mich added.

"I was only two years old!" said Paul.

"Youthlet," countered Mich.

Jon laughed. "Well, Princess Anne's bodyguard pulled out a 9mm and it jammed. He took a bullet for her and was lucky to escape with his life. The reason the automatic jammed was that he left the rounds in all the time and the spring got permanently compressed and wouldn't work. That was why I used to empty my magazines once a day when I was in Africa."

"Was that when you were in Zimbabwe?" asked Sonia.

"Yes," replied Jon. "I was a security officer on a gold mine."

"A gold mine? Did you see any gold?" someone asked.

"Yes. I once held a 17kg ingot of almost pure gold in my hand," Jon recalled. "It was the last smelting before we closed the mine down. It was surprisingly small and the most beautiful thing that I've ever seen in my life."

"How much was it worth?"

"Gold was $17 a gram, in those days. So, eighteen times seventeen thousand," Jon did a quick calculation. "Almost $300,000."

"What did you do with it?"

"We locked it in the safe."

He thought back. Greg, his crazy American colleague, had suggested that they steal the gold. They had both been armed, Greg had a four-wheel drive Land Rover, and they were only 15km from the Botswana border. He had briefly been tempted, but they would have left their boss, John, in the shit, and anyway, what the hell would he do with a 17kg ingot of gold? He couldn't exactly go into a shop and spend it. Jon smiled as he thought about it. He wondered where Greg was now. He was a 6ft 4in. blonde American, whose father had been a Hollywood golf pro. Greg had tried his hand at that, but he said that although he was winning upwards of $10,000 a year, the expenses were so high that he couldn't make any money. He had been married for a month before he had gone out to Zimbabwe. His wife had looked as if she had been made of plastic.

Sonia's voice broke into his reverie. "You really are a bit of a dark horse, you know."

Donna, Mich and some of the other recruits had gone off to RAF Brawdy in Wales on a liaison visit to 14 Signal Regiment. Jon declined to go as he had no intention of joining 14 Sigs, even though he found the concept of electronic warfare quite interesting. Instead, he had volunteered to help out in the Intelligence Corps library as he had never really had time to see what they had on their shelves.

The library was literally stuffed with books; piles of them were stacked on the floor awaiting classification and placement His sister, Aggie, should have been here. She had been a librarian at one point, working in the main library on George IV Bridge in Edinburgh, but had abandoned the delights of books for more lucrative work in a building society.

"Could you just sort out that pile over there?" asked a small, birdlike woman in a quiet voice.

She looked like she was probably the wife of one of the officers, who was running the library for something to do. She seemed very timid and was pathetically grateful when Jon and Simon had volunteered to help her.

"Would you like a coffee?" she enquired, almost flinching when she asked, and Jon wondered what it was that made her so nervous.

"I'm Captain Gewächshaus's wife," she told them, as they drank their coffee, and Jon understood her submissive attitude.

Gewächshaus had the reputation for being a complete and utter bastard. He was something to do with the stores. He might even have been the Quartermaster, although Jon seemed to remember that that was a Major's post.

On the odd occasion that the recruits had had anything to do with him, he had seemed to be a thoroughly unpleasant person and particularly so to the females. It was rumoured that he was a completely different person when his wife was away, and Jon wondered if he was gay.

Gewächshaus's wife jumped up with a terrified look on her face and almost dropped her china teacup. Jon looked up to see Gewächshaus walk in the door with a thunderous look on his face. Jon leapt to attention, followed immediately by Simon.

"Who are you?" he demanded of the two recruits.

"Private Comyn, sir," barked Jon.

"Private Tollsland, sir," said Simon, just after. "We're helping out in the library."

Gewächshaus's face softened as he looked at Simon, and Simon smiled back.

Kindred spirits, thought Jon.

"Well done, boys," he said, and disappeared through the door after his wife.

Jon looked at Simon, who reddened.

"He seems to like you."

"Well... you know," mumbled Simon.

Jon smiled. "Well, as long as he leaves us alone, I don't care."

They made themselves busy and Gewächshaus left without seeing them. Jon couldn't help but feel sorry for his wife. She seemed like a nice person who was trapped in a world not of her making. After they tidied up a few piles of books, they browsed through the collection. Jon was amazed at the variety of books on military subjects that there were. He had never thought that there would be anywhere near that many. It would take years to read them all; he wished that he had time to do so. It would be great to have a cosy little house, maybe a cottage, where he could burrow down in the winter next to an open fire and spend the cold months never going out, with plenty to eat and drink and read.

The Captain's wife thanked them profusely for their help and they wandered back to the billet.

"Have you ever been to the Intelligence Corps Museum?" Simon asked.

Jon admitted that he hadn't. It had been closed for refurbishment when they had arrived, and they hadn't had the opportunity to go and have a look.

"It looks like it could be quite interesting," offered Simon.

Jon agreed. They would have to have a look before they left the depot.

It was only a couple of weeks now. Time seemed to be flying now that they were getting near the end.

The trip to RAF Brawdy had gone well and those who had asked to join 14 Sigs were happy that they had made the choice. The next visit would be from Intelligence Corps members from JSIW, the Joint

Services Interrogation Wing, who ran the advanced questioning techniques school in the depot.

The recruits had been trained in how to conduct an interview. This was one of the jobs that they might find themselves carrying out if they were posted to a Security section, but advanced questioning techniques was on another level altogether.

It was rumoured, so Jon had heard, that JSIW could break anyone in three days, although the process would leave the subject brain damaged, but this might have been an urban myth. What was certain was that the Resistance to Interrogation part of SAS selection was sufficiently hard that a fair number of SAS recruits failed it. The problem is that people can resist physical pain far more easily than they can resist mental pain, and those trained in the techniques can be very good at it. This was apparently why the SAS called the Intelligence Corps green slime and demonstrated how much they disliked the procedure.

"Physical torture works if all that is wanted is a confession," one of the instructors told them "The Spanish Inquisition proved that, back in the sixteenth century, but any information gained will be of no use in the short term, because the person being tortured will eventually say anything to stop the pain. This is no use to us as, apart from it being illegal, it takes too long to sort through the data to determine what is true and what has merely been said under duress.

The art of extracting information, therefore, is to get the subject to voluntarily offer information that can either be easily verified or is likely to be true. This is where skilled interrogators come in, and they are extensively trained in the various techniques for this to happen."

"What do you do if you get caught and are about to be interrogated?" asked the JSIW WO2 in response to a question from one of the recruits. "It depends on the circumstances but, if you can, try to hold out for two days. After that, anything you know will hopefully be obsolete and of no use to the enemy."

He paused for a moment.

"However, if they are going to torture you, I would advise you start talking and don't stop. Tell them anything you can think of and then make it up. Overload them with information and they will waste time trying to decipher it."

"How long can someone hold out, under torture?" someone asked.

"That's a good question, and it depends on the individual. Have you heard of Noor Inayat Khan?"

Some of the recruits nodded, but most had never heard of her.

"She was an SOE agent during the war and was betrayed and captured in France in 1943. She was interrogated many times, but never gave anything away until she was finally shot in 1944."

To allow the recruits to get a feel of what real warfare was actually like, the training wing staff organised a visit to a firepower demonstration run by the Land Warfare Trainer in Warminster.

Once again, the recruits got on a coach and were bussed to their destination. They sat, transfixed, in purpose-built seating as firstly a section of infantry fired their SLRs. Next came the GPMG and mortars. The noise of battle increased, and the visual effects of tracer rounds and mortar explosions added to the action. After that, it was the turn of the Warrior Armoured Fighting Vehicle (AFV), which had been introduced in 1986 and gave an infantry platoon the benefit of its 30mm Rarden cannon. Added to the infantry was a battery of AS90 self-propelled guns, dropping their 155mm shells from several kilometres away.

Things started to get really heavy when a squadron of Challenger tanks roared up and blasted away. Finally, to round things off, an A10 Warthog appeared and fired off a two-second burst consisting of an estimated 2,900 rounds, with an ear-splitting *thrrrrrp* sound.

The A10 had been designed as a tank killer, and the recruits could understand how the average Soviet tank would have little chance, if hit by that many rounds in such a short period of time.

One more reason why you wouldn't want to be a Russian tank crew, thought Jon.

It was a wonder that soldiers could hear anything after that and, although it was great to watch, it would be a totally different matter if the same, or more, ordnance was coming the other way. It was no wonder that soldiers got shell shocked during the First World War.

There was a story from the Falklands about when Lieutenant Mills and his men from the Royal Marines tried to defend South Georgia against the Argentinian invaders, at the beginning of the campaign. At the end of the assault, when Lieutenant Mills had been forced to surrender, one of the Marines asked why the Carl Gustav – an 84mm anti-tank weapon – hadn't been used. The operator told him that he had fired it several times, but the other soldier hadn't noticed it going off. Jon remembered the noise it made and had wondered how one could miss it, but the firepower demonstration had just explained why.

It all made the SMG, which the Intelligence Corps was issued with, seem like a popgun.

He suddenly remembered Linda and realised that, although it was a small weapon and not very powerful, it could still kill in close quarters. He wondered if they would ever find out the reason for what she did. He hadn't known her very well, but she had been a colleague. He looked over at Simon, who was sitting staring out the window. He had been on duty that night. He had blamed himself for not being there for her. Had he got over it?

As if he had been talking out loud, Simon looked over at him and gave him a sad smile and then looked away again.

Jon drifted away into a world of his own, as the coach rumbled along the motorway on its way back to Ashford. There was a low hum of conversations, and he noticed that Paul and Sue were sitting next to each other – again. There must be something going on.

Good on them.

After a while, he dozed off and woke up as the coach pulled up at the depot guardroom.

CHAPTER 21

The Territorial Army Intelligence Corps' Corps Training Platoon (CTP) arrived on Saturday 8 July, exactly one week before Corps Day. This gave them six days to practice their drill, before the pass out parade, and constituted their Drill and Duties 3 course. They had done their trade tests at the end of their Security and Combat Intelligence phases like their regular counterparts and would be eligible for promotion to Lance Corporal by the following Saturday, if all went well.

They were in a buoyant mood as they entered the bar of the NAAFI and seemed to be little different from the regular recruits, Jon thought as he watched them come in. They seemed to split into two distinct groups, with some, but not much, interaction between them.

"Hi. We're the TA, mind if we sit here?" one of them asked in what sounded to Jon like an east coast of Scotland accent.

"Sure," he said. "Help yourself."

"Are you regulars?" a tall, blonde girl asked him, which was a pretty stupid question, considering they were in the regular Intelligence Corps depot NAAFI, but he shrugged it off. They weren't to know better, he supposed.

"Yes. Most of the people in here are Squad 49. We're due to pass out with you lot."

"Oh! That's nice," she said, happily.

"East or west coast?" he enquired.

She gave him a look. "East coast. I'm from Edinburgh."

"Are you all from Edinburgh?"

"No. Some of us are from Glasgow, and they're all English." She indicated the other TA personnel, sitting at separate tables.

"How does it work, then? Aren't you one squad?"

"No. We're 23 and 29 companies, and they're the London ones."

"I don't know much about the TA Int Corps," Jon admitted. "What do 23 and 29 companies do?"

"Oh!" she said, realising she had assumed that he would know what she was talking about. "23 Security company does Security and 294 section does Security and Intelligence. 23 company is the Scottish company and 29 company does home defence and covers the whole of the UK. The London companies do Security, Combat Int, Imagery Analysis and Advanced Questioning Techniques. There's four of them. We also have sections in Newcastle, York, Manchester and Birmingham. They're the northern squad, but there's no one from there at the moment."

"Right," said Jon, not completely following her, but getting a better idea of why they seemed to be two separate groups.

"So, what's it like in the regulars?" she asked.

"I don't know yet. We'll find out once we've passed out."

"Oh. OK."

Something caught Jon's eye, and he looked up at the bar.

What the hell is he up to? he wondered

Paul 'Biff' Dobson had approached one of the TA Intelligence Corps who was standing at the bar. Jon could just make out what he was saying over the hum of conversation.

"You look pretty fit," said Paul to a well-built male recruit. "I bet you a beer that I can do between two and three hundred press-ups."

The TA recruit looked at him in disbelief. "Two and three hundred press-ups? No way!"

"I'm not going to specify an exact number, but I bet you I can do between two and three hundred press ups," repeated Paul.

"Somewhere between two and three hundred press-ups?"

"Yep. You gonna take up my bet, then?" asked Paul.

"Sure," came the confident reply.

There was a pause in the conversation as Paul made a space, and people stopped their conversations to watch.

Paul got down into the press-up position and slowly did five press-ups as everyone watched and waited. After doing the five press-ups, he got up.

"There you go," he said.

"You only did five!" objected his opponent.

"It's between *two* and three hundred," said Paul, with a sly smile. "I told you I wasn't going to specify a figure."

A huge cheer went up from the regular recruits as they realised that Paul had scammed the TA.

"Bastard!" said the TA recruit, but he bought Paul a beer.

That broke the ice, and the two squads started mixing. It carried on until the bar closed at 2230 and they all poured out of the NAAFI and went to bed.

The following morning, Jon saw the TA out doing a Basic Fitness Test, first thing. He could see that some of them were struggling, and it didn't really surprise him. He had heard stories about people drinking in the mess all night and then going out to do a BFT, but one would have to be a really hardened drinker to do that.

The army had a serious drinking culture, which wasn't helped by the fact that booze in Germany was tax-free. This meant that alcohol was so cheap that people drank huge amounts, and the only thing that stopped the statistics from revealing this was the fact that one didn't get tested for it.

Jon's cousin, who had been a Lieutenant in the Royal Signals in the early 1970s, had told him that he had seen a questionnaire that stated that if you answered yes to three or more questions out of twenty, then you might have a drinking problem, and that he had answered yes to almost all of them.

Virtually all of his friends who had committed criminal offences, including himself, had done so because of alcohol. But in the army, soldiers were positively encouraged to drink. From the messes that had little or no options for non-alcoholic drinks, to an almost bullying culture where it wasn't considered 'manly' *nor* to drink, there wasn't much scope for teetotallers. It was surprising that there weren't more alcoholics. Although, saying that, maybe that was one of the reasons why so many homeless people were ex-services.

The TA stragglers finally finished, and Jon wondered if the run was an important test. The TA got a tax-free 'bounty' each year that was dependant one passing certain tests, and he was pretty sure that the BFT was one of them. He would have to ask someone when they came to the NAAFI tonight.

The regular recruits were sitting in the classroom, wondering what today's lessons would be about, when Major Elswick came in with another officer.

"Good morning, ladies and gentlemen. This is Captain Smythe and he's going to tell you all about our counterparts in the Territorial Army," announced Elswick, in a jovial tone.

There were a few quiet groans, but not loud enough to be heard at the front of the room.

Captain Smythe was a small, thin man with a slightly untidy haircut and thinning brown hair.

"Good morning, everyone," he started, sweeping the room with his eyes. "Firstly, I'll tell you a bit about myself. I was originally in the regular Intelligence Corps, like yourselves, and reached the rank of Corporal. After that, I left the army and went to university to study accountancy."

Well, that explains a lot, thought Jon. *An accountant.*

"While I was at university, I joined the Officer Training Corps (OTC) and, on completion of my degree, I was commissioned into the Intelligence and Security Group (Volunteers). The TA Intelligence Corps was created on 1 April 1967, in case anyone is interested."

"April Fool's Day!" someone muttered.

"So, I've seen the Corps from both sides," he said.

He went on to tell them that the Int & Sy Gp (V) was made up of six companies and a headquarters element. He then went on to list the various companies, starting with 20 Security company (V).

"The role of 20 Sy Coy (V) is rear area Security in Belgium. This was to secure the supply ports from the UK to Europe in the event of World War Three breaking out, although with the fall of the Berlin wall, this is seeming less and less likely. 20 company is based in Fitzroy House, Hampstead, London in a building that it shares with 24 Int coy (V)."

Next came 21 Intelligence company (V), the Imagery Analysts.

"They spend most of their weekends at JARIC, and the joke is that they are all weedy little people with glasses who get locked in a cupboard for the weekend. They aren't really. Some of them don't wear glasses," he laughed. "If you've got any questions, by the way, please ask."

No one did.

He then talked about 22 Intelligence company (V) which is the TA Human Intelligence company who are trained in advanced questioning techniques.

"The members of 22 Company are generally a bit older than in other TA units. That's because they are generally linguists—"

"Cunning linguists. I might have known," one of the recruits said, quietly.

"—and they mostly speak Russian. You can do advanced questioning through an interpreter, but it's a lot more difficult and it's very easy to lose control of the narrative, if you're not careful."

That's interesting, thought Jon. *I never knew that.*

"There's a funny story about 22 company," continued Smythe.

"I bet there is," came the rejoinder, although too quietly for Smythe to hear. He was an officer, after all, even if he was TA and not a proper soldier.

"One weekend, the company went out for a field weekend," narrated Smythe, oblivious to the indifference of most of his audience. "The Permanent Staff Instructor (PSI) who was a regular Intelligence Corps Warrant Officer, went into the centre on Saturday morning to do some paperwork and found the company camped out in the drill hall. 'What are you doing here?' he asked. 'You're supposed to be in the field'. Only to be told, 'Oh! It was raining'."

Smythe obviously thought that this story was highly amusing and didn't notice that it went down like a lead balloon as the recruits thought about the various field exercises that they had had to endure.

Jon thought about what would have happened to an infantry regiment if they had done a similar thing; they would have been crucified. He remembered being freezing cold, wet, tired and hungry, living in a trench for days on end.

Wrong audience, mate! he thought.

Next up was 23 Security company (V) and like 20 Sy Coy (V), the role of 23 company was rear-area security, although their area of operations was the Netherlands rather than Belgium. 23 Security company also had a detachment in Belfast although they did all their training in Scotland.

That's quite bizarre, Jon thought.

He wondered what it was like being, in effect, a civilian living in Belfast but also a member of a unit of which PIRA would take a special interest.

Major Smythe continued talking about 24 Int coy (V) who were the Combat Inters and had a section that was supposed to support the SAS. He told them that they were co-located with 20 Sy coy (V) in Hampstead Training Centre. And finally 29 Intelligence and Security company (V) which was the home defence company and had sections covering most of the UK.

The regular recruits mostly listened with disinterest, but Jon thought that the lecture was very helpful. The guys and gals who were going to Security sections would very likely have a close liaison with their TA counterparts, and it was useful to understand them a bit more.

"You said that 23 company has a detachment in Belfast, sir?" Jon asked.

"Yes," answered Smythe.

"How do they find day-to-day living under those conditions?"

"That's a very good question. Surprisingly enough, they don't seem to have too many problems. We've even got one Warrant Officer who is Catholic and has never told his family that he is in the Intelligence Corps."

"What about the bombs?" someone asked.

"That's an interesting point. One of the detachment told me that although there are IEDs going off almost every day, unless you are close to one going off, you don't know anything about it until it's reported on television."

"I don't know if I could live like that," said someone.

"You'd be surprised. I always wondered how they managed at the siege of Leningrad. It lasted almost three years and yet they survived. That's humans for you, I suppose."

They trooped out of the lecture theatre and went to lunch. The cookhouse had a glass frontage, and they watched as the TA squad was marched up and halted just outside.

"To your duties... Fall out!" came the command.

They all turned to their right, except one recruit who turned the wrong way and ended up facing his colleagues. He quickly spun round as the squad marched the regulation three paces before splitting up. A huge cheer went up from the cookhouse, similar to when someone drops a glass in a busy pub or restaurant.

The unfortunate recruit who had turned the wrong way gave the watching regulars a flourishing bow, as if he was on a stage in front of an appreciative audience.

He's got a brass neck to do that, thought Jon.

Most people would have been really embarrassed and slink away, but the TA recruit had shrugged it off with aplomb.

The regular recruits continued with a mix of lessons while their TA counterparts carried on with their drill practice. Corps Day was the following Saturday, and the squad had been having drill lessons and practice for the best part of a year, so Sergeant Thompson saw no need for them to do even more drill, particularly now that they were all trade qualified.

Most of the recruits took the opportunity to have an evening out in London, but the CSM asked for volunteers for guard duty. Jon volunteered, as he had no wish to spend vast amounts of money on dubious beer in the country's capital city. He had drunk in London often enough when he lived there in the early eighties and the novelty had worn off.

Sonia volunteered too, so the two of them found themselves

patrolling the depot in the early hours of the morning. They were checking that the doors to the accommodation were secured when Jon noticed a light on in one of the classrooms. He pushed open the door to find two TA members engaged in 'manoeuvres' on the floor. One was the tall blonde girl whom he had spoken to on the first night that the TA squad had arrived. She looked up and smiled at him as he backed out the door.

"Bloody hell," he muttered.

"What is it?" asked Sonia.

"Two of the TA, going at it like rabbits."

"What, on the floor?"

"Yes."

Sonia laughed. "A bit uncomfortable, I would have thought."

"You can say that again."

Thursday morning was the final drill period before the full dress rehearsal on Friday, and the TA squad joined the regulars on the square at 0900. They were formed up as two separate squads, with the regulars on the right as they were the senior unit. There were roughly the same number of recruits in both squads, which helped the symmetry of the parade.

They would be wearing Number Two dress uniform for the actual parade, but today they were dressed in lightweight trousers and shirts.

Jon noticed that the TA were told to remove their berets at every opportunity, and he found out that this was because the recruits from the Belfast detachment of 23 Security company would put themselves at risk of being compromised if they went back to the province with tan lines from the headgear. It had never occurred to Jon that something like that could happen, but the army had probably found out the hard way and learned their lesson.

They were also parading with SMGs, and this made the drill slightly more complicated. The SMG can be folded up or used with the butt extended. For the purposes of the parade, the weapons were extended but didn't have magazines fitted.

Unlike the SLR, where the operator would go from the 'attention' position to 'order arms', so that the weapon was held tucked under the right arm for marching, the SMG had to go from the 'stand at ease' position, to the 'attention' position, to 'order arms', where the weapon was held across the chest. This meant that there were three sets of commands to be given before the squad was ready to march off.

They practiced arms drill for most of the morning, until Sergeant Thompson was happy that they could carry it off, and then they marched around the parade square a few times to accustom both squads to marching together.

Later on they had the sports afternoon, which consisted of a number of events with the TA on one side and the regular Intelligence Corps recruits on the other. The regulars gave the TA a good thrashing, although the TA didn't seem to be particularly bothered. They appeared to be competing just for the fun of it and seemed to enjoy themselves far more than the regulars, some of whom were taking it far too seriously, to Jon's mind.

There were a couple of incidents where angry comments made about other members of the team were verging on unacceptable insults, particularly when the TA team came close to winning. There were one or two excellent sportsmen and women in the TA, including the guy who had turned the wrong way when falling out. Jon found out later that he was ex-regular infantry and that, between them, three of the TA squad had more regular experience than the whole of the regular squad put together.

The TA didn't seem to care who won and laughed if someone

messed up rather than berating them, which Jon thought was the correct way to play sport if one was to properly enjoy it and to work as a team.

That evening in the bar, things got a bit nasty when one of the regular recruits took offense at something one of the TA said and a fight almost broke out. Jon could see why there was an element of jealousy involved in the rivalry between the two factions. The TA seemed to get it easy compared to the regulars, and on top of their pay they got a (not unsubstantial) bounty each year.

The difference was that the regulars were in full-time employment, with a regular promotion pattern, pensions, adventurous training and leave, whereas the TA gave up their weekends and one night a week, and were only allocated thirty-five days a year, including a two-week camp. Anything over that had to be authorised and so it hardly counted as a part-time job. There was no way anyone could live on a TA salary without some other form of income. But some of the regulars couldn't see that. Or they didn't want to.

The weather was pretty hot as it was the height of summer and even at 0800 it was still quite warm. What it was actually going to be like on the day of the parade was anyone's guess, but it didn't look like it was going to rain.

Major Elswick stood in for the Director during the dress rehearsal and the CSM took the place of the adjutant. It was the adjutant who would actually give the orders during the parade, not the Regimental Sergeant Major. The Corps RSM played no actual part in the ceremony, except to be there in full dress uniform with an impressive amount of medals.

The format of the parade was that the two squads would march onto the square, where seating had been arranged for the guests.

It was rumoured that Prince Philip, as Colonel in Chief of the Intelligence Corps, might be the guest of honour, but Jon doubted that. The security arrangements would have been just too much for what was a fairly low key ceremony.

The squads would be halted, turned to the left and put in open order and told to stand at ease. The guest of honour would then inspect them and then they would have the presentations. Sergeant Thompson had made sure that those being given awards were positioned so that they wouldn't get in each other's way as they marched out to collect their awards and back to the squad.

Jon wasn't really bothered about being the centre of attention on the parade, but Paul was incredibly nervous. He had never been particularly good at drill and previously had managed to hide within the squad, but now he would be in the open, in front of the Director and his guest. Sergeant Thompson tried to calm him down, and eventually he deemed him capable of going through the ceremony without throwing up or making a complete mess of it. There were instances of people watching from the sidelines instead of being part of the squad due to their lack of competence on the square, but Paul seemed like he would be able to pull it off.

The TA went out for the obligatory curry on Friday night as the end of their course was looming, which meant that they wouldn't be in the NAAFI that night which Jon thought was probably a good idea considering the simmering tensions between the two groups. He noticed that many of the recruits were missing from the bar. They were probably doing last minute adjustments to their kit and trying to get an early night before the big day.

"What are you doing for leave?" Sonia asked him, as he sat nursing a bottle of Becks.

"I don't know yet," he admitted. "I'll probably go back to Edinburgh for a bit and stay with my parents. I suppose it depends on where we go after here."

They had still not been told of their postings. They would get the written orders on Monday, after the pass out parade and Corps Day were over. They would also get their Lance Corporal's stripes from the Director and then be granted two weeks' leave before they reported to their new units.

Jon felt a twinge of sadness at the thought. He might never see some of his colleagues again. The Corps was pretty small but there were plenty of places for them to go, and unless they all stayed in, which was unlikely, they would be scattered around the world. They might meet up again on the A2 and Drill and Duties Two, but that was going to be a couple of years away at least and, in the meantime, they would almost all be separated after the best part of a year together.

"How about you?" he asked.

"I'm not sure," Sonia replied. "I quite fancy going somewhere, but I don't know if I can afford it."

Privates didn't get paid much and, although they hadn't really had much in the way of expenses with their food and accommodation being provided, they still didn't have much left at the end of the month.

He was just about to ask her if she fancied going somewhere together, when Paul and Sue came into the bar and interrupted them, and the moment was lost.

The next day was Corps Day. The parade wasn't due to start until 1100, so there was a fair amount of time spent milling about. They made last minute preparations and then killed time by drinking tea in the cookhouse until, finally, they got the call to arms.

The day was blazingly hot already. Even at 1000, they were sweating in their heavy Number Two dress uniforms.

"I hope no one faints on parade," Jon heard Major Elswick saying to Sergeant Thompson.

"As long as they do it to attention, it'll be all right," he replied, with a laugh.

Anyone foolish enough to have overdone it with the alcohol last night is going to suffer the consequences, on a day like this, thought Jon.

They were standing in small groups round the back of the cookhouse, waiting to go on. They had their berets off and were trying to get as much shade as possible.

Guests had been arriving all morning and Jon could hear the band tuning up. He loved marching to music. There was something about martial tunes that made you brace up and want to show off.

"Don't worry about the parade," Thompson was telling the recruits. "We'll be there in case anything goes wrong."

There was a feeling of excitement growing as the time drew near. Some recruits were ashen-faced but that might just be nerves. Jon's own hands were sweating, but he knew that once they got the order to march and the band started playing, it would be fine.

They had been told that the guest of honour wasn't going to be Prince Philip, after all, which came as no surprise to Jon, but was obviously a bit of a disappointment to some of the recruits. Instead, the guest of honour was going to be the Master of the Worshipful Company of Painter-Stainers which was a livery company of the city of London. Apparently, according to the TA Intelligence Corps, who called him the Mattress stainer and bed wetter, the Worshipful Company of Painter-Stainers had been used by Sir Francis Walsingham, who was Queen Elizabeth I's spymaster, as agents and that gave the link to the Intelligence Corps. The TA had a competition called the Master's Competition, which was held each year in honour of this association, and the winning company was called the Master's company for that year.

It all sounded like a typical load of bollocks to Jon, but he didn't really care. They had to have someone as guest of honour, and it could have been worse – at least it wasn't a politician.

"Form up. Three ranks," came the command, informing them that they were just about to go on.

There was a last minute flurry of nerves as the recruits shuffled into position and got ready to go.

"By the right... Quick march!"

They all stepped off and the sound of everyone's heels hitting the ground at almost the same time gave a gratifying noise.

"Left, right, left, right, left, right, left," Sergeant Thompson called out, as he guided the squad onto the parade square.

They marched on, their left arms hitting the SMGs as they swung them so that they would be parallel to the ground, and halted with a resounding crack in front of the seating, where the Master and the Corps Director were sitting.

"Squaaaads will advance. Left turn!"

This brought both squads to the position where the right-hand marker was at the right of the parade, and they faced the stand.

"In open order... Right dress."

The front rank took one pace forward and the rear rank one pace to the rear as the centre rank stood still. This drill movement was so that the Master and Director could walk between the ranks for the inspection without standing on anyone's highly polished boots or catching themselves on the barrel of an SMG.

At this point, Sergeant Thompson marched round to the front of the squad so that he could pass over command to the adjutant. He halted at the front and awaited the arrival of the adjutant, who was waiting on the sidelines. The adjutant marched onto the square and Thompson turned and marched towards him. They halted three paces apart and Thompson threw up a salute. The adjutant brought his sword up to the present in a graceful gesture, acknowledging the salute to the Queen's Commission.

"Squads 49 and 40 formed up and awaiting your disposal, sir," Thompson bawled in his best parade-ground voice.

"Thank you, Sergeant," the adjutant replied.

Thompson saluted again and the adjutant responded with his sword. Thompson, his task completed for the moment, turned to his right and marched to the back of the squads, and the adjutant took over the parade. He turned towards the squad with his sword held upright before him.

"Squads. Stand at... ease!"

There was a tiny hesitation from the regular squad, while the TA squad dropped their SMGs from the 'order' straight into the 'at ease' position, without going through the 'order arms'. The adjutant had given the wrong order and the correct thing to do would have been for the squads to stand completely still. Unfortunately for the regular squad, some of them had done this whilst others had done what the TA did and moved directly into the 'at ease' position, and they were now split between those who were still standing at 'order arm' and those who were 'at ease'. The adjutant hadn't noticed his mistake as he had done an about-turn just after giving the order and now stood with his back to the squads.

It was any easy mistake to make; the adjutant wasn't a drill instructor. In fact, he was an Imagery Analyst by trade. However, that didn't help the fact that the regulars looked like they had made a mess whereas the TA looked like they had done it properly.

Typical fucking officer, thought Jon, bitterly.

At least this wasn't Sandhurst, where the press would have had a field day if the Officer Cadets had been caught out like that on their pass out parade.

No one seemed to have noticed, not that anyone could have done anything about it, and the Master and Director were now on their way to inspect the squads.

"Stand at ease," hissed Thompson, and those who still had their SMGs in the 'order arms' did so.

The Master and Director wandered along the lines of recruits, oblivious to the drama that just unfolded, with the Master giving the odd compliment and asking the occasional question as he went along. They then sauntered back to their seats for the start of the presentations.

The heat was beginning to become oppressive, and Thompson moved through the ranks, checking that no one was going to keel over.

Those who were getting awards had started marching out in order of presentation and Jon awaited his turn.

"The award for best at drill... Private Comyn," the Master announced, to a round of polite applause.

Thompson took his SMG and Jon turned to his right and marched around the back of the front rank and out to the podium, where the Master waited to give him his prize.

"Well done, well done," gushed the Master effusively. "I've always loved drill, myself. I was in the infantry for national service, don't you know."

"Thank you, sir," replied Jon, taking the wooden shield from the tall, thin man dressed in ceremonial robes.

Someone behind him relieved him of the prize and Jon made his way back to the squad and took up his position. The Master stood up to give a speech.

"Christ! I hope he hurries up, before we lose anyone," snarled Thompson from the back of the squad.

There were a few wobbles that Jon could see, and the sweat was dripping down his back, soaking the shirt under his jacket.

Finally, the Master finished his speech, and the squads marched off. It was over.

CHAPTER 22

Jon handed in his SMG and headed back to his room to get out of his sweaty uniform. Some of the recruits had headed straight to the bar from the armoury, but Jon didn't fancy getting his best boots ruined by a careless drinker and, anyway, they had the rest of the day to get rat-arsed drunk, if they wanted to.

There was going to be a barbeque later on. Stalls had been set up to cater for the children of staff and guests who had arrived, and were still arriving, for Corps Day. There was a real party atmosphere, and everyone seemed to be happy.

Corps Day is a big thing for the Intelligence Corps. Being a small Corps, there is a good chance one will know most, if not all, the people there if they have served for anything more than a couple of years.

Jon took his time. He looked at the small, wooden shield that displayed the Intelligence Corps badge and motto along with a plaque reading 'Private Comyn, Best at Drill, Squad 49' along the bottom. He carefully packed it away in his top drawer and took off his boots. He hung his Number Two's on a coat hanger and changed into casual civilian clothes. They were now off duty, and it would save him having to salute officers or get 'dicked' for duty by a passing Warrant Officer or Sergeant.

The bar was packed with recruits and guests trying to get served. Jon knew that there would be a mobile bar outside later, but for the moment, the NAAFI had been declared an all ranks' mess.

It was nice of them to do that, he thought. *They wouldn't open their own fucking messes, instead the officers and senior ranks were invading the juniors' territory.*

He saw Paul, who waved at him and indicated that he had a drink already waiting.

"Thanks, mate" he said gratefully, helping himself to a bottle of Becks. The table was packed with beer bottles, and Jon realised that the recruits had anticipated the invasion of their bar and had taken measures to ensure that they all had drinks before the staff and guests barged them out of the way.

The noise in the NAAFI was incredible as everyone competed to be heard above the others. Jon looked around, but he couldn't see any of the TA recruits. Maybe they had gone to get changed?

"Anyone seen that big, blonde TA girl?" Peter asked, waving his bottle of beer about. "I reckon I could get lucky with that one."

Jon and Sonia exchanged glances.

"They've gone," said someone else.

"What! Gone where?" asked Peter.

"They've all fucked off," said another. "A WO2 came in while some of them were having a beer and told them that they had to catch the train."

"Bloody hell, that's a bit rough," said Jon.

"Bugger!" remarked Peter, seeing his chances of getting his end away disappearing down the tubes.

"Probably for the best. Corps Day isn't really a TA thing," added one of the staff, who had overheard the conversation.

"No?" queried Jon. "Why not?"

"They've got their own traditions," explained the Sergeant. "They're different from us."

Great way to integrate, thought Jon, but he supposed that was what the army was like, individual units who all claimed to be the best and who all had rivalries that bordered on the hostile. The only thing that got them together was a common enemy, like the TA.

The heat in the bar was stifling, so they gathered up their bottles and spilled outside. This would normally be frowned upon, but it was Corps Day, and the rules were different. It was fantastic to sit on the grass, drinking beer and chatting away. There were no more tests – at least, not at the moment – and they now had a little bit of status; they were no longer the bottom of the ladder. Even if it was only on the first rung, they had to start somewhere.

They watched as a group of old men with huge moustaches came out of the bar with pints of beer in their hands. They looked like they were probably old hands who had continued to live in Ashford after leaving the Corps. They were loudly discussing the 'good old days', and Jon decided that he would try to avoid them, if he could. He was in no mood to be condescended to by a bunch of has-beens.

The smell of roasting meat drifted towards them, and they all realised that they were quite hungry. They had missed lunch, and they had got accustomed to regular mealtimes. They wandered across to the barbeque, where volunteers were dishing out plates of well-done meat from the grill of a slowly turning hog roast.

"Wow! This is fantastic," said Rob, through a mouthful of roast pork.

"It's a bit masculine," retorted Donna. "It would be nice to have a bit of salad with it, instead of burnt meat."

"Burnt meat? What more could a man ask for?" stated Peter.

Donna just rolled her eyes.

They saw the Director guiding the Master towards the food and decided that a tactical withdrawal was in order.

"We need a 'replen' with beer," announced Paul, and with that, they trooped back to the NAAFI.

One of the outside bars had been opened, and the wives and more senior personnel seemed to be congregating around it, so it was a bit quieter. They saw there was a bouncy castle set up, and this led to a discussion about having sex on one.

"Has anyone ever done it?" Peter asked.

"I doubt it," said Jon. "But I've heard that a waterbed can make you seasick."

"It would be fun to try," said Paul, giving Sue a look.

She just smiled back at him.

The afternoon melted into early evening. There was a shuttle going back and forth between the barbeque and the bar. The guests gradually departed, leaving a hard-core of recruits and staff who seemed determined to see who could last the longest.

Eventually, Jon gave up and wandered off to bed. Someone would have to clear up in the morning and he had a strong suspicion who that someone would be. He lay for a while, listening to the quiet sounds of merriment from outside and then drifted off into a deep sleep.

Jon was proven right the next morning, when the recruits found themselves on cleaning detail.

"God. What a mess!" Peter complained, although he had probably added his fair share of empty glasses and discarded bottles to the carnage.

They spent the morning with black bags, picking up cigarette ends and paper plates, while another group collected the glasses to be washed, and another the bottles to go into the huge metal container behind the NAAFI.

Lunch consisted of leftover steaks and burgers, much to Donna's disgust at having to eat virtually nothing but red meat for two days.

"What's wrong with red meat?" demanded Peter.

"It gives you bowel cancer," said Donna, rather offputtingly.

They had the afternoon to pack up their kit as they would be going on leave after they received their posting orders. Equipment and uniforms that they couldn't easily carry were packed into boxes which would be forwarded to their new units.

"What does MFO mean?" someone asked.

"Moving Forces Overseas," interpreted Mich, who had come across the lightweight wooden crates before.

"What happens if you're not going overseas, then?" someone asked, pedantically.

"Then you don't use them," replied Mich, snappily.

He wasn't someone who suffered fools gladly, and it was a pretty stupid question.

The boxes were perfect for webbing, sleeping bags and other large items of kit that would be a drag to carry on the train. Virtually none of the recruits had their own vehicles, and lugging more than two bags was a real pain.

Jon had a flashback to when he, Andy and Richard had been posted to Bridge of Don. One of them had held the train door open as the other two lobbed bags through the door. It seemed like a lifetime ago. He wondered if either Andy or Richard were still in the army. They would be Captains by now if so. Would he meet them at some army camp sometime? He wondered about how they would react to him being a Lance Corporal and them being officers. Would they be friendly, or would the social divide be too large to cross? He would only find out if and when it happened, he supposed.

It was a subdued night in the bar. The atmosphere was totally different from the previous day and quite a few of the recruits were nursing soft drinks, rather than alcohol.

Jon sat with Donna, Sonia, Steve, Mich, Paul and Sue.

"Well, tomorrow's the day we find out" announced Jon.

They had been sitting quietly, talking about the future and musing on the past.

"Will you miss this place?" Donna asked.

"Ashford? No," said Jon. "But I'll miss the people. Not all of them, of course, but most of them."

They all agreed.

"To tomorrow," said Jon, raising his glass, and they all toasted the undiscovered country.

"Good morning, good morning," said Elswick, as he came into the classroom.

The recruits all looked at him. "Good morning, sir," they replied, almost in unison.

"Posting orders and promotion," he said, as he pulled a sheaf of large brown envelopes from his folder.

He went through the recruits alphabetically and handed them their envelope as they answered their names. He knew most of them, if not all, by now but it saved any discrepancies to check.

Jon broke open the glued flap and pulled out the Lance Corporal stripes and the letter with his posting orders. He felt a moment's reluctance to open them, a vague fear that this was the point of no return. But it would happen regardless, so he crossed the Rubicon and opened the letter.

He had got what he had asked for: an Intelligence company. He would be going to JHQ Rheindalen in West Germany. He looked around the room to see smiles on most of the faces. Nearly everyone had got the posting that they had asked for by the looks of it.

In reality, there wasn't really much choice. The vast majority of posts were either in Security sections or Intelligence companies. Only people who had an aptitude for languages would generally request to be sent to 14 Sigs, and one had to pass the test to be accepted as an IA.

This meant that, unless you had requested something unreasonable, you were likely to have got your first choice. He couldn't understand why anyone wouldn't be happy with their posting preference but, unless the person told you what they had put down, you would never find out, as the information was classified confidential.

It took a while for Elswick to get through everyone and then he gave a speech, thanking them for their efforts and wishing them luck in the future. All the staff who had given them lectures then added their congratulations, and then the recruits broke up into little groups, like A level students swapping results.

Donna and Mich, unsurprisingly, had been accepted for 14 Sigs and Paul was going to the Security section based in Imphal Barracks in York. Steve had also asked to join an Intelligence Company and would be joining Jon in JHQ, Rheindalen, which only left Sonia and Sue. Sue had been posted to a Security section based in Abingdon, wherever that was, and Sonia had been given a wildcard and was posted to DIS.

Peter was dancing around, saying, "Yes! Yes! Yes!"

"What've you got, Pete?" asked Mich.

"Gibraltar!" announced Peter, with a huge grin.

"Wow!" said Mich. "Did you ask for that?"

"No," admitted Peter. "I just put in for a Security section. I didn't even know we had a section in Gibraltar."

"Well, there you go," replied Mich. "Congratulations."

After that, it was just a case of filling in a bit of paperwork and being issued with rail passes.

"You will get joining instructions through the post," said Elswick. "And those of you going overseas will be advised of your travel arrangements. Best of luck, and I'll see you all back here for your A2."

That was highly unlikely, as Elswick would probably have been posted by the time they did their A2, but no one contradicted him, and they all filed out of the classroom.

There was a shuttle to the station as the minibuses soon filled up with baggage, and Jon found himself standing outside the guardroom with a group that included Sonia.

"You'll have to give me a shout if you're ever in London," she said, with a smile.

"Yes, I will do," he agreed.

"We never got round to going to the Intelligence Corps Museum, did we?" she said.

"No. Maybe next Corps Day. You never know."

"Are you ready to go, Corporal?" asked the driver.

"Yes," said Jon, and got on the minibus.

9 781803 782638

The Silent One
...and Other Stories

By Bank Street Writers

Printed in the United Kingdom

First Printing, 2016

ISBN-13: 978-1540518422

"I brought milk, but
forgot the teabags."

— Bank Street Writers

Contents